reborn

j.f.r. coates

j.f.r. coates

Text copyright 2019

Cover by Ilya Zyor

www.artstation.com/ilyar

Reborn 2nd Edition

Originally published 2015

978-1-922061-68-3

J.F.R. Coates

Queensland, Australia

acknowledgements

No book is ever the work of just one person.

This particular book has been a process like few others. It has gone through so many different iterations, including one previously published version that I realised was flawed in several ways. This version has sought to correct those issues, and I hope I have been successful.

I have had a lot of help through this process.

Firstly, I have to thank my husband, Jamie. It's probably not the easiest to live with a writer, but he puts up with me and all the weird little quirks that come with it. Thank you for your ongoing support!

My friends and family have also been really good in supporting me and my efforts. They have been readers, editors, and cheerleaders. I couldn't make it without them.

I also have to give special thanks to Shane Jason Taylor, a fellow local writer, who has helped make Reborn into a much better book. His feedback on my drafts was incredible, if a little painfully harsh at times. This story would not be as good without his efforts. You should all check out his work too!

I would like to give a huge shout out to my supporters on Patreon. Writing isn't always the most financially rewarding endeavour, and my backers there help provide that little bit more income to pay all the bills. You are all incredible people, and every dollar you pledge is so wonderfully appreciated.

Finally, and most importantly of all, I would like to thank you – the person reading this book. Whether you're a returning reader or discovering my work for the first time, thank you! I really hope you enjoy this book, and that you'll return for more.

about the author

J.F.R. Coates was born and raised in picturesque Somerset, England, but she moved out to Brisbane, Australia as a teenager. She grew up reading from a young age, starting with Enid Blyton's *The Famous Five* and *Secret Seven*, before finding her calling with J.R.R. Tolkien's *The Hobbit*. Speculative Fiction has gripped her ever since, and now she calls amongst her favourite authors Maggie Furey, Phillip Pullman, and Robin Hobb.

She still lives in Brisbane, where she lives with her husband and – as seems ubiquitous for authors – her two cats.

You can follow her on Bluesky at @jfrcoates.bsky.social, or Facebook at /jfrcoates.

She also has a Patreon, which allows for sneak-previews of what's to come, as well as additional stories that fit in around her novels. All support is always gratefully received. https://www.patreon.com/jfrcoates

Reborn

chapter one

"I don't think she's coming tonight, Captain."

Captain Rhys Griffiths didn't abandon his search of the Cerian skies. He stood at the top of the Normandy Observation Tower, through whose glass-domed ceiling he could see the entire expanse of the darkening sky. There were many stars dotting the inky black vista above their heads, but nowhere was there any sign of an approaching spaceship.

"Let's face it, Captain. We'd have seen something by now if the *Dawn* was coming before nightfall," said the other man in the observation room. Lieutenant Giles Cooper was a powerfully built man with no hair on his head at all, and a permanent expression that looked like he was trying too hard to think. Despite appearances, he was a smart man and had served as Rhys's first officer for almost two years.

"No, Captain Lee isn't one for being late. Especially not on a route this short. He'll be here tonight," Rhys said. It was the first time he had spoken in over an hour, ever since he had climbed the stairs to the top of the tallest building on all of Ceres to begin his vigil for the *Terrestrial Dawn*. The *Dawn* was one of the finest ships ever produced by the Terran Interplanetary Empire. It was captained by Rhys's old friend and training partner, Aaron Lee.

"He should have been here three hours ago, Captain," Cooper pointed out. He pulled himself to attention as Rhys turned around to stare at his first officer. The lieutenant wasn't to be perturbed though. "I'm just suggesting that there must have been a delay on Mars we didn't hear about. You know what it's like here."

Rhys tutted and shook his head, preferring not to respond to his first officer for the moment, instead starting to pace back and forth around the watchtower. He glanced down at the communicator at his hip, but the red light above the screen was flashing, indicating that it was out of service range. If Normandy Control had been trying to contact him, they wouldn't have gotten through. He ground his teeth together, his hand twitching at his side as he resisted the urge to hurl the communicator across the watchtower as hard as he could.

"Are you in range?" Rhys eventually asked, turning around to face Cooper. His pacing had paused, though his leg still twitched, foot tapping against the floor.

Cooper checked his communicator. An amber light flashed, interchanging with an occasional gleam of green. Service was spotty, but it was more reliable than the constant red from the device at Rhys's hip.

"Contact Control, would you? Ask for any updates," Rhys instructed his first officer.

No sooner had Cooper reached for the communicator did it flare to life. A burst of static boomed out from the struggling speaker. It would have deafened the lieutenant had it been held to his ear.

"Christ and Veritas," Cooper muttered, waiting for the static and white noise to clear. He fiddled with the volume before holding the temperamental device up to his ear. "Cooper here."

Rhys couldn't hear anything that was said to Cooper, so he turned his attention back to the sky. The glare from the lights behind him reflected off the thickened glass, making it harder to see anything clearly through the distorted image of his face. His brown eyes glared into the darkness. The last of Sol's light shone off the small satellite that orbited Ceres, barely visible in the darkening sky. Soon the stars would be the only light on the dwarf planet's surface.

"Captain Griffiths, we've been summoned back to Control," Cooper said as he returned his communicator to its holster. His voice was terse. He paused and looked towards his captain, waiting for Rhys to make the first move towards the stairwell that led down to the spaceport.

"What happened?" Rhys replied. He was wary. Control would only have summoned him back if they had good reason for it. He was, strictly speaking, off-duty for the rest of the night.

"They say they've received some contact from the *Dawn*, and that it's not good news."

"Shit." Rhys ran for the stairs. He took them four at a time, his left shoulder bumping against the wall several times as he spiralled down to the below-ground level. Caught off guard by his captain's sudden movement, Cooper trailed some distance behind, taking the stairs at a more reasonable pace. His stocky body couldn't match the lean strides Rhys was able to manage.

At the lower level, several corridors opened up. All descended even further down, cutting deeper into the rocky surface of Ceres and keeping the spaceport away from the dangerous, airless surface of the dwarf planet. Though the narrow corridors of the spaceport were busy, Rhys was able to push his way through, the privilege of his rank helping to part the crowd.

Another staircase led up to the control tower. It wasn't as tall as the observation tower, but Rhys's legs were already burning from that rapid descent, and by the time he reached the summit his chest was heaving from exertion. He took a few moments to compose himself, resting his hand on the thick glass window that overlooked the barren landscape. The few towers of the spaceport that rose above the surface were old and grey. What little colour they once possessed had faded away from the two centuries of exposure to the near vacuum of the Cerian environment. The rise of Ahuna Mons loomed on the horizon, but otherwise the surface of the dwarf planet was mostly flat.

At the end of the short, poorly-lit corridor was the control room, where the small military port was overseen from. Making sure his shirt was straight and his coat was buttoned up, Rhys punched his access code into the panel by the door and entered, not waiting for his first officer to catch up.

Control was a hive of activity as Rhys entered. Around the edge of the room, beneath the windows that dominated three of the four walls, was a large array of computers, monitors, and sensors. A few were inactive, but those that were still working were surrounded by a few dozen white-shirted operators. They scurried back and forth, exchanging messages across the room as they tried to make sense of the information their dated equipment was giving them.

All this was orchestrated by three of the four men around the table in the centre of the room. Jacques Favre, the resident captain of the port, was at the centre of it all, conferencing with his staff and taking input from the veteran Admiral Garter by his side. The Cerian's wiry black hair was messed up, and he ran his hand through it several times to further displace it.

John Baron, captain of the *Odyssey*, was conversing with the fourth man at the central table. Rhys was unfamiliar with him, though his red and gold robe marked him as a cardinal of the Vatican of Mars. The cardinal was a sour-faced man who looked to Rhys with an expression of intense dislike. The captain took no offence to it, as the cardinal had not reserved that expression just for him. Wherever the cardinal looked, he wore it like it was permanently affixed to his face.

Rhys saluted the admiral as he approached the table, before glancing down at the papers strewn across it. He cast a wary eye across at the cardinal, but the servant of the Vatican seemed content in talking to Captain Baron. The captain was nodding zealously on occasion, the dark skin on his bald head gleaming in the light.

"What's the situation, Admiral?" Rhys asked, after the admiral had gestured to come to ease.

"In short, the *Terrestrial Dawn* is in the hands of the Centauran Governance of Planets and is enroute. Now, we haven't picked anything up on the *Odyssey's* short-range sublight scanners, so we have at least three hours before we can expect any form of attack," Admiral Garter said gravely. The admiral peered over the rim of his glasses.

"And the long-range scanners, Admiral?" Rhys asked, knowing the answer already.

"Inactive," Admiral Garter replied with a shake of his head, confirming Rhys's fears.

"We have mechanics working on it, but I doubt it'll be fixed that quickly," Favre cut in. He rubbed his brow wearily, fending off the attentions from one of his staff. "Our ground defences aren't fully operational, but we're working at getting online what we can before those terrorists get here."

"So, what have we got? Captain Lee was ousted? Captured?" Rhys asked.

Admiral Garter shook his head and uttered a single word that felt like a physical blow to Rhys. "Defected."

"Captain Lee defected? That's... that's not possible. He's a friend, I've known him for years. He would never do that," Rhys said. His throat was dry. He tried swallowing, but he couldn't quite manage it.

"I'm afraid he sent the transmission himself, Captain Griffiths. There can be no doubting Captain Lee himself was responsible for this defection," Admiral Garter replied.

"May I see the recording, Admiral? There must be something else here, his loyalty to the emperor has always been absolute," Rhys said. He wasn't sure he wanted to see it, but he would never truly believe the admiral until he saw the proof of Aaron's defection with his own eyes.

Admiral Garter fumbled with the unfamiliar and old holographic projector for a few moments, before he was able to bring up the insignia of the Terran Interplanetary Empire up on the white wall between the large windows. The insignia then faded to display a still frame of a middle-aged man with black hair that pushed the limit of the strict, military-enforced permitted lengths. His face was very familiar to Rhys, from the thick eyebrows to scarred chin. It was Aaron Lee. He was captain of the *Terrestrial Dawn*, sworn servant of the Terran Empire. Or so Rhys had believed.

The still frame began to move, and sound followed a few seconds later, emerging from the large speakers either side of the image. Audio and visuals remained slightly out of sync. It would normally have annoyed Rhys, but he had other things to worry about.

"Good evening Admiral Garter and Captains Favre, Baron... and Captain Griffiths. As I'm sure you're already aware, the *Terrestrial Dawn* will not be docking around Ceres tonight. Instead I'm heading to Alpha Centauri to join up with the CGP. I will however stop by the port to pick up anyone who may wish to join me. A similar message has been broadcast on all military and civilian frequencies, so you can't hide this offer from the citizenry." Though it was impossible for Aaron to know where Rhys was going to stand when viewing the message, he felt that Aaron was looking right at him as he gave the invitation to betray the Emperor of Terra.

Aaron was not yet finished. He took a deep breath, a steely glint that Rhys recognised only too well entering his eye. "I trust you will do nothing to hinder those who wish to join me. I do not desire hostilities, but we will protect those who choose to join us."

The screen went black as the projector turned off. Any lingering doubt in Rhys's mind that Aaron had not switched allegiance had gone. There was no mistaking it. Captain Aaron Lee was part of the CGP now. He now had to be considered an enemy. Something drastic had changed since he had seen him last, only a few months prior. One question remained. Why?

"You know Captain Lee. Is it possible he truly does not want to open fire?" Admiral Garter asked Rhys after allowing him a few moments of silence.

"I don't know if this is Captain Lee calling the shots. He must be under duress, or someone has tricked him. He has always been true to his word and loyal to the empire, so I can't see how he could have willingly defected." Rhys paused and took a deep breath. "Having said that, the man I have known all these years would never attack without provocation. I hope those principles remain, no matter what is happening on the bridge."

Admiral Garter nodded, before clasping his hands behind his back as he looked around the table. "We can't risk a mass exodus, but Captain Lee's broadcast would have been picked up by the mining base. We could have defectors on our door within twenty minutes, expecting safe passage through to the *Dawn*," the admiral explained. He adjusted his glasses, letting them sit a little further down his nose. "They will expect us to acquiesce to Captain Lee's demands. Any suggestions on how to proceed, gentlemen?"

"We cannot let them reach the shuttles, Admiral," Captain Favre said immediately. The captain placed his hands down on the table and looked around at the other men. "If we let them escape, then we risk a revolt."

"So, what do we do, have armed guards at the gate?" Rhys asked with a shake of his head. "They're unarmed civilians. We can't open fire on them."

"But nor can we let them just defect like the traitors they are," Captain Baron intervened, his deep voice reverberating around the table. "We have more ships than them, why is this even a problem? We scramble the *Odyssey*, *Harvester*, and the *Europa* into defensive positions around the port. We shore up the ground-based defences as much as we can."

"We force the *Dawn* into a surrender or a defeat," Captain Favre added, slapping Captain Baron on the shoulder. He laughed. "I like it. We have nothing to fear here, Admiral. The port may be old, but the ships protecting it are not.”

The admiral nodded, but Captain Favre was not yet finished. A malicious grin cracked open his weathered face. “Open the gates to the traitors. Let them on board the shuttles and keep them there until justice can be brought down upon the infidels.”

Admiral Garter nodded again. He grimaced and ran a hand over his forehead. “Very well. I will remain on the ground with Captain Favre to organise our defences, just in case they launch a ground assault. Two ships will be enough to protect against the *Dawn* in orbit,” he said. He tapped his fingers against the table. “We should arm the starats too. God only knows we could use any help we can get.”

“With all due respect, I don’t think that’s a good idea, Admiral,” Captain Favre said with a considerable amount of distaste in his words. At the same moment, the cardinal cleared his throat and sneered.

“Explain please,” the admiral commanded. He raised one bushy white eyebrow as he took the glasses from his nose to give them a quick wipe down on his sleeve.

Favre hesitated, but after a moment of thought he answered. “They don’t have the intelligence to be of any use in combat. They barely even know one end of a gun to the other. We may as well give weapons to cats and dogs for all the use they’d be. Simply put, we can’t trust them to do anything they aren’t used to doing, that they’ve been trained their entire lives for.”

“And besides,” Captain Baron added, wagging a finger in the direction of Captain Favre. “We’ve no guarantee they wouldn’t flee with the rest of the traitors if they were made aware of the ship’s presence. We can’t risk them escaping or getting silly thoughts in their heads. It would cost too much to replace them. Better they were left unaware of the entire situation.”

Admiral Garter turned to Rhys. “And you, Captain Griffiths?”

Rhys shrugged. He was uncomfortable about the whole situation. Aaron was not an idiot. He should know he was outgunned. There was something else at play here, he was sure of it. The starats were merely an additional worry he didn’t want to concern himself with.

"I mean, they are just starats. What good could they do?" Out of the corner of his eye, Rhys could see the cardinal nod.

"I suppose you're right. Very well. Keep it from them, but arm every human you can," Admiral Garter said, though Rhys could see a shadow of doubt pass across his eyes. Was the admiral sharing the same concerns Rhys had over Aaron's apparent brashness?

"Consider it done. I'll have this port defended as much as I can manage," Favre said, saluting Admiral Garter before giving a polite nod to the others around the table. He left the control room without once looking back.

"I will expect," the cardinal said, speaking to Admiral Garter, "that shuttles will be prepared for anyone who wishes to come from the *Dawn*?"

"If Captain Lee is willing to cooperate, then of course we will do all we can to ensure those still loyal to us will be looked after," the admiral replied. He then turned his attention to the two captains. "Go prepare your ships. We still have at least three hours before we can expect Captain Lee. He'll be restricted to sublight speed through the Belt, so we will be able to detect him with plenty of time." He dismissed the two captains with a wave of his hand.

Both captains saluted Admiral Garter, before turning to leave. To Rhys's surprise, the cardinal followed behind them.

Cooper was waiting for them just outside. Lacking the access code for the control tower, he hadn't been able to follow Rhys inside and had been forced to wait for his captain to emerge once more. He looked more than merely disgruntled that he had been left outside, but for once was smart enough not to mention his discontent. They descended the stairs in silence, all three of them uncomfortable in the presence of the cardinal.

Once they were underground and back in the network of tunnels, Rhys felt a hand on his shoulder. "Captain Griffiths, a word if I may?" Rhys turned at the oily voice, shrugging the hand from his shoulder. It was the cardinal who had spoken.

Rhys didn't answer the cardinal immediately. Instead he addressed his first officer. "Mr Cooper, follow Captain Baron to the shuttle bay and head up to the *Harvester* if I don't catch up in time. Prepare the ship for launch and wait for further instructions. Captain Baron, if you could fill Mr Cooper in on what's going on, that would be most appreciated," he said. Only after seeing the two men off did he turn back to the cardinal. "Make it quick."

"Cardinal Erik Aurealiusson of the Vatican," he introduced himself as. With what seemed to be an afterthought, he offered his hand to the captain. Rhys took the offered hand, but barely had they touched before the cardinal withdrew his arm again, a sneer on his face that suggested he still took great offence with everything he saw.

The cardinal then frowned and pursed his lips. "Captain Griffiths. I feel like I know that name from somewhere." He scratched his chin, but Rhys didn't volunteer any information. He had never heard of the cardinal before the priest's recent arrival on Ceres. After a few moments, the cardinal shrugged his shoulders and continued. "I have been speaking to everyone of rank in this port. Pope Adamantius is concerned about the starat treatment here," he said with a slight sucking in of his breath.

Rhys glanced back to find the reason for his reaction. One of the starats was approaching. The short, brown-furred creature was one of humanity's greatest creations; a skilled slave manufactured only to serve. The starat squeaked quietly and bowed its head.

"Adamantius is concerned about their treatment?" Rhys asked, turning back to face the cardinal as the starat turned down a different corridor before it reached them. The Vatican had always opposed the mere existence of starats. No one affiliated with the Vatican would ever champion for their rights.

Cardinal Erik nodded once. "His Holiness is very concerned. Word has reached his ears of starats gaining promotions within the ranks of the space corps," he said as he licked his lips maliciously. "He believes there is a... sympathiser somewhere within this spaceport. We cannot allow this sort of thing to happen. For two hundred and fifty years we have struggled against them, casting their blasphemous souls into the fires they belong. Any human that protects them will be met with the same fate."

Rhys folded his arms and stared down at the cardinal. "I know all this. Everyone in the space corps is instructed in their use."

"I know someone here is supporting them. I just have to ask enough questions and they will crack eventually," Cardinal Erik said with a smile that filled Rhys with dread. He didn't dare let any of that fear show on his face. Even knowing his innocence wasn't enough to suppress that fear. "So, tell me, Captain Griffiths. What are they to you?"

"Starats are tools, nothing more. They work hard and without complaint, but that's all they're good for. I am not, as you say, a sympathiser," Rhys said, choosing his words carefully. "I follow imperial and Vatican guidelines on their treatment. Nothing more or less than that."

Cardinal Erik twisted his face into a look of concentration. "Are there any starats on your ship?"

Rhys paused. "Two, I think. Both in the services crew. You'll have to speak with Simon Briggs if you want more information on them. He's my services commander," he said. It had been quite a while since he had seen either of the starats in his employ. He'd had nothing to do with them since he'd signed the paperwork that designated them to his ship. "But if you'll excuse me, we have a situation I must attend to."

The cardinal frowned. "Very well. I'll let you get back to your duties. If you learn anything that may be of use, please contact me immediately. Protecting the sympathiser is just as blasphemous as protecting the starats. Remember, the Vatican has eyes everywhere. Veritas keep you," he said.

"And you too," Rhys mumbled in the traditional response, before the cardinal stalked off, heading in the opposite direction to Captain Baron and Cooper. Rhys shook his head and made his way to the shuttle bay. He had work to do.

***

The long corridor of the shuttle bay was almost completely empty when Rhys arrived. Small windows provided a few glimpses of the barren Cerian surface, where the dozen or so automated shuttles were docked, linked to the port by small walkways that were withdrawn when it was time to launch. Rhys was met by one of the operators, who informed him that he had just missed Captain Baron and Cooper. They had just launched, but there was still a spare shuttle to transport Rhys up to his ship.

The shuttle was little more than a square box with engines, and inside was no different. The hard, metallic floors were bare, and the rows of seats that ran down the shuttle were rigid and uncomfortable to sit on. At the front of the shuttle was a large screen, currently switched off. There was nowhere for a pilot, as the shuttles on Ceres were all fully automated, without any need for human guidance. They were slow and clunky compared to the shuttles elsewhere in the system, and especially compared to the teleporters that were starting to become the prevalent means of short-range transport. Though the Normandy port was equipped with teleporters, they were only used when the shuttles were unavailable, due to the stress the immense electrical loads placed on the port's fragile infrastructure.

Rhys had barely strapped himself into his seat before the onboard communicator pinged. He leaned forward to accept the call, pressing a button on the side of the screen which briefly threatened to flicker to life, before falling into blackness again. The gruff voice of Admiral Garter strained through the speakers.

"We've received word from Remus, on behalf of Romulus, who were unable to open a communications channel with us," the admiral explained, not bothering with any pleasantries. His voice was urgent, and Rhys sat back as far as he could in his rigid seat, hands gripping hard onto the armrests. "In short, the *Terrestrial Dawn* left Romulus eight hours early."

"Early? How? Why aren't they here already?" Rhys asked, more musing to himself than asking the admiral directly. The hairs on the back of his neck prickled. Aaron was up to something, but he just didn't know what.

"We don't know," came the terse reply from Admiral Garter. "We're running some simulations back here, but at the moment I just can't explain the delay. Unless they ran into some mechanical or subspace issues, there seems to be no reason for it. We need to be prepared and ready as soon as possible. I don't like this situation one bit. Are you about to board the *Harvester*?"

"Not yet, Admiral," Rhys admitted. He looked around the small shuttle, but there was no evidence it was ready to launch just yet. "I was delayed by Cardinal Erik, but Lieutenant Cooper has gone on ahead of me."

"Good. Get him to prepare your ship. I want it in place above the port and ready to fire if necessary," Admiral Garter said. He waited for an affirmation from Rhys before ending the call.

Rhys sat back in silence for a few moments, before trying to contact the *Harvester*, up in orbit at the small docking station a safe distance from the dwarf planet. The response was almost immediate.

The screen flickered to life and stayed that way, displaying Lieutenant Cooper standing in the bridge of his ship. Behind the first officer, Rhys could see a few others from his crew, flitting back and forth as they readied their stations.

"Captain Griffiths, are you on your way now?" Cooper asked.

"Almost, there seems to be a small delay in getting me off the ground, but I should be soon," Rhys replied, before he passed on the message from the admiral, ordering Cooper to get the ship ready for possible action.

Cooper nodded and rubbed his unshaven chin. "We're in deep shit, if you'll pardon my language, captain. I'd say we just open fire on the *Dawn* and hang the consequences. We outnumber him, so why are we giving him the chance to get away?"

"Better to lose a few traitors to the CGP than risk the lives of everyone on board our ships," Rhys replied. He paused as he felt a shudder run through the small shuttle as the engines finally switched on. He still didn't like thinking of Aaron as a traitor. "Get Mr Scott to have the coordinates ready for Romulus as well. And for goodness sake, make sure Mr Briggs has refuelled the ship. We don't want another fiasco like we had in Moscow."

"Romulus, Captain?" Cooper asked in surprise.

Rhys nodded. "I want to know why Captain Lee chose to defect. Once this is all over I'll seek permission from the admiral, and we can go to Lee's last posting so I can work this all out. There has to be a reason for all of this." It had also been the last place he had seen his old friend, when the *Harvester* had briefly docked in Romulus before coming to Normandy. Aaron had been the same as he had ever been, and Rhys certainly hadn't picked up on any signs of discontent. This seemed to be quite a sudden shift in Aaron's thinking and Rhys wanted to know what had caused it. Good, loyal men like Aaron didn't suddenly decide to pack up and leave for Alpha Centauri without reason.

"Understood, Captain. I'll have the ship ready by the time you arrive," Cooper said. He saluted his captain before the screen went dark.

Rhys leaned forward and put his head in his hands. He could feel the beginnings of a headache starting to form, but he forced himself to ignore the pain for the time being. He'd be able to see the ship's doctor for some pain relief once this crisis had been resolved.

Finally, the shuttle launched without any countdown to prepare Rhys. There were no windows to look out of, so Rhys could only rely on the internal pressure of the shuttle changing subtly as it ascended through the virtually non-existent Cerian atmosphere. He knew he had about ten minutes before he would be docking with the *Harvester*, plenty of time to compose himself and think over what had just happened. He could still scarcely believe that Aaron had defected. It just didn't sit right with him. He was missing something, he was sure.

Rhys had no warning before the shuttle suddenly jolted hard. He would have been thrown from his seat had he not been strapped in; instead the protective belts just cut in hard to his shoulders. A red light started to flash, and the screen started to display a warning. 'Proximity Alert'. A second alarm followed almost immediately, warning Rhys that the shuttle was about to suffer an imminent engine failure.

Cursing loudly, Rhys tried to contact the *Harvester* once more. It took a few tries, but through the chaos he managed to succeed. Once more it was Cooper who answered.

"Christ and Veritas, Captain. It's the *Dawn*," Cooper swore as a manner of greeting. Rhys could hear his crew barking out orders to each other, with the navigator, Scott, being loudest of them all. "It's positioned between us and your shuttle. I think you may have been hit."

Rhys glanced up. Between the shouting on the bridge and the alarms blaring in his ear, he could barely even hear Cooper. But that wasn't what he was most concerned about. "How though? How is the *Dawn* here? You can't jump into the Belt like that. And certainly not this close to Ceres. Are you sure?"

"I didn't think so either, but I'm looking at the *Dawn* right here, and she's shrouded in Denitchev radiation. Somehow the bastard did it. That ship jumped here," Cooper replied. The lieutenant rubbed his chin and looked back towards the bridge. He bellowed some orders towards Scott, before turning back to face Rhys. "We can't lock onto your shuttle. The *Dawn* is in the way. I think... Christ, I think they've got a mag-lock on you..."

The signal cut out, leaving the screen to display just static. At almost the same moment, Rhys felt another jolt shudder through the shuttle. Something had a hold of the shuttle and was pulling it in.

Another loud bang echoed through the small shuttle, and the power abruptly switched off, plunging Rhys into total darkness. The alarms mercifully went quiet too. Rhys blindly struggled to release the straps of his harness and slowly stood up. He fumbled for the backs of the seats, before carefully walking towards the back of the shuttle, feeling around for the door. Before he could reach it, the door began to hiss and slowly slide open. Light poured in, and Rhys flung his arm across his eyes to shield himself from the bright light.

A voice spoke out of the light. "Sorry about the rough landing, but welcome aboard the *Terrestrial Dawn*."

chapter two

"It's… just you?"

A hand rested on Rhys's shoulder, which he quickly pushed away. His eyes got used to the harsh light shining right in his face, and he was able to squint to see someone standing over him, trying to peer into the dark shuttle.

"What?" Rhys asked. He stepped fully out of the shuttle and brushed down his uniform, hoping it hadn't been too ruffled in the rough landing.

"No one else chose to join us? Just you? The captain was hoping for a few dozen at least."

"I… what?" Rhys replied, stumbling over his words as he realised the implications. He frowned and shook his head, resisting the urge to shout his denial at the accusation. "I can assure you my presence here is entirely accidental. In fact, it would be best if you put me back in a shuttle and send me on my way."

The crewman took a step back from Rhys. "I'm afraid I can't do that without Captain Lee's permission," he said, before pausing for a moment. He glanced down to the epaulettes on Rhys's shoulders. His hand moved to his wrist, pressing a small button on his wristband. "Who are you… sir?"

Rhys was about to answer, but he stopped himself just before he started speaking. He had suddenly realised just how severe the situation was. He wasn't just onboard his friend's ship. He was onboard an enemy ship. Should Aaron decide it, Rhys could be considered a hostage of war. He sighed. He should have realised that before the shuttle had been opened and attempted to obscure his identity then. There was nothing he could do about it now.

"I'm Captain Rhys Griffiths of the *Harvester*," he said after a short pause. His hand slowly reached down to his hip, but to his dismay he realised he didn't have a weapon on him. He had left his pistol holstered on the *Harvester*, not having expected to need it when he left his ship that morning. His eyes flicked down to his potential captor's hips. He was armed. If Rhys was to get back off the *Dawn* in a hurry, he would need to take one of the other shuttles, but he doubted he would be allowed to do so without resistance.

Rhys watched as the crewman's gaze followed his own, his hand drifting down to protectively rest over his hip. "I see," he said slowly, pushing another button on his wristband. "I think you should come with me to see the captain, sir."

Rhys flashed a nervous smile, knowing that the crewman had probably just called backup down to deal with him. He knew he didn't have any time, nor any opportunity to fight. His enemy held all the cards. He was left with nothing. He did not doubt his ability to fight one crewman, but if backup was on its way, then he risked a fire fight. Outgunned and outmatched, he would be killed without question or mercy. His shoulders slumped, and he took a deep breath.

"Very well. Take me through to him," Rhys said, admitting defeat. Heavy footfalls announced the arrival of the summoned armed backup. Pistols were held in hands, not yet pointing at Rhys, but he was well aware that should he misstep now, he would be dead in seconds.

Rhys allowed himself to be led through the shuttle dock. His was the only foreign shuttle docked in the *Dawn*, but Rhys couldn't help but notice that a number of the evacuation shuttles appeared to be missing. Rhys said nothing of it to the guards leading him through, but he couldn't help but wonder what had happened to the other shuttles. Had there been an evacuation of crew who hadn't wished to defect from the empire?

A woman was waiting for them outside the shuttle dock. She was dressed in the uniform indicating a senior member of the operations crew, but Rhys noticed the empire insignia had been stitched over with plain white fabric, and she had no epaulettes on her shoulders.

"Stand down gentlemen," she said, waving towards the guards either side of Rhys. They released him, and he straightened the cuffs of his shirt. The woman stepped towards him, holding out her hand. "Lieutenant Carter, first officer of the *Terrestrial Dawn*." Rhys didn't take the offered hand. Carter dropped it after a moment. "If you'll follow me, I'll take you through to meet the captain."

Rhys remained silent as he was led him through the lower levels of the *Dawn*; Carter in front and the four guards right behind. Rhys kept his head high as his eyes scanned around him, trying to find any clue about what was truly going on here. When he had last seen his friend on Mars, his first officer had been Lieutenant Uwele. What had happened to the former first officer? That, and a hundred other questions, burned within Rhys's mind, but he kept his mouth shut. Those questions needed to be addressed by Aaron. Rhys was also acutely aware of how he needed to behave. He did not wish to antagonise Aaron at all, lest he run the risk of his friend deciding that Rhys shouldn't be sent back down to Ceres after all. He had no desire to be held as a prisoner here.

"I suppose you're wondering why we're doing this?" Carter asked Rhys, breaking the silence in the elevator. Rhys didn't respond, keeping his head held high and looking straight ahead, eyes boring into the closed doors. Carter was stood next to him, her hands clasped behind her back. She didn't turn to face him, but out of the corner of his eye, Rhys could see her shoulders slump slightly.

"It was not a decision anyone made lightly," Carter continued, ignoring Rhys's silence. "But I think we all had different reasons. I would have had the church after me, had I stayed. There were some who were... less than impressed with some of my recent choices. I do not regret them, but I couldn't stay."

Rhys chose not to answer, keeping his lips pursed. As terrifying as the church could be when they disagreed with you, it still sounded like a flimsy excuse to throw away everything, to betray the empire and all it stood for.

Thankfully, Rhys was saved from further pitiful explanations by the elevator doors opening. The guards took hold of his wrists again and guided him out with more force than he felt was necessary. He remained quiet, not protesting the strong grip or gentle shove in his back to get him moving. Once again, Rhys felt a flutter of nerves but refused to let it show. Normally he would be excited to meet Aaron, but this time he really didn't know how his friend was going to react.

The bridge was bustling with activity as Rhys was led onto it. Everything felt calm as Aaron's crew prepared the ship for combat defence as they came out of their impossible jump. At first, everything appeared normal to Rhys, but then he saw a flash of brown fur and he froze. There was a starat on the bridge, breaching every regulation for all Terran ships. Not only that, but it was sat in the position usually reserved for the ship's navigator. As he stared, the starat turned around and looked right back at him. Its eyes flashed with recognition as they narrowed, lacking the usual humility and deference ubiquitous in their usual behaviour. It unsettled Rhys enough that he had to turn away again, instead dragging his attention on the back of Aaron's head.

Aaron hadn't yet turned around as he focused on orchestrating the preparations for combat from his chair in the middle of the bridge, but after a few moments Carter let go of Rhys's hand and approached her captain. She tapped him on the shoulder and whispered something in his ear.

"So soon? That can't be right," Aaron said. He stood up and turned around, before recoiling in shock. It took him a few moments to regain his composure, a small smile forming on his face. He rose from his chair. "Rhys? It is a surprise to see you here. Are you here to…"

Rhys shook his head, cutting off Aaron's question before he had chance to finish it. "I am not here to defect or join your cause. My presence is merely an unhappy coincidence and nothing more," he said sharply, surprising even himself with the accusation in his voice. He had seen nothing to exonerate Aaron. Carter had returned to his side, but she hadn't taken hold of his wrist again, though his other was still gripped tight by the other crewman.

Carter spoke up. "We mag-locked his shuttle as soon as we came out of the jump. It was just him onboard."

"I was trying to get to my ship before I was abducted," Rhys protested, shaking off the guard still trying to hold onto his wrist. "What's this all about, Aaron? Why are you doing this?"

Aaron took a step back, gripping his hand onto the back of his chair. He ignored Rhys's question. "Are the other ships being prepared for combat?" he asked, his eyes turning to Rhys, piercing through him almost without seeing.

Rhys nodded. There was little point in hiding it, as the two ships would appear on the *Dawn's* sensors as soon as they were fully powered up. "Both the *Odyssey* and the *Harvester* are being readied right now. They should be minutes away. You lose, Aaron."

"Shit, we weren't quick enough," Aaron muttered under his breath, turning away from Rhys. He called out to his communications officer. "Bokhari, patch us down to Normandy. I need to speak to Admiral Garter."

Rhys was completely ignored in the short time it took to bring up a grainy visual display of the Normandy Control Room was displayed over the screens at the front of the bridge. The admiral frowned and spoke before Aaron could. "Captain Lee, you will stand down. Our port is defended, and we have two ships enroute. We are not afraid to open fire if necessary."

Aaron took a step to one side and turned his body to gesture back at Rhys, who was clearly revealed to the admiral. "We have Captain Griffiths on board," Aaron said, before turning back to face the screen, leaving Rhys unable to see his friend's face. "He is our hostage, but we will provide his safe return if you stand your ships down and facilitate the safe passage of all those who wish to join us."

Admiral Garter muttered something quietly, too quiet for the microphones at his end to pick up. He grimaced, but otherwise didn't show much emotion. When he spoke again, his voice was strained. "We still outgun you and outman you. We can take the ship without destroying it, but we will not let you escape."

"Are you sure, Admiral Garter?" Aaron laughed, his voice cold. "You saw the precision of our jump. We're ready to leave at an instant's notice, and you will not know where we've gone until it's too late. And then? We will be waiting for your guard to drop, and we will strike without warning. We have the firepower to destroy your port with the snap of my fingers. Do not test me."

A second voice spoke through the speakers, one that made Rhys shudder slightly. "Can he really do that?" Cardinal Erik asked. He remained off-screen, still speaking solely to the admiral. "We cannot risk the death of a servant of the church."

Admiral Garter's face twitched. "I thought your aim was peaceful, Mr Lee."

"You threatened me first, Admiral. I am merely responding in kind. It's your call. Stand down, or we lie in wait," Aaron replied. His voice was harsh and uncompromising. Rhys was glad he couldn't see his former friend's face, as he was sure Aaron's face was thunderous.

Admiral Garter stepped back from the screen slightly. He rubbed his jaw. "Very well, we shall concede to your demands. The *Odyssey* and the *Harvester* will be called back. A shuttle had already been prepared for civilians and staff who wish to leave behind the empire."

Aaron turned and flashed a quick smile towards Rhys, before facing Admiral Garter again. "Good. I'm glad you can see reason, Admiral. I have no wish to harm anyone, after all. Once the shuttle has been received, I shall send Captain Griffiths back down in it. Of this you have my word."

"Forgive me if I don't trust you, Captain Lee. We will maintain our defences, but will otherwise accede to your requests," the admiral replied. He then leaned forward, and his image disappeared from the *Dawn's* screens.

Rhys took in a deep breath. Aaron had confirmed his fears. He was being considered a hostage aboard the *Dawn*, but nor could he blame Aaron for taking full advantage of the situation. That the admiral was still willing to open fire on the *Dawn* if necessary was chilling. All he could do was trust Aaron would be good to his word and allow him to return down to the dwarf planet once the traitors had boarded.

Aaron turned around and sighed. "You're not even going to try and stop me, are you?" He waved away Carter and the other crewman, leaving Rhys unguarded. He placed his hand around Rhys's shoulder and guided him back off the bridge.

"Why would I waste my breath?" Rhys replied, allowing himself to be led outside. Aaron didn't take him far, stopping as soon as they were out of earshot range from the bridge. "I just don't understand why. On Mars you were… normal. Where did this come from?"

Aaron sighed and bowed his head. "I don't know where to start, and I don't think you'd believe me anyway." He fell silent, not daring to look up at Rhys, instead staring down at the floor. Rhys just waited for his friend to say something else, not wanting to speculate on what reason could have been important enough for his friend to betray everyone he had ever known. Aaron smiled nervously. "I just… feel like it's the right thing to do. I wish you could see what I see, but you… you would never consider the other viewpoint."

Rhys shook his head. "No, never. I will never turn my back on the empire."

Aaron's smile grew a little wider, but it was a smile of sadness, not joy. "That wasn't what I… Yeah, I know. You will remain loyal to Terra no matter what, won't you?"

"Unless Emperor Neicwyk himself tells me I am no longer welcome in the empire, then I will always remain loyal to TIE," Rhys retorted.

"A shame, but not entirely unexpected."

"That's what loyalty is, Aaron. Never wavering from the cause, no matter what may try to turn your head," Rhys replied. He half turned away from his oldest friend, stopping himself before he said something he would regret. He didn't want to goad his friend into going back on his word, trapping him aboard the *Dawn* while he made his way to Alpha Centauri.

"I have remained loyal, Rhys. Just not to the same people as you," Aaron said. He looked back towards the bridge, avoiding the incredulous stare Rhys gave him.

"What you've done here? That's not loyalty."

Aaron sighed reached into his pocket. Rhys tensed, but his friend pulled out a flash drive and nothing more. He held it out for Rhys to take. "When you get this down to the surface, you'll be able to find the co-ordinates from a tracking beacon. Follow it, and you'll be able to pick up the rest of my crew," he explained. Once Rhys had taken the drive, he rubbed his hand over his forehead. "Look, Rhys. I'm sorry it's come to this."

"No, you're not," Rhys replied sharply. "If you were sorry, you would never have betrayed your duty and your emperor."

"Not of that," Aaron replied, his voice dull and listless. Gone was the authority he had held when speaking to Admiral Garter. His arm raised slightly, as though to place his hand on Rhys's shoulder, but Rhys stepped back. The arm fell down to Aaron's hip again. "I'm sorry you can't see things from my point of view. I've always tried, but I don't think you ever even realised what I was trying to say."

Rhys didn't get a chance to respond, as Carter stuck her head out of the bridge. "Captain. The shuttle is approaching."

Aaron let his arm drop back down to his side. He sounded weary when he spoke. "Alright. I'm coming. Get Mr Chen to lead Captain Griffiths back down to the shuttle bay. And… the cardinal?"

Carter shook her head. "He's staying. I asked him before we jumped," Carter replied, but the two turned their back to Rhys and offered no explanation for their words. He was left alone for just a few moments before they instructed one of the crew out of the bridge to meet him.

Rhys said nothing as he turned to leave, ignoring Aaron's pained goodbye. He didn't see Aaron's shoulders shaking as he shuffled back onto the bridge.

The walk back down to the shuttles was difficult. Rhys had not expected to see Aaron again after he had seen the message from his old friend. The shock of the parting still hadn't sunk through too deep, but Rhys already knew that the next time he saw Aaron, they would have to consider themselves enemies. Rhys would be fighting for TIE, and Aaron for the CGP.

Rhys tried not to look at those who disembarked the shuttle. He didn't want to know who they were, and he certainly didn't want to know why they had chosen to come to the *Dawn*. Every single one of them was human. It appeared that Admiral Garter and Captain Favre had been successful in keeping the situation from the starats, even though their initial plan to apprehend the defectors had been foiled by Rhys's unfortunate capture. Once the shuttle was empty, Rhys stepped in.

"Have a good flight, Captain," Chen said. His sincerity made Rhys turn around to face him. Then Rhys remembered. Sun Chen had served on the *Harvester* until a few years ago. He had transferred to the *Dawn* a month before Rhys had been promoted from first officer to captain. He had always been a good man to work with.

"You too," Rhys said, quickly and reflexively. His hand twitched at his side, almost going to hold it out to Chen. He suppressed the motion. He had been a good man. Now he was a traitor. Chen turned to leave as the shuttle door hissed shut, leaving Rhys alone with his troubles. He took the closest seat and sat down, resting his head in his hands. What had Aaron meant? What reason had he seen? He could recall nothing on the *Dawn* that could have resulted in his friend's defection.

He could feel the shuttle detach from the *Dawn*, and the engines began to rumble as they activated, guiding the shuttle back down to the dwarf planet. He was about to strap himself in when he caught sight of something gleaming on the floor. He picked up a small necklace, a glinting pendant with a small disc of gold, inscribed with the TIE insignia. Without thinking, Rhys pocketed it. Most likely one of the previous passengers had dropped it, whether deliberately or not.

***

By the time the shuttle slowed down on its approach to the surface, all thought of the necklace was already pushed from Rhys's mind. With no windows to look out of, there was no way of knowing how far from the surface he was. All he could do was guess the distance judging on how long the flight had been. It was a situation that threatened to bring back some old memories he would rather forget. He gripped onto the armrests of his chair until his knuckles turned white. He didn't expect the sudden landing, the abrupt jolt too strong even for the stabilisers to negate.

It took a few minutes after the shuttle landed for the walkway to extend out and latch onto the shuttle before the doors could be opened. It gave Rhys plenty of time to compose himself again. He smoothed down his shirt and adjusted his cuffs. He didn't know what sort of reception he was about to receive.

Once the doors finally opened, Rhys stepped out to find Admiral Garter was the only person waiting for him back in the shuttle dock. He was standing a little straighter than before, a hint of a smile on his weathered face.

"Welcome back, Captain," the admiral said, waving away Rhys's salute and reaching out to shake the captain's hand. "The *Dawn* has already departed. It jumped mere moments after your shuttle disengaged. We've had no further communication from Lee, so now that we have you safely back, all appears well."

"I was given this, sir," Rhys said, holding out the small flash drive. The admiral took it, looking at the little device curiously. "Lee told me it contained coordinates to the rest of his crew."

Admiral Garter nodded and slipped the flash drive into his pocket. "I'll have someone verify it's safe. If it appears to be legitimate, we'll have a search group sent out. For now, I think we need to discuss what happened."

"I'm sorry for what happened up there, Admiral," Rhys said, but the admiral waved his hand to silence him. "We would have had him otherwise."

"I can hardly blame you for that, Rhys. Wrong place at the wrong time, it can't be helped," the admiral said. It was one of the first times Rhys had ever heard him speak without the rigid formality of his rank. He gestured for Rhys to start walking further down the dock, away from the door into the rest of the port. The admiral sucked in his breath as they approached the end of the docking bay, looking out the windows over the barren dwarf planet. Away to one side was a small atmosphere dome, which housed a few of the other external buildings, allowing people to walk on the surface between them with enough oxygen to breathe. "Besides, I think we can work this into a good thing."

"What do you mean, Admiral?" Rhys asked. There was something about the tone of the admiral's voice that confused him. He stood slightly behind the admiral, looking out towards the dome, where he could see a couple of starats carefully creep across the surface to run external repairs on something.

"I think public knowledge could be how Captain Lee wished to fire upon Normandy, using your position as hostage aboard the ship to prevent any return fire," Admiral Garter said, speaking quietly and quickly, glancing back to make sure there was no one around to overhear them. "Of course, you intervened, putting yourself at great risk. You managed to subdue the traitor Lee and force your escape, demanding that the *Dawn* leave before it was destroyed. Through your actions, you saved everyone in Normandy and on Ceres."

Rhys leaned against the wall beside the window. "He was a good officer once. Why would we want to slander his memory further?"

"He was a good officer. Once. Emphasis on the past tense. He is now a traitor to the empire. A little false truth will not hurt him any more than he has hurt himself," Admiral Garter said, turning around to face Rhys.

"I'm not sure this covers a little false truth. It sounds pretty blatant, and I'm just not sure why," Rhys replied. He grimaced and turned away from the admiral, tapping his foot nervously on the floor.

Admiral Garter removed his glasses, rubbing them clean on the hem of his sleeve. "Are you defending his actions, Captain?"

"Of course not, sir. I just don't see what benefit it can bring for us to slander him," Rhys replied. He knew he needed to be quick to defend himself from any potential accusations of sympathy towards Aaron.

The admiral nodded, returning the glasses to his nose. "I've known you for twenty-five years now, Rhys. Ever since you graduated I have been watching your progress. You're every bit the officer your mother was. She would have been proud."

"I... thank you," Rhys said, caught off guard by the sudden change in subject.

"To tell the truth, I'm being pressured into retirement within a year," the admiral said. He looked outside again, and Rhys followed his gaze, though there was no longer any movement on the surface. "I get to nominate a successor, but the final choice of my replacement will be up to Chancellor Roberts. As things stand, you're my nomination to replace me. You're a sharp man and are quick on your feet. You aren't afraid to make the big calls, and I think that will be very important to maintain stability within the Belt."

"Again, thank you, Admiral. I'm honoured you think I'm worthy to step up," Rhys replied, his shock at the recommendation making him slip back into his usual formality.

"Chancellor Roberts is not an easy man to please. He will have his eye on other candidates, so you will need to impress him in order to get his consideration. Single-handedly saving Ceres will go some way," the admiral explained. Rhys stayed silent in the face of the praise. He was honoured by the recommendation, but he wasn't sure he agreed with the insinuation that he needed to lie or cheat his way to a promotion.

"It's getting late. Sleep on it for now and we can discuss the matter further tomorrow. Come see me in the control tower when you rise. We'll likely need to provide an official explanation for Terra," Admiral Garter said. A small smile flashed across his face.

Thanking the admiral again, Rhys stayed where he was as he watched Admiral Garter leave. He was left alone in the shuttle dock, with the only sounds being the occasional creak of metal and quiet pop from the flickering lights. His thoughts were a mess, with a wide range of emotions fighting within his mind. Relief, concern, confusion, panic, worry. He didn't know what to think, but that he needed some time to rest and enjoy a good drink.

***

By the time Rhys made his way up to his ship, Cooper was waiting for him. "No one else to come on board tonight, sir?" the first officer asked as Rhys stepped out of the shuttle. When Rhys shook his head, Cooper followed his captain onto the ship and closed the shuttle bay behind them.

"We have two more on board at the moment, just so you're aware, sir," Cooper said as the two walked through the narrow corridors of the ship, towards the bridge. His mouth twisted in distaste. "Not for long. Just a couple of starats. One was injured while working on some external repairs. Doctor Sparks insisted we take them in to give them treatment."

"I see," Rhys said slowly, pursing his lips up in thought. "They down in the medical bay then?"

"Until morning, yes," Cooper replied.

Rhys nodded. "Good. Make sure Doctor Sparks knows he is to keep them down there. Please remind him that he's to consult me before taking anyone on board. I don't like not knowing who is on my ship."

"Of course, sir. I can see him right away."

Out of habit, the two had walked into the bridge, waving a greeting to the communications officer, who was the only other person present. Rhys and Cooper stood in the middle of the wide, circular room, around the walls of which were the various terminals used by the operations crew necessary to maintain a safe and quick flight between the planets and stars. But for the communications officer, Jermaine McDonald, it was deserted. There was no need for anyone else to maintain a presence on the bridge. The ship was no longer in a situation where it needed to prepare for combat, and all non-essential communications would be automatically redirected to Normandy Control. McDonald's presence was only required should the ship need to be alerted to any urgent updates from the surface, or if the ship needed to be scrambled in a hurry.

"Nothing else I should be aware of?" Rhys asked. He glanced around the bridge. Everything else was quiet and still. The shutters were drawn closed across the small windows at the front of the bridge, hiding the view of the dwarf planet beyond.

"Nothing, Captain. If we needed to, we could scramble and be ready for launch in ten minutes," Cooper replied.

"Very good then. Once you've spoken to Doctor Sparks then you're relieved. I'll take emergency call tonight," Rhys said, taking one last look around the empty bridge. Though they had never been in any real danger, Rhys still felt drained and needed a drink to wash away the last of the nervous tension that was stiffening his body. He turned back to his first officer. "If you care to, you're welcome to share a drink in my quarters."

"Not for me, Captain, no thank you," Cooper said. His face was twisted into a grimace and his hands clenched slightly by his side. "I don't drink. Not anymore."

Rhys nodded his head. The two had worked together for five years now in various forms, but Rhys still knew very little about his first officer. But then, no one did. Of everyone in the military, Rhys was one of the few privy to some of Cooper's darkest secrets, not that the first officer was aware of that. "Very well. Don't forget to shut down the lights on your way back."

"Of course, Captain," Cooper said with a quick salute. He turned and disappeared from the bridge. Rhys could hear him open the emergency stairwell door. His footsteps echoed down, taking the stairs two at a time as he descended to the medical bay, several floors below the main deck. Once these sounds faded, Rhys was left alone with only the creaks and groans from the ship, and the occasional squeaks from McDonald's chair as he leaned back.

"I need to get away from this place." Rhys whispered to the near-silence. He hated everything about Ceres. Despite being so close to Terra it was unable to properly defend itself from even a single enemy ship. He had much preferred his time on Mars, with the vast resources of the Vatican's coffers able to produce probably the most advanced network of spaceships and ports between the three star systems settled by humanity. Rhys had only travelled out to the Sirius System twice, but his experiences there had been much better than what he was finding on Ceres, as few structures there were older than a couple of decades. The very latest technology had gone into work out there. Naturally, Rhys had never been Centauri System. That was the province of the CGP, and it had been almost as long as the system had been colonised.

"Just forget it Rhys. Think of the positives," he told himself. He could well be on his way to admiral, and that was definitely something worth thinking about. Admiral Griffiths. He liked the sound of that, even if he disagreed with some of Admiral Garter's suggestions on how to acquire that rank.

"Did you say something, Captain?" McDonald asked, lifting his headpiece up and swivelling on his chair. It broke Rhys out of his reverie.

"Oh, no. Sorry. Just thinking out loud. How long until Ms Watkins relieves you?" Rhys replied.

"Another couple of hours. We're not expecting any more dramas tonight. The *Dawn* is certainly long gone," McDonald said. He spun a pen around in his fingers, ready to take down any transcripts if needed. "The *Odyssey* is providing scanner information tonight."

Rhys nodded and bade the communications officer good night. There was little else that needed to be done, so he thought he may as well attempt to get a restful night's sleep.

Locking himself in his quarters on the level above the bridge, Rhys kicked his shoes off, and stretched his tense shoulders. He stripped out of his uniform and bundled it to the floor without any care for creases and dirt. There would be a clean uniform for him already in his wardrobe, and the dirty set would be picked up in the morning by one of the starats aboard the ship.

Pouring himself a glass of red wine, Rhys slumped against the wall and ran his spare hand through his short brown hair, exhaling deeply. His wine cabinet had an extensive collection of bottles sourced from all corners of the empire. There had been many times during his training at the academy that Rhys had shared a bottle or two with Aaron. He raised his glass in a silent toast for who his friend had once been. Limiting himself to the one glass before he ended up consuming a whole bottle, Rhys closed his wine cabinet and shut off all the lights in his room. No light came through the cracks around his door from the corridor outside, so Cooper had already switched all the lights through the ship but for those on the bridge.

The wine had helped loosen some of the tension in his shoulders, but it had done nothing for the questions that swirled around his mind. He settled down in bed and closed his eyes. He still had no real answer behind Aaron's defection. Just vague hints and further questions. Should he lie to the chancellor to earn his respect? Should he be concerned about Cardinal Erik's presence and probing questions?

Despite his worries, Rhys slept well that night, quickly falling into slumber. But for the familiar sound of scurrying claws through the corridors, the *Harvester* was silent.

chapter three

Rhys woke early the following morning. It would be close to twilight at the Normandy spaceport, but because of the dwarf planet's rapid rotation, everyone used the Terran clock to keep track of the daily routines. Likewise, most of the empire's ships were also keyed in to operate under Terran schedules.

The skeleton night crew had yet to retire when Rhys left his quarters, though he was one of the first of the day crew to have risen. He was out of uniform and in casual wear, but he still received a couple of salutes and greetings of, "Good morning, Captain," from the few he passed. He even caught sight of a furred tail disappearing around the corner as one of the starats fled him.

He made his way down towards the small gym in the lower levels of the ship. Ever since his early teens, Rhys had kept his body in good shape, both through the gym and sports, and this had held him in good stead during his mock combat trials at the academy. He had never worked on building his muscles like his first officer had, but he had the lean, athletic tone of a long-distance runner.

He was the only one present in the gym, and as he pounded the treadmill he watched a small television in one corner of the room, using signals transmitted up from Ceres. The grainy image was of a news report from Terra. There was a brief discussion on a CGP raid on the Denitchev mines in the Sirius system, but there was no talk at all about the defection of Aaron. Rhys had expected some news on it given how close it was to Terra, but perhaps it had all been kept internal for now. A second news report followed, detailing a private investor's attempts to purchase a stake in the mining colony near the Normandy spaceport, as well as the construction of civilian ports around the Asteroid Belt.

Rhys was only halfway through his usual set before his isolation was broken. He heard the door slide open behind him and footsteps come in, but he didn't turn around to see who it was. There were usually a few other early risers who used the gym on the days there were no scheduled sessions. Occasionally he was able to recruit a sparring partner from them too.

"Thought I'd find you here, sir."

Rhys sighed and switched off the treadmill, his run slowing to a jog before he hopped off the side. He ran a towel over his forehead and turned to face his navigator. Edgar Scott was a tall man and towered over most. Rhys was no exception.

"What can I do for you, Mr Scott?"

The navigator had a quick look around the otherwise empty room, making sure there was no one else present. "Were you expecting a class this morning, Captain?"

"Not today, no. We have one tomorrow morning, though," Rhys replied. He took a few deep breaths and then a long drink of water. He normally led his crew through their morning physical exertions, but the gym wasn't large enough for his whole crew. Usually they would use the facilities in the port they were stationed at, but Normandy was lacking a modern gym.

"Oh good. I thought I'd missed it," Scott said, holding his hand to his chest in relief. "But if you're about finished here, then the admiral was searching for you, sir."

"Did he say how urgent it was?" Rhys asked. He glanced back at the treadmill, wondering if he had time to complete his set.

"Urgent enough, but not so urgent you can't make yourself presentable first, he told me," Scott replied.

Rhys sighed again. He reached for the television remote and switched it off, leaving the small gym quiet once more. He towelled his forehead dry again, pushing his hair from his eyes. "If you see the admiral first, let him know I'll be on my way," he said. He would be expected to shower and dress in uniform before presenting himself to the admiral, unless the situation was desperate.

"Understood, Captain," Scott said. The navigator gave Rhys a quick salute, before ducking outside the gym to head through the dark corridors of the ship. Rhys left in the opposite direction, returning back towards his quarters.

Before he made it back up to his quarters, he ran into Cooper, who was also dressed in his casual exercise gear. "On the way to the gym?" the first officer asked, after the formal greetings were completed.

"Already been. Got a summons from the admiral."

Cooper grimaced. "Ah. Sounds important, if it's this early. Perhaps another call from the *Dawn*."

Rhys shrugged his shoulders, but he decided not to speculate on what news the admiral had to share. It could be completely unrelated to the *Dawn*. He would have to wait to find out. The two prepared to leave in their opposite directions; Rhys to the shuttle bay and Cooper to the gym.

"Those two starats are gone, by the way," Cooper said, turning on his heel and turning to face Rhys once more. "Doctor Sparks discharged the wounded one under my supervision about fifteen minutes ago. They were escorted off the ship and sent back to Captain Favre."

"Much appreciated, thank you," Rhys said, before Cooper gave his captain a quick salute. The first officer headed down towards the gym, while Rhys made his way back up to his quarters to prepare for his meeting with the admiral.

***

It took Rhys half an hour to prepare himself for the meeting with Admiral Garter, cleaning his body of the sweat from his run on the treadmill, and then making sure his fresh uniform was perfectly presented. By the time he was back on Ceres, the spaceport was starting to wake up, with a number of starats scurrying around. The small creatures largely kept to the shadows as Rhys passed them, keeping their heads low and tails tucked in between their legs. They didn't offer so much as a squeak of greeting towards him, and Rhys largely ignored them back. He barely even noticed their presence.

Another cluster of rooms had been closed off overnight, with yellow tape plastered across the doors. Just what had caused these closures, Rhys couldn't be sure. They were situated near a number of other rooms that had been closed off due to structural instability in the ceilings, threatening a collapse and exposure to the thin, freezing

Cerian atmosphere. Given the rooms hadn't been sealed off, a collapse hadn't occurred yet. It was surely it was only a matter of time. There was only so much the starats could do to maintain the place.

Rhys was followed up the stairs to the control tower. A quick glance back revealed the unpleasant face of Cardinal Erik just behind him. The captain had no desire to slow down and allow the cardinal to join him, so he picked up his pace so that he could reach the control room first. Unfortunately, he wasn't quick enough to make it through the door before the cardinal was able to put his foot through. Servants of the church were not permitted to be removed from any location once they were present, so despite the aggrieved looks from Admiral Garter as he looked up, there was nothing anyone could do to dislodge the cardinal once he slipped inside after Rhys.

None of the other captains were yet present, with only a skeleton crew on the communications array manning their stations. Out of the few windows, light was creeping across the barren, Cerian landscape. All was still and quiet out there.

"Captain Griffiths, glad you could make it," Admiral Garter said gruffly, making a point to avoid making eye contact with the cardinal behind Rhys. As the captain approached the table, Cardinal Erik turned to look out the windows, hands clasped behind his back as he surveyed the barren terrain.

Admiral Garter looked weary as he sat at the table, a steaming cup of coffee clutched in one hand. His uniform was scruffy and unkempt, as though he had worn it all night. He waved away Rhys's salute. A number of printed transcripts were scattered over the small table, covering up the maps and blueprints they had studied the previous day. Rhys quickly made himself an instant coffee before he took his place at the table.

"We've received a number of messages overnight. It has taken me a number of hours to sort things out, after yesterday's debacle," the admiral said. He leaned back in his chair and ran a hand over his brow, before taking a small sip from his coffee.

"Are we not waiting for Favre and Baron first, Admiral?" Rhys asked, surprised that the admiral would begin without the presence of the other two captains.

"I'll be speaking to them individually. Some things I need to say concern them, but others concern just yourself, Captain Griffiths," the admiral said with a weary sigh.

Admiral Garter picked up a bundle of papers as he stood up, taking a couple more sips of his steaming coffee as he did so. "This is the transcript of a conversation I had with Chancellor Roberts a couple of hours ago. He has expressed his… displeasure at the loss of the *Dawn*, and a full-scale investigation will be held into the conduct of everyone involved, and if there were any actions that could have been taken to prevent the loss of such a prized military asset."

"Permission to speak freely, sir?" Rhys asked, biting back his immediate retort. He waited for the admiral's curt nod before proceeding. "He does know there was nothing more that we could do, right?"

"I understand that. But the chancellor is adamant that protocol must be adhered to. He will find fault somewhere, even if it is not from this port. He expects to be here in a day or two to conduct interviews," Admiral Garter explained, doing little to assuage Rhys's worries.

Taking the transcript from the admiral, Rhys started to read through the chancellor's words, confirming everything Admiral Garter had said. The chancellor had been careful in his words to not attribute any blame at this stage, but it was clear that he was less than impressed with the actions the admiral had taken, and through extension, Rhys's own.

"Is he serious, sir?" Rhys asked, the transcript lifted up in his hands. "He's threatening expulsion if he's not satisfied with our response? What did he expect us to do?"

Admiral Garter didn't respond at first. His lips were pursed tight. "It seems that way."

Rhys put the transcript back down on the table and gripped his coffee in both hands. "This is… complicated," Rhys said quietly, before glancing up to see if the cardinal was listening in on them. He dropped his voice a little lower. "Our story hasn't changed yet, I assume, Admiral?"

"Still the same, yes," Admiral Garter replied as he slumped down in his chair. He rubbed his eyes and stifled a yawn behind his hand.

"Excuse me, I'm sorry Captain. I've been up all night trying to clean up this mess."

"And what about the mess with the Vatican?" an oily voice interjected. Both Admiral Garter and Rhys turned around to face the cardinal, who had moved away from the window.

"I beg your pardon?" Admiral Garter asked. A spasm of annoyance had run over his cheek before speaking, but his voice remained calm.

Cardinal Erik frowned. "I speak of the cardinal who was aboard the *Terrestrial Dawn*. He was to assist in my attempts to eradicate this unfortunate blemish of starat sympathy in this hovel," he said, brushing some dust from his bright robes. "That I have received no word from him, nor have there been any attempts from empire forces to retrieve him, have left His Holiness most concerned."

Admiral Garter and Rhys briefly glanced towards each other. It was the admiral who spoke first. "We have knowledge some of Captain Lee's crew who were left behind at an old mining station. It is possible your cardinal is still with the crew there, but beyond that, we have had no word of any cardinal's presence on the *Dawn*. If there have been any communications from the Vatican regarding this matter, then we have not received them."

"I see. That is disappointing news," the cardinal said, folding his arms across his chest. His lips pulled up in a sneer. "I shall pass this information on to the Vatican. We shall see what their next move shall be, but should it be found that you are withholding information from the Holy See..." The cardinal trailed off, letting his threat remain unspoken. Everyone already knew that the punishments for disobeying the Vatican were severe indeed.

The cardinal then dismissed himself without another word, leaving Rhys and Admiral Garter alone once more. Rhys was about to express his confusion at the situation, before remembering a casual word from Aaron directed at his first officer. "I think the cardinal was still on board the *Dawn*," he said quietly, tapping his fingers on the table as he looked up towards the admiral. "Captain Lee mentioned him, and it seemed the cardinal had no wish to come to the surface."

"You believe the cardinal defected too? That would be difficult to prove, and it could create a lot of other problems that I have no desire to deal with now," the admiral replied. He rubbed his eyes again and drained the last of his coffee. Immediately he got up to make a new one. By the time he had finished preparing it, Captain Favre had arrived.

The Cerian glanced back at the door with a foul look on his face, and he muttered something beneath his breath. Rhys didn't need to ask who had annoyed him. He was sure the cardinal had mentioned something unpleasant to the Cerian captain.

Captain Favre and Admiral Garter greeted each other, before the admiral began to brief the Cerian on the events of the night. There was no new information for Rhys as the admiral went back over the chancellor's messages, so he sat down at the table with his coffee and poured over the transcripts again. He sifted through the pages, then stopped and stared in shock at the heading over one of the pages, one the admiral had not discussed with him.

Admiral Garter glanced down, noticing the cause of Rhys's sudden concern. He took the page of the transcript and held it close to his chest. "This is not to become public knowledge at this stage. It is not to leave this room, or to be discussed with anyone," he said, staring Rhys and Favre in the eyes. Both nodded and agreed. "Chancellor Roberts has warned that a review will be done of the Normandy spaceport. This review will cover a number of points, ranging from its strategic use to the practical value of maintaining and operating the port. The chancellor was particularly vociferous in pointing out that should it be found wanting, the port faces risk of decommission."

"Decommission?" Captain Favre said, his back stiffening. His voice was higher pitched than normal. "They can't be seriously considering that? There's been a port here for centuries now, they can't just rip it up! The people of Ceres rely on us to survive. Without a port, they have no food, no water."

Admiral Garter raised his hands towards Favre. "I understand your concerns, Captain, but it is not to me you must appeal. It is the chancellor who will make that decision. He will come speak to you and draw his own conclusions." The admiral paused and ran his hand over his cheek. "Nostalgia and history aren't enough. You will need to convince the chancellor yourself why this port should remain, and what strategic value it offers to the empire. I believe there have already been rumours of a privately-owned civilian port being built to replace this one."

"This is ridiculous," Favre spat, reaching out for the transcript from the admiral's hands. Like Rhys before him, Favre dedicated a few minutes to reading through the transcript, and all the while his face grew paler as he read on. "He's really serious about doing this, isn't he? We should… we should go and fix whatever we can, before he gets here. Get this port running as smoothly as we can manage. Captain Griffiths, do you have any crew you can spare to assist?"

Rhys nodded. "I'll speak to my services commander and see who he can spare," he said. Commander Briggs would be able to provide some men for emergency repairs on the port. It wasn't like there was much else for them to do. There could well be rumblings of annoyance from the service crew at having to be drawn from their usual work, but some could well enjoy the change from their day to day monotony.

"We should tour the grounds, captain," the admiral said, gesturing towards Captain Favre. "You can show me exactly what is still functional, and what is beyond repair so that I can prepare a report to the chancellor."

"That would be most appreciated, Admiral," Favre replied, giving the admiral a quick salute. "Anything we can do to get this place up to standard, I will do it. This place has been my home for almost my entire life. I will not see it abandoned."

"We can do what we can," Admiral Garter said, before gesturing to Favre to leave the control room. He then turned to Rhys as the Cerian exited the room. "See to your services commander. Inform any recruits that they're to serve under Captain Favre for the time being. Have them meet at the mess hall in two hours."

"Understood, Admiral," Rhys said, giving his superior officer a quick salute. The admiral then left Rhys, the captain alone with just a couple of the tower crew, trying to wrestle with the ancient Cerian communications systems. None appeared to have listened to anything the admiral and two captains had been discussing. The situation was not ideal from a security perspective, but the usual briefing room the admiral summoned the captains to was one of the many locations in the port that had been rendered unusable. The control tower was only a temporary measure, though it had lasted for the several months Rhys had been stationed at the small port.

Rhys sighed as he looked out over the bleak vista from the dirty windows. Outside, he could see a few people walking the desolate surface. Out of necessity, they were clad in protective suits and tethered to the railings that were affixed to the surface. It was probably too soon for them to be surveying the outer perimeter defences, but Rhys couldn't think of any other reason to leave the port. There was nothing out there.

Knowing he couldn't linger long, Rhys started on the walk back to the docking bay once more. The route had become so familiar over the months on Ceres, he didn't need to put any concentration into where he was going, even though the first few weeks it had felt like an indecipherable labyrinth.

Rhys simply sent a message up to his ship to inform Briggs of the orders from Admiral Garter. He was in no mood to speak to the services commander face to face, instead choosing to remain on the surface even though he had no official duties until he was able to assist with the port maintenance. The training session he had been scheduled to oversee in the rifle range had been cancelled the previous day due to a series of electrical faults in the local artificial gravity systems that had rendered the rooms unusable.

It hadn't been long since he had been buoyed by his prospects, surprised by Admiral Garter's recommendation for a promotion. Now there was a dark cloud on the horizon. Unless he could convince Chancellor Roberts otherwise, he could find his career diminishing or even ending. The same threat hung upon the very port he resided in.

Until Briggs responded to his message and sent some of the services crew down, all he could do was think over his defence before the chancellor.

There was nothing to prepare but words.

***

The Normandy spaceport was transformed into a hive of activity. Rhys had never seen so much work taking place in the dark corridors, but he couldn't help but think it wouldn't be enough. He patrolled through the port, overseeing some of the construction work, assisting Captain Favre in coordinating the efforts when he could. But there was only so much that could be done with the materials they had on hand. Breaches in the atmospheric shells couldn't be repaired with ease, and there was nothing that could be done about the inoperative weapons system that was meant to protect the port from attack. Rhys doubted it would be enough to impress the chancellor.

Word reached Ceres that the *Olympus* was due to arrive at Normandy the following day, with the chancellor on board. When advance messages had come through that the ship was preparing for its final approach to the dwarf planet, Rhys retreated back to his ship to prepare. In an attempt to make himself appear more impressive for the chancellor, he put on his formal dress uniform. The long, thick coat was almost unbearably hot to wear, even in the cool, air-conditioned port, but Rhys had to admit it helped project an aura of power and confidence.

Finally, he was given the summons to make his way to the *Olympus*. He was instructed to take a shuttle directly from the *Harvester* to board the chancellor's ship. It didn't take long for that to be arranged, and soon afterwards Rhys was waiting in a small room just off the shuttle bay in the *Olympus*. He had been left to sit down and wait for the chancellor to finish his other interviews. He was to be spoken to last, after Captain Favre and Admiral Garter. He tapped his foot as he sat back, alone in the small room as he let the minutes tick by. He kept his coat on, fanning himself to keep himself cool, convinced that the air-conditioners had stopped working.

After what felt like hours, but had only been about forty-five minutes, the door opened, and a young woman came through. "Captain Griffiths, welcome to the *Olympus*," she said with a bright smile. She extended her hand out for Rhys to take in greeting. "I'm Melanie Carpenter. If you'll follow me, I can take you to the chancellor. He will be ready to see you now."

It had been a long time since Rhys had last been on a civilian spaceship. Whilst the bridge was identical to a military vessel, it was beyond this that there were major differences. Instead of the utilitarian corridors of the crew's quarters, there were spacious dining and recreation areas, and the quarters themselves were more attributed to comfort than the military crafts. The ship was also somewhat larger than those used by the military to accommodate all this. However, as the *Olympus* was on official business with the chancellor, it was mostly empty, with just a small crew to operate it.

Melanie didn't even try to breach the conversation barrier as she led Rhys up to Chancellor Roberts' quarters, though she glanced back a few times to make sure the captain was still following her. He stayed right behind her, keeping pace as he clenched his fists by his sides.

Rhys's heart was hammering at his ribs. He couldn't remember being so nervous before; not the day he had first gone into the Cardiff Academy; not the day he had graduated; not even the first time he had captained his own ship.

Eventually, after a short wait inside an elevator, Rhys found himself waiting outside the chancellor's quarters. Melanie directed him to wait on a couch just beside the closed double doors while she slipped inside. A few murmured voices could be heard from within, and after just a few moments Rhys was permitted inside.

A large office opened up, lavishly decorated in a manner that would never have been seen on a military ship. A number of ornate artworks were hung from the walls, including a rare Van Gogh replica. Rhys couldn't help but glance around the room, at the opulence on the walls, before his eyes were directed to the mahogany desk before the back wall, behind which sat an elderly man with wiry grey hair. A notebook was open on the desk, with a series of notes scrawled across a number of pages.

The chancellor gestured to the three chairs in front of the desk, before flicking the notebook over to a fresh page before Rhys could read any of it. "Please sit down, Captain Griffiths," he said in a soft voice. Rhys took the centre one, flicking the tail of his coat to the side so he didn't scrunch it up badly.

"It's a pleasure to meet you, Chancellor," Rhys said. He was unsure if he should offer to shake the chancellor's hand or not. The chancellor didn't show any sign of offence when Rhys's hand remained beneath the desk.

"Melanie here will be transcribing our conversation," the chancellor explained. He leaned forward in his chair and steepled his fingers.

"Of course, sir," Rhys said. He tried not to let his nerves at having the conversation recorded show.

"Admiral Garter will be returning to Ceres momentarily. He explained everything that occurred on the ground to me; especially the inadequacies of the defences here, which will be looked into. Captain Favre was also quite… vociferous on the matter. But I now need to know what happened with Captain Lee. I need to know what went on inside his head, and I think you're the best person to explain that," the chancellor said. His voice was calm and even, betraying nothing of his internal thoughts or emotions. A politician's voice.

"I'm not sure where to begin," Rhys said, tapping his fingers on his knees beneath the desk.

"Try the start," the chancellor said, not unkindly.

Rhys exhaled heavily, running through his mind some of the speeches he had planned the previous day, using Admiral Garter's concocted version of the events that had happened on the *Dawn*. Most of it had already fled, leaving him mute before the kindly gaze of the chancellor.

"I was enroute to my ship via shuttle, when I was intercepted by the *Dawn* as it made an unexpected jump into the orbit of Ceres," Rhys said, before the chancellor raised his hand.

"Not that beginning, Captain. I'm more interested in before that for the moment. In fact, I don't really care what you say happened on the *Dawn*. Admiral Garter has already explained what happened there, but I need to know the reasons why Captain Lee chose to defect. When was it you last spoke with him?" the chancellor asked. Though his voice remained calm, there was the slightest hint of steel in his question. Accusatory.

"I… I last saw him on Mars, briefly, a few months ago. He was stationed at Romulus, and we needed to refuel," Rhys replied, furrowing his brow as he tried to remember that previous encounter, wanting to get everything correct. He knew every word was being recorded, the tap of Melanie's fingers on her electronic keyboard distracting him slightly. He had been caught off guard by the chancellor's area of focus, and he struggled to remember. There hadn't been much, just a brief encounter in the couple of hours he had on the surface. Nothing about it had given away that it would be the last time they would meet as friends.

The chancellor was evidently not content to let the matter sit there. "And what was discussed during that meeting?"

Rhys had to pause to think. "Nothing important. How my time in Moscow was, mostly. There was certainly no indication then that he was considering defection," he replied, choosing his words carefully. He had no desire to accidentally incriminate himself in anything the chancellor may be suggesting.

"No talk of future plans?"

"No. It never came up. We didn't have much time. I spoke of my displeasure at being assigned to Normandy, but nothing more than that," Rhys replied with a shake of his head. He was beginning to calm down, just focusing on answering the questions truthfully.

Once again, Chancellor Roberts leaned forward in his chair. His fingers drummed on the desk. "So, he knew that you'd be stationed on Ceres?"

"Of course. That was always open knowledge," Rhys replied, a little confused by the insinuation.

"And if Captain Lee wished to communicate with you during your time on Normandy, he would have been able to do so with ease?"

Rhys paused before answering. There hadn't been any communication between him and Aaron since leaving Mars. He didn't know why the chancellor would want to know such things. "I suppose that would have been possible, yes."

"I see. So, let's move on to your more recent meeting with him. Was there anything untoward you noticed on his ship that may explain his defection?"

Rhys went to shake his head again, before he was suddenly reminded of something. "Yes, there was. There was a starat there, acting as navigator."

That got the chancellor to sit up. "A starat? Are you sure? Well now, that is interesting indeed," he said. He scribbled down a few notes of his own, before turning to Melanie. "I assume you never managed to question Captain Lee about the starat's presence?"

"There were other things on my mind, Chancellor," Rhys said. He tried to relax in his chair. He knew he had nothing to worry about. He just had to convince the chancellor that. "An errant starat was the least of my concerns. I was just worried about securing the safety of those on Ceres and making my own escape."

"Of course, I understand that was of course your primary goal. Though I must ask if you confronted Captain Lee about his defection. Did you question him about it?" Chancellor Roberts said, as he slowly started to lean back in his seat again.

Rhys paused, trying to think back to everything Aaron had said. Beneath the table, his hands tensed, gripping his knees firmly. He could feel a few trickles of sweat run down his back, the thick coat far too warm for him, despite the cool air circulating through the room.

"I asked him, but he didn't give a clear answer," Rhys replied. He took a deep breath and furrowed his brow. "He told me that it felt like the right thing to do, but it didn't seem like he was willing to elaborate. His first officer, a Lieutenant Carter, volunteered some information. She insinuated she had a conflict with the Vatican, but again she refused to specify."

Chancellor Roberts nodded, and again both he and Melanie took down a few notes. The chancellor kept his arm across the page, preventing Rhys from seeing what he wrote, though his spidery writing looked difficult to decipher anyway.

The chancellor was about to speak again, when Melanie coughed loudly, attracting his attention. She tapped the watch on her wrist. He nodded at her and sighed, removing his glasses and carefully placing them down on the desk.

"Very well, Captain Griffiths. It seems we're out of time, but I don't think there's anything more to be said here," the chancellor said, much to Rhys's surprise. He had expected a much more intensive line of questioning, and the sudden end to the interview confused him. "I am disappointed in the loss of the *Dawn*, but I believe it when you say there was little more that could be done. Naturally my investigation will be ongoing, and I have no conclusions to make just now. I will be in touch after I've spoken to further witnesses on Mars. You may leave."

"That's all, Chancellor?" Rhys asked, as he slowly started to rise to his feet. At the same time, Melanie stood up from her seat and approached them.

"Yes, that's all. Thank you, Captain. As I said, we'll be in touch should we need more information from you," the chancellor replied. He didn't look up from his notes, just waving his hand in Rhys's direction.

"Well, thank you, Chancellor. Good luck with the investigation," Rhys said. He got no reply back, and he left the chancellor without another word being spoken. He felt strange, leaving so suddenly. He had expected so much more, and he couldn't help but feel underwhelmed by it. Worse still, he still didn't have a clear understanding of what it meant towards his future. The chancellor had clearly suspected he had some involvement in Aaron's defection, and that thought chilled him.

Melanie followed Rhys outside to guide him back through the ship. He barely even noticed where they were going, keeping his head down and pursing his lips as he wondered if there was anything else he could have said to better his position with the chancellor. They took the elevator back down to the shuttle bay.

"Here you are, Captain Griffiths," Melanie said, extending her hand for Rhys to take again. She held it for a couple of seconds, before pointing out one of the mechanics further into the dock. "Pierre there will sort you out for a shuttle back down to the surface."

"Thank you, I appreciate it," Rhys said, before Melanie made a hasty exit, leaving Rhys by himself. From deeper in the dock, Rhys could hear the mechanic swearing at something, with the clatter of a spanner against the floor following shortly afterwards. He called out to the mechanic. "Is everything alright?"

The mechanic appeared from behind one of the shuttle doors. He was read in the face and had grime halfway up his arms. "Another one to go down? Ah, well you're out of luck. Navigation's down. I had a starat up to fix it, but I think it's made things worse."

"The shuttles aren't working? How long will it take to fix?" Rhys asked, working hard not to groan in frustration.

"More time than we have at the moment. We're departing in about ten minutes to get the best jump to Mars," the mechanic replied. He shrugged his shoulders and banged his spanner on the side of the nearest shuttle. "Got no choice other than the teleporters, unless you want to risk smashing into the surface in one of these. I just sent the starat there, so if you hurry you should be able to go down before it."

Rhys rubbed his hand over his eyes. He hated the teleporters, but he did not want to risk being stuck on the *Olympus* until it arrived in Mars, forced to find his own way back from there. "Where are they?" he asked Pierre.

The mechanic gave him directions. It wasn't far, just out of the shuttle bay and the third room on the right after that. Rhys thanked him and left, walking briskly to give himself the most amount of time before the ship departed to Mars. He found the right place and opened the door to step inside, finding a small room with three chairs backed up against one wall. On the opposite side was the teleporter pod; an imposing structure of metal and wire. In the corner was a small desk and computer, behind which sat the operator. She glanced up as Rhys entered.

"Same place?" she asked.

Rhys nodded as he sat down, realising only then that there was a starat in the middle seat. It squeaked and darted away to the right seat, as far from Rhys as it could manage whilst still staying seated. Rhys ignored it as he removed his coat, draping it over his right shoulder. His nose wrinkled at the smell of oil and grease emanating from the starat's dirty and stained fur and overalls.

For several minutes, the two remained in silence, with just the furious tapping and muttering from the operator in the corner as she communicated with her counterpart on the surface. Rhys could hear the tension in her voice, and that made him nervous. He had always hated the teleporters. He knew they were perfectly safe, and that there had never been an incident with them since they had been in early testing, but there was still always a concern at the back of his mind. Especially when he considered the patchy nature of the Cerian port.

"Captain Griffiths, would you like to go through first?" the operator said after a few minutes.

Rhys shook his head. "Send the starat through before me," he said. The air was cool on the *Olympus*, and he wanted a few extra moments to sort his thoughts out before the inevitable meeting with the admiral on the surface.

"If you're sure, Captain. Step forward, starat," the operator said, a noticeable coldness entering her voice as she addressed the starat.

The starat leapt from its seat as though an electric current had suddenly surged through it. With tail tucked between its legs, the starat scampered for the teleporter. The door slid shut behind it, and the last thing Rhys saw of it was the bright flash of a nervous smile. A second flash, this time of light, and the starat was gone.

Rhys breathed out a heavy sigh. He had a few more seconds to compose himself as the operator reset the teleporters, getting them prepared for his transfer down to the dwarf planet. Wiping the small amount of sweat on his brow with his coat sleeve, Rhys waited to be called forward to step into the teleporters, but that moment didn't come. He glanced to the operator, who had returned to her furious typing.

"Sorry, Captain. Having difficulty staying connected to the Ceres end. It's been disconnecting after each use. Nothing to worry about though, just delays things more than they should," she said, noticing Rhys's worried glance. The explanation did nothing to ease his trepidation, but when the operator finally declared it was ready, he stepped forward anyway. He had no choice.

Now cleared to enter the teleporter, Rhys stepped inside. The floor was a white disc that glowed slightly. As Rhys closed the door behind him, he could just about see the operator through the small glass window, half-obscured by the myriad of wires that ran around the outside of the pod.

"Alright Captain, just stand still," the operator said, her voice emanating out from an unseen speaker from somewhere above his head.

A bright white light filled the tube, blinding Rhys. He fought hard to stop his arm coming up to shield his face. He had used the teleporters before, so he knew what to expect, even if he didn't like it. The tingling sensation that spread across his body always unsettled him, but he was soon able to dismiss it.

There should have been absolute silence, but something clicked loudly.

Everything went black.

chapter four

Rhys opened his eyes groggily, slowly becoming aware of two different things. The first was that he was in a medical bay. Judging by the flecked paint of the white walls, it was the barely functional ward of the Cerian spaceport. The second was that he couldn't move at all. He couldn't feel any restraints holding him down, but his limbs felt numb and inactive. Panic gripped his mind as he tried to work out what had happened. The last thing he could remember was stepping into the teleporters on the *Olympus*, but then there was nothing. He thought he could remember screaming and panicked yells.

"Good morning-evening-night, insert patient name here. You are awake. I am glad of this," a flat and emotionless voice said. Rhys tried to move his head to find the source, but he found he could not. Nothing responded. A small medical helper bot moved into his field of vision. Its dull, unreflective metal casing was covered in many scratches and dents, and its movements were slow and clunky. It was an old model. An MHB-2, if Rhys's identification was correct.

The small screen on the MHB-2's front casing flickered on to display a female face, smiling in a most unrealistic manner. Even the most recent models, the MHB-13s, such as those he had on the *Harvester*, still could not fully comprehend the subtleties of human emotion. At least the MHB-13s had a voice that could sometimes be confused for a human one, rather than the mechanical drone of the MHB-2s.

"I shall alert Doctor Name to your alertness. Remain in your current location and expect Doctor Name's return," the MHB-2 droned before slowly moving away, the whine of its anti-grav motors fading into silence, leaving Rhys alone to stare at the blank white ceiling.

Rhys's face itched, but though he tried to reach up a hand to scratch it, his body simply didn't respond to his will. He was utterly paralysed. Not a single muscle responded, despite his best efforts. Even his eyes remained completely still. Something was blocking part of the bottom of his vision, irritating him further. He couldn't work out what the dark shape was, but it remained still and seemed to take up space around his nose.

Before long Rhys heard the sound of a door slide open. Some part of the door was clearly broken on the underside, for something dragged along the floor too, emitting a terrible screech that would have had Rhys clamping his hands over his ears were he still able to move. Then there was the sound of footsteps, and the face of the *Harvester's* doctor peered down at Rhys.

"The old piece of junk was right. Welcome back. Captain?" Doctor Sparks said in a cautious voice. He shone a torch into Rhys's eyes, testing his responsiveness. "We're sorry about these measures, but I'm afraid something went quite amiss when you used the teleporters yesterday morning. A monumental cock-up would be an appropriate term, I believe."

Rhys struggled to speak, but he couldn't make a sound. He could only stare up at the concerned face of the doctor.

"We had to put you under full mindlock, just in case. We weren't sure how… how you'd react," the doctor said as he paced around Rhys's bed. He disappeared in and out of Rhys's limited view. Rhys couldn't help but notice the doctor failed to look in his direction even once.

Sparks took something from the MHB that was still hovering around the doctor's shoulder, before Rhys felt the pinch of a needle against his neck. "That should start wearing off the mindlock in a few minutes. Nasty thing, usually used for torture, don't ask me how I got hold of some. But we had no choice, you see. Before you properly wake up, you need to understand… I was told how those teleporters work, in layman's terms, at least. They essentially save three things; organic matter, non-organic matter, and the mind of the occupant is turned to code. This is then all passed on to the receiving machine, and you're replicated." Sparks paused. He turned and started to pace beside the bed as he struggled to find his words.

"What happened?" Rhys asked, his words slurring into one another, like he was drunk. His jaw didn't feel right, a strange weight to his mouth that didn't seem natural. Something was odd about his teeth. But there was something more. That wasn't his voice. It was higher pitched than it should be, sounding weird that the mumbled slurring couldn't account for.

"I just need you to answer a few questions first. I need you to state your full name, your age, your place of birth, and your military ID," the doctor said. He still didn't meet Rhys's eyes. "Standard procedure for anything like this. Well, not like this, but..."

Rhys struggled to move again, but he could barely twitch still. An itchiness was starting to spread from his extremities. He sighed and closed his eyes for a moment as he leaned back into his pillow. "Rhys James Griffiths. Forty-three. Merthyr Tydfil. Six-six-four-two-seven-nine," he said slowly. He tried to stop his words slurring, but they still mumbled together. He assumed it was just the anaesthetic he had been given. "Can you please tell me what is going on?"

The doctor stopped his pacing and rubbed his hand over his mouth. "The teleporter here is an older model. They don't like using it because of how much power it uses. Transporting so many people down so close together put the electronics under even more strain. There was a brief power failure right as you came down. There shouldn't have been one. There are backups of the backups, but somehow it happened. The machine failed. It didn't receive any genetic information, so it used what it had. The previous user. It gave that to you instead. They called the *Olympus*, in case something was saved at their end, but, you know..." The doctor trailed off awkwardly.

Rhys took an involuntary breath. The starat...

Sparks pulled across a small mirror for Rhys to see. The reflection of Rhys Griffiths did not look back out of the glass. It was that of a starat.

"Jesus Christ in Heaven," Rhys whispered, watching the starat's mouth move as he spoke. The blue eyes ringed with brown fur that stared back in revulsion could not possibly be his. He muttered beneath his breath. "This can't be happening. There's no way this is happening."

The numbness was starting to fade from his extremities, allowing Rhys a little movement in his hands. With a great effort, he curled up his fingers. Then, shaking, he lifted his arm up in front of his face. It was not the arm of a human. Dark brown fur covered it, and his fingers were tipped with short, black claws. Rhys's head felt light, but he was damned if he was going to faint now.

"Are you alright, Captain Griffiths?" Doctor Sparks asked. The doctor pushed the mirror back to the side. The ghastly sight of the repulsed starat that had been reflected there was gone. Rhys squeezed his eyes closed.

"Can this be reversed?" Rhys asked, trying to fight the growing sensation of nausea in his stomach.

Doctor Sparks sighed. Even with his eyes closed, Rhys could hear the gentle movement of fabric as the doctor folded his arms. His ears had never been so sensitive before. It took Rhys a lot of effort not to move his arms up to the top of his head to feel the rounded ears he knew he'd find there.

"It's complicated. If they can find your genetic information on the *Olympus*, then maybe. If not…" Rhys felt the bed compress as the doctor sat down by his feet. Rhys's eyes snapped open as the doctor continued. "You have to understand, this is unprecedented. This has never happened before, not even in testing. No one knows what to do."

Rhys slowly sat up with a groan. His limbs ached as sensation flooded into them. He inspected his body with revulsion. For the first time, he noticed that he was still wearing his uniform, though it was many sizes too large for him now. Rolls of fabric obscured most of his body, but he could feel an uncomfortable itchiness as it rubbed over his fur. He leaned forward, and a sudden catch of unexpected pain gave him another unwanted surprise.

"Jesus fucking Christ, I have a tail."

After that particular revelation Rhys felt like he was about to faint again. Determined not to, he gritted his teeth together. That was considerably harder than he was used to, given the needle-like things he now had for teeth. He placed his head in his hands, only to yelp out loud as his claws dug into his skin. He swore again under his breath and looked up at Doctor Sparks, a pleading look in his eyes. Surely there had to be something he could do to help? In his heart

Rhys knew it was hopeless. If there was anything the doctor could do, he would have done it already.

"What the hell am I going to do?" Rhys asked in desperation, knowing there could be no answer. He choked back a sob. He had little dignity left. He wasn't going to lose the last of it by crying in front of the doctor.

Sparks sighed and shook his head. "I know this must be hard for you…"

"No shit."

"…but I know that if anyone can get through this, it's you. I've hunted down the starat who went through the teleporter before you. I'll have him sent down to you. He needs to know what happened, and I think he could help you too."

"No," Rhys said bluntly. He had no desire to meet the starat that had caused all of this.

"He can help you."

"I don't want help," Rhys snapped, his voice breaking into a cracked squeak. It was a pitiful shadow of what his voice had been. "Not from him."

"You need it though. Trust me, Captain. He can help you."

"Get out," Rhys said, pointing to the door in a manner he intended to be forceful, all the while trying to avoid putting his arm into his field of vision. That ruined a lot of the effect he was going for.

Sparks had the tenacity to ignore his captain's orders. He stood resolutely by the door, but he didn't open it just yet. "It'll be best for you. You need to learn, and the starat is the logical option for you," Sparks said, evidently not giving up.

"I don't want to see him," Rhys shrieked, his voice reaching a far higher register than he was used to hearing. He grasped for the first thing close to hand. He gripped onto his pillow and hurled it towards the doctor. "I don't want to see any goddamned weasel, and I definitely don't want to see you!"

Doctor Sparks barely recoiled, despite being struck in the chest from the pillow. He simply dusted himself down and stood up from the bed. He took a couple of steps towards the door, before turning on his heel and looking back at the seething Rhys. "I think you'll find you are one of those goddamned weasels now, Captain. As difficult as that is to accept, as challenging as it must be, it is the truth. And you need help to come to terms with that. I'll come back for you in an hour. Call for me if you need me before then," he said, before sliding the door shut behind him.

Rhys was alone, with just the MHB-2 for company. "Patient designation 42B. I am here to attain to your every need or want or desire or requirement or service – delete as necessary," the bot droned, its display screen still portraying the woman with the absurd smile.

"Oh, shut up," Rhys snapped at it. He rested his hands in his lap and squeezed his eyes shut, trying to choke back another sob. The MHB drifted serenely back, screen smiling all the way, before disappearing into a service hatch. Now Rhys was truly alone with his thoughts. He hated every single one of them.

Filled with a desire to pace the room, Rhys slipped off the bed, only to completely misjudge the distance to the floor. He ended up sprawled on all fours, a position that felt far too natural for Rhys's new body. The attempt to push himself back up onto his feet was harder than he cared to admit. His torso was longer, and his legs shorter than he remembered. Not only that, but the structure of his feet was all wrong. He tried to put his heels down, but only succeeded in toppling back onto the bed, striking his head against the frame as he fell.

Crying in pain, Rhys just stared at the unfamiliar sight of his furred hands. It was like a dream – or a nightmare, Rhys corrected himself – because those hands and arms just could not be attached to his shoulders. Somehow, they were, and his shoulders were covered in the same dark fur as his arms. As though needing confirmation, Rhys plucked the too-large white shirt away from his chest and looked down. The fur was lighter there. And down his legs, the fur had returned to dark brown with occasional black patches, right down to his feet that had long lost his shoes. The legs of his trousers bundled up on the floor, but he rolled them up so he could see his claw-tipped toes poking out the end. He turned away from those paws in disgust and tried to haul himself back up to his feet once more.

His frustrations were building, and his hand tapped restlessly on the table beside the bed, but he soon stopped that as the noise his claws were making on the cold metal began to annoy him further. Then he rubbed his hands down the side of his head and neck, but the feel of his fur passing between his fingers repulsed him.

Even the various medical tools on the table were annoying him now, and he hurled a sensor array across the room, watching the metallic tube clatter into the far wall, unbroken. The action had as little effect on his mood as it did the wall. He snarled. A genuine, animalistic snarl. That chased the rage away in an instant as he felt a cold shiver run down his body. The last thing he wanted was to lose the tenuous hold on what little shred of humanity he still had left.

He forced his mind to calm down and remind himself exactly who, and what, he was. He was Rhys Griffiths, captain of the *Harvester*, one of the finest ships in the empire. What was more, he was on course to become the youngest admiral in many years. Had been, at least. The insidious thought had crept unwanted into his mind. Now it was there, he had to admit it may be his reality. Would the chancellor want to appoint someone who, to all physical appearances, was a starat? Or would he remember the person he had been?

Rhys could see his career crumbling before his eyes. He couldn't help it. He began crying. Everything he had ever worked so hard for was now completely and utterly futile. He knew the treatment he would have to face as well as any. No starat was even allowed on the bridge of a ship in flight, so what chance did he have of even keeping his position as captain, let alone promotion to admiral?

But no, he would not give in, he thought to himself as he tried to sniff back the tears that came to his eyes. Doctor Sparks had been right. If anyone could pull themselves through this, then he was that person. He would go out there and prove any doubters wrong. He would not only hold his position as captain, but he would strive to achieve admiral, and why stop there? Why limit himself? Just a day ago he wouldn't have done so, so there was no reason why he should start doing so now. He knew he possessed the same, capable human mind. That was what mattered.

He wiped dry his eyes, shuddering again at the touch of his fur. He clenched his fists, ignoring the pain of his claws digging into the soft flesh of his palms.

Rhys staggered towards the door like a drunkard, throwing his hands out to catch his regular falls. He didn't know where he was going or what he was going to do, but he had to get out of the ward. He needed to occupy himself before he slipped back into depression. It was only once he finally reached the door did Rhys pause and think about what he was about to do. How would people react to his new form? Would they even accept his word that he was Rhys Griffiths?

His hand trembled above the control panel that would open the doors. He had to admit he was terrified. He knew full well what reaction he would get out there. He would be invisible to the human eye, ignored and pushed aside except when something was needed from him. He knew that, because that was how he had treated starats. He pushed his head against the cold metal door as a few more tears fell from his eyes. He was the mind of a human, trapped in the body of a beast. It was a miracle he was still able to think properly.

The moment he moved his hands away from the door, he tottered and fell back to the floor, wincing as he landed right on his tail. Pain shot through it as he rolled up onto his knees and shuffled towards the bed. He growled and muttered beneath his breath, doing his best to ignore the strange sensations in the new limb. It felt wrong as it draped over the back of his legs. Alien. Foreign. Like it wasn't really a part of him. Like it shouldn't be a part of him.

Despair threatened to well up inside him, but he forced it back again. He couldn't give in so easily. He forced himself to take a few deep, slow breaths. His heart raced in his chest, and he placed a hand over it to try and calm himself. He was glad to discover that his heart was still in the same part of his chest. Despite all the changes, at least that had remained the same.

What Rhys needed was a plan, and for that he needed Sparks. He glanced back to the door. The doctor can't have gone too far.

Rhys whistled to summon the MHB. Or tried, at least. The shape of his mouth was all wrong, and the only noise he made was a small squeak. He gently ran his clawed fingers down his muzzle, shivering at the bizarre sensation of his elongated face. A silent snarl remained on his lips. There was a remote by the bed that would summon the bot, but that table looked so far away when he couldn't trust his legs to support his weight.

Even crawling on his hands and knees was difficult. His trousers kept trying to slip free, forcing him to hold onto the waistband with one hand to keep them up. There may not be anyone to see him, but he still had his modesty. With that, he knew he was still human where it mattered – in his mind. He would cling to every last scrap of his humanity if it meant overcoming this adversity.

Finally, he was able to reach the small remote. It took several presses of the right button for it to beep. Almost immediately, the MHB emerged from the small service hatch near the door. It really was an ugly thing, with its paint chipped and scratched, with even a few wires hanging loose beneath it. The anti-grav engines that kept it afloat were starting to fail, give it a slight list to one side. The screen on the front still beamed its unnatural smile.

"Patient Designation 11S, you are recommended-advised to return to the bed. This is for your safety or well-being," the bot said, beeping a few times as it scanned Rhys.

"Shut up," Rhys muttered under his breath. The bot's memory had clearly begun to fail. He dragged himself up to his elbows as his eyes tracked the medical machine. "I need you to-"

"Default apology not found. Understanding not found. Please repeat or say again." The MHB's screen smiled widely.

"I said shut up. Just listen to me," Rhys said, his voice rising as he glared at the small machine. His ears curled in on themselves as he struggled up to his feet, using the bed behind him as a support.

"Subject not found. State what needs to be shut." The MHB bobbed in front of Rhys as the screen flickered and died, leaving a surface in which Rhys could just about make out his reflection.

Realising what was happening to his ears, Rhys grabbed them with his hands and tried to hold them straight. His claws pinched into the soft flesh, making him whimper in pain. His hands dropped down to his sides again. "Just fetch Doctor Sparks and go away."

"Please state reason for Doctor Name to attend."

"Does he need one? Just go," Rhys snapped, but the bot steadfastly refused to move anywhere. Instead it just scanned Rhys again, almost blinding him as the light shone right into his eyes. "Just say it's a medical emergency if you need to say anything. You understand that, right? Medical emergency."

Rhys didn't know if it was his slurred words or the bot's old programming that was making it so difficult, but it beeped a couple of times at his words and completed its scan. The screen flickered a few times, but it didn't turn back on.

"Patient Designation 12B. Diagnosis. Depression. Recommended treatment. Euthanasia. Please stand by. Doctor Name will be present presently to administer your treatment."

Rhys could only stare in confusion as the bot drifted away at last. His ear flicked in a subconscious motion as he grasped at his tail, twisting it in his hands. It took him a few moments realise what he was doing. When he noticed, he let go of it in disgust, planting his hands down firmly on the thin mattress. He shuddered and took in a deep breath, once again trying to calm his mind and lessen the despair within him. He was Captain Rhys Griffiths. He could not give up hope. Not now, not ever.

***

Rhys felt like pacing impatiently as he waited for Doctor Sparks to return, but he didn't trust his feet enough to try. Instead he was restricted to his bed, twisting knots into the sheets as he tried to keep his hands away from his restless tail. It was often a futile thing. His hands seemed magnetically attracted to the strange new limb, even though every time he touched it he felt another welling of disgust at his new body.

Finally, the door opened, and Doctor Sparks returned. The doctor was cautious as the door slowly opened, glancing down at Rhys with his hands held up close to his chest. "How are you feeling? The bot said..."

"I'm depressed, yeah," Rhys replied. He closed his eyes and turned away from the doctor, not wanting to see the pity in his eyes.

"And are you?"

"Well I'm not exactly bright and cheerful," Rhys replied, before sighing and slowly opening his eyes. He spread his furred palms wide, forcing himself to stare down at them. "This is painful. I... I still don't think I truly believe this is happening. This... can't be me. I really don't know what I can do, but I know I can't give up and do nothing."

"So, do you want the starat?" Doctor Sparks asked. Rhys could hear him walk closer, before he felt the weight of the doctor sitting on the bed by him. "I can have him down here in a few minutes."

Rhys shook his head. "I don't need him. I need you."

"I can't fix this."

"I know," Rhys said, his voice cracking a little as he turned away from the doctor. He trembled and felt his nausea return, unable to believe that he was accepting he could never become human again. "I just need to know who else knows about this."

"Not many yet. A few of the teleporter attendants here and on the *Olympus*, and Admiral Garter," Doctor Sparks said, before pausing, tapping his fingers together. "Well, the admiral is aware of a situation, but I haven't told him the specifics just yet. I wanted to see if it could be fixed first."

Rhys nodded and sucked in his breath. His nose twitched, subconsciously trying to clear the obstruction at the bottom of his vision. It took him a couple of moments to realise that it was just his muzzle. He sighed and rubbed his hand over it. "He should know soon. If he... if he accepts that I'm still capable, then things could still be alright. If he doesn't... well. He will. I know he will."

Doctor Sparks rose to his feet. "Would you like me to fetch him now?"

Despite his resolve to speak to the admiral, Rhys felt his heart flutter in his chest. He gripped onto the bed hard, feeling his claws piercing the sheets. He shook his head and forced himself to exhale, releasing the breath he had been holding in. "No, not just yet," he squeaked, before breathing in deep again to calm himself further. He forced himself to speak at a more normal level. "No. I'd like to go back to the *Harvester* first."

"I'm sure that will be fine. I don't think I need to do much more active monitoring of your condition. Everything seems stable, at least," Doctor Sparks said. He gestured a hand down towards Rhys. "I can get you something to wear that fits a bit better if you'd like."

Rhys glanced down at his clothes. They didn't fit at all, dangling loosely from his body. His trousers and underwear were barely staying on, requiring a hand to hold them up whenever he moved around on the bed. He nodded to the doctor. Though he was loathe to lose them, his clothes being one of the last points of status he still had, he knew he couldn't continue to wear them. If he needed to prove to the admiral that he was still the same, capable human mind, then he needed to present himself accordingly. Wearing ridiculously oversized clothes would not give that impression.

He did not have to wait long for Doctor Sparks to return, and he shirked away from what the doctor carried. He wasn't sure what he had expected, but seeing the work overalls the doctor held out to him made his heart beat faster again. Wearing those, he would be indistinguishable from any common starat. His mouth felt dry as he took it from the doctor. "Is this the only way?" he asked in a small voice, knowing that the answer would be.

Doctor Sparks turned around, giving Rhys the privacy to change. He tried not to see the symbolism of replacing his captain's uniform with the starat's one. He slid his epaulettes off his old shirt and slipped them into one of the many pockets on the overalls. It took him a few minutes to work out what to do with his tail. Having it inside the overalls hurt him, but poking it out the side just looked and felt ridiculous. Why did he even have it? It was all he could do to not give it a firm, angry tug.

Fully dressed again, he slid back off the bed, landing clumsily on his feet. A twinge of pain stabbed through his left ankle as he tried to place it down on the floor. He tottered and swayed, staying upright for a few moments before collapsing in an undignified heap. He almost pulled the doctor down with him, his claws grabbing onto Sparks's shirt as he fell.

"These feet," Rhys snarled, slamming his fist into the floor in frustration. "They're fucking ridiculous. How can anyone walk on them?"

Doctor Sparks held his hand out for Rhys, who swatted it aside. "It's just a matter of practice," the doctor said as his hands moved to his hips.

"I don't want practice," Rhys retorted, his voice descending into a frustrated growl that he couldn't prevent. He shot the doctor a look of irritation before attempting to stand again. He couldn't find his balance, trying to press his heels down on the floor only to rock back, almost falling over again before digging his claws into the mattress of the bed as he scrambled to stay upright. "I just want… I want…"

Rhys planted his face into the mattress, trying to fend off tears again. What he wanted was to be human. To have feet that worked. No ridiculous tail getting trapped in his clothes. He couldn't have it.

He felt close to breaking again, but he forced himself to take slow, deep breaths.

"Would you like me to carry you?" Doctor Sparks asked, placing his hand on Rhys's shoulder.

"No," Rhys growled, brushing the doctor's hand away. He tried to push himself back and stay upright, but once more he could feel himself swaying, completely off balance still. He leaned back against the bed, his shoulders drooping. "Yes. Please."

To his shame, Rhys allowed the doctor to scoop him up and carry him out of the medical bay. His skin burned beneath his fur, ears sub-consciously flattening down on his head. He squeezed his eyes shut as his newly-sensitive ears caught distant sounds echoing through the corridors. No one seemed to be close as the medical bay was located in one of the quieter, more isolated corners of the port, but the sheer embarrassment of his position lingered.

Rhys was thankful Doctor Sparks didn't try to speak to him along the way to the shuttle bay, instead remaining in silence. They passed few, and no one had anything to say about the doctor carrying a starat through the port. No one stopped them. No one had need to. They were just a ship's doctor and a starat.

Rhys didn't open his eyes once during the journey to the shuttle bay, not wanting to risk seeing anyone he knew; someone who would not recognise him. His heart was pounding hard, unrelenting.

Doctor Sparks had no issue securing a shuttle to transfer up to the *Harvester* in orbit. It was common enough for crew to move between ship and port while it was docked. The attendant on duty didn't even question the presence of Rhys. He forced himself to stay quiet, not wanting to attract any undue attention to himself. Not yet at least. For the moment, he was not a captain. He was a mere starat. Unworthy of attention.

The journey up to the ship was uneventful. The doctor strapped Rhys in and took a seat next to him. Still they remained in silence, letting Rhys brood and compose himself before he potentially met his crew. He wasn't even sure what time it was, whether the ship would be busy or deserted. Without any windows to look through, it was impossible to tell the time of day.

When the familiar shudder of the shuttle docking arrived, Rhys felt his whole body tense up with fear. His tail was held rigid, unsure what to do with the additional limb. He struggled to extricate himself from his seat, needing the doctor's help to even undo the buckles holding him down. His hands trembled, and his vision was starting to blur. He barely even felt it when the doctor picked him up again.

Rhys tried to compose his breathing as he was carried into the *Harvester*. He squeaked as he caught sight of someone. Lieutenant Cooper passed them by, barely giving them a second glance. It was a shocking blow to Rhys, not seeing a trace of recognition in the eyes of the man he had worked with for over five years. It only cemented the realisation that he would never be the same person again.

Edgar Scott was the first to stop them. The ship's navigator had also worked with Rhys since before he was promoted to captain. And like Cooper, had no trace of recognition as he looked down, briefly, at Rhys.

"Any sign of Captain Griffiths, doctor? I've not seen or heard from him all day. Captain Favre was looking for him," Scott asked.

"He's taken unwell, I'm afraid. Suffered a bit of teleporter sickness, but there shouldn't be any, uh... any lasting effects. I'm sure Lieutenant Cooper will be able to take any queries intended for the captain at the moment," the doctor replied. Rhys felt a small pinch on his back, warning him to remain quiet, but it was wholly unnecessary. The sheer terror at being discovered was enough to keep him silent.

"I hope he recovers soon. Pass my well wishes on to him, would you?" Scott said. He briefly glanced over Sparks' shoulder in the direction Cooper had just gone, and looked about to follow after the first officer, before he paused and glanced down at Rhys again. "And what's with the starat?"

Rhys trembled with fear.

"He twisted his ankle quite badly, so I'm just going to strap it up for him and send him on his way," Sparks replied without a moment of hesitation.

Scott looked like he just about resisted the urge to roll his eyes, a small smirk tugging at the corner of his mouth. "Another one, Ant? We can't keep treating every starat you find, no matter how hurt they are. I'm sure the captain won't appreciate a Vatican inquest with that cardinal skulking around the place," he said, before pausing with a slight frown. "And isn't the medical bay down that way?"

"Of course. But my notes on starat anatomy are in my quarters. Now, if you don't mind, he's heavier than he looks, so if I may be on my way…" Sparks said. He shifted his hands against Rhys, who had to cling on to the doctor's shoulder a little tighter to avoid slipping.

Scott took the polite and veiled rebuff. "I'll leave you to it then. If you'll be seeing the captain, can you please pass on this message? And keep me updated on his condition."

Rhys closed his eyes as the doctor adjusted his grip on Rhys to take hold of the small envelope Scott had produced from his pocket. He was filled with fear about how Scott would react if he found out that his captain's 'condition' was barely over a metre tall, furry, and right under his nose. Probably very poorly.

No one else intercepted them on the route up to the quarter deck. Those that acknowledged them simply greeted Doctor Sparks as though Rhys wasn't even there. He couldn't even be sure some of them even saw him, despite his obvious presence in the doctor's arms. It was like being a ghost, and that terrified him.

The upper levels above the bridge were largely for the crew quarters and dormitories, as well as the mess hall and other amenities. Thankfully for Rhys, they were mostly empty as he was carried through them, and up to the captain's quarters.

Rhys was set down just in front of the sealed door, where he immediately slid down the wall to sit down. He leaned back and closed his eyes to avoid looking down at his body. His tailtip twitched.

"Do you want me to come in with you?" the doctor asked.

"No."

"Should I send up the starat to see you?"

"No."

Doctor Sparks sighed. "Is there anything I can do to help you?"

"No. I need to be alone."

"If you insist. But Rhys, please call for me if you need help. You need it."

"Whatever. Sure." Rhys struggled back up to his feet, turning to face the door. He rested his forehead against the cool, metallic surface, wincing as he bumped his muzzle against it. He was thankful of the doctor's help, but right now the trauma of seeing the lack of recognition in the eyes of two of his most senior officers had brutally revealed just how difficult things were going to be.

Sparks shrugged and forced the message from Scott into Rhys's hand. He then started to head back down the corridor. He paused and turned back. "I'll come back in the morning to check in on you, alright?"

Rhys didn't respond. He stayed silent and still until he was sure the doctor had left him alone. It was only the knowledge that he was still exposed that forced him into action at last. He crawled to the door and placed his hand on the control panel, but it wasn't until it lighted up red and refused to open that he realised the obvious problem. The doors operated with a fingerprint scanner.

"Jesus fucking shit!"

Rhys slammed his fist against the door and tried to pry it open. It remained firmly locked. He tried the scanner again once more, in vain hope, before rubbing his hands over his forehead and yelping in pain as his claws snagged in his fur.

Muttering beneath his breath, Rhys started the override process, a series of passwords and log in details so that he would be able to change the saved details to allow him to use the door. The unauthorised reconfiguration would probably flag a system administrator somewhere in the ship or on the port below, but he didn't have any other option. It took him a few minutes, and he twitched to every sound that reached his sensitive ears, terrified that someone was about to discover him. There wouldn't be any reasonable explanation he'd be able to provide should someone see him. He was just a starat, breaking into the captain's quarters.

"Come on you... fucking bastard, just open... finally!" Rhys growled, before the scanner finally beeped and flashed green, allowing him to reconfigure the fingerprint scanner and voice recognition. He wasn't sure how the fingerprint scanner would work with all the fur in the way, but it flashed green as he updated the new details. He struggled to keep his voice even and flat as he provided a new vocal pattern. Erasing his old self. The human self. He shuddered and felt bile rising in his throat as he finalised the new details.

At last, the door slid open without any further complications. Rhys staggered inside and collapsed on the floor. His tail was almost trapped as the door closed again, but he was able to pull it free at the last moment. As an afterthought, he locked the door so that no one, not even Sparks, could disturb him.

"Fuck," he swore, looking around his quarters in despair. This place was little better than the medical ward, but at least now he no longer had to worry about the blasted MHB floating around and irritating him. And he had other luxuries in here he hadn't had access to in the port. His eyes were attracted up to his wine cabinet. He felt like something much stronger than wine, but all the hard liquor was stored in the ship's storage rooms in the maintenance levels. He was damned if he was going to ask Briggs for some now. Wine would have to do.

The bottles had more weight to them now, and Rhys struggled to lift the bottle he selected at random. He didn't care where it came from or how valuable it was, he just needed the contents to try to alleviate his woes.

Half-crawling to his bed, Rhys clambered up to lean back against the backboard. He tossed the slightly crumpled letter from Scott onto the bedside table, before realising he had failed to bring a glass. After a quick shrug of his shoulders, he simply twisted the bottle open and took a drink straight from it. He neglected to take into account the design of his new mouth. Crimson liquid poured from the side of his muzzle, spilling on to his cheeks and shoulders, staining his overalls red. Suppressing an irate growl and filthy curse, Rhys tried again with greater care, taking just a small swig from the neck of the bottle. Still the wine wetted the fur on his cheeks, but more of it reached the back of his throat.

Gradually the weight of the bottle diminished. With nothing to do, he only had his thoughts for company. In his mind he played out every potential scenario he could think of. Though he tried to inject some form of hope into the fantasies, in every imagined scenario his timid shred of optimism was firmly crushed by his rampant pessimism. The best situation he could envisage was expulsion from the military. It was not an attractive proposition.

The hours he spent moping trickled by slowly. Whenever a bottle of wine was depleted he staggered across to gather a new one, until he could no longer focus on just a single image of the cabinet. No one tried to bypass the locked doors. He was left alone with the misery that had slowly overwhelmed his earlier optimism.

He couldn't sleep, no matter how many bottles of wine he drained. Every time he shut his eyes he was plagued by visions of his likely fate. He felt almost feverish, racked by a cold sweat. Several times he was forced to purge the alcohol from his system, only just reaching his private bathroom before throwing up. For a while he just laid on the cool tiles, almost comatose as his head spun, the taste of vomit coating his throat. Though he tried to hold them back, tears came to his eyes and he silently cried to the darkness.

At one point in his sleepless vigil, Rhys tried to tear the fur from his body, but only took out a handful from his arm before realising the futility of it. Taking out his fur wouldn't give him back his lost height, or remove the tail from the base of his spine, or change the structure of his bones. The body of the starat was his body now. The thought rankled in his mind, but it was the truth. He couldn't continue to deny it.

***

Morning came painfully to Rhys. He lay on his bed, eyes closed as he tried to fend off a stabbing headache. He knew he must have dozed off to sleep at some point, as he couldn't remember crawling onto his mattress, but he certainly didn't feel rested. He felt nauseous still, but he was feeling wretched enough that he didn't make any attempt to move towards the bathroom again.

In the corner of his room, the small service hatch beeped. His breakfast and morning tea had been automatically delivered, but he had no desire to stagger over to retrieve it. He certainly didn't feel hungry enough to eat. Instead he just groaned and stretched out his legs, feeling a small twinge of pain in his left ankle. Everything ached, especially his right hand. He was only half-surprised to look down and see a little blood matting the fur around his fingers, though he certainly couldn't remember punching anything hard enough to open up the wounds.

Even thinking too hard was painful, but the other needs of his body were starting to become more insistent. He slowly pushed himself off the bed and tentatively placed his feet on the floor, which seemed to rock and pitch. His vision spun alarmingly as he staggered towards the nearest wall for support. He barely made it, almost forced down to his knees by his impossible feet.

Practically crawling into the bathroom, he was able to relieve the aching pressure from his bladder, though he was annoyed anew by the different anatomy he now possessed down there. It all felt strange and unusual, but he didn't have the mental capacity to look down and explore it just yet. That would be for a time when every movement didn't send piercing pain through his head.

The cup of tea that had been delivered was his next target. This time he did drop down to his knees, not even bothering to try walking normally. The smell of bacon and eggs made his stomach churn again, so he left the plate in the hatch, instead just taking the cup in his trembling hands. Steam drifted over his face, the heat somewhat soothing as he sat back, remembering to flick his tail away at the last moment.

It took Rhys a few attempts to work out how to properly drink from the cup, wanting to avoid spilling the hot liquid down his cheeks and chest. He had to settle for an odd lapping sip, only taking a small amount of tea into his mouth at a time. The small compromise almost brought the tears back again, as it made him realise that even a simple act like drinking would be forever changed for him.

Needing something to distract him, he placed down the cup and reached back to pull the crumpled letter down from his bedside table. He looked down at it as his hands trembled. His claws tore through the envelope with ease and he unfolded the single piece of paper within. On it was a hand-written transcript. Rhys recognised Scott's neat and efficient handwriting. Some of it appeared to be an official report, but some of Scott's own thoughts had been added to the side.

Situation Report – Oberon – 20/02/2616 – 03:35GMT (approx.)

Britannia *and* Blazing Fury *assaulted and disabled by hit-and-run assault by CGP craft. Later identified as the traitorous scum* Terrestrial Dawn. *– **Confirmed by one of my old training friends stationed on the** Blazing Fury.*

*The traitors jumped in closer than anticipated to Oberon and opened fire on the defenders of the empire without warning – **this sequence of events conflicts with the report I got from Lieutenant Davies** – and disabled the* Britannia *and* Blazing Fury *before a counter-attack could be initiated. A boarding party was performed by the traitors onto the mining colony, though it is not currently clear what their objective was. Personnel counts report that no one is missing or killed in the raid.*

King's Hammer and Requiem *both scrambled from Miranda, but the traitors fled before backup forces could assist the disabled defenders of Oberon.* King's Hammer *suspected lost to subspace as no further contact has been initiated. Inventory checks are underway, seeking for any lost equipment. No computer systems or data was accessed or compromised. An internal investigation is underway how the traitors could slip through our defences, and jump in so close to Oberon.*

Lieutenant Davies claimed that the* Dawn *had kill shots on both defending ships, and that it came after attempted negotiations from Captain Lee. He believed he was going to die for his empire, but for some reason the shot wasn't taken. This was a surgical strike, and the* Dawn *specifically targeted engine and weapon systems to cripple the ships. I am sure Captain Lee had a target in mind, but at the moment his motives are unclear. Are you aware of any ties Captain Lee may have to Oberon?

I have taken my concerns about the conflicting reports from Lieutenant Davies to Admiral Garter, but these issues appear to have been ignored. Perhaps your voice might hold stronger weight. I look forward to discussing this with you personally.

E. Scott

Rhys frowned and read over the letter a few times. He took a couple more sips of tea and leaned his head back against the side of his bed. "What are you doing, Aaron?" he whispered. He wished he could see his friend again, to ask him why he had turned his back on the empire and raided the colony on Oberon. He could think of nothing in the rings of Uranus that would be of value to Aaron.

But Rhys couldn't see Aaron again. Not only were they enemies now, but Aaron would never even recognise Rhys anymore. Aaron would look at him without recognition.

Rhys choked back a sob, holding the hot cup close to his chest. His head throbbed, and his body was sore, but even then he didn't want to break down completely. Barely had he regained his composure before his ears flicked upright as the door beeped. Somehow it slid open. He was momentarily too surprised to even worry about his identity being revealed.

A starat stood in the door. It was familiar to Rhys in a way that was both vague and uncertain, yet also as though he had known the creature all his life. The starat's ears were folded completely back against its head as it slowly passed through the threshold, so slowly the door beeped again in protest as it tried to close. It eventually gave up and secured itself in the open position.

"Who the fuck are you?" Rhys asked, finding his voice before the starat. He made no attempt to stand up, instead just rising to his knees. "Why are you here?"

"I'm… I'm…" the starat stammered, blinking a few times. It took a couple of slow steps forward, finally letting the doors close behind it. "You saw me. On the *Olympus*. Before…" The starat gestured one hand towards Rhys. This was the starat who had, albeit unwittingly, made Rhys who he was now.

"How did you get in? Only I can unlock that door. Only my… only my fingerprints…" Rhys said, before his tired mind came to the obvious realisation. He leaned forward and grabbed the starat's arm, pressing their hands together. Though it was impossible to see the tiny genetic quirks, their furred hands were completely identical. He glanced up at the starat. The same pattern of black fur over its ears, the tear-drop markings around the eyes, it was all identical. "You're me," Rhys breathed.

A shadow of a smirk flashed across the starat's face. It pressed its finger against the control panel again, and the door audibly locked at its command. "I think you'll find you're me, actually."

Rhys felt faint. A combination of the alcohol still in his system, his feet, and the shock at seeing his mirror image in front of him were all combining to threaten to overwhelm him once more. He was no longer himself. It was the starat's finger and voice that controlled the door, not his. He was just using them, a perfect copy of the original.

He dropped from his knees and sat back. Once more he sat on his tail and yelped in pain, falling to the side and spilling his tea across the floor. He buried his head in his hands and tried not to cry. His claws drew blood as he ran his fingers through his fur, leaving three small, thin scratches behind.

"Captain Rhys, are you hurt?" the starat asked, crouching down next to Rhys and placing a hand on his leg. The contact made Rhys recoil away, trying to roll beyond the reach of the starat.

"Why do you care?" Rhys wiped the moisture from his eyes as he glared at the starat.

The starat crouched down in front of Rhys. Its eyes were wide and its tail flicked back and forth. "Well, because you're clearly upset about this all. Little bit panicked. Certainly confused. Which is understandable, I suppose. Big changes for you. I can only imagine it must be… overwhelming."

For a few moments, Rhys's disgust about his body was replaced by confusion. Starats couldn't feel emotion. They weren't capable of it. They couldn't understand it. Everyone knew that. But this starat was different. This starat was holding a conversation. Every starat he had ever known had barely been able to give a squeaked response to orders. "How… how do you know that?"

The starat tilted its head to the side and flicked its ears. Its tail didn't stop moving. "What do you mean?"

"Feel. Emote. You're… not meant to do that," Rhys said. He tried to shuffle back, escaping those big, wide blue eyes of the starat.

A brief shadow passed over the starat's eyes, and it took a few seconds before it smirked brightly. "I must have missed the memo. We're a lot more intelligent than humans give us credit for. We know, we think, we feel. And we resent. We don't like humans all that much, though most of us don't really blame them. If there's one thing we make sure we remember from Essie's experiences, is that humans treat us how they're taught. You did the same."

"Essie?"

"The first starat. Now, shall we get you up on your paws?" the starat said, extending its hand out to Rhys, but he slapped it away.

"Don't touch me."

The starat blinked as it withdrew its hand, holding it to its chest. Its ears curled up again. "Captain Rhys, is everything alright?"

"Nothing's alright. Everything is wrong. I mean, just look at me," Rhys said, his voice rising as he was struck by unexpected anger, his brief confusion and curiosity blown away in an instant.

"I don't see anything wrong with you," the starat said, with a quick shrug of the shoulders. "Just different, that's all."

"I don't want different," Rhys growled in response. He looked up to the starat, pleading with his eyes. His anger drained away, replaced anew by cold fear. "I just want to be me."

The starat nodded, its eyes dulled in sympathy. "I know. But this is you now. The nice doctor told me so. There wasn't any way back for you."

Rhys choked and closed his eyes. "You don't know that." He shook his head, before rolling over to the side and curling up in a tight ball. He knew he was lying even to himself, but it still sickened him to hear the starat say it so bluntly. "You don't know that…"

The starat rested a hand on Rhys's shoulder, and this time he didn't recoil away as another round of sobs racked through his body. He couldn't stop them this time. There was something about the gentle concern from the starat that cut him deeply, and made his predicament feel even more real than Doctor Sparks had ever made it feel.

"No, I don't know," the starat said. It gently stroked Rhys's head, between his ears. He was ashamed to realise the motion soothed him somewhat. "But I do think you should learn how to be a starat, just in case."

"You assume I want to become one of you." Rhys only argued for the sake of arguing.

"You were a human for how long and you still think everything works out the way you want?" The starat giggled as it continued to stroke between Rhys's ears.

"No. I won't let this beat me though. I have to believe my friends will still trust and believe in me." Even to his own ears, his words rang false. Hope that he had no right to feel. It sickened him more than the hangover.

"Your friends, maybe. But what about the rest of TIE? There aren't many humans around here who'll readily admit to liking us. And as for the Vatican, well, they wish that we'd never existed in the first place, and they hold a lot of influence over the emperor." The starat shuddered. "That cardinal prowling around sets my fur on edge."

Though the starat's words did hit a vein of truth, Rhys refused to believe them completely. He wanted to put faith in his friends and allies to remain so, despite the changes he had gone through. Still, he thought that it might be beneficial to integrate himself with the local starats, to get to know them at least. The logical part of his mind, unbiased by emotion, saw the sense in what the starat was suggesting. If the worst of his fears came true and he was rejected by the military or the empire, then he would have no one to fall back to but the starats. He didn't know how he could adapt to living with them. Would he be forced to live as a servant like they were?

Rhys slowly sat up, wiping some of the tears from his eyes. "Alright, you can take me to them if you feel it's best," he said, trying not to think about that horrific outcome. It would be a terrible fall to go from captain of his own ship to servant.

The starat didn't stand up or even move anywhere for that matter. "Not when you look like that I'm not," it said, gesturing vaguely in Rhys's direction. "Look, I didn't want to say it because you're, well, fragile at the moment, but you do look a bit of a disgrace. I just can't let me be seen in public like that."

Rhys stood with his mouth agape. His mind was finding it a little hard to process. The starat was vain about Rhys's appearance. It was such an odd concept to come across, and yet, he also understood that in some bizarre way it made sense.

"It's true. Your fur is an absolute mess. It looks all tangled and filthy. I don't even want to know what you've spilled all over it, and you haven't groomed it at all," the starat said, perhaps misinterpreting the exact reason for Rhys's silence. It bounced on its toes, tail flicking back and forth, a constant movement that never stopped.

"Groomed it?" Rhys asked uncertainly. He looked down at his body and for the first time really permitted himself to inspect what he saw thoroughly. His fur was coarse and, as the starat had observed, deeply stained and matted with many small knots.

"Yeah, grooming. You thought fur like this was all natural and didn't need any work?" the starat said with a grin, even giving a little pose with its nose held high. But that smirk quickly twisted into a grimace. "If you go out there like that, they'll all be saying 'oh Twitch, he's really let himself go now', and I have a reputation to uphold."

Rhys blinked. "Twitch?"

The starat giggled again, scratching just behind its ear. "I never introduced myself, did I? I'm Twitch. It's been… interesting to meet you, Captain Rhys."

Rhys bowed his head. "I didn't even know you had names," he said, in a small voice. He didn't look up to see Twitch's reaction. He felt like he had been blind to starats, and Twitch had just uncovered his eyes and revealed the truth. The knowledge conflicted within his mind greatly. It – no, he – he was more intelligent than Rhys could ever have thought. More intelligent than any human had thought.

Whether Twitch had heard him or not, the starat continued as though he hadn't. "Is there a shower in this cubicle somewhere?" the starat asked with an inquisitive glance. Rhys nodded, pointing back to his bathroom. He had never been as glad of the private bathroom as he had in his nine years as captain. Using the communal showers with the rest of his crew was a terrifying prospect.

"Good," Twitch continued. "Now get in it. You need a very good clean."

It took Rhys a few seconds to realise that he had just heard a starat giving a direct order. It wasn't until he had opened the door to his bathroom that he realised he was obeying it, slowly walking with one hand on the wall for balance. It was another few seconds still before he noticed the starat following him in.

"What are you doing?"

Twitch shrugged. "Nothing I haven't seen before. Besides, you need someone to show you what needs to be done and how to do it," he said, giving Rhys a gentle nudge to push him onwards. "And what the hell are you doing with your feet. That's... wow, that's all wrong." The starat didn't even try to suppress his giggle.

Rhys shook his head incredulously. Though the starat was technically correct, he had done nothing to alleviate Rhys's concerns. However, Rhys could also tell that Twitch was not to be deterred. He settled for a compromise that was, whilst not exactly comfortable, at least bearable. He stripped down to his loose underwear, held up only by his tail that was forced through one of the leg holes.

"These stay on," he said firmly as he bundled up the uniform and threw it into the usual corner.

"Whatever you like, Captain Rhys. Now get in. Water as hot as you can," Twitch said. An almost sadistic smile lit up his eyes and perked his ears. Rhys turned around, not wanting to see if Twitch would share his modesty. He placed one hand on the wall as he adjusted the shower knobs, then yelped as Twitch placed his hands on him. His protests quickly descended into a restrained purr that was barely audible over the cascading water that drenched them both. He was glad Twitch didn't comment on the sounds. He didn't want to think about how much he was enjoying the animalistic act of being groomed. Twitch's hands moved all over Rhys's body in a firm and fast brushing motion. He started around Rhys's head and neck before slowly working his way down. And down. And down.

"Away from there," Rhys said, slapping Twitch's wandering hands away. Again, the starat shrugged but this time said nothing as he turned his attention to smoothing down Rhys's tail, freeing it from its confines within Rhys's underwear. If Twitch had hoped Rhys was distracted enough to let them fall, he was disappointed. The captain still had enough presence of mind to hold them up with one hand, while he leaned against the shower wall with his other.

A full bottle of shampoo and another grooming session later, Twitch told Rhys to turn off the water. Rhys felt at least twice the weight he did before, and it took considerable effort to raise his arm to shut off the shower. Despite the extra weight, he appeared considerably smaller as his fur was plastered close against his body. He felt a little light-headed from the attention Twitch's hands had been giving him.

"Dry off and give yourself a good brush down. You'll look almost lovely when you're done," Twitch said, passing Rhys a towel before taking a second one for himself and finally giving Rhys some privacy.

Rhys almost slipped on the wet floor the moment he took his hand away from the tiled wall, but somehow remained upright long enough to stagger against the sink. Once his feet felt stable enough, he looked up into the mirror that was now too high for him as he dried himself with a towel that was ridiculously large. In his unfamiliar pale blue eyes he could recognise the determination to succeed that had made him one of the youngest captains in the history of the empire. It was still there, waiting to drive him on to his next goal. That had been to strive to become an admiral, but Rhys knew that he now had to alter that and be realistic. What he wouldn't do though was lose hope in his situation again. He would make this work for him. He supposed he already was the first starat of any rank now. He vowed to keep that rank.

With his new goal in mind, Rhys could feel the hopelessness slowly draining out of him. He would not go as far as to say he was happy with his new situation – far from it, but he was resolved to at least make the best out of it. He flashed a nervous smile at his new reflection as he brushed down his fur. When he was satisfied, he tightened the towel around his waist and carefully stepped out of the bathroom to return to Twitch.

"I think I'm ready to go to the starats now," he said, but Twitch shook his head.

"I said almost lovely. We still need to do something with those feet. What are you even trying to do there?"

Rhys glanced down at his feet. "I don't know. They don't work right." He held onto his bed and lifted his left foot. "This one hurts a bit whenever I walk. Around the ankle."

"Yeah, it'll do that. Has been hurting for years." Twitch giggled and approached Rhys, crouching down in front of him. At first Rhys tried to recoil, thinking the starat was going for his towel, but Twitch's hands just moved down to his ankles. "These shouldn't be so low, you've got to lift them up a bit," the starat explained, giving a firm tug at the same time. It almost unbalanced Rhys entirely, but he was already holding onto his bed for support.

Rhys tried to let his feet settle into the position Twitch moved them into, but he didn't feel confident in letting go of the bed. "No, that's worse," he muttered, having to lean his shoulders back to avoid toppling forward.

Twitch stood back up and placed his hands on Rhys's shoulders, before pulling his hand off the bed. The starat then released him, letting him stand freely. It lasted for just a couple of seconds before Rhys overbalanced and crashed into the starat, knocking them both to the floor.

"Oops, yes. Much worse. Try again," Twitch said with a giggle as he helped Rhys back up to his unsteady feet. This time, the starat stood behind Rhys, nudging Rhys's ankles with his foot until it was held in the right position. His hands then dived down into the towel around Rhys's waist. He fished around for Rhys's tail and pulled it out before the yelp of protest even made it to Rhys's lips. "But this time use this. It's there to help you balance."

Rhys growled in protest at the starat's actions, but he couldn't help but admit that he could already feel the difference with his tail free behind him. He chose to ignore the wide grin on Twitch's muzzle as the starat moved back in front of him.

"Isn't that much better?" the starat asked.

Rhys grumbled quietly and gave the starat the middle finger, but there was a small smile on his lips as he attempted to take a step forward. Once again, he crashed down to the floor, squeaking in surprise and pain as he landed hard on his outstretched hands.

"Oh dear, this is going to be harder than I thought," Twitch muttered as he helped Rhys back up to his feet once more. The starat bounced on his toes and swished his tail. "Look. Just watch at what I do for a few minutes, okay?"

Rhys leaned back on his bed and nodded, paying close attention to how Twitch walked around the room, what the starat was doing with his feet and tail. It didn't look much different to how Rhys thought he had been walking, with the exception that Twitch's ankles never moved close to the floor at all. Instead the starat walked solely on his toes, adding a slight bounce to his gait.

Twitch seemed to view everything as a game. Rhys lost track of how many times he tried and failed to keep his balance, but Twitch was never anything but positive and encouraging. He was always there to pick Rhys back up, though the falls slowly became less frequent. The starat giggled as Rhys finally made a decent attempt at walking across the room, after what felt like hours of work. "I think you're getting the hang of it all now. Think you'll be able to keep practicing without me?"

"Without you? You need to go?" Rhys replied. He felt a flicker of disappointment that Twitch was going, and immediately wondered where that thought came from. There was something about Twitch that made Rhys comfortable.

"Yeah, got a bunch of stuff to do. Busy life of a starat and all," Twitch replied. His ears flattened against his head for a moment before they perked up again. He flashed a quick smile. "Keep practicing and get some rest later. If you can walk properly and you're well-groomed in the morning, then I'll take you to the others."

"I'll keep practicing, don't worry," Rhys said. He was amused by Twitch as the starat poked his tongue out, betraying the brief authority that had been present in his voice.

"And don't drink any more of those," Twitch added, pointing to the stack of wine bottles that had built up. Rhys looked away. The lingering pain behind his eyes was the only reminder of that binge that he needed – he didn't want a physical reminder of it too.

Rhys shook his head. "I won't touch it, don't worry. I'll see you tomorrow."

Twitch's grin returned as he waved goodbye. The door opened and closed to the starat's touch, reminding Rhys anew that it operated to Twitch's genetic code now. Rhys stared down at his hands as he slowly sank back onto his bed. He winced and rolled to the side as he sat on his tail, eventually settling with lying on his belly to avoid crushing the new limb. His hand idly stroked his arm. His fur was still soft beneath his fingers from his grooming, and it possessed a shine that had been decidedly lacking beforehand.

He still harboured fears about his crew's reaction, but they were buried down that little bit deeper to a more manageable level. He wasn't about to open the door and loudly announce himself, but he knew that there would soon come a moment when his new identity would be revealed to his crew. He would not shy away from that. Anyone who objected to serving under him would have to find a new ship to work on.

He was Rhys Griffiths, the first starat captain of the *Harvester*. He was going to succeed.

chapter fiue

He dreamed he was human that night.

Only vague memories remained, but he had been standing alone on a desolate planet with no air to breathe. The rock beneath his feet had shattered and crumbled, before he had been left as a bodiless mind observing the inky darkness of space. It had woken him in terror, and it took him a few minutes to realise where – and even who – he was.

Troubled by his dream even hours later, Rhys felt doubt creeping back into his mind. He sat on the edge of his bed, staring down at the steaming cup of tea in his hands. He had only fallen over once so far, having momentarily forgotten Twitch's advice on how to properly stand up. Now that his mind was clearer and the starat was no longer present, he was beginning to worry he had made the wrong decision in choosing to trust the starat. Just because one of them was eloquent and intelligent enough to communicate properly, didn't mean he should be so easily swayed by his arguments.

He sighed and picked at his breakfast. He knew that he'd need to speak to Admiral Garter as well. Even thinking about that meeting was making him nervous. What sort of reaction would he get from the admiral?

Clothed once again in his borrowed overalls, Rhys resigned himself to simply waiting around for either Doctor Sparks or Twitch to return. He didn't feel comfortable going out of his quarters by himself, even if there was no one who could recognise him. He simply feared be treated like a starat.

The door beeped, dragging Rhys out of his thoughts. Given that it started to slide open, he knew that it was Twitch who had come. He spun around on the bed to face the door, but the greeting died in his throat when he saw who was with the starat. Lieutenant Cooper had hold of the collar of Twitch's overalls, bundling it up in a tight fist. The lieutenant's face was a worrying shade of red.

"Get down from there, starat. Where's Captain Griffiths?" Cooper demanded of Rhys, who found his voice completely lacking. Cooper waited for a few seconds for Rhys to splutter wordlessly. "Answer me weasel. I know you're up to something. I followed this one away from here yesterday." He pushed Twitch to the ground, who fell with a brief cry, but did not resist as Cooper placed his foot against his back. Twitch was bleeding from a cut on his forehead.

Rhys slowly jumped down from the bed, placing one hand against the wall to keep himself upright as he found his balance. He was terribly aware of how short he was now compared to Cooper. Whereas he had once been the taller, he now barely reached halfway up his first officer's chest. One of the things Rhys had never tolerated on his ship was violence of any kind. Though he had always assumed it went on behind his back, he had never condoned his crew to assault starats either.

"Let him go," Rhys said quietly in a voice that quivered with equal measures of fear and fury. His hands formed fists by his hips, prepared to fight if it came to that. He would not act passively like Twitch had, like starats did. He was not one of them. As he looked up at Cooper, he feared he had made the wrong decision. While as a human he had been competent at hand-to-hand combat; it had been part of his training, he wasn't as confident as a starat. Not only could he barely stand up, but his body didn't feel strong.

Cooper just laughed. "I'm sorry. What? You don't get to speak back to me, weasel."

"I'm not a weasel, Lieutenant Cooper. I'm Captain Griffiths. There was an incident," Rhys replied, patting around in his pockets for his captain's epaulettes. That was as far as he got before Cooper started to advance on him, a steely glint in his eye that made Rhys take an alarmed step back. He stumbled and almost fell.

"It would take a starat to tell a lie so blatant," he said coldly. He covered the distance between them in a couple of steps and snatched the epaulettes away from Rhys's unmoving fingers. Cooper took him by the collar and slammed him against the wall. Rhys whimpered as his muzzle struck the rigid metal, dazing him and sending him sprawled across the floor.

Lieutenant Cooper stood over him. "Why are you in here, and where is the captain?" he demanded.

Rhys slowly stood up and spat blood on the floor. So much for not acting passively. He felt his ribs tentatively and ran his tongue along the inside of his teeth, making sure nothing was broken or missing. He glared at Cooper. "No matter what you may think, or what I look like, you have just struck a superior officer," he said. Twitch sidled to his side and stood just behind him.

"You are not the fucking captain of this ship. You're not even human," Cooper said, raising his hand to strike Rhys again.

Acting instinctively, Rhys blocked the attack and struck out with his own hand, jabbing Cooper in the stomach. Though it lacked the strength he could usually muster, the blow was still enough to shock Cooper into taking a couple of steps back. "I did notice that, Mr Cooper. There was an incident with the teleporters. They made me like this. Now, will you please get out of my quarters before you destroy your career further," Rhys said. With difficulty he managed to keep his voice calm and even.

"I don't know what's got into your mind, weasel, but I will never believe you're Captain Griffiths, no matter how many times you say it. In his absence, this is my ship. And I am giving you two minutes to get your fucking ass down to the shuttles, or I will throw you out the airlock," Cooper said, his voice beginning to rise to dangerous levels. His hands were flexing repeatedly by his side as though it was a struggle simply not to throttle Rhys there and then.

With that observation in mind, Rhys had no good options left. He knew he was taking a risk of fuelling Cooper's anger further. He spoke quickly and as clearly as his awkward tongue would allow him. "Emile Salazar."

Cooper's fury seemed to collapse in on itself. Again, Rhys feared he had made a misstep. He would have taken a step back from the white-faced officer had he not already been pressed against the wall. "How do you know that name?" Cooper said in a voice barely more than a strained whisper. The colour returned to his face as his rage violently exploded with far more force than before. "Answer me, you fucking rat!"

Rhys struggled to remain calm with the tempest raging before him. "Admiral Garter told me all about your history when he appointed me captain. To my knowledge, only myself and Admiral Garter know it," he said with the slightest squeak of fear in his voice.

Something snapped within Cooper's mind. "Shut the fuck up," he bellowed, bringing down a rain of blows to Rhys's body.

Though Rhys tried to defend himself, Cooper's strength was too great. He took powerful punches to his head, neck, and body before he was forced to the ground. Cooper reached down to grab Rhys, who then reacted on pure instinct. He tasted blood as he bit down on Cooper's outstretched hand.

Cooper howled in pain and forced his hand from Rhys's grip. He picked Rhys up by the collar and threw him right out the still-open door. "Get out of here you disgusting creature. I never want to see you on this ship again," he yelled.

Cooper then turned to Twitch, but the starat fled before the human could grab him.

Moving quickly, Rhys reached up to the control panel just above his head, fumbling blindly for the right button. Before Cooper could react, the doors slid shut with a hiss, slamming together with an abrupt finality.

"Great. Thrown out of my own quarters. That won't hold long. He has override codes as well," Rhys said, rubbing the back of his head where he had hit the corridor wall. He grimly got to his feet and for a moment entertained the thought of opening the doors and confronting Cooper again, but thought better of it. The back of his head was pounding from the impact with the wall, and his first officer's furious bellows easily penetrated the thick metal door. It sounded like the first officer was trying to hammer his way through the door with his fists. Rhys knew it was only a matter of time before Cooper cleared his head enough to override the controls.

Twitch was staring at Rhys, his mouth open and ears perked upright.

"What?" Rhys asked.

"I've never seen a starat stand up to a human before. That was amazing," he said in absolute awe.

"I shouldn't have bit him."

"No, that was cool. You know how much respect you'll get when you tell the others that you stood up to him like that? You'll be a hero to them."

Rhys shook his head, not to disagree with Twitch, but more as the reality of what had just happened overtook him. This was an incredibly bad situation. He had been assaulted by his first officer, who had refused to believe his new identity. Rhys had to go to Admiral Garter about this, but before that he needed to see Doctor Sparks. He needed a mediator to help inform his senior officer of his new body. Admiral Garter had to be told the truth before he was made aware of Cooper's misinformed opinion.

"Come on, change of plan," he told Twitch. Together, they hurried through the ship down to the medical bay as quickly as Rhys's stumbling run could manage. Three times he fell over, losing balance on unfamiliar feet. Every time Twitch helped him back up, offering further advice on where he should be holding his tail to better keep his balance, as well as reminding him what part of his foot should be touching the ground first. Rhys clearly hadn't inherited his new body's natural instincts, though he had sometimes noticed his ears moving in reaction to his thoughts. His human mind rebelled against the actions he tried to do, and his tail invariably ended up stiff and straight behind him.

As they ran and stumbled, Rhys glanced nervously up at everyone they passed, but no one even spared them a second glance. He felt invisible to everyone. This was his own crew, people he had worked with for years, and now he was a stranger amongst them. Rhys was just thankful they didn't try to order him around. Instead he was ignored. A mere ghost. Had this been how he had reacted to starats? Had he really been blind to them? Rhys already knew the answer to that. Of course he had. He had never seen them unless he needed one. It was how starats were expected to behave.

Doctor Sparks was clearly surprised to be interrupted by the two starats. It also took him a few moments to recognise Rhys. His eyes widened slightly as he looked from one to the other. "Glad to see you up and about again," he said as he gestured for them both to enter his small office, just off to the side of the medical ward. Rhys noticed that instead of focussing on him, Doctor Sparks looked at the foot of empty space between him and Twitch.

The office was cramped. A small desk dominated the centre of the room. It was barely big enough for the computer, books, and paperwork that had been spread over it. Each wall was completely covered in filing cabinets and bookshelves, which were themselves overflowing with various reference books. There wasn't much room to stand.

Rhys wasted no time in informing Sparks of the reason for their visit. "Have you told Admiral Garter about this yet?"

"What happened?" Sparks asked, instantly aware that something had gone amiss.

"Cooper followed Twitch up to my quarters. He refused to believe me when I said who I was. He physically assaulted me, and I fear he's going to take his story to the admiral," Rhys said quickly. "We need to make sure Admiral Garter knows the truth first."

"Cooper attacked you? That would mean..."

"He'll never work on my ship again," Rhys finished for the doctor, but that hadn't been his train of thought.

"Well, yeah, obviously. But it's more than that. You stood up to him. You must have fought back," Sparks said. Silently, Twitch vigorously nodded his head.

"How did you know that?"

"Because you're not a sorry, bloody mess of broken bone. I know all about Giles Cooper's temper. And his background. I know he served with Emile Salazar on the *Emperor's Revenge.*"

Rhys stared in absolute shock. He had just told Cooper that only two people knew about his past because that's what he had believed to be the case. Doctor Sparks was definitely not on that list, and yet, the evidence to the contrary was obvious. How the doctor knew beggared belief.

"People in my trade get access to a lot more information than you may think," Doctor Sparks explained. He opened one of the many filing cabinets around them, revealing rows of thick files, all labelled with a name, some of which Rhys recognised. "Patient histories. They give a lot of information, including what ships a person has been treated on. The *Emperor's Revenge* was no different to our ships. Emile kept records of everything, even if it wasn't stored digitally. I have them all in here."

"Emile? You mentioned him before. Who is he?" Twitch asked, looking between Rhys and Doctor Sparks.

"Emile Salazar is the real name of the Silver Fox. You've heard of him, right?" Doctor Sparks said.

"Yeah, of course. The pirate," Twitch said, brandishing an imaginary sword as he spoke. The Silver Fox had been rumoured to carry one of the archaic weapons. "Even we have stories about him. You know he had a starat on his crew?"

"I don't know about that, but he was the greatest threat to the empire, discounting the CGP. Hardly anyone knew his real name, or where he was based. Giles Cooper was his first officer and most trusted ally for many years, but he turned traitor and handed Emile over to empire authorities. We never knew what his motives were, but as a reward he just asked to be enrolled in the military. Probably wanted a more stable life," Rhys said. This had all happened before he had completed his training, but the admiral had told him the full story. There had never been any troubles with Cooper's conduct, though Doctor Sparks was right to point out his short temper. There were more urgent concerns than Cooper's past though. It was what Cooper was doing at the present that filled Rhys with worry. He tapped his fingers on the desk and looked up at the doctor. "What have you told the admiral already?"

"He knows there was a teleporter incident, but I haven't told him the specifics. I wanted to wait until it was clear it couldn't be reversed first," the doctor explained. He ran his hand through his hair and checked his watch. "I'll go find him and see how we can break the news. Wait here. I'll bring him up."

"Thanks," Rhys replied. He gripped onto the desk, his claws digging in to the wood. He didn't look up as the doctor left the two starats alone together. Rhys had to sink down into the vacated chair while he waited, his tail tucked to the side. His feet ached as he struggled to find the right balance on them.

Twitch gazed at Rhys with a look of pure admiration in his eyes. An awkward silence stretched out, until Twitch finally broke it. "I have never seen a starat stand up to a human before, you know. Never even heard of it happening." He started pacing the room restlessly. Rhys could sense the thought that was forming in Twitch's mind, as though he was weaving it with his footsteps and creating a banner proclaiming his mind. Sure enough, Twitch added, "You could help us – inspire us. We don't like our position, and with you we could change that."

"Hang on a minute. You want me to lead a revolt?"

Twitch shook his head with his eyes wide. "It doesn't have to be violent. If it doesn't have to be. You can talk to them. The humans. Make them see things from our point of view."

"I… I'm not able to do anything like that." Rhys said weakly.

"Why?"

Rhys sighed and leaned back with a wince, the chair not accommodating his tail too well. "I can't be seen at the front of an army or rebellion against the empire. Think how the Vatican would react if I started doing that. I won't stand idly by and let starats be abused, but I can't lead a revolt."

"I hope you'll keep that promise," Twitch said before falling silent. The starat twisted his tail in his lap. There were times when it looked like he was about to speak again, but every time he closed his mouth and kept his silence. They were momentarily interrupted when Edgar Scott poked his head into the office, but he didn't even look down to the two starats before leaving again.

Doctor Sparks returned twenty minutes later. He was in the middle of an animated conversation with Admiral Garter. Rhys jumped to his feet and tugged on Twitch's hand, pulling him through into the main ward.

The admiral started when he saw the two starats emerging from the office. "These are your ulterior motive for bringing me here, Doctor Sparks?"

"Yes. I'll make it brief, don't worry. I want you to tell me, Admiral, can you tell any difference between these two starats?"

Admiral Garter pulled his glasses from his pocket, wiped them on his shirt, and put them on. "Most humans can't tell apart two starats aside from any obvious height and fur colour differences. I, however, have worked with a lot more starats than most, and can identify individuals with relative ease. Between these two though, I can't see a single difference," he said, looking intently at Rhys and Twitch through his glasses.

"That's because there isn't any. These two are completely identical, Admiral," Sparks said.

Admiral Garter didn't appear too impressed by such a revelation. "I'm sure there are identical twins amongst starats as well as us,

Doctor. Now can you please take me through to Captain Griffiths," he said as he removed his glasses again.

"I'll take you in a moment, I promise. This is important though. These two starats weren't born identical. They became it."

This time Admiral Garter's interest was betrayed by the slightest rise of his eyebrow. "Go on."

"When the teleporters malfunctioned the other day, they lost the second one's genetic information. Instead it replaced it with an exact copy of the first starat, who had gone through about thirty seconds earlier, effectively creating a clone of the first with the mind and personality of the second." Doctor Sparks spoke quickly. Rhys could feel the tension rising. His fingers grasped the side of the desk behind him.

Admiral Garter appeared struck dumb. He looked again at the two starats, closed his eyes for a moment and took a deep breath. "The teleporter attendant told me Rhys came down just after a starat when the system malfunctioned," he said eventually in an emotionless voice. He turned back to Doctor Sparks. "Which is he?"

Wordlessly, Doctor Sparks pointed to Twitch. Twitch then pointed to Rhys, and the doctor quickly corrected himself.

"Good afternoon, Admiral," Rhys said, not quite able to meet Admiral Garter's eyes. He noticed his hands were fiddling with his tail, so he placed them flat against the gurney again.

Admiral Garter had to sit on the closest chair to him for support. "Captain Griffiths? Well, I must say, when I heard you had been taken ill, this was not what I expected."

"The illness was…" Rhys paused and sighed. He closed his eyes for a moment, before looking to the admiral's chest. "It has taken, and will take, a lot of getting used to."

"And you feel you'll be ready to resume your usual duties soon?"

Rhys's ears perked up, an involuntary reaction he wasn't aware of. Admiral Garter wouldn't have asked that question if he didn't still have trust in him. "As soon as I've cleared some trouble I'll need your help with, Admiral."

"Could we have some privacy, Doctor Sparks?" the admiral said, turning to the doctor. The doctor nodded and gave the admiral a quick salute before leaving the ward. Twitch glanced to Rhys, but

Admiral Garter didn't address the starat to dismiss him, or even look in his direction. Rhys gestured for him to remain where he was.

"Do explain," the admiral said, once he was sure Sparks had left.

"Lieutenant Cooper came up to my quarters just before. He reacted... unfavourably towards my new, uh... condition," Rhys said quietly. He barely dared to look up towards the admiral, scared to see his superior officer ignoring him. He was surprised to see Admiral Garter looking right at him, hands clasped beneath his chin. As Rhys paused in surprise, the admiral gestured with a hand for him to continue. When Rhys spoke next, a little more confidence crept into his voice. "He attacked me and struck me several times. I gave him the chance to apologise, warning him for his behaviour, but he attempted to assault me once more. I fear he will no longer work for me, and that he will spread misinformation to the rest of my crew."

"You are right of course," Admiral Garter said once Rhys had finished. "Lieutenant Cooper's position has become quite untenable. And yes, I will make your new identity public knowledge. I shall take your doctor here and get him to inform your crew, with my backing. Then I'll spread the word to the rest of the port, and finally on to Chancellor Roberts."

"Thank you, Admiral. That would be most appreciated. Has there been any news from the *Dawn*?"

"Nothing at all," the admiral said. "It would seem that Captain Lee has now left the Sol System. I certainly haven't heard any reports from his ship in the last twenty-four hours. As for Chancellor Roberts, there's been no meaningful updates in his investigation. He has returned to Terra for consultations. He will advise us when he requires our presence. He also, upon hearing of your illness, wished you a prompt return to... well, your usual self."

"I think we can both agree that's a long shot, Admiral," Rhys said quietly.

There was a smile on Admiral Garter's usually taciturn face. It was the closest Rhys had seen him come to humour. "Indeed," he said, nodding his head in dismissal of the captain. He turned to take his leave, before pausing to add one last thing. "You will continue to be excused from your regular duties for the rest of the day, but be present at briefing tomorrow at 0900 hours in the control tower. I can tell you more about the chancellor's report then, but right now I have other pressing matters to deal with. I will give you special mitigation for the time being, given your... shall we say, exceptional circumstances, but do try and find a uniform more suitable for your rank."

"I'll be sure to get that arranged as soon as possible, sir," Rhys replied.

The admiral nodded. "Most appreciated, Captain Griffiths. Good luck with the rest of your day," he said. For a moment, the admiral's eyes moved across the room to glance at Twitch, but then he left the office without another word.

Rhys leaned back in his chair and took a deep breath. He accidently hit himself in the muzzle as he rubbed his hands over his face. Wincing in pain, he tried to ignore Twitch's giggle.

"I can only hope that will be enough," Rhys said quietly. He could not have hoped for his first talk with Admiral Garter to go any better, and it had helped loosen the knot of panic in his chest, but he also knew that the next day would be far from easy. Cooper's reaction was a perfect example of that.

"Yeah, but enough of boring old humans for one day," Twitch said, sticking his tongue out at Rhys. The starat grinned, showing off all of his needle-like teeth, before tugging on Rhys's arm to drag him from the ward. "Come on, I want you to see the other starats. And trust me on this, they're going to absolutely love you."

No one gave a second glance at the sight of the two starats walking through the *Harvester* and then out through the port. In fact, Rhys wasn't convinced anyone even noticed their presence at all. There certainly wasn't any of the salutes and muttered greetings he was used to; just pure indifference. Everyone looked so tall, too. Already he was beginning to understand why starats were intimidated around humans. He had never felt so insignificant before.

Without a need for urgency, they walked at a much slower pace this time, one that Rhys was able to manage without falling over. He tried to take on Twitch's advice, but he had to keep consciously thinking about where to place his tail and how to take the next step. It was mentally exhausting.

Rhys had no idea where they were going. He had been to Normandy many times before and had spent most of the last few months in the spaceport, but he wouldn't even know where to begin looking for where the resident starats lived. Never once before had he ever felt the need to go find them.

Twitch led him to the outskirts of the port. It was one of the newer sections, which actually surprised Rhys a bit. He had expected them to be holed away in one of the older and shabbier corners of the spaceport. It was also one of the few structures in the spaceport that rose above the ground. Only the control tower and a half dozen other small buildings cleared the surface.

The starats' residence was a tall and sprawling warehouse-like building consisting of just a single level, or so it appeared from the outside at least. There was only a single entry that Rhys could see; a large double door that was absurdly tall for use by the starats. Rhys would have considered it too tall even if it had been used by humans. Around the building was a thick, metal dome with a number of windows around the base, protecting them from the harsh, airless void beyond. Beneath their feet was the bare rocky surface of Ceres.

Then Twitch pushed open the doors and pulled Rhys inside.

"Oh shit, they've cloned Twitch," was the first thing Rhys heard as he stepped inside. A flood of other comments followed shortly after.

"Not with a cardinal around they wouldn't. Church banned that stuff ages ago."

"There's a cardinal here? Better not go out unless it's really necessary then. You know what they're like."

"I know, right. Always after our fur, the religious pricks."

"So why the two Twitches then? One was bad enough. No offence to you Twitch."

"None taken."

"Come on, start explaining then. Don't say you're out of words 'cause we won't believe you."

"Yes, we'll explain everything," Twitch said, pulling Rhys closer to him. For a moment there was a bit of silence, and Rhys was able to catch up with his senses and take stock of where he was. The entire building appeared to be just a single, massive room. Down each wall was a row of beds, but there was little else to furnish the room. At the far end was a woefully small kitchen, where a couple of starats were working, creating a tantalising aroma of fried fish. Near the ceiling there was a collection of vents that regulated the temperature inside.

As soon as the doors had opened, all the starats within, which Rhys had made a conservative guess was around fifty, had gathered close. They were all wearing the same blue overalls Rhys and Twitch were wearing. Everything all seemed very... normal. Rhys was surprised by it. But for the fur and tails, this could easily be a group of humans gathered together.

Rhys would admit it to no one, but he was absolutely terrified, and he hoped no one would be able to see him shaking. He was no longer quite sure if this had been such a good idea. If the starats rejected him, then he would be running short on options.

"This must be all the starats in the port, surely?" he whispered under his breath. He hadn't realised there was so many of them here.

"Yeah, this looks about everyone. Can't be too much work for us to do at the moment, for once," Twitch replied, just as quietly. Then he turned his attention back to the starats, who were starting to crowd in close, eager for answers. None of them showed any signs of being the emotionless, simple creatures Rhys had always believed them to be.

"Well come on, out with it," a starat called out again, bringing Rhys's attention back to the revelation that was to come.

Of all the tactful and diplomatic ways that Twitch could have explained the situation, he chose the bluntest and simplest. "My new twin here is none other than Captain Rhys."

His name was evidently not unfamiliar amongst the starats.

"Captain? Did he say captain?" was the most repeated response to that piece of news.

"He has to be joking, right?" usually followed straight after, but the starats soon came to realise that Twitch had not, in fact, been joking at all. Though it was hard for some of them to believe, they were really looking at Captain Rhys Griffiths.

"He hasn't been seen for a couple of days..."

"And there was that thing with the teleporters..."

Then one of them laughed. A female near the back. "If this is true, then it is good for us. He's a captain. He has more authority than any starat has ever had. He can help us," she said as she started to push her way towards the front of the crowd.

Then another piped up. "But does he consider himself a starat?" he said sceptically. At once, all eyes turned on the pair of Rhys and Twitch. They appeared a little unsure as to which one precisely they were meant to be staring at, so they settled for both at the same time.

Rhys knew he had to say something now. "I doubt I can be human again," he said, diplomatic where Twitch had been blunt. A few giggled at him. His words still came out slightly slurred. "If I don't consider myself a starat, then what else am I?"

"Neither us nor them," the sceptical starat said. A few others murmured in agreement.

"He doesn't care for us," another said. "He only comes here asking for our help because no one else will give it. Just because he looks like one of us doesn't mean he's like us on the inside. He didn't care about us before. He doesn't care about us now."

Rhys looked down at his feet. "I know I have done nothing to deserve your help. You have no reason to trust me. I don't know how much sway my word as captain has here, but I promise you I will try to change my ways."

"If you want to stay with us, then you must," one of them growled. "And get rid of any beliefs that you're better than us, because you're not."

"I understand that," Rhys said. Without seeing who had just spoken, he wasn't able to look towards his accuser. Instead, he slowly looked around at all the starats as he spoke. "I won't lie, it will not be easy. We are taught that starats are our inferiors, that their only purpose is to serve humans. I… I can already see that this is incorrect. I don't know what I can do to change the minds of my colleagues, but I will do my best."

"And how did you treat us? I've never spoken with a starat who has served on your ship."

Rhys sighed and placed a hand on his forehead. "With indifference. I never cared about starats. They were just there, and they did what they were required to do. But never with cruelty, I can guarantee that. I have never been cruel to a starat."

"I can only hope that's true." A few starats murmured and nodded. Rhys knew he wouldn't be able to walk in and get every starat to believe him. There were still so many who appeared unconvinced, but his heart was warmed by those who believed that he was capable of change. He would do his best to justify that faith.

Rhys placed his hands to his chest. "Please. Tell me how I can help you."

His question opened a floodgate of answers, with many of the starats eager to make their opinion heard. There were so many voices speaking over the top of each other that Rhys couldn't make heads or tails of anything anyone was trying to tell him. He couldn't even pick up on whether the dominant emotion was hope at his acceptance to help or anger at his ignorance of how they needed it. Rhys was paralysed by the hopelessness of trying to decipher everything.

Then someone displayed a bit of common sense. "Quiet!" a powerful voice yelled across all the babble. Silence soon fell at the request of the one starat, a large male with coffee-coloured fur and particularly pronounced black tear-drop markings around his eyes.

"That's David," Twitch whispered for Rhys's benefit. "He's my partner."

"Partner? That makes sense," Rhys muttered, thinking back to how fascinated Twitch had been with his body. He glanced across at David, who was staring with intent at them both. "Just... make sure he knows which of us is which, alright?"

Twitch smiled nervously. Both his ears were pulled back on his head in a movement Rhys was keen to remember. If he was to learn this body, he would need to know every emotion, and he had the slight feeling he would be rather nervous quite a lot in the upcoming days.

Rhys felt a little embarrassed by David's rapt attention, especially knowing his relation to Twitch. His comment to Twitch had been flippant and he had spoken without thinking, but what if David did think he was Twitch? Rhys told himself to forget it. The two were partners. He was sure that David would be able to tell if the starat he was with was his partner or someone still trying to come to terms with his new identity as a starat.

A starat pushed the way through to the front of the crowd. She was short even for a starat, and her fur was so dark it was almost black. "That's Steph. She's always had a bit of a thing for me," Twitch whispered in Rhys's ear with a giggle.

"We do need help, Captain Rhys," Steph said, her voice strong and without fear. "We're sick of being treated like we are. I'm sure you contributed to that somewhat, but I don't judge you for that. You were simply acting as you were taught. I just hope you use this experience to see what we're really like, and to end this treatment of us." Her words made Rhys feel even more guilty for his past behaviour to starats. He was already finding it hard to reconcile the dumb creatures he had thought them to be with this mass of faces before him. They simmered with excitement, tempered with distrust.

"He was never as bad as some of the others," one starat said, alleviating a little of the guilt. Even as a human, he had been disturbed about some of the reports on how starats were treated, but never once had he done anything about it. Captain Baron was often mentioned with such reports, which sent a tremor of fear down his spine.

"It's just TIE though," another starat added.

"And the Vatican," a third said.

"The CGP humans treat starats as equal, I've heard," the second starat continued.

"We haven't got any proof of that though," a fourth said. "And besides, the CGP don't send their ships here, and we have next to zero a chance of leaving this desolate rock. Our only chance of escaping here is by punching a hole through the dome and letting the vacuum deal with us."

Rhys felt physically sick as the guilt returned with the force of one of Cooper's punches. The mere rumour that the CGP treated his new kind well would have been enough to make him uneasy. But he had been aboard a CGP ship, albeit a recently acquired one. And what was more, he could confirm the rumour. Rhys did not like the fact that he could find equality amongst humans again if only he would fight against the empire. But then he reminded himself that the emperor had not turned his back on him. Yet, added some insidious part of his mind, which he told to shut up and leave him alone. Still, the starats had a right to know. He had to tell them.

"I think I know the answer to that," he said before anyone else could speak. "The *Terrestrial Dawn* defected a week or so ago. I was a hostage aboard it when it passed Ceres to pick up any who wished to join them. Their navigator was a starat. I don't know if that's what the CGP is like always, but I doubt a starat would be trusted if they weren't capable."

"A CGP ship? Here? Why didn't we know about this?" David asked, regarding Rhys with suspicion. He wasn't the only one. Everyone's attention, even Twitch's, was now on Rhys.

"I told you he was no different to the others," a dissenting starat grumbled. His voice was not alone. Others called for Rhys to be thrown back amongst the humans.

Rhys held his hands up defensively. "That was Admiral Garter's decision, not mine. Though we were willing to inform you of the situation, and assist in the defence of the port if we were attacked, Captain Favre and Captain Baron both recommended against it. They thought you were more likely to flee to the *Dawn*," he said. Then a small smile touched his lips. "You can't deny they were right in their reasoning, but I understand now why you would be frustrated by his decision. I would have probably felt the same way."

Rhys almost clapped his hand over his mouth, shocked at the words that had spilled out. Was that really true? Had Rhys been a starat already, would he have turned to the CGP at the first given opportunity? He decided he wouldn't even attempt to answer that question until a few more days had passed. Only once he knew the true opinions of TIE and his superiors would he try and work out the truth.

Steph's voice rose above the growing clamour. "He deserves another chance," she said. She turned around to face the starats, her back to Rhys and Twitch. "We shouldn't judge him on his past actions, just on those he makes from now on. If he is truly willing to help us, then we should be willing to accept that help."

"So, Captain Rhys," David said in a loud voice, clapping his hands together. "Are you with us?"

Rhys didn't even need to think about his answer. "I can't lead a revolution. I can't do anything that will risk my position as captain, but I will do anything I can to help change human perception of you," he said, repeating his sentiments he had told Twitch earlier. The next moment he was bowled over as Twitch hugged him tightly, clearly expecting Rhys to stay on his feet. His balance wasn't good enough, and the two were sent sprawling across the floor.

Twitch's hands pressed down on Rhys's shoulders, pinning him in place as the starat grinned down at him. "I knew you'd be alright, Captain Rhys," Twitch crowed, before David came over to disentangle the pair.

Rhys didn't get back up to his feet right away, instead sitting down on the floor. He could hear the starats all talking around him, but for the moment he was too lost in his thoughts to focus on them.

He knew that if he spoke out against the treatment of starats, he would be stripped of his rank in an instant. He would be lucky to keep his life if he was taken away by the Vatican. His career stood on a knife edge. He would have to balance his duties as a captain and his desire to see starat treatment improve. One misstep and he would lose all chance of personal gain and influence to benefit starats. Equality was a far-off dream he could never hope to see himself, but he had to try. That way they wouldn't have to risk everything in a desperate attempt to flee to the CGP. There would be people who would oppose. They would oppose vehemently. He understood there would even be some starats who would feel he was meddling in affairs that were not his own. But he was determined to succeed.

***

The starats were insistent as they relentlessly approached Rhys, and soon he had no choice but to start listening to them all. David organised all the waiting starats into some loose order as Rhys tried to absorb all the requests for help. Before long though, they turned into questions about humans. Some questions were rather personal, and he didn't feel he could answer them in a public location. But most he was more than happy to give answers to. Even simple things like their diet were asked. One younger starat even asked why the humans didn't have fur. Rhys had no idea how to answer that one, but tried nonetheless. He actually rather enjoyed the entire experience. Given the chance, the starats weren't so different from humans.

Rhys had sat on the edge of one of the many beds that lined the warehouse-like room, with just under half the starats gathered around by his feet as he spoke. He had his own questions too. When the starats' queries seemed to be exhausted for the time being, about halfway through the afternoon, Rhys was able to ask the gathered crowd something that had been pressing on his mind all day.

"Why do you need me to help you? If you so desperately want to change things, why have you waited for someone like me to happen?"

There was a short period of uncomfortable silence before an answer was offered. It was the same little starat who had asked Rhys for help in the first place, Steph.

"We've been dominated by humans for over two hundred years. Not since Essie have we had anyone speak up for us. We have no authority amongst them and they never listen to us when we speak out. They just look down at us and laugh, if they even pay attention to us at all. To them we're just another animal to do their bidding." She held her tail in her hands and looked down at Rhys's feet bashfully.

"If one of us is successful, then others will follow," another added. He was one of the few young starats that Rhys had seen. His furry face was beaming with youthful hope. It was an expression that was prevalent throughout the twenty-strong crowd gathered around Rhys. He had never seen it on a starat before he had arrived in their home.

"So, I'm to be the inspiration for better things for you all?" Rhys said. That was something not too alien to Rhys. He had been idolised by the new recruits in the Cardiff Interstellar Academy when he had last visited to give some motivational speeches. Inspiring others was within his means.

"We need you to make some noise too. It's not just starats here that need your help. Every starat in TIE needs to have someone to look up to," Steph said.

Rhys looked around at the expectant faces. This was a chance they had all hoped for, yet had never believed would actually happen. The true realisation of the task at hand hit Rhys. It wasn't just the fifty starats here he would be fighting for. It would be the millions spread throughout the reaches of the empire, across two star systems. The thought of standing up against the empire and Vatican terrified him. He bowed his head and closed his eyes. "If I do that, I will lose everything. I don't think you realise what you're asking me to do. What you're asking me to risk."

A few mutters spread through the crowd, and a couple of starats wandered off. Steph's voice took on a steely edge. "I know exactly what I'm asking you to do. I know what the risks are. If you truly care about us though, if what you say is true, then that risk is something worth taking."

"If I speak up too loudly, I lose everything. No more captain, no more ship. No more influence. If I'm lucky, I become a... I become an ordinary starat, like you all. If that happens, I can't help anyone," Rhys replied. He hated himself for bringing that up, but he couldn't see any way around it. If he took direct action now, he would be stripped of everything and thrown in amongst the other starats without hope of returning to his human life.

"So, you'll do nothing?" one of the starats gathered around asked.

Rhys quickly shook his head. "I never said that. My attitudes will change. I will correct behaviour against starats where I can. It will be slow, but I will always be looking for ways to help change people's minds about starats... about us."

"I hope you will. We'll certainly know if you don't," Steph said. Her ears flicked a couple of times before she sat beside Rhys on the edge of the bed. "I think you will though. You were always one of the better humans. As one of us I think you'll be even better, even if you do look like another Twitch."

Rhys leaned back, resting his elbows on the firm, rigid mattress. "I don't know why I let Twitch go first into that teleporter. I still don't know if I'd make the same choice if I had that time again, but... I'm seeing it less as a curse now," he said, choosing his words carefully as he looked around at the starats gathered around him.

"He's going to be unbearable if he realises what he's done. I can hear him now, Christopher –the twin of the starat saviour," Steph said, drawing a couple of giggles from the young starats, though they could also have come from Rhys's grimace at calling him a saviour.

"I'm not a saviour," Rhys muttered with a frown, before he took in the rest of what she had said. His ears flicked up. "But, Christopher? That's Twitch's name?"

"Yeah. Just don't tell him I told you. He hates that name. Not even David dares to call him it," Steph said in hushed tones and a conspiratorial giggle.

"I'll keep that in mind," Rhys said. He looked around again at the starats who remained and smiled. Most of them had already moved on, sensing that Rhys had nothing further to say. Out of the dozen left, six were children, or kits, Rhys had learned what the correct term for juvenile starats was. They were all gazing at him with awe, but they all started sniggering at him.

"What?"

"Your ears. They're angry but your face is always happy," one of the kits piped up. Both her ears perked upright as she smiled widely. "You look happy like this."

"I have a lot to learn, it seems," Rhys said. He resisted the urge to reach up and feel what his ears were doing.

"Curious, questioning, and intrigued," another of the kits said, paying attention to Rhys's ears. His left ear had curled in on itself.

"Alright, that's enough. You don't need to commentate on everything," Rhys said.

"Slightly amused!" the second kit said excitedly. "You're starting to get the hang of it, I think. Oh, and that one means you're annoyed, and – oh, sorry." The kit fell silent as he realised exactly what was annoying Rhys.

"You're going to get a lot of that," Steph commented as the kits scampered away, probably to annoy some other poor soul.

"It'll get much worse tomorrow," Rhys said with a sigh. Even though he had Admiral Garter's personal support, he was still terrified about the morning briefing. He had Captain Favre and Captain Baron to contend with, as he was sure there had to be some form of confrontation. Then there was also the matter of the cardinal. If the Vatican's emissary was present, then matters would likely get heated rather quickly. Even as a human he'd been all too aware how the Vatican treated starats.

Steph put her hand on his. "Don't worry too much about it. For now, they can't touch you. If, as you say, your admiral supports you, then everyone else must too," she said.

"I wish it were that simple," Rhys said. He stood up and intentionally broke the contact between the two of them. He glanced back at her and felt a sensation welling within his chest. He took a deep breath. A shudder travelled down from his shoulders all the way to the tip of his tail. "I knew another Stephanie, once."

"Was she nice?" Steph asked brightly.

Rhys nodded and closed his eyes. He pinched his clawed fingers over his muzzle. "She was. Haven't thought about her for a long time. Don't know why I remembered her then."

Desperate for a distraction from his thoughts before they went down a road he had long ago blocked off, he looked around the warehouse to find Twitch. He was falling asleep in his partner's arms on the other side of the large room, amongst a throng of starats. Rhys then glanced up to the row of windows just beneath the warehouse's ceiling. Beneath the large dome, there was little indication of the position of the sun, but Rhys felt like it had to be getting close to the second sunset. It would soon be night again. This was not where he needed to be. No captain fit of their rank would be seen in the starats' quarters.

"What am I doing here?" he muttered, not intending for anyone to hear him, but a starat's hearing was better than that of a human.

"What do you mean?" Steph asked. She was perched on the edge of the bed, her claws digging in to the tattered mattress. Both ears had pulled forward and the tip of her tail was twitching.

Rhys stumbled as he hastily took a couple of steps away from the diminutive starat. He yelped as he thrust his hand out for support, only to lean against a boiling water pipe that stuck out from the wall. Regaining his balance, he cradled his burnt hand against his chest, fending away the concerned attentions of Steph with his other.

"I... can't be here. I'd better get back to my ship so I can get ready for tomorrow," he said, trying to suppress a whimper as he moved his injured hand slightly.

"You can always sleep with us for the night," Steph said.

He looked down at her, but he shook his head. "I can't."

"Why?" Steph asked, before shaking her head and sighing. "Let me at least look at that hand." She reached out to touch Rhys on the arm, but again he pulled away.

"I'm fine," Rhys said, before ruining the illusion by crying out in pain as he tried to brush Steph away with his right hand. He felt tears spring to his eyes, so he turned his back to the smaller starat. "It'll look better to the others if I'm staying on my ship and fulfilling my duties still. I have... I have paperwork to catch up on," he said. He grasped his tail in his left hand and started to walk away. This time Steph did nothing to stop him.

Keeping his excuses short, Rhys quickly left before anyone else was able to hold him up. No one called him back. He emerged outside alone. As the doors slammed shut behind him, Rhys paused for a moment, hugging his injured hand close to his chest. For a moment, he was tempted to walk back inside, but instead he started to walk towards the stairs back down to the underground part of the port.

A few paces from the stairwell, Rhys's unsteady feet slipped on the rough stone. He staggered for a few steps, but without anything to hold on to for support, he couldn't control where his feet went. Each impact of the soft foot pads hurt, but the last was the worst. He shrieked in pain as a jagged shard of rock punctured through his flesh, piercing his pads with ease.

He collapsed to the floor, once more yelping as his injured hand struck the unyielding rocky ground. With an agonising wrench, he pulled his foot free from the protruding spur that had punctured the soft pad. Blood flowed freely, splashing across the slate-grey stone. He tried to crawl, but with one hand he was barely able to reach the top of the stairs before collapsing. He curled into a ball and whimpered, his cheeks wet from fresh tears.

It would be so easy to go back into the warehouse for help. So tempting. Rhys gritted his teeth, knowing at the same time that he simply couldn't do any such thing. Fighting through the pain, Rhys dug the claws of his left hand into his overall, tearing off a strip of fabric.

"Ah, fuck..." Rhys whimpered as he tied the strip around his foot. It was dirty and crude, but it would last long enough to get to his ship.

Getting to his feet was one of the most challenging things he'd ever had to do. He couldn't place any weight on his left foot at all, and he staggered down the stairs, almost falling again. With his left hand on the wall, he slowly limped through the port. He walked by many humans along the way, but not a single one stopped to look at him, let alone offer any assistance. He was alone and invisible to them, the only traces of his passing being the smudged bloody pawprint he left with each step.

By the time he made it to the shuttle bay, Rhys could barely walk anymore. The strip of blue fabric around his food was soaked red, and his burned hand ached with a constant, pulsing throb. He could barely even mumble to one of the shuttle attendants where he needed to go, which probably played into the act of being a simple, submissive starat. At least it didn't take long before he was bundled into a free shuttle and transported up to his ship. No one said a word to him, not even when he squeaked out a weary word of thanks.

He made it a couple of steps off the shuttle before his strength finally gave out. He collapsed to his knees and tried to crawl, but his hand prevented him from doing that. Footsteps approached just as Rhys fell to the floor.

Rhys closed his eyes as he felt two strong, human hands pick him up. "Damn it, we've got another one." Aleksandr Chekolin, the ship's pilot. Rhys was hauled over the pilot's shoulder like he weighed nothing at all.

"We've got to tell Sparks not to keep welcoming them all in," another voice said, this one of Edgar Scott.

They didn't recognise him. Bleeding and wounded, Rhys didn't feel like re-introducing himself to his crew. Instead he just slumped over Chekolin's shoulder, letting the pilot carry him through to the medical ward. Rhys could hear Scott following along behind them.

"We're going to get that cardinal breathing down our necks if this keeps happening," Chekolin said as he shifted Rhys's weight on his shoulder.

Scott clicked his tongue, and from the sound of it, was tapping his knuckles against the wall as he walked. "We definitely can't have that," the navigator replied. "Or there'll be trouble for us all."

"Well you tell Sparks about it, he doesn't listen to me," Chekolin replied. Rhys flicked his tail and groaned in pain, but neither of the humans seemed to pay any attention to him at all.

"I'll speak to Ant. And the captain, when he's back."

A door was kicked open, and Rhys got a strong scent of medicines and the clean, sharp tang of the sterile ward. He was dumped on one of the beds as Scott called out for the doctor.

Rhys whimpered and opened his eyes, shielding his injured hand close to his chest. Chekolin had turned away, looking towards the open door to the small office. "Thank you, Alek," he whispered, too tired to even think of the consequences of addressing his pilot with familiarity.

The pilot spun on his heel. "Huh?"

Chekolin's confusion went unanswered as Scott and Doctor Sparks emerged from the small office off to the side of the ward. The navigator had always appeared tall to Rhys, but now he looked absolutely massive. He couldn't help but feel intimidated.

"Again, Twitch?" Doctor Sparks said with a sigh.

Rhys shook his head. His eyes flicked up to Scott and Chekolin.

"Ah," Sparks said. He also looked across to the other two standing by his sides. He gestured them towards the door, bustling them away from the side of the bed. "Thank you for bringing him down here, but let's give him some space and rest now. Thank you."

At first, both Scott and Chekolin went to leave without protest, but just before they left, the pilot turned around suddenly. There was recognition in his eyes as he looked towards Rhys, and he silently mouthed his captain's name. Rhys tensed in fear, but before anything could be said, Sparks closed the door and locked it.

"What have you been doing to yourself?" Sparks asked. He briefly inspected the strip of blood-soaked fabric wrapped around Rhys's foot. He sucked in his breath and shook his head as he gently lifted Rhys's foot up, before gently lowering it to the bed again. He then turned aside and started to rummage through the supply cabinet.

"Stood on some rocks," Rhys muttered. He lifted up his arm. "And burned my hand. This body is too clumsy. Can I have a new one?" Rhys felt almost delirious as he lay back on the bed. He couldn't help but chuckle. He felt so weak, like all the strength had drained from his body. He knew he'd probably lost too much blood, and he didn't even notice the doctor preparing a small injection.

"I don't think I can give you that, Rhys, but I can give you something to sleep and give your body the chance to heal," the doctor said.

Rhys turned his head to the side in time to see Sparks stab him with the needle in the shoulder. He grimaced and gritted his teeth together, before he felt his body relax completely. "Oh, that's good, thank you," he muttered. His head rested back on the pillow, and within a moment he was asleep.

chapter six

Rhys woke slowly from a dreamless sleep. For a few moments he didn't remember where he was. The sheets felt tight around him, the mattress firmer than he was used to. He wasn't in his quarters. Slowly, it all trickled down into his mind. The last time he had woken up in a medical ward, he hadn't been able to move in an attempt to protect him from that life-changing incident in the teleporters. At least this time he was still on his ship, and not in the derelict ward on Ceres.

His eyes gradually opened. With a little effort, he pulled his right hand out from the sheets and held it up. It was wrapped in white bandages, but between the tight rolls of gauze he could see brown fur poking through. He was still a starat. It hadn't all been one, long dream.

He sat up, wincing as he accidently crushed his tail for a moment. He still wasn't used to it, and he doubted he would be for quite some time.

His other wounds didn't hurt anymore. Whatever Sparks had done whilst he'd been asleep had worked very well. His foot felt stiff, but he was confident he'd be able to put pressure on it once he summoned the energy to get out of bed.

It took Rhys a few moments to realise he wasn't alone. A starat in white overalls was lying back on another of the beds, though by the look of him he didn't appear injured or ill. His eyes were closed, foot tapping to some tune in his head. "Twitch?" Rhys asked.

The starat opened his eyes. "I beg your pardon?" he said. His ears perked up.

Rhys cursed beneath his breath. He should have known. The starat was clearly not Twitch. His fur was the wrong colour; a much lighter shade of brown, and his muzzle was thinner and longer. He also spoke with a Welsh accent, much stronger than Rhys's own military-suppressed twang.

"Sorry. Thought you were someone else," Rhys said. He lifted himself up and started to untangle himself from the bed sheets. It wasn't until he swung his legs out to the side before realising what was missing. Sometime during his sleep he had been stripped completely naked, with nothing but his fur hiding his modesty. He hastily pulled the sheets over his lap.

If the other starat noticed Rhys's nakedness, he made no indication of it. He leaned forward with a small smirk. "I'm Richard. I've served on the *Harvester* for nearly two years now, but I don't expect you to recognise me," the starat said. His ears drooped, an expression matched by Rhys.

"I'm sorry, I should…" Rhys said, before he was interrupted by a raised hand from Richard.

"I didn't expect anything else from you then. To be honest, I'm still not sure what I expect from you now. I just wanted the spare bed, and to bring you some clean clothes," Richard said. The starat scratched behind his ear with one hand, gesturing to the clean white overalls draped over the end of Rhys's bed. "I know you'll be busy, but when you get a chance, come down to the service levels and see me. I can get you measured up for some proper stuff. Assuming you're still captain by then."

Rhys narrowed his eyes at the starat, who didn't appear to have been joking at all. "I'll keep that in mind. Now give me some privacy."

Richard hopped up from the bed with a grace that made Rhys envious. He mock bowed. "Of course, Captain. Whatever you command." The starat flicked his tail as he left.

Rhys pulled down on his ears and groaned. Two years the starat had been on his ship, and Rhys hadn't even known his name. Nor had he thanked the starat for the clean uniform to replace the overalls he had bled all over. If he wanted to help starats, then he needed to treat them as he did any human. That was not what he had just done. Even a human of inferior rank deserved thanks for their tasks. There would be just as many changes needed to his habits and mentality than there would be physical changes.

After checking to make sure he was truly alone, Rhys slipped out from beneath the sheets again and tested his weight on his injured foot. There was still a little pain there and the tight bandaging was annoying, but he would be able to walk at least. The first few steps were gingerly taken, but he quickly became more confident with pressing his weight down on it.

He made his way into the small bathrooms to relieve himself. His new anatomy down there was still causing him a few troubles as he tried to work out the best system to avoid making an unpleasant mess. Once he was done and his hands washed, he made his way back into the ward, rubbing his eyes and yawning. He wondered if there was anywhere down here to get a coffee, but a quick search of the ward, and then into the empty office, revealed nothing. He wasn't yet confident enough to acquire one from the ship or port cafeteria, so he resigned himself to going without. A quick check of the clock warned him that he had a little time to waste before he was expected in the control tower.

He used that time to shower. He groomed his fur and dressed in the starat uniform Richard had provided. He pinned his captain's epaulettes to the shoulders. Breakfast could wait. His stomach was too unsettled for food. He was ready to leave well in advance, but he couldn't muster the courage to leave the security of the ward. He hesitated and started to pace. Out there, the eyes of everyone would be on him. They would not view him as a human, or as a captain. He would be a starat. A slave. He didn't know what he would do if someone tried to give him an order.

Then the time came when he had no choice but to leave. He couldn't permit himself to be late, so he took a deep breath, gave himself a mental dressing-down and reminded himself of who he was. He took a few confident steps towards the door and opened it. That was as far as his confidence took him, and from there he scampered through the shadows, avoiding eye contact with everyone until he reached the control tower.

His hand shook as he keyed in his passcode, sliding open the door. Admiral Garter and Captains Favre and Baron were already present. To Rhys's dismay, so was Cardinal Erik. There was only one control operative present; a young man who seemed to be doing his best to studiously ignore the meeting happening in the middle of the room. Whatever reaction Rhys anticipated, he didn't expect none, but that was what he received. No one gave any indication that he had entered the room.

Clearing his throat, Rhys took a couple of steps forward, trying his hardest to walk properly. Now would not be a good time to stumble and fall.

Captain Favre was the first to look up. "Yes?" he asked with a cold edge in his voice Rhys had never heard before.

"Captain Griffiths," Rhys said, tapping his chest, hating how small his voice sounded.

At the sound of his voice, the other three men looked up. Their expressions could hardly be more varied. Captain Baron was quite indifferent and seemed to look right through him before returning to the paperwork on the table. Cardinal Erik looked as though he was bearing witness to the single most unpleasant thing to have occurred in his life, while Admiral Garter simply looked relieved.

"Ah, Captain Griffiths, you're here just in time," the admiral said. Rhys simply nodded his head in acknowledgement. He was rather unnerved by the look of absolute loathing and hatred in Cardinal Erik's eyes, and didn't quite trust his voice at the moment. Rhys couldn't recall seeing such passionate fury in someone's eyes before. He quailed slightly under the cardinal's gaze and stood at the table as far from the red-robed Martian as he could.

"What's the latest then, Admiral?" Rhys asking, silently cursing how timidly he spoke. He shouldn't have to be afraid of these people; he had known them all in a working capacity for many years. He had never felt the need to fear them before; he didn't know why he needed to start now. Trying to divert his mind from such matters, he started to look through the nearest papers, but the table was almost as high as his shoulders. He wasn't able to see much at all.

"Surprisingly little," Admiral Garter admitted, seeming to not notice or ignore the various reactions Rhys's arrival had sparked. "CGP movements within the Sol System are minimal and, though I had expected some by last night at the latest, there has been no contact from Terra. Beyond that, a distress call was received from the mining expedition on the Silvestro Comet, but that was passed on to the base on Ganymede, as they're much closer," Admiral Garter concluded, discreetly sliding some papers across the table to Rhys could grab them, before clasping his hands together.

"I suppose they discovered no sign of Denitchev's particles?" Rhys asked, focusing solely on the admiral, ignoring the presence of everyone else around him. "And has there been any updates from Oberon?"

"Oberon, Captain Griffiths?" Admiral Garter asked in surprise.

"Didn't Captain Lee just strike Oberon?" Rhys replied. His ears pinned back slightly. He hoped Scott hadn't given him false information about the *Terrestrial Dawn's* movements.

"He did," Admiral Garter said. He straightened his glasses. "I'm just surprised you've been able to keep up to date with everything, given your... situation. But no, there has been no further updates, nor any sign of the *Dawn* since. It is probable he has left Sol entirely. We don't think it had anything to do with the resource piracy in the outer system."

Rhys frowned and flicked his ears. "I just wish I knew why he'd done it, but I don't think Captain Lee had ever gone out there before."

"I have received word from the Vatican," the cardinal interjected before Admiral Garter could respond, stepping forward and keeping his eyes anywhere but looking at Rhys. "His Grace, Pope Adamantius has expressed his displeasure at the perceived lack of effort given down to tracking his missing disciple, Cardinal Iain Jones."

Though Admiral Garter had appeared surprised and a bit alarmed to hear of the cardinal's communication with the pope, this had quickly turned to exasperation. He removed his glasses and rubbed the sides of his nose. "Please inform Adamantius that there is nothing we can do. His cardinal boarded the *Terrestrial Dawn* in Romulus and did not disembark here, nor was he amongst the rescued crew, so we can only assume he is still on-board, enroute to Alpha Centauri. Also remind Adamantius that he has far more influence within the CGP than we do, so it would be a better use of his time to conduct the search himself, rather than pestering us about it."

Cardinal Erik looked like he had been struck in the face.

"If Cardinal Iain had wanted to make himself known, he had opportunity enough to do so when I was on-board," Rhys added, forcing the cardinal to look at him for just an instant – plenty of time for a patronising sneer to form on his face. Rhys turned away, not liking the self-righteous hunger he saw in the cardinal's eyes.

Admiral Garter's intervention was a welcome one. "We simply cannot afford to waste its resources looking for a man who clearly does not wish to be found by us. Cardinal Iain must have had his reasons for staying on the *Terrestrial Dawn*. This is a Vatican matter now. Not a TIE one, and certainly not one for Ceres."

"I see," Cardinal Erik said, his disappointment evident. His face was twisted in the manner of one used to getting their own way without exception. He pursed his lips together as his eyes glanced between the three humans in front of him, studiously avoiding Rhys again. Everyone waited in silence to hear what his next words would be. When they came they were surprisingly accepting.

"Very well," he said tersely. "I shall inform His Grace of your recommendation." Without another word, Cardinal Erik stalked out of the control tower.

"Well, now he's gone, perhaps we can move on with more relevant matters," Admiral Garter said, for a moment glancing down at a sheet of notes on the table in front of him. "The comet –"

Whatever the admiral's ideas of what relevant matters were, Captain Favre clearly had his own agenda to follow as he cut across Admiral Garter before he even had chance to look back up. "Lieutenant Cooper has applied for a transfer to my ship," he said loudly and confrontationally. He looked down at Rhys for just a fraction of a second. Rhys knew why. The Cerian was assessing his reaction.

Rhys glanced across at Admiral Garter, who looked every bit as surprised as Rhys felt about the sudden announcement.

Though he was tempted to remain silent, Rhys was the first to respond. "I think you might want to think twice about accepting that transfer, Captain Favre," he said quietly. "Mr Cooper is currently facing charges of insubordination and assault, and is not free to apply for any other position without his current captain's approval, which I have not granted."

"I have the paperwork with me, Admiral, for you to sign and make it official," Favre said, completely ignoring Rhys and speaking over him. "He says he cannot work under such an abomination masquerading as his captain, a reason I understand completely, and am willing to back as exceptional circumstances."

"Abomination? Is that what you think of me now?" Rhys snarled, clenching his fists by his side. His anger had been kindled now, and it quickly overcame his nervousness. He had already stood up to one human in this body and fared reasonably well. He did not doubt his ability to do the same again.

"I will not be signing that paperwork," Admiral Garter said. He raised his voice slightly, his tone warning for no further arguments. He turned towards Favre. "As Captain Griffiths mentioned, Mr Cooper is facing charges of insubordination, and has been barred from speaking to any military personnel. If he has breached this, then I shall have to investigate."

Captain Favre started in surprise. Rhys doubted the more experienced captain had expected Admiral Garter to speak against the Cerian. Captain Favre's reaction, however, had been exactly what Rhys had anticipated.

"But, Admiral Garter..."

"I will hear no more of it, Captain Favre. Mr Cooper does not have authority to apply for a position on your ship for the reasons Captain Griffiths has already explained," the admiral said sternly. He peered at the Cerian captain over the rims of his glasses.

Captain Favre was not finished though, and in the moment he seemed to forget just who he was speaking to. "You're defending him? The starat? You know the protocol. We would be the laughing stock of TIE if we allowed him to continue like this," the Cerian cried, his voice in danger of rising out of control. Rhys couldn't help but take a step back from the table, fearful of the hatred evident on the captain's face. "We're trying to save face here after the debacle with the *Dawn*. If the chancellor gets word of this..."

Admiral Garter slammed his hand down on the table, bringing an end to Captain Favre's protests. "Enough of this at once. This is not how you treat a captain of the empire. Until you can both clear your heads you will stay apart from each other. We shall re-convene tomorrow at the same time. I trust you will both be on better behaviour then. Until then, you are dismissed."

Rhys, surprised by the sudden adjournment of the meeting, turned to leave first, eager to be away from the Cerian captain, but

Admiral Garter held his hand out towards him. "I want you to remain behind a few moments, Captain Griffiths."

Captain Favre leered at Rhys as he left, obviously expecting some kind of trouble to befall the starat. Captain Baron hung back a few moments to exchange a brief, quiet conversation with the admiral about some maintenance that still hadn't been completed on his ship. As he refused starat workers, the necessary repairs were taking longer to arrange. When he left he did so without even looking at Rhys. Baron hadn't once even acknowledged Rhys's presence. The door slid shut the door behind him, leaving Rhys with the admiral and the lone operative in the corner.

Admiral Garter had removed his glasses and placed them in his pocket. No trace of his previous anger lingered. "Just two questions on my behalf, Captain. Nothing to concern yourself with," he said. He pointed Rhys to one of the chairs around the table, which he declined. Rhys was still more comfortable standing up, despite the ache in his legs. The admiral however did sit down, which brought him almost to the same height as the starat. "I need to know if you're capable of speaking at Mr Cooper's hearing, which starts tomorrow afternoon. And have you been able to identify a new first officer to replace Cooper with?"

Rhys took a deep breath. With everything that had been going on, he hadn't even thought about having to replace Cooper in his crew. The appointment would be crucial. He'd need to bring someone in who would support a starat captain and command the respect of the rest of the crew. It wouldn't be easy.

"Yes to the first," Rhys said, after taking a few seconds to compose his thoughts. "But no to the second. I still want to meet my crew first, before thinking about any new appointments."

Admiral Garter nodded. "Perfectly understandable, but I would advise not delaying that for too much longer. Given you could be tied up with the hearing for a day or two, try to see them before it starts."

"I can try, Admiral," Rhys said with a nod. He tried to hide his nerves, hoping that his ears weren't being too expressive and that the admiral couldn't read them anyway.

"That's all I can ask. But for now, I just need to update you on a few more details from Chancellor Roberts. I'll be speaking to Captain Favre later too," the admiral said. Rhys flicked his ears and frowned, wondering what further there could be to add from the previous day.

"The chancellor has sided with us that the status of the defences here meant there was little we could do to fend off a possible attack from the *Dawn*, and in that regard he holds all of us blameless. I don't yet know if he wishes to rebuild the port, or to sell it off to private investors. For that, we can only wait and see," the admiral said, before pausing to glance down at some of the notes he'd prepared.

"I'm sure they might spare more than a few words about me, too," Rhys said, filling the brief moment of silence without even thinking.

"Why do you say that?"

Rhys sighed and rested his arms on the table. He felt his tail tuck between his legs. "You saw Captain Favre's reaction. Look at me and say that the chancellor or the emperor is going to want me as captain of one of their ships."

"You've told me that you feel you're fit for command still, and I shall inform the chancellor of that in turn. Until you believe you are no longer suitable for command, you will remain captain of the *Harvester*, and you will still receive my recommendation for admiral."

Rhys struggled to contain the choked sob that threatened to overwhelm him. He felt light-headed. Hearing those words, that support, from his superior officer removed a tangible weight of worry from his shoulders. "Thank you, Admiral," he eventually managed to say.

"I trust your judgement," the admiral said, waving away Rhys's attempted thanks. "I'm expecting more updates through the day, but I'll be speaking with Favre and Baron, so I think it's best if you steer clear of them for the remainder of the day, until our next meeting at 0900 tomorrow. Go about your duties as normal, and I hardly need remind you not to lose your temper and provoke anyone else."

"Understood, Admiral," Rhys said, accepting the rebuke without any argument. He turned quickly to leave. He didn't want the admiral to see the broad smile on his face, displaying so proudly his elation and relief that he still had allies amongst humans. Behind him his tail arched up and quivered, broadcasting his joy to the admiral anyway.

***

Though Rhys was tempted to head back to the starat quarters, he found himself, more through habit than anything else, heading towards the shuttle bay. He hesitated for a moment, but then decided to just carry on walking. Like Admiral Garter had said, he had to reintroduce himself to his crew sooner or later. There was little point in continuing to put it off.

Given the lack of duties his crew would have around the ship, Rhys didn't expect to see many about. He hoped not to run into Captain Favre or Captain Baron on his way through the port, and thankfully there was no sign of either of them in the corridors or the shuttle bay. He didn't know which he preferred, the cold indifference of Baron, or the open hostility from Favre.

The bridge of the *Harvester* was empty, but Rhys expected that. In orbit over the port, there was little reason for anyone to be present on the bridge. In most ports, there were no reasons to be on the ship at all. It was only because of the port's poor crew quarters that they had chosen to sleep in their ship in the first place.

Four immensely complex workstations lined the walls of the bridge, with three further in the centre. These were what the crew used to operate a ship through the emptiness of space. Of an operations crew of thirteen, there were always at least six present on the bridge at any given moment when the ship was in flight. It went against policy for that number to ever be breached.

Rhys perched on the edge of the captain's seat, raised on a small dais in the middle of the bridge, so that he could see everything that was happening at once. In front of him, the large screens were dark and blank. In flight they would display important information, and a live feed from the ship's exterior cameras.

To his right would sit the sensory officer and the weapons officer. To his left would be the pilot and navigator. And directly in front of him sat the first officer and the communications officer. Each position in the operations crew had one cadet officer, to rotate during the long hours at space so that at least one person from each role was present. Given the gruelling work manning the ship's complex sensory array, the sensory position was always filled by three officers.

Every single one of the *Harvester's* operations crew had been hand-picked by Rhys. They were amongst the very best Earth had to offer. They should be loyal to him. They had vowed to serve him as captain for as long as they were a part of his crew. He didn't know if any of them would uphold those promises now.

Pulling his aching feet up onto the chair, Rhys idly stroked his tail. The bridge sounded so quiet when it wasn't active, and the silence drew him in. His thoughts wandered, fantasising about where his future was going to lead him. He tried to picture himself as he was in uniform with the five gold stripes of an admiral on his shoulder, rather than the four red stripes of a captain. The image never materialised in his mind. It didn't help that he could barely even remember what he looked like now. He didn't even recognise his own reflection.

"Can I help you?"

The sudden voice was like an electric current through the chair. Rhys leapt to his feet and spun around, his eyes wide and tail still in his hand. It was James Sutherland, the sensory cadet officer. At only two years younger than Rhys, Sutherland was much older than most cadet officers. He had moved into the military from commercial spaceflight, having spent many years in Galactic Aviation. There were two others behind Sutherland. Cameron Riley, the cadet navigator, was one. Sarah Pool, the senior sensory officer was the other.

"I'm sorry?" Rhys asked. He had to suppress a small flutter of fear as he was reminded anew about his physical limitations. Sutherland wasn't a particularly tall man, but now he positively towered over Rhys, having the advantage of over half a metre. However, this was his home, his element, and his crew. As quickly as the fear had come, it was crushed by an upwelling of confidence.

"Well, come on. Spit it out if it's important. Otherwise, just leave or I'll send for..." Sutherland said, before pausing and turning to face Pool. "Who is in charge here at the moment?"

Pool shrugged. "The admiral, I guess. We just go straight to him?" she said, though she sounded far from certain.

"Me." Rhys had spoken quickly, before they could get lost in their own debate. Suddenly all three pairs of eyes were boring into him.

"I'm sorry?" Sutherland said.

Rhys took a deep breath and squared his shoulders. He tried to make himself look as tall as possible. A futile act. He hadn't measured himself yet, but he knew he had to be only a little over a metre tall. "I'm in charge. I trust the admiral has spoken to you about my… situation."

"Oh shit," Sutherland said. He took a couple of steps back. Behind him, Riley saluted and came to attention, though Pool was a little more hesitant to follow his lead. "Captain Griffiths, is that really you?"

"At ease," Rhys said, his voice barely audible. They had treated him like a captain. He struggled to contain his relief, but his ears still pinned back against his head as he looked up to the three humans. His words sparked Sutherland into action, realising he should have been to attention in the presence of his superior officer on the bridge. He quickly saluted, before coming to ease with Pool and Riley.

"I'm sorry, Captain. I didn't recognise you," Sutherland said, quickly blurting out his apology.

Rhys nodded. "That's perfectly understandable, Mr Sutherland. I barely recognise myself anymore either."

"I thought it was some sort of joke, when Admiral Garter told us yesterday," Riley said. He took a couple of steps past the motionless Sutherland. "Now I can see... Now this is... It's real." Riley shook his head in amazement. "This is revolutionary."

"I don't intend on starting any revolutions, Mr Riley," Rhys said, keeping his voice firm. Internally, he had relaxed greatly. It didn't seem like any of the three were going to be rejecting him as captain, as Cooper had done.

"Intend to or not, this is going to change things, sir," Pool said, finding her voice at last.

Rhys sighed and looked down at his bare feet. He didn't want to lead any great cause or revolution against the empire. He just wanted to continue as he had been, to be treated no differently. And while he admitted that would require change in the mentality of many humans, he still felt deeply uncomfortable with the idea of being a figurehead for rebellion.

"Change is not necessarily bad, Captain," Riley said. "There are good people out there. They're not all people like Cooper. The admiral won't let something like this stand in your way. You shouldn't either."

"I know. I try, but it's hard. I can't hope on everyone supporting me like Admiral Garter does," Rhys replied. He turned away from the cadet navigator, crossing his arms across his chest and gazing out at the empty bridge. There was no view to appreciate but the collection of computers and instruments used to pilot the ship. It was such a familiar sight. Rhys knew everything on the bridge of his ship.

"Initially, no, of course not," was Riley's response. "But in time people will see how little you really have changed, and you'll earn their respect back."

Rhys turned back to face the three humans. "And I'll have your support, no matter what?"

There was no hesitation from either Riley or Sutherland as they pledged their continued support for him, but Pool just frowned and glanced down at him for a few seconds longer. "For now, Captain," she said eventually. "If I can see you've changed, if I feel that at any point you are unfit in your duties, I will withdraw my support. Having said that, I don't think that will happen any time soon."

"I appreciate that," Rhys said simply. That was the response he wanted most, for he had expected no differently from his crew as a human. "I can only hope the rest of the crew will be so accommodating."

"If your crew has learned anything from you, Captain, then I'm sure they will be," Sutherland said.

"I'm glad of that, thank you," Rhys said. He took a deep breath and glanced up to the clock above the shuttered windows. "I shouldn't put it off any longer. I'll get in contact with everyone and schedule a meeting with the whole crew at midday, so make sure you're there."

"Understood, Captain," Sutherland said. Both Pool and Riley also confirmed that they would be there, before giving Rhys a last salute as he dismissed them. They left him alone in the bridge once more.

A fresh wave of nerves washed over Rhys. He couldn't believe he was actually going to do this, to step out in front of his whole crew as a starat. He clutched at his tail and twisted it in his hands. There wasn't much he could do about it now. He'd already told three of his crew what he was going to do. He couldn't turn back now.

Rhys hurried back to his quarters for a little time alone before he had to face his crew. It was his first time back since he had been thrown out of them by Cooper. The memory made him shudder, and he could see the remnants of his former first-officer's rage. The door had been buckled slightly from Cooper's fists, and several items had been thrown to the floor, though Rhys was thankful to see his wine closet had been untouched.

He took a few moments to straighten everything back up again, before flopping back on his bed. Once again he yelped as he crushed his tail. It took a few attempts to get comfortable, and once he did he pulled across his communicator. It was time to summon his crew.

chapter seven

There was a small briefing room by the mess hall. Rhys made sure he made it down there half an hour early, so that he could sit quietly in one corner and wait for his crew to arrive. He perched on the edge of his seat, tapping his claws against the table in front of him. In the front pocket of his overalls, he could feel the weight of his tablet. It was one of the newer models that were only really useful within the ship, as the port's wireless systems were incompatible with the modern tablets, forcing them to use the more antiquated communicator models on the dwarf planet.

One by one his crew started to arrive. Rhys checked them off his list as they came in. Jordan Dewson was the first to arrive, along with Pool. The two sensory officers were engaged in deep conversation with each other, and neither seemed to notice the starat in the corner at all as they took some seats towards the front of the room. Rhys chose to remain where he was rather than approaching them.

The communications officer, Jermaine McDonald, was next, and he was closely followed by his cadet officer, Marianne Watkins. Once again, neither even looked towards Rhys as they joined the first two. The weapons officer was Kim van den Burgh, and she was the first to notice Rhys's presence in the corner, but she just turned her head to the side and otherwise ignored him. Doctor Sparks was next, and while he saw Rhys as well, he gave no sign he had recognised the starat. Rhys was sure he had though, and assumed the doctor was just letting Rhys identify himself when he chose to do so.

Donald Mathers and Deborah Simms, the cadet pilot and weapons officer respectively, entered the small room together and took their seats. Rhys's ears flicked as he listened to the conversations between his crew. He was surprised no one was talking about his situation. He thought back to Riley thinking it some joke. Did the others all think the same? Did they really not believe that their captain was a starat now? He wondered if he would have believed it too, had he been in their position.

Scott, Riley, Sutherland, and Chekolin all came in together, leaving just one person short from those expected. From the moment he walked in, Chekolin stared at Rhys with wide eyes. Rhys flashed a small smile and nodded, a quick gesture for the navigator to continue on his way. He turned to the side and scratched behind his ear as he waited for the last person. The services commander was a tough man called Simon Briggs. He controlled everything below the bridge in the *Harvester*, and it was his crew who kept the ship functional. His support would be critical to the smooth running of the ship.

Conversation amongst the gathered crew quickly grew. Those who knew Rhys's identity said nothing of it to their fellow crew, while the others expressed their confusion about just what the meeting would be about. Of just the three who had noticed Rhys's presence, two of them couldn't be certain of his identity and had said nothing of the starat sitting in with them.

Briggs finally arrived a few minutes later. His face was dirty with oil and grime, and he stank of it too. Rhys wrinkled up his nose at the powerful odour. Everyone on the crew was present, but for the first officer, a position that still needed to be filled.

No one noticed as Rhys stood up. No one even looked at him as he walked towards the front of the room, not until Van den Burgh called out to him. "Hey starat, go fetch us some drinks." Rhys tried to ignore her, though he nearly missed his footing and stumbled. At the front of the room he turned around and leaned on the nearest table. Van den Burgh looked shocked at being ignored, and there were more than a few confused looks being cast in his direction.

"I see some of you weren't paying attention to Admiral Garter yesterday," Rhys said. He fought hard to keep his tail still. "I'd like to re-introduce myself to you. Despite all appearances, I'm Captain Griffiths."

"Impossible," Simms said. She was the only person to speak. Those who already knew his identity had sat back in their seats, while the others were all struck dumb. Rhys was about to assure the cadet officer that it was indeed true, but she wasn't finished. "A starat captain? Whoever even thought of such nonsense?"

Rhys's ears folded forward, and his tail thrashed from side to side. A growl rumbled deep in his throat. Simms shuffled in her seat. No one else had spoken, either to side with her or to speak out in defence of their captain.

"If you have a problem with that," Rhys said in a cold but firm voice. The fur on his tail had puffed up. "I can have a resignation letter ready for you to sign. You will not receive a recommendation for service on another ship."

"You wouldn't dare," Simms said, but she was interrupted by a raised hand from Rhys. He was actually surprised she stopped talking.

"I am your captain. I need not remind you that insubordination is a punishable offence," Rhys said. He glared at the cadet officer until she looked away again. His gaze then moved around the room, stopping at every member of his crew for a few seconds before moving on. "You may notice there is one person missing. Mr Cooper was dismissed from the crew yesterday, and I expect he will find himself stripped of rank for striking his commanding officer. I do not want to discipline any of you, but if you leave me no choice then I will not hesitate. Yes, Mr Dewson?"

Dewson had raised his hand like a child at school asking for attention from his teacher. "If Cooper's gone, then who will be first officer?"

Rhys smiled, but the fur on his tail was still raised. "I'm glad you asked that. I'll be accepting applications for the position as I'd rather hire from within." He paused to pull out his tablet and placed it on the table in front of him. "I would expect anyone who wishes to become first officer to be capable of working with a starat without argument and without prejudice. Just as I would expect it of anyone who wishes to remain on my crew. Are there any objections?"

Once more Rhys challenged his crew with nothing more than his eyes. He expected a protest from someone. Van den Burgh or Simms were the most likely to cause trouble, but to his surprise they both remained silent, even as his eyes passed over them.

The only person who spoke was Edgar Scott. "I'd like to put myself forward as a candidate for first officer."

Rhys nodded in the navigator's direction. He had hoped for that. Of all the people in his crew, Scott was the one he considered the most capable. His frazzled fur slowly started to settle back down, now that it appeared likely he wasn't going to get any significant conflict from his crew. He waited for a few moments for any further responses, but no one seemed willing to compete with Scott for the promotion. The navigator was well respected by the crew already, and in many ways he had already been acting as the first officer, even with Cooper around.

"Very well, Mr Scott. I'll be speaking with you later to discuss details on your promotion. Mr Riley, I'll want to speak with you too," Rhys said. He waited for both men to nod. Then he clasped his hands together in order to resist the urge to grasp at his tail tip. "Finally then, does anyone have any concerns with serving beneath a starat? This will be the only time I will allow anyone to step down quietly and without fuss. If you remain beyond today, then I will expect the exact same respect I have earned from you before. No exceptions."

Rhys expected someone to speak out. He looked towards Simms and Van den Burgh, anticipating their complaints, but to his surprise they remained silent. Neither met his eyes. He wondered if they had both expected a bigger voice to speak out against him. Faced with being in the minority, they had chosen to keep their tongue and their jobs. He could only hope that he didn't have to deal with them later.

"I know it's going to be difficult to get used to this," Rhys said, after letting the uncomfortable silence draw out for a minute. "I know as well as you all how starats are usually treated in the empire. This will be tough, and I am willing to forgive any minor lapses in behaviour. However, I will not be tolerating any abuse towards myself, or to any other starat – deliberate or otherwise. Do I make myself clear?"

A few mumbles of "Yes, Captain," rippled around the room. While he would have preferred a more vociferous response, he had to settle with what he was given. It was still more than he would have expected a couple of days prior.

"Does anyone have anything further to add?" Rhys asked. His eyes swept around the room once more. He could definitely see two differing reactions amongst his crew; two sets of emotions. Those who were able to meet his eyes seemed eager for this new experience. About half the room though, including Simms and Van den Burgh, shifted awkwardly in their seats. They were uncomfortable. Rhys could only hope that didn't develop into something more. No one spoke up.

"Very well, dismissed."

Van den Burgh and Simms couldn't wait to be gone, and they were the first out of the room with Briggs following just behind. Scott, Riley, and Chekolin lingered, as though wanting to speak to Rhys. He wearily waved them closer.

"I'll discuss the specifics of your promotion later, Mr Scott. And you too, Mr Riley. Naturally you'll be taking on the role of senior navigator," Rhys said.

"Understood, sir," Scott said with a nod. "But I was more intending to speak to you about a message I got from Lieutenant Davies on the *Britannia.*"

Rhys's ears flicked up. "That's the one Captain Lee attacked, wasn't it?"

Scott nodded. His lips pursed slightly. "It was, sir. Lieutenant Davies sent me through some more information, but there doesn't appear to be any further official updates. They ran an... uh, inventory check and realised three starats were missing. Nothing or no one else had been taken."

"Just three starats?" Rhys asked. He frowned, confused. He chose to ignore the fact that starats were accounted for by an inventory check, instead choosing to focus on why Aaron would have gone out of his way to take three starats. It didn't make any sense based on what he knew of his old friend.

"There hasn't been any official recognition of their loss. This all came from Lieutenant Davies," Scott said.

"But why would Captain Lee risk everything just for a few starats?" Riley mused. Rhys cleared his throat, but he said nothing. Immediately Riley's eyes widened. Flustered, he was quick to clarify. "Not that starats aren't worth going after, but I just meant..."

Rhys raised his hand. "At ease, Mr Riley. I know you meant nothing by it this time."

"Of course not, sir."

Rhys nodded, then turned his head to his new first officer and navigator. "I'll speak to you two later though. For now I have a few things to think about. Thank you for bringing that information, Mr Scott. If you hear anything further, please let me know. Until then, you're all dismissed for now."

The three all saluted Rhys before they made their way out of the briefing room. When they were gone, he collapsed down in a chair. His limbs felt numb as the adrenaline dissipated from his body. He felt wearied, like he had been running all morning, even though he hadn't once been to the gym since the teleporter incident. He supposed he should at some point, in the quiet hours of the night when he wouldn't be disturbed.

Rhys felt too mentally drained to even think of going down there. Instead he just leaned back in his chair and closed his eyes. It was not comfortable. The hard plastic chair dug into his back, and his tail was pinched between the seat and his leg. But there was no one judging him, no glares cast in his direction, no one to ignore him completely. It was a chance to just sit back and relax, to drop his guard for a few minutes and feel the giddy elation that his crew had, largely, accepted him spread through his body.

"Captain Rhys? Doctor Sparks said I'd find you here."

Rhys groaned and pulled down on his ears. "Why are you here, Twitch?"

"Just here to make sure no one's attacked you again. And look. I brought some friends along," the starat said. His voice was bright and cheery, seemingly unaware of Rhys's desire to be left alone.

Peeking out from between his wrists, Rhys saw two other starats behind Twitch. He was surprised he recognised them both. David stood almost a head taller than Twitch, who in turn was about the same height taller than the dark-furred Steph.

Rhys slowly lowered his hands down over his muzzle. His ears and tail both drooped low. He then gestured to the room in general. "Well, welcome to my ship, I guess."

Steph was almost vibrating. "I've never been on a spaceship before. This is all so cool," she squeaked. She didn't stop moving, her eyes wide as she tried to take it all in.

"Never?" Rhys asked, curious despite himself.

Steph shook her head, then flattened her ears against her head. "Never. I don't have the skills usually needed to work on a spaceship, so I never got assigned to one."

Rhys frowned. He slowly rose to his feet, forgetting for a moment to keep his ankle raised and stand on his toes. He wobbled and grabbed hold of the table for support as he regained his balance. "So, what is it you do?"

The starat shrugged her shoulders. "Whatever I can," she said quietly. "We're given a list of everything that needs doing through the day or the week, and we delegate out the tasks according to who can do what."

"Means we're never doing the same thing twice," Twitch interjected. He was bouncing on his toes as he gripped hold of David's hand.

"Lucky for some."

Rhys was startled by the sudden voice. All four starats turned to face the door. It framed a fifth starat, and it took Rhys a few moments to recognise Richard. "Briggs was complaining about having to come here, so I thought I'd come and see what the fuss was about."

The Cerian starats all glanced towards each other, before Richard held out his hand. "I'm Richard. It's nice to see a friendly face around the place."

Rhys hung to the side, not getting involved with the introductions. The Cerian starats didn't know Richard, and he had to wonder why. His ears curled in on themselves. Had the starats on his ship been confined to the *Harvester*, not allowed to interact with their brethren in the port? In his brief exchanges with the starats, he had learned that they were incredibly social creatures, and he had to think he'd been depriving his starat workers of that opportunity.

He had to do something to fix that. He gripped hold of his tail in his right hand as he approached the group. "Uh, Richard. Who was the other starat you worked with?"

Rhys did his best to ignore the disappointed looks he got from Steph and David. He tried to stop his ears from falling flat to his head. It was unacceptable for a captain not to know who his crew was. Starat or human, they deserved the same respect.

"That would be William. I think he should be down in the kitchens at the moment. Why do you ask?" Richard replied.

Rhys exhaled heavily. "I should right a wrong and go down to see him. I…" he paused and closed his eyes. "I'm sorry for how you've been treated, Richard. I have no excuse other than simply being a human and doing what was considered normal."

Richard held up his hand. "Apology accepted. But remember, I still need your measurements for a new uniform. I have an hour free now, if you wanted to come with me."

Rubbing his hand over his muzzle, Rhys thought about it for a few moments, before his eyes drifted across to Twitch. "You could do it, couldn't you?" Rhys asked him. "You're the same as me, so you could go with Richard and get measured up, and I can speak to William."

Twitch grinned widely. "Of course I could do that. Would be fun. I could pretend to be a captain for a bit." He giggled and flicked his tail back and forth.

"Don't you dare start talking to my crew. I think I've got them convinced to support me, so I don't need you ruining that," Rhys warned.

Twitch stuck his tongue out. "What? Don't trust me?"

"I'll keep him under control," David promised. It didn't calm his nerves much.

"Come on with me then. I'll show you where to go," Richard said, gesturing towards Rhys. The starat turned and took the lead as he guided the four of them through the ship. Rhys rarely went down to the service levels located beneath the bridge. Usually it was just to visit the gym or to have a quick meeting with Briggs, so everywhere beyond those two rooms was mostly unknown to him.

As they walked, Richard talked about his history in the military, exchanging some stories with Twitch, Steph, and David. Rhys was surprised to hear none of the latter three had ever left Ceres, spending their whole lives on the small dwarf planet. Richard, by virtue of his posting on the *Harvester*, had visited many more planets, but to Rhys's shame, had rarely been able to see much of them. Though he was asked several questions about his life before he had served, Richard never mentioned anything about what he had been doing before getting signed up. He just shook his head with a faint smile.

Richard bundled them all into a small elevator and pushed a couple of buttons. After descending just two floors to take them directly below the bridge level, the doors opened again. Richard held them open.

"This is your stop, Captain Rhys. Just around to your left and you should find William down near the kitchens," Richard explained. For a moment, Rhys thought the starat was about to reach out and touch his shoulder, but then his hand dropped down again. "I'm sure William will tell you where to go when you want to find me again."

Rhys nodded and flicked his tail in anticipation. "Thank you. I appreciate it, I really do," he said as he stepped out of the elevator. He spun around to look at the four starats. Twitch was grinning as widely as always, but he couldn't work out what the other three were thinking. Their ears were all perked upright, eyes bright as always, but their expressions were completely unreadable. Rhys smiled nervously as the door slid shut, and he could hear the elevator take them all down another level.

Muttering beneath his breath, Rhys turned again and looked around. It was all pretty quiet beneath the bridge. In the middle of flight it would be different, but with the ship docked there was significantly less to do.

The bare grey walls all looked the same to Rhys, and without the familiarity he had of the upper levels, he would have soon gotten lost had it not been for Richard's directions. There weren't even any signs anywhere, but Rhys found the kitchens anyway. Gleaming metal and the strong scent of food were the first two things he noticed. Ship food was never particularly glamorous, but when docked in port the cooks were able to produce a little more than the usual rehydrated rations.

However, there wasn't any starat present. Just one human was inside, with her back turned to Rhys. He cleared his throat, and though the human glanced around briefly at him, she didn't greet him at all, instead turning back around to what she was doing. He sighed. It looked like he'd have to go find the starat himself.

As he turned to leave, Rhys's nose twitched as he caught hold of a different scent amongst that wafting out from the kitchen. It made him pause. The smell was both familiar, yet not at the same time. It reminded him of starats. He was sure that it was William. All he had to do was find out where the scent was stronger and follow it.

Rhys knew he would never have been able to detect the starat's scent before. He'd noticed his improved hearing since his transformation, but this was the first time he'd truly recognised how much better his sense of smell was. He took a deep breath, his nostrils flared wide as he allowed the sense to wash over him. The smell from the kitchens still overpowered almost everything else, but there was that other scent, of grime and fur and metal.

A burst of cinnamon spice distracted him. Rhys wrinkled his nose and almost sneezed. He had half a mind to go back in and see just what the head chef was doing, but instead he turned his focus back to finding William's scent.

Lacking the knowledge to know how old the scent was, Rhys could only hope that following it wouldn't lead him on a mad chase around the lower levels of the ship. He was relieved, therefore, to discover the scent getting stronger, until he was sure that the starat was behind the door he was standing next to. It was only a few corridors away from the kitchen, easy enough to get back. To Rhys, it appeared to be a small storage room. The spicy prickled still lingered at the back of his nose.

He tapped on the door gently, but no answer came from within. He was sure this was where the starat had gone though, and he pressed his finger on the control panel to open it up. It was a storage room. On all three walls were rows of tall shelves, rising well above Rhys's head height, but about right for a normal human to just about reach for the top. In one corner, half hidden behind some boxes, was a large bundle of rags and sheets.

At first Rhys thought he was mistaken, and that there wasn't anyone present at all. But then he caught sight of some movement amongst the rags. He cautiously approached, unsure of whether it was a starat buried amongst them. Then a furred muzzle poked out from within, but the starat didn't seem to notice that he was no longer alone. The starat was breathing heavily, as though he was sleeping.

"William?" Rhys called out, but the starat didn't stir. He tentatively approached, repeating the starat's name as he placed his hand down on where he thought William's shoulder would be.

William jerked awake in an instant, his limbs flailing amongst the blankets as he tried to sit up. "I'm awake, I'm awake," he yelped. His eyes darted around the room. When they finally settled on Rhys, his brow furrowed, and the tips of his ears curled in confusion. "You're not Richard."

"Captain Griffiths," Rhys clarified, holding a hand to his chest.

William's ears straightened for a moment, before folding down entirely. "I heard about that," the starat snarled. "Funny how you suddenly think I'm worthy of your attention."

Rhys raised his hands. "I know I've made some mistakes in the past. I'm sorry for those, but I'm here to make amends now," he said, pleading with the starat. There was more aggression in William's voice than he had been expecting. This wasn't just distrust. It was outright hatred.

"Oh fuck you," William retorted. His mouth was twisted into a snarl, showing off every one of his sharp teeth. "You're here now? Where were you when I fucking needed you? Where were you when… forget it. You're nothing but the same oblivious human you always were."

Rhys had to scramble back as William rose to his feet, the starat chucking a bundle of rags and blankets at Rhys as he did so. By the time Rhys had composed himself again, William was already walking past him. The starat had an unusual limp, with his left leg kept rigid, forcing him to swing it around to step forward. An odd, metallic noise followed each step the starat made with his left foot.

"William, please. Just listen to me," Rhys pleaded.

The starat spun around on his left foot, which screeched against the bare floor. Rhys had to resist the urge to slap his hands over his ears at the noise. As much as he wanted to know what was causing the noise, he didn't want to break eye contact with the irate William.

"Listen to what? What could you possibly have to say to me that will make anything better?" William growled. He approached Rhys with that same, awkward limp, and for a moment Rhys thought the starat was about to strike him. "I have suffered more than you could ever know, and you have done absolutely nothing to prevent that. I don't like you, Captain Rhys."

Rhys's ears drooped. "I understand that, and I know it will take time to change that, but please, let me prove myself to you."

William scoffed and turned his head to the side, but he didn't refuse. The starat's tail thrashed back and forth, and his right foot tapped against the floor. When he spoke again, it was in a low growl, barely above a savage, bestial snarl. "If only you knew what we go through." He hugged his arms close to his chest and turned away, hunching his shoulders though his tail remained high. It flicked from side to side.

Rhys felt the temptation to place his hand on William's shoulder, but he wasn't sure the starat would appreciate that. "I want to help you. I really do. Whatever I did before, whatever mistakes I made and acts I overlooked, I swear to you I will not do any of that again."

If William was swayed by Rhys's arguments, he didn't show it at all. "One time they decided to play a prank on me," the starat said. He shuddered and gave off a little growl, before spinning around and facing Rhys with fury in his eyes. "They deliberately weakened the support on one of the replacement power cells before I ran some maintenance on it. It fell. It crushed my leg and..."

William pulled up the leg of his trousers. Instead of fur, Rhys only saw metal. The starat had a prosthetic leg, and not a good one by the look of it. The metal was dirty and damaged, with parts of it twisted out of shape, scraping along the floor with each step he took. Scraps of carbon fibre casing still lingered in some places, but most of what Rhys saw was simply the metallic skeleton.

"I didn't know," Rhys whispered. He shook his head in horror and gestured to William's leg. "How... how much?"

William's ear flicked. He pointed to a point a couple of centimetres below his hip. "To here. And I was lucky to get this leg. Commander Simon found an old spare one of his crew used a few years ago. Of course, it doesn't fit properly. The knee is fucked and barely works. Then they had to cut a bunch off to get it the right size and the foot is all wrong." He grimaced as he lowered his trousers again, hiding most of the humanlike foot away. "They thought they were making up for it by giving me this. As though it was as good as my leg."

"I'm sorry. I really didn't know. Please, believe that," Rhys said. He dropped back and leaned against the nearest shelves.

William growled. "And now that you do know, what now?"

"I don't know. I'll do what I can. I'll speak to Briggs. I'll fix it," Rhys said, even though he didn't know how to do any of that. He doubted Briggs would take to heart anything he may say to him.

William shared Rhys's scepticism. "Yeah, sure you will," he muttered. The starat sank to the floor, sitting amongst the pile of rags. His mismatched feet were on clearer display. His prosthetic was clearly designed for a human, forcing him to walk with his left ankle down on the floor. "Now if you don't mind, I was trying to sleep. I've got an hour free, and you've just wasted enough of it."

"Sleep? Here?" Rhys spluttered. He straightened up in shock. "You don't even have a bed?"

"Of course not," William scoffed. "I sleep where and when I can. Richard too."

"That changes now. You hear me? I will not let this happen any longer," Rhys said with a snarl. Now it was his turn to get angry. "Come on. Get up. You're going to come up to my quarters and rest there until you need to. Then I'll deal with Briggs."

Rhys extended his hand down to William. The starat looked confused for a moment, the force of his anger diverted. He hesitated, before taking the offered hand and allowing him to be hauled up to his feet. "Do you think this makes up for anything?" he asked, letting go of Rhys's hand the moment he was balanced on his mismatched feet.

"Of course it doesn't, but I want to make a start. A sign that I'm willing to help," Rhys said. His tail twitched nervously. He was more scared of William than he had been meeting the rest of his crew.

William snarled. "Yeah. You have a lot of work to do. Give me the bed for the night, and I might just start to think you're being serious. But don't think I'm going to forgive you so quickly."

Rhys nodded. He wanted to assure William he was being genuine and true, but he knew the other starat wasn't going to be quick to believe him. William couldn't walk quickly, but he refused any help Rhys offered him as they approached the elevators. They were left undisturbed to go all the way to Rhys's quarters.

Once they entered the room, Rhys gestured to the bed, but William just stared at it as though he didn't know what to do with it. Rhys sat on the edge of the mattress and waited for the starat to come across.

Slowly William approached, lowering himself gently onto the bed. To Rhys's surprise he stripped off his trousers, revealing the full extent of his prosthetic leg. There was only small amount of flesh remaining of his left leg, before giving way to metal and carbon fibre. The knee looked like it had once been a flexible joint that moved with each step, but now it was just welded metal that barely flexed at all. The starat reached down and twisted the leg to the side, unclipping it and letting it fall onto the mattress. A half-corroded metal ring was left embedded into the remnants of the limb.

"You have no idea how nice it feels to have that wretched thing off," William said as he leaned back into the soft pillows, groaning as he stretched out his remaining leg. "Thank you for this. I suppose."

"You're welcome," Rhys said as he stood up. He tried not to stare too much at the half-naked starat, or his missing limb. He wasn't sure why, but something about William unnerved him. "You rest here for as long as you need. You won't be able to lock the door, but no one will be up here to disturb you. I'll check in on you later, once I've spoken to Briggs and dealt with a few other things. Is that alright?"

No answer came from William. Rhys glanced back to the starat, but he already appeared to be asleep. Rhys sighed. The starat's fur was matted and filthy, much like his had been before Twitch had first come to see him. He couldn't believe he had ever let any member of his crew get as mistreated as Richard and William had been. He clenched his fists at his side. He had trusted Briggs to act decently to everyone beneath him, human or starat. Now he knew differently. Things would be changing on the *Harvester*. And then, once he had sorted out his ship, he would work on fixing things beyond.

Rhys stalked out of his room to find the service commander.

***

Unfortunately for Rhys, the service commander was not the first person he ran into. There was someone else on board his ship, someone who had no right to be skulking around the bridge, but Rhys recognised the red robes immediately. Why Cardinal Erik had been given permission to enter the *Harvester* was beyond him. He paused, debating whether to go on before straightening his shoulders and stepping into the bridge.

The cardinal turned from searching around the control panels when he heard Rhys approach. He didn't even bother concealing a look of absolute hatred. "You dare come onto this bridge, beast?" he said in a tone that was laced with blatant malice. Rhys could tell there wasn't much stopping the religious man from attempting to harm him quite severely.

Rhys knew he had to remain calm, though inside he was seething. He did not much appreciate being called 'beast'. The words of Admiral Garter were still burnt into his mind though: don't lose your temper.

"I believe the correct form of address is 'Captain', is it not, Cardinal Erik?" Rhys replied in what he thought was a creditable imitation on nonchalance. He inspected his claws; partly to keep up the act, but mostly so he didn't need to look the cardinal in the eye.

"Captain? Ah, but for how much longer, hmm? I hear you're attending a disciplinary hearing tomorrow morning. Do you think the admiral will keep you as captain after that, now that they've seen the beast you've become?"

Rhys frowned, momentarily confused, before realising what the cardinal was talking about. "The hearing? You mean the one that will see my former first officer dismissed for insubordination? That's a military matter, so I'll ask that you keep out of matters that do not concern you."

Cardinal Erik only laughed. A cold, cruel laugh. "You really think you're going to get out of this, don't you? You must have inherited more than just their behaviour; you have their intelligence too."

Rhys only just caught the snarl before it escaped his lips. Acting like a starat would only make matters worse. He had to show that he was still human in his mind. He could do nothing about his thrashing tail. He swallowed hard, not wanting to give Cardinal Erik the satisfaction of drawing a bestial response from him.

Cardinal Erik stalked away, pushing Rhys to the side as he passed. "Don't be so sure of yourself, beast. As long as I am present, there will always be a voice clamouring to bring you down from your lofty ideals and delusions of self-righteousness," he said as Rhys struggled to stay on his feet.

"As always, the Vatican's opinion is always welcome, but if you'll excuse me, I have official business to attend to. If you could please leave my ship," Rhys replied, again keeping his voice even and low.

There was nothing he could do about the cardinal. The Vatican were an entity to their own; completely independent from TIE. They were responsible for their own actions, and Rhys knew enough about them that they would turn a blind eye to even the most blatant and cruel misbehaviour if a starat was the target. He had heard stories of cardinals torturing starats in attempts to 'cleanse their souls', for, according to Vatican doctrine, starats were an abomination to nature and thus inherently evil. However, in an attempt to maintain compassion for all intelligent beings, something they only begrudgingly admitted starats to be, they offered their services to all starats whether they wanted it or not – the latter being exclusively the case. It sickened Rhys to think that, to the Vatican, showing compassion meant weeks upon weeks of unimaginable pain so that the afterlife could be tolerable. Even before his transformation he was quite disgusted by it, but of course had never spoken out against it. No one spoke out against the all-powerful Vatican.

They were a terrible enemy to have.

Looking out across the bridge, Rhys knew that he would lose this all if the Vatican were to have their way. His ship, his career, and quite possibly his life would all be taken from him. He had to stop that. The only way he could do so was to garner enough support that the likes of Admiral Garter would not crack under the pressure exerted from the Vatican. He needed his crew to back him. But right now, he needed Briggs.

chapter eight

"Captain Rhys, over here!"

Rhys's ears perked up as he tried to find who was calling him. The voice wasn't human, and as he spun around he finally caught sight of Steph, waving at him from down the corridor he'd walked past. He tried to hide the anger he still felt, but he knew he must have failed. Steph slowed as he approached her.

"Is everything alright, Captain Rhys?" she asked. She bounced on her toes before she turned to guide him down a narrow flight of stairs.

"Yeah, sorry. Just ran into Cardinal Erik up there," he replied with a low growl. She flinched at the sound of the cardinal's name. Though Steph had not been the focus of his search, he was still glad to see her. She was a moment of comfort after the frustration of dealing with the cardinal.

Still keeping his ears alert in case he could hear Briggs, Rhys followed Steph down a level. When they left the stairwell, they stepped out into a dark corridor. Gone were the crisp, clean walls and floors. Everything down here looked and felt grimy. The floor beneath their feet was a metallic grill, exposing a series of pipes and bundles of cables running underneath.

The ship wasn't even in flight, but it was still noisy. The dull roar of the ventilation systems was unfiltered, and the thrum of the distant engines, idling only to keep the ship's critical systems active, was a constant buzz in Rhys's ears. Even the pipes that ran overhead seemed to move, grinding against each other as the pressures within changed. It felt alive down here, a sense Rhys never got in the sanitised upper levels. There were so many different systems on display, none of which Rhys knew how to operate. He would be utterly lost without his service crew.

Steph led Rhys into a small laundry room. Here the floors were tiled, and the walls were covered in various washing machines and driers. A little workshop was crammed in between a couple of the machines in the far corner of the room. The ceiling was a network of pipes, some coming down so low that a human would have to duck beneath them. Two flickering lights swung between the pipes.

A starat was hunched over the workshop desk, a bundle of clothes before him. Richard didn't turn around as Rhys entered, but his tail did flick to the side. There was no sign of David and Twitch.

"I've got it ready for you. It should all fit," Richard said, still without turning around. He was smoothing down a white shirt on the table.

"Already? That was fast. I didn't expect it to be done so soon," Rhys replied. His ears flicked up in surprise.

Richard shrugged. "It's what I'm here for."

"Well, you're clearly very good at your job," Rhys said as he approached Richard. At last the starat turned around, and the look on his face froze Rhys where he was. There was a mixture of sadness, anguish, and anger in the set of his ears.

"Job?" the starat said in a quiet whisper. Then he laughed and shook his head. "No, Captain Rhys. Job implies payment. We're not employees, or have you forgotten what we really are?"

Rhys shrank in on himself. His ears folded low and his tail tucked between his legs. "Please don't say it."

"Why not? Because it will hurt your feelings?" Richard spat.

"Because it makes me realise how much of a monster I was," Rhys replied. He couldn't meet the fury in Richard's eyes.

"You should feel like a monster," Richard snarled. He grabbed hold of Rhys's muzzle and forced his head up to look at him. "It isn't clean and pretty down here. We're slaves, Captain. Property. I was bought by the military, not hired, or employed, or any other fancy, clean word you want to call it. I am owned, and I don't like that."

"I'm sorry," was all Rhys could say. He struggled to pull himself free of Richard's strong grip, and eventually the other starat pushed him away.

"Of course you are. That's all it ever is with you. Words." Richard padded away and placed his hands down on his desk. He hunched over and appeared to be on the verge of tears. Steph pushed past Rhys and placed her hand on Richard's back.

Rhys knew he should say something, but he couldn't think what. He didn't know how to make this better, because his words weren't enough. He shuffled on his feet as the silence between them dragged on, watching Steph comfort the other starat. He felt like an intruder, like he was trying to fit in where he didn't belong. And he was. He wasn't a starat. He had never suffered like they had. What right did he have to be comfortable amongst them?

He couldn't take it. He slipped outside the laundry and sunk to his haunches, leaning against a small patch of bare wall for support. His hands idly brushed over his tail as he tried to sort through his thoughts. He couldn't help but hurt the starats. He had been implicit in their abuse for so long, so he couldn't blame them for pushing back against him.

"Captain Rhys?" Steph poked her head out the door and looked down at Rhys. "Are you alright?"

"Is Richard?"

"He'll be fine, yeah. I just… think we had it easier in the port than he did," she explained. Her hand came down to rest on Rhys's shoulder, her fingers lightly rubbing through his fur. "I believe you when you say you never mistreated starats out of spite, just out of ignorance. I think Richard will understand that someday too. But right now he is hurting."

"What can I do to help him? I can't just click my fingers and make everything better for him. It just doesn't work that way," Rhys protested.

"I know. And so does Richard. I think that's why he's so upset. But you can start by treating him as you would anyone else on your crew. Treat him as an equal, and slowly he'll realise you've really changed your ways." Steph's hand moved around to the back of his neck. Her claws felt nice. "But come on. Let's get you looking more like a proper captain."

"Some would argue I'm too short and furry to ever look like a proper captain," Rhys retorted, but he allowed Steph to help him back up to his feet anyway. "But I suppose I can do what I can to look the part."

The small starat led Rhys back into the laundry room. Barely had they entered, had Richard held out his hand for Rhys to grasp. When he did so, the starat pulled him close and embraced him.

"I'm sorry for my behaviour, Captain. I spoke out of frustration," Richard said.

Though surprised by the embrace, Rhys returned it, before pulling back after a few moments. "And I apologise too. For being a blind, ignorant ass of a human."

Richard patted Rhys on the shoulder. Gone was the simmering anger that had been there just moments earlier. It was like being in the room with a wholly new starat. "I won't blame you for that, Captain Rhys. Just... remember why I said those things, and hopefully I won't need to say them again." The starat gestured towards the pile of clothing on the desk behind him. "But come on, let's see how well these fit you. I hope you won't need your combat gear for a while, as they're tougher to make."

Richard first held up a plain white short-sleeved shirt. Above the left breast was the empire insignia threaded in gold. Other than being a bit smaller in size, but relatively a little longer, it was otherwise no different to those Rhys was used to. It would be good to get back into something a little more familiar, rather than being forced to wear his borrowed overalls. There were four shirts, all identical.

The black trousers were different. The bottom of the leg was wider to better accommodate his altered feet, but there was also a small hole at the back of the waistband that could be done up with a single button. Holding the trousers in his hand, he poked his finger through the hole. "What's this for?"

Steph giggled and held her hands in front of her muzzle. "For your tail, silly."

Beneath his fur, Rhys blushed a crimson red. "Oh, right," he muttered, feeling a little foolish. He hoped his embarrassment wouldn't show, but he must have been broadcasting his emotions somehow as Steph giggled again.

"Well, are you going to see if it fits? Better to adjust it now if we need to," Richard said, offering Rhys a timely distraction.

Rhys nodded and glanced around the small room, looking for anywhere that may have a modicum of privacy. There was nowhere to hide behind. Rhys sighed and folded his ears. "Can you, uh... turn around or something?"

"That's just your human morals speaking," Steph replied. She remained still, not looking like she was about to turn around at all. She grinned, showing off her teeth. "We don't share the same restrictions when it comes to modesty. Call it our animal origins if you will."

Richard took pity on the flustered Rhys. "However, if you're uncomfortable with undressing in front of us, then we shall look the other way," he said. He gave Steph a little pull on the arm, and though she protested a little, they both turned around to look towards the rumbling washers on the wall.

Rhys decided to get it over with quickly, and he stripped down out of the overalls and went to put on the trousers. He then promptly lost his balance as soon as he tried to stand on one leg and fell to the floor. He could hear Steph laughing, though she didn't look around thanks to Richard's arm, which was still around her shoulder. He finished sliding on his trousers where he sat, and then twisted around to button up the back. It was difficult as he couldn't actually see the small button, and he had to rely on touch alone. He eventually found it, and he was soon able to return to his feet.

"Very nice," Steph said as his shirt covered his chest. It was hard to tell if she was talking about the clothes or his body. Again he felt his cheeks flush, and again she giggled.

"It fits you well," Richard said. At least Rhys was certain he was talking about the clothes. He looked down at Rhys's bare feet and added, "Our legs and feet don't owe much to shoes, so you'll have to get used to going without them. Unless you stand on anything sharp, your footpads will give you just as much protection, so I doubt you'll really notice much of a difference."

"So I discovered, yeah," Rhys replied. It had felt strange not wearing shoes at first, but Richard was right. Shoes just did not work with his feet anymore. His pads were tough, but as he had already learned, they were vulnerable too. He flexed his injured foot, still wrapped in bandages. It was difficult to be careful when he was still trying to work out how to properly balance on them.

Moving his attention away from his feet, he twisted and turned, trying to see how well the new clothing sat on his body. It felt reasonably comfortable at least, though his tail felt a little pinched. The fur spilling out the sleeves of his shirt and around his collar looked strange. Too smart, too formal for a starat. It would have to do.

Richard moved his weight from one foot to the other as he waited for Rhys's opinion. "So, how is it?" the starat asked.

Rhys flashed a smile. "It's great, thank you. I couldn't ask for anything better." He raised his arms up, making sure he wasn't restricted in his movement. Though it tickled slightly as it pulled on his fur, it otherwise didn't irritate him at all.

Exhaling heavily, Richard leaned back against his desk and returned the smile. "You were right. I am good at what I do. Now..." The starat paused suddenly, his ears twitching. His eyes grew wide as he turned towards the door. "It's Commander Simon."

Rhys heard it a moment later. Footsteps approached; a dull clunk of heavy boots on the loose metal flooring. He turned around to face the door, taking a half step to the side. Steph retreated back to Richard's side.

When Briggs appeared in the doorway, he was even redder than usual. Sweat dripped from his forehead and his greasy black hair shone off the flickering lights. Rhys's nose twitched at the unwashed scent wafting off the service commander. The human only had eyes for one starat in the room – Richard. "Where is the other?" Briggs demanded.

Richard quailed, pressing himself back against the desk. He shook his head and lowered his eyes, looking down towards the human's feet and keeping silent.

"Answer me," Briggs barked. He approached Richard and raised his fist. For a moment Rhys could only watch on in terror, before he remembered himself. He didn't need to watch this. He stepped forward and cleared his throat to attract Briggs' attention. It took the service commander a few seconds to recognise who was standing in front of him.

"He's in my quarters," Rhys said before Briggs could say anything. His voice was stern, trying to instil a sense of command and authority that had always been present in his human voice. His new, starat throat wasn't as good at projecting a powerful tone.

Briggs blinked a few times, his mouth hung slightly open. He looked to be having difficulty processing what he was experiencing. Rhys tried again. "The starat. William. He's in my quarters, resting."

"He has work to do," Briggs growled, snapping out of his reverie.

"Not until he's rested," Rhys said, quickly holding up his hand to silence further protests from the service commander. "You work him too hard. Richard here too. I'd like to know why they seem to do much more work than anyone else on your crew, Mr Briggs."

Again, Briggs' mouth worked up and down a few times without any sound. His fists clenched, then he exhaled slowly like he was releasing high pressure from within his gut. "Jesus Christ and Emilio Veritas in a fucking tree, that didn't take you long to sink to their level, did it?"

Rhys drew himself up to his full, diminutive height. "Explain yourself, Mr Briggs."

Briggs gestured to the two starats, but he seemed to smartly hold back the first words that had come to his tongue. He took a couple of deep breathes. "You know what? Fine. Just fine. Whatever you like, Captain," he said. There was a clear distaste on his voice as he addressed the starat captain. "If you're going to be protecting them, giving them special treatment, then whatever. I won't argue with you. I'll go do it all my fucking self."

Rhys frowned and twitched his tail. That hadn't been at all what he was saying, but by the time he could sort his thoughts out, Briggs had already turned and started to walk out the laundry room. He tilted his head and flicked his ears inquisitively towards the other two starats.

"Thank you, Captain Rhys," Richard said. He smiled warmly and nodded his head to the captain. "That was good."

"Yeah, I think it was. I hope it was," Rhys muttered. He knew there would be some price to pay for that later. He didn't expect Briggs to let him get away for such open support for the starats with such ease. He would be planning some way to retaliate, subtly, in some way that couldn't be traced back to him. Rhys feared he may have made things worse for the two starats on his ship, as well as possibly himself too.

He looked to the two starats, both beaming with hope. If he wanted to succeed, then he needed to familiarise his crew with more starats, to teach them to treat the starats as equal. He needed more starats on his ship. It took just a moment to come to a decision. "Hey Steph. How would you like to work on a spaceship?"

***

Rhys's ears were still ringing from Steph's excited squeals, even half an hour later. She had embraced him tightly, saying over and over again that she would be so happy to join Rhys's ship, even if it did mean working under Briggs and his heavy boots. He hoped he had made the right decision, and that he hadn't just made a promise he couldn't keep. He would need to get permission from Captain Favre to transfer any starats over from the port and into his care. With the way Captain Favre had been treating him, he wasn't sure that permission would be granted.

He had managed to extricate himself from an excited Steph, and placated Richard, when his communicator had warned him of a message waiting for him from Admiral Garter. Scott had received it, and he had been waiting for Rhys on the bridge. It had not been anything too interesting; just the admiral advising Rhys that the disciplinary hearing for Cooper would take place directly after the captain's meeting in the newly repaired briefing room.

A few words were exchanged about the details of Scott's promotion to first officer, but the two agreed to put most of the discussion to a time after Rhys was no longer occupied with the looming hearing of his former first officer. It was one less thing Rhys had to worry about, and the two arranged a time to meet up the day after the hearing.

Checking the time, Rhys was surprised to see how much of the day had managed to escape him. It was already fast approaching the evening sunset. He had heard nothing from Twitch and David since leaving them with Richard in the afternoon, so he assumed they had gone back to the port for the night.

Given another early start in the morning, Rhys soon made his way back up to his quarters. He had delayed as long as possible, but when he opened the door to his quarters, the bed was empty. He flicked his ears, unable to detect the presence of William at all. The starat's scent still lingered, but Rhys couldn't tell how fresh it was. A little steam drifted out between the gaps around the door through to his bathroom. Evidently the starat had recently enjoyed a hot shower. For a moment, Rhys was tempted to have one himself, but instead his weary feet directed him to his bed. He could have one in the morning.

He placed the bundle of clothes he'd been carrying on his bedside table before perching on the edge of his mattress. His feet ached, and all down the back of his legs too. The pain in his left ankle was particularly bad. It was all the constant adjusting of his weight that was doing it, he was sure. He gritted his teeth and leaned back, rubbing his feet firmly between his fingers. He could feel the raised ridge of a scar along the pads of his left foot, all that was left of the deep gouge he'd suffered the previous day.

Slowly, Rhys started to strip out of his new clothes. By habit, he threw them all down to the floor, but he had the sudden mental image of Richard coming around to pick them all up the next day, when he was out doing his own errands. With a weary sigh, Rhys slipped out of bed and picked them up again, before folding them in a neat pile near the door.

His tail flicked as he padded back to his bed. It felt strangely nice to be completely nude, his fur unrestricted. He idly brushed his fingers over his belly, before collapsing back onto the bed. Face down to keep his tail free, he slowly pulled himself up to rest his head on his pillow. A small seed of worry planted itself in his mind as he thought about the prospect of coming face-to-face with Cooper again, but it was not enough to keep him awake for much longer.

He drifted off to a deep sleep where his worries no longer bothered him.

chapter nine

When his alarm woke Rhys up the following morning, he fumbled around blindly to switch it off, then pulled the sheet up over his head and kept his eyes closed for a little longer. Everything was peaceful here. The bed was warm, and the arm around his waist was comforting. He didn't want to get up and face the troubles of the day just yet. He shifted to stretch out a leg, feeling the warmth of another body pressing against his back. It was like being back with...

Rhys flicked his ears and frowned. He hadn't shared a bed with anyone for years now, and he certainly couldn't remember getting into bed with anyone the previous night. He lifted the covers and glanced down, seeing a furred arm wrapped around his chest. The fur was lighter than his own, and it was silky smooth and clean. Craning his neck to look behind him, Rhys saw William pressed up to his back, the starat still deeply asleep.

Rhys flattened his ears. He had given the starat permission to use his bed for as long as the starat needed. He just didn't expect William to use it while he was occupying it.

Taking care not to wake the starat, Rhys reluctantly slipped out of bed and made his way towards the bathroom. He took a quick piss, before kicking aside a couple of wet towels that had been left on the floor and replacing them with some fresh ones from the small cabinet beside the sink.

It may only have been a day since his last shower, but he felt like he hadn't been clean in weeks. His fur seemed to attract dirt and grime, and he was grateful for the cascade of steaming water to wash over his body. Though it was time consuming, grooming his fur could actually become one aspect of his new body that he could grow to enjoy. Brushing through wet fur and smoothing out the knots felt so relaxing, except for those few moments when he snared on a particularly firm tangle.

After cleaning his fur to a satisfactory level, Rhys got out the shower and start to pat dry his fur with the towel, letting some of the excess moisture drip away from his tail. He was about to walk out into his quarters again, before he remembered the presence of William. Not knowing whether the starat was awake again or not, he wrapped the towel around his waist and opened the door.

William was awake. The starat was sat up in bed, rubbing his eyes. His prosthetic leg was propped up against the wall. "Sorry about that, Captain. I wasn't sure where else to go."

"Don't worry about it. I'll make sure you have somewhere of your own to sleep for tonight," Rhys said, brushing away the starat's apologies. When it all came down to it, he knew it really should be him apologising to William. It had ultimately been his fault that William had been left without anywhere to sleep.

Seeing that the starat didn't seem to be about to move anywhere, Rhys collected a clean set of his uniform and retreated back into the bathroom to finish getting dressed. The starats certainly did seem less hung up on modesty, but Rhys didn't think that was any part of him that was about to change. He still wasn't used to his altered anatomy, and he wasn't about to show it off any time soon.

Even though his fur was still a little damp, Rhys quickly dressed himself, grimacing as damp patches showed through on his white shirt. He knew he needed to get some better way to dry himself, as fur just took so much longer than skin, but he didn't have any more time to waste. He didn't want to be late down to the captain's meeting.

He left William in his quarters, letting the starat know that the door would remain unlocked, so he could return to his regular duties as soon as he wished. From there, he made the way down to the surface and into the derelict corridors of the spaceport. Out of habit, he started to walk towards the control tower, before reminding himself of the new location. He had never been to the briefing room before, as it had been damaged since long before his arrival at the port. Something about the atmospheric containment structures being breached, leaking precious air and temperature into the barren Cerian environment. Work to fix it had been slow, as a multitude of higher priority fixes had always taken over immediate focus until, finally, it had been declared safe for use once more.

With his new uniform, Rhys received more attention than had been directed his way previously. Most humans he walked past did a double-take, with a few providing a reluctant salute. Others sneered and turned on their way, arms kept resolutely by their sides. His ears caught some muttered comments that weren't meant for him to hear.

"What does it think it is doing?"

"That's not right."

"Look at that, it still thinks it is human."

Rhys hurried on his way.

The briefing room was about halfway between the control tower and the shuttle bay, towards the outskirts of the port. As he approached, he wondered what sort of reaction he would get from his fellow captains. Would an extra day allow them both to warm towards him, to treat him as they did before his incident with the teleporters?

From the moment Rhys stepped into the briefing room, he knew that much more than a day would be needed. Both Favre and Baron turned when the door opened, then looked away again without a word. A small sneer appeared on Favre's lips, which he made no attempt to hide. Rhys shivered.

The two captains returned to their own conversation, with the admiral not yet present. From the sound of it, they were discussing the actions of the resident cardinal, about how he had been questioning several of their crew in an attempt to weed out any starat sympathisers. Baron mentioned his time growing up in Nairobi, and the strong presence of church officials ruling with a firmer fist than the local government ever did. Neither included Rhys, and nor did he want to discuss such matters. It made his skin crawl, thinking back to how Cardinal Erik had spoken to him the previous day.

Instead, Rhys sat well away from the other two, perched on the edge of one of the cheap plastic chairs that surrounded the several tables. He glanced around the room. There was nothing interesting about the place, just a simple square room fitted with tables, chairs, and a projector that Rhys doubted worked properly. The ceiling was a network of colours and uneven concrete patches to fix the damage caused by age and wear.

Time crept on, and yet there was still no sign of Admiral Garter. Even Favre and Baron seemed to be showing a little concern for their superior's tardiness. It was most unlike the admiral to ever be late.

Finally, over half an hour after the arranged time for the meeting, the door opened and Admiral Garter entered. His brow was riveted with a deep frown. "Apologies gentlemen," he said as he swept forward to the front of the room. "I was delayed. I had some important communications with Terra to deal with."

"About the animal in the room?" Captain Favre drawled.

Admiral Garter stared at Captain Favre for a moment, before he turned to the other human in the room. "Captain Baron. You're required to prepare your ship. Ganymede can't spare the resources to answer the Silvestro distress call, so you're to offer your assistance to the miners there."

"Understood, Admiral. Would you like me to go now?" Baron replied. His eyes flicked down towards Rhys for a fraction of a second.

"If you would, yes. Radio through when you're ready to launch."

"Of course, sir," Baron said. He saluted the admiral and turned to leave without another word.

The door had barely closed before Favre spoke up again. "And the animal, sir?"

"Captain Favre," Admiral Garter warned. His voiced was raised slightly as he glared towards the Cerian captain. "I know you may not, but I continue to have absolute faith in Captain Griffiths' ability, and I will not hear you speak of him in such terms again. Do you understand me?"

"He's not fit for duty. He never will be," Captain Favre countered.

"He's also sitting right next to you," Rhys bristled, suppressing with immense difficulty an animalistic snarl that would not have gone down well in present company or circumstances.

Captain Favre shook his head sadly. For the first time, he actually turned to look directly at Rhys. "No. Rhys Griffiths is dead. You may think you're him, but you're not. He died the moment that teleporter failed," he said.

Rhys stared at him, dumbfounded. "Excuse me?"

Captain Favre ignored Rhys entirely and turned back to face the admiral. "I've been watching him, Admiral," Captain Favre said with a dismissive shrug. He continued to talk as though Rhys couldn't hear him. "He's no longer human. He looks, thinks, and acts like a starat because that's all he is now."

"And who are you to know what a starat thinks, Favre?" Rhys spat back.

Captain Favre looked back to Rhys, a sneer on his lips. "They don't. They don't think. They respond, that's all."

"Exactly. You just treat them as mindless slaves."

"Well, yes, that's what they are, essentially."

"No they're not." Rhys's voice had dropped to a whisper that still reverberated around the room, such was the silence that accompanied it. He took a deep breath to try and contain his anger, which utterly failed. He rose up out of his seat, trying to gain as much height as he could. "Have you ever seen a starat smile? Have you ever seen one happy? Or sad? Have you seen one scared? Have you seen a starat love?"

Rhys breathed heavily as Captain Favre took his time answering. "No, I haven't," came the eventual reply. "They're not capable of it. They're built to serve. That's what you're made for."

"They're so much more than that, but you don't give them the chance. They're every bit as intelligent as humans, and a damn sight better company," Rhys yelled. His voice wasn't as powerful as it had once been, but it was still loud enough to stun Captain Favre into a few seconds of silence. Before Captain Favre was able to recompose himself, Admiral Garter cut in.

"That's enough, both of you. Captain Griffiths, your passion for this is admirable, but this is not the time to discuss such matters. And Favre, you disappoint me. You will cease this vindictive behaviour against your fellow captain immediately," he said, looking between the two sternly. Rhys's back had stiffened the moment the admiral had interrupted them, his mouth held firmly shut. Favre remained slouched over and tapped his fingers against the table, a silent snarl still on his lips. "Either you both act civil to each other or you will keep silent. Am I clear?"

"My apologies, sir," Rhys said quietly, his head bowed.

"Yes, sir." Captain Favre said after a pause.

Admiral Garter sighed and removed his glasses. He wiped them on his sleeve. "Captain Favre," the admiral eventually said, before pausing for a moment. He tapped his fingers on the table Rhys was sat at. "Some of the parts for the upgraded defences came in overnight. I want you to go and supervise their construction."

"Of course, admiral. And perhaps later, may I speak to you privately about the..." the captain said, before trailing off at the look he received from the admiral. "Of course, sir. Am I dismissed?"

The admiral nodded, and Favre beat a hasty retreat. He still kept his eyes away from Rhys as he left the room. Once they were alone, the admiral sat down opposite Rhys.

"I would say control your temper, but that seems to be a bit of an impossibility with you, Captain Griffiths," the admiral said, removing his glasses and placing them on the table.

"I... Admiral...permission to speak freely?" Rhys blustered. The admiral nodded permission. "I have had to control my anger in front of my crew despite insubordination, in front of the cardinal despite his zealous demands, and in front of my peers. I am a captain, and I do not deserve to be treated that way."

"Of course, Captain. But if you can control your anger in front of the cardinal, then you can in front of your fellow captains," Admiral Garter replied, his voice calm and even. "No matter what your intentions may be, you are playing a dangerous game. Justifiable or not, you must be your very best self, no matter what."

Rhys bowed his head. He rested his hands on his muzzle. "I understand, sir."

Admiral Garter leaned forward and drummed his fingers on the table. He cleared his throat. "In the past hour we have had communication from both the Holy See on Mars, and Windsor Castle. In short, Pope Adamantius has expressed his personal displeasure that a starat has been permitted to hold a position of power within our organisation."

Rhys rested his hands on the briefing table, losing confidence in his ability to remain standing without aid. His throat felt constricted as Admiral Garter continued.

"Windsor Castle was in contact ten minutes later. They reminded us that neither they nor the Papacy can directly interfere with our organisation, they nevertheless advised against defying Adamantius's wishes. However, until I get explicit orders from *my* superiors, you will be maintaining your rank with us."

Rhys breathed a sigh of relief, though his head spun that such important people were talking directly about him. "So, I'm safe?"

"Safe? No, Captain. From the moment you had fur, you were not safe. Nor can I see a time when you ever will be," Admiral Garter replied. His voice was harsh, tinged with sadness.

Rhys slumped in his seat as his ears drooped. "Of course, sir. It was never going to be any other way, was it?"

Instead of answering, the admiral changed the subject. "Lieutenant Cooper has not been stripped of his rank, nor of his position within the military," he said. As a distraction, it worked perfectly.

Rhys jumped out of his seat in shock. "What? I thought that was after the meeting. How could that have been decided already?" he yelped. He was sure he hadn't forgotten it.

"It was meant to be later. But my hands were tied, I'm sorry. Those were the orders that came through this morning," the admiral replied. He held his hands up in a signal of defeat. "He is to join up with Captain Favre's crew in the port here, as per his transfer request."

"He assaulted me, Admiral!" Rhys exclaimed. He started to pace back and forth past the table. The admiral remained seated where he was, following Rhys's movement with his eyes as the starat blustered. "Why should he get to remain after assaulting his captain? No, don't answer that. I know why. It's because I'm a starat, right? If I were human still, he'd have been out on his ass faster than you could say 'dismissed'. Deny it if that's not true."

Admiral Garter shook his head. "I won't deny it, because I know that's probably the reason. But it was not my call. Those were my orders, Captain," he said, raising his hands again to forestall Rhys's next wave of protests. "I had no choice. You are still, and always have been, my choice for admiral. But I fear my opinion is being disregarded."

Rhys's ears flicked. He stopped pacing and turned to look up at the admiral. A sudden thought had come to his mind. "It's you, isn't it? The one Cardinal Erik is looking for? The starat sympathiser?"

For the first time, Rhys saw Admiral Garter's face break into a genuine smile. "I believe in the fair treatment for everyone. Starat or human," he explained. His smile didn't last long, but for just a few moments his taciturn demeanour had been replaced by something new and almost unnerving. "I have been trying to improve starat attitudes here, yes. But as I'm sure you're aware, Captain Favre is not an easy mind to convince."

"Don't you fear the cardinal, Admiral?"

Admiral Garter shook his head. "No. I am not worried about him. But we're not here to talk about him. We're talking about you."

Rhys's ears dropped again. "There's more, isn't there?"

"There is." Admiral Garter leaned forward in his chair and clasped his hands together. "The chancellor isn't convinced Captain Lee defected without any inside help or influence. You have been summoned to Terra to answer further questions regarding your involvement in the loss of the *Dawn*."

Rhys slumped back, suddenly feeling quite numb. "They think I helped him defect? That's... that's nonsense," he whispered. He held his head in his hands, staring down at the plastic table. "He can't possibly believe that."

"I can help you where I can, but with your presence on Terra, then my influence will be severely limited," the admiral explained.

Rhys nodded his head, still not looking up. It didn't feel right. Surely there couldn't be any real cause that had them thinking he had helped Aaron. There had to be some other reason for it all. Of course. There wasn't any legislation in the empire's military branches to allow any removal of a captain for being a starat, simply because it was impossible for any starat to ever become a captain. They were trying to pin this on him simply to remove him from his post. His fists curled up beneath the table.

"It just isn't fair."

"No, it is not. I really wish it could be different for you, Captain. You will need to be the light that shines to change the way in the future, but I'm afraid there's not much we can do for you now. To be the light means you must look into a lot of darkness," the admiral said.

Rhys glanced up. His muzzle twitched as he tried to hold back a couple of tears. "A light?" he asked.

"If you must go down, then don't go down quietly. Make noise. Don't make this easy for them," the admiral replied. He reached forward and took hold of Rhys's hands in his own, gripping them tight. "Be the future the starats deserve."

His ears and tail drooping, Rhys looked up to the admiral and nodded. "I can do my best, Admiral. When do I leave, and where am I going?" he asked. He felt a new fear growing within him. Being asked by the starats to help further their cause was one thing. Having someone as influential as the admiral ask the same question was truly terrifying. He really didn't know if he would be able to live up to such expectations, and the weight of them pressed down on his shoulders already.

"You will leave tomorrow. I haven't been informed where on Terra you'll be, but you'll rendezvous at the Star Hub and receive instructions from there. I'm sure you'll do just grand," the admiral assured. He peered down at Rhys as he released the starat's hands and returned his glasses to the bridge of his nose. "I still believe in you, Rhys. No matter what."

"I wish I shared your optimism."

***

Rhys trudged back to his ship in a daze. The conversation with the admiral rung in his ears, adding yet more turbulent thoughts to his troubled mind. He didn't know what to do. This wasn't how any of it should have gone. He should have been excited about the prospect of becoming an admiral within the coming months, when Admiral Garter stepped down. Instead he had to worry about the prospect of being branded a traitor or considered nothing more than a slave.

This would be the last night he'd spend on Ceres, which was something else he should have been looking forward to. He was finally going away from this derelict little port that no one particularly cared about, other than the few local Cerians who had remained. He should have been so excited to finally be going back to Terra, but all he could feel was absolute dread for what was waiting for him there. He would be leaving early in the morning. It could not come soon enough, yet he would do anything to delay it for as long as possible.

He wanted time to brood on his own, but he wasn't even given that luxury. He'd made it through the port, and then through his ship, without being stopped by anyone, but when he got back to his quarters he found that they weren't empty.

"Captain Rhys!" Twitch cried. The starat beamed widely from where he was perched on the edge of Rhys's bed. "Did you miss me?"

Rhys just shook his head and closed the door behind him. His tail was held low as he stumbled across the room, doing his best to ignore the starat bouncing on his toes. He went straight into the bathroom and splashed water on his face, wetting his fur in an attempt to disguise the small damp patches around his eyes. He didn't even bother towelling his fur dry before going back into his quarters. Twitch was still grinning.

"I'm leaving tomorrow," Rhys told the starat, whose smile only reduced by a fraction.

"Where to?" Twitch asked.

"Terra. I've been summoned. I... don't know what's going to happen there. I doubt I'll ever be allowed back here again," Rhys replied. He wouldn't be able to see any of the starats here again.

Twitch didn't seem too concerned by that. "Oh!" he exclaimed, clapping his hands together. "I've never been there before. That will be exciting. I can't wait to leave."

"You? I... I don't think you can come too."

Twitch leapt up from the bed, quickly covering the distance between them and wrapping a confused Rhys in a tight embrace. "That's just the thing!" Twitch squeaked in excitement. "I spent all night with your doctor and navigator with David. Doctor Anthony said that he needs a new assistant, and that David has always been good with that sort of thing, so he was going to ask your permission to hire him. And then Edgar and Aleksandr showed me how to do all their navigation and piloting things. It's all a bit confusing, but I think I might be able to understand it all soon as I've always been a quick learner."

"I... never heard about any of this," Rhys said slowly, trying to take stock of what he was being told. He had wanted to bring more starats onto his ship, but he doubted that he would be allowed to do such a thing, especially with his summons to Terra.

"Well of course not," Twitch exclaimed. He stroked down Rhys's arms before he took a couple of steps back. "We were talking about it last night. Edgar was going to find you this morning to talk about it with you, but you'd already gone. We thought you'd approve of it." The starat's smile faltered a little. "You do approve, right?"

"I do, yeah. I just..." Rhys trailed off. He wandered over towards his wine cabinet, which was looking very tempting. "I'm not going to be allowed to take you. Captain Favre won't even listen to me, and I don't think Admiral Garter will be able to approve it."

Twitch frowned and swished his tail. Then his face brightened in another smile. "Well, then we'll just hide on the ship until we leave tomorrow. Come on Captain Rhys, it will be exciting!"

"I... I can't just do that. They'll brand me as a sympathiser. I'll be stripped of rank. I'll lose my ship, I'll lose everything," Rhys said. He groaned and pressed his head against the cabinet door, gazing in longingly through the glass to the bottles within. It went against all protocol.

"You think they won't do that anyway? They probably already are," Twitch pointed out. He placed his hand on Rhys's shoulder.

Rhys frowned. That thought had swirled at the back of his mind for a long time, but now that Twitch brought it up, he was able to focus on it fully for the first time. Admiral Garter had been trying to protect him from it, but even his influence had dried up. They were looking for any excuse they could muster to kick him down into what they believe was his proper place. His thoughts hardened, and a silent snarl formed on his lips. "Fuck them. Fuck Favre. Fuck what any of them think. You're coming with us, no matter what any of them say. They don't own you anymore."

Catching sight of Twitch's reflection moving in the glass, Rhys had barely a moment to prepare before the other starat barrelled into him, knocking him to the floor in another tight embrace. Twitch giggled and gave Rhys a firm kiss on the lips. "I knew I could trust you, Captain Rhys!"

Rhys could feel himself burning crimson red beneath his fur. Judging from Twitch's howls of laughter, the other starat was fully aware about the reaction he was causing. He curled up and tried to extricate himself from Twitch's embrace, without much success. The starat's grip was firm.

"I need to sleep," Rhys protested, arching his head back to keep his mouth away from Twitch's. "We're leaving early tomorrow, so I need to be up before prelim checks."

Twitch giggled and released Rhys, his eyes flicking towards the bed. "Want another starat in bed with you?"

"Anoth... William told you?" Rhys blanched.

"Oh yes. He's quite cute, don't you think, Captain Rhys?" Twitch teased, sticking his tongue out at Rhys's discomfort.

"I don't... I'm not..." Rhys protested, but he wasn't able to even complete his denial. He had enjoyed the comfort of waking up to William's embrace. He couldn't deny that. He just rubbed his temples and slowly stood up as Twitch released him. "No. I don't want another starat in bed with me. I... there should be a spare room a few doors down. It should already be unlocked. Find Scott if you need more help."

"Sure thing, Captain Rhys," Twitch said as he jumped up to his feet. He gave Rhys another tight hug, before scampering towards the door, which he unlocked with his thumbprint. He turned to grin at Rhys again. "I'll see you again when we're in space. Space! Actual space! I can't believe it! I've never been out of orbit before. Is it cold? Will we be floating? Actually, no! Don't say! I want to find out for myself. Good night, Captain Rhys!"

"Good night Twitch," Rhys replied, waiting for the door to close on the starat before flopping down onto his bed. A small act of rebellion. He would be stealing away three starats from Ceres. Twitch, David, and Steph would all be welcome additions to his ship, in his eyes at least. He was sure there would be some dissenters, not least back on Ceres. But if he was to make a stand and let the empire realise that he wasn't going to step aside and let them strip him of all his ranks and powers, then he needed to make a statement of intent somewhere. Freeing five starats from their ownership, two on his ship and three from Normandy, was a small start. But it was still a start. Change had begun.

chapter ten

"Captain, we're all prepared to leave."

Acting-Lieutenant Scott was stood in the centre of the bridge, just in front of Rhys who oversaw the entire operation from his seat. The starat was nervous and his tail twitched fitfully. He knew this could be his last flight as a captain. It was also the first time a starat had ever been present on the bridge while his ship was in flight – even if that starat was him. He acknowledged the call from his first officer with a wave of his hand, then he gestured down to his communications officer, giving him the permission to pass on that information to Normandy Control.

There were a few moments of silence after Jermaine McDonald spoke. When a response finally came through, it was not a calm permission to depart. It was a voice Rhys would rather not hear again.

"Where are they?" Captain Favre's voice spat through the speakers.

Rhys gestured to McDonald to hook up his microphone so he could speak directly to the Cerian. "Apologies, Captain Favre. We're in the middle of launch. You'll have to be more specific."

"Don't play coy with me, rat," came the immediate, furious response. "Three starats are missing, and I know you've taken them. Acting-Lieutenant Scott, are they on your ship?"

A few sharp glares turned towards Rhys from his crew, but he was glad that no one spoke out. Rhys gestured towards Scott to advise his new first officer to answer the question from the Cerian captain. "I'm afraid you're mistaken, Captain Favre," Scott said, his voice low and even. "There aren't any starats on this ship, other than those who are meant to be here."

Blustered sounds came through the speakers, before a calmer voice started to speak. Admiral Garter. "Apologies for that, Captain Griffiths. Captain Favre has misplaced three starats, one of which is the one whose genetic information you share. Have you seen them?"

"Can't say I have, Admiral. Though I did notice some of my clothes had gone missing this morning. If the starat wished to pose as me, he could be anywhere by now," Rhys replied. He had practised that lie all morning, and he was glad that he'd been able to avoid stuttering as he told it.

Captain Favre's disbelieving voice could be heard through the speakers, ranting about Rhys, but it was once more the admiral who spoke clearly. "Very well, Captain. We shall continue our search here."

"I'm sure you'll find them somewhere," Rhys replied. He could barely hide the grin on his face, glad that neither the admiral nor Captain Favre could see him.

The sounds of Admiral Garter and Captain Favre talking could still be heard over the speakers, but it was clear they had moved a little further away, as their voices were easily drowned out by a new speaker. "Alright *Harvester*, this is Normandy Control. You are cleared for launch and may depart in your own time."

"Alright then Mr Chekolin, let's get this ship moving," Rhys said to the ship's pilot. With barely a moment's hesitation, the ship began to shake as the engines began to rumble and power up. The ship gradually started to move, the massive engines sending vibrations all through the ship as it started to navigate far enough away from the dwarf planet for a safe switch to the faster subspace travel.

The massive screens flickered on as the ship started to move, displaying the impressive vista of the dwarf planet below as it gradually receded. Then the view flicked to what lay in front of them – the inky blackness of space. It looked cold and empty, but also beautiful. Here and there was the glint of sunlight shining off an asteroid, but there was little close by. Certainly nothing that would present a danger to the ship.

"Alright Mr Riley, it's time to work your magic. Set course for orbit around Terra," Rhys said.

Riley was already at work, filling in many series of numbers and coordinates into his computer to determine the exact course they would need to take. There were so many variables that had to be considered, notwithstanding small objects that may, and probably were, in the way. Because of the distance being covered, even the slightest miscalculation on Riley's behalf could result in being massively off course. Even on such a relatively short journey, absolute precision was necessary. It was the young man's first time navigating the ship solo, but he did have Scott looking over his shoulder. The acting first officer didn't say anything, with no need to correct the *Harvester's* new navigator.

"Coordinates set. Four minutes and fourteen seconds until correct trajectory is acquired from our current orbit and speed," Riley said after barely a minute. With the navigator confident, Scott started to patrol around the bridge, keeping a calculated eye on the rest of the crew.

Riley and Chekolin were in constant communication. The navigator and pilot were the two of the most closely linked roles. One couldn't function without the other. Riley needed to inform exactly how much thrust Chekolin had to apply from the ion engines, and the precise moment when he had to do so. Chekolin checked his computer's clock was synced to the tenth of a second to Riley's computer for the fourth time. There could be no margin for error.

Rhys counted down the seconds in his head. The moment came. Without a sound, the ship threw itself forward in sudden acceleration, leaving Ceres well behind in an instant. Instead of the rumbling roar of the hydrogen engines, the ionic power manifested itself as a low hum that radiated through the ship.

"Correct trajectory acquired," Riley said after a glance at his computer confirmed it. "We're on course for Terra."

"Well done Mr Riley, Mr Chekolin," Rhys said. He turned to the ship's systems officer. "Mr Dewson, we're relying on you now."

Though Sarah Pool was also on the bridge, she had delegated her duties to her assistant for the relatively simple journey to Terra. They usually shared the shift with a rotation period of about six hours, with the junior officer, Sutherland, filling in when necessary. Of course, on such a short trip as this one, neither Pool nor Sutherland would be required. Given the likelihood of any CGP craft so deep into TIE territory was miniscule, Dewson's presence was only required to detect any piece of space debris that Riley's computer had failed to detect at either end of the journey. A rogue meteor or comet could cause significant damage to a spaceship. Such a collision was best avoided.

"Mr Chekolin, status?" Rhys asked of his pilot.

"Engines running at full strength, captain," was the quick reply from Chekolin. The navigator pulled up on his computer screen a display of several graphs and pie charts of red, green, and yellow. The green was by far the dominant colour. "Temperature, power, and energy insertion all normal. Countdown initiated before Denitchev Drive activation."

"Mr Scott, everything as it should be?" Rhys asked, turning to his first officer who had taken a seat just behind him and to his right. From there he had access to a computer that gave him information on all the non-essential and critical systems of the ship. If anything were to go amiss in any section of the *Harvester*, then Scott would be the first to know.

"All online, all systems optimal, captain," he replied instantly. "Tiny leak of hydraulic fluid, but small enough to be burned off by the ionic engines without negative effect. Denitchev Drives ready and primed for activation."

Rhys raised his hand, ready to give the final order to launch the Denitchev Drive as Chekolin's countdown progressed, but then he held his hand to his ear. He frowned for a moment and listened into his communicator. He made sure to hide it from his crew so they didn't realise that it wasn't active. He then groaned and held his hand over his muzzle.

"Mr McDonald, could you please send a message back to Ceres to say we've found their missing starats. They're held below deck and we will return them when our business on Terra is concluded. We would love to return them now, but we don't want to delay our launch to Terra," Rhys ordered. His eyes swept across the bridge. Though McDonald raised his brow at the latest request, everyone had obeyed his every command.

"I'm on it, Captain," McDonald replied. Moments later he was in communication with Ceres, informing them exactly what Rhys had requested. He spoke quickly as Chekolin continued to countdown.

"Ready to deploy the Denitchev Drive in five seconds," Chekolin called out once McDonald fell quiet. The pilot glanced over his shoulder for confirmation from his captain. It came from a quick nod from the starat. The ship's shields were activated, and a stream of Dentichev particles shrouded around the craft. A burst of electricity quickly followed, and there was a barely perceptible shift in the tone of the ionic engines as the ship was displaced from realspace. The external screens showed nothing but pure white light before they were switched off.

With his muzzle still hidden by his hand, Rhys turned to Scott. "I'll go check on our stowaways. You have the bridge, Acting-Lieutenant."

"Aye, sir."

***

Briggs scowled as he looked down at Rhys. They were down in the brig, a rarely used part of the ship that was used to house the occasional dissenters or prisoners the *Harvester* took on board. The three starats from Ceres had been held there for a short while. Conditions weren't great, and it was incredibly loud with the rumble of the engines close by. None of the starats seemed concerned though, and Twitch was being true to his name. His tail vibrated as he gazed wide-eyed around the room.

"So I'm to find work for them, sir?" Briggs asked. He twisted a length of cloth in his hands as he spat out Rhys's honourific.

"Fair work for two of them, yes," Rhys replied. He wanted to be quite clear with Briggs that he wouldn't accept any further unfair treatment of the starats under his care, but nor did he wish to antagonise the services commander. He needed Briggs on his side, or else he would risk losing the support of a large swathe of his services crew. Without them, the ship would not function, no matter how loyal the operations crew on the bridge remained to Rhys.

"Just two?"

Rhys nodded and glanced back to the three starats behind him. He gestured for Twitch and Steph to step forward. "Just two, yes. I have other things in mind for David here. Talk to the starats and see what they'd be best at."

"Talk to them, sir?" Briggs said. He raised a brow and tightened his grip around the cloth.

"Talk to them, yes. Have a conversation with them. You might be surprised," Rhys said. He couldn't help but smirk slightly. His ears perked up. "Talk to Richard as well. He might be able to tell you some things you weren't aware of."

"I don't know which one that is." Briggs started to turn away.

Rhys's tail twitched. "The one with both legs."

Briggs paused and looked back down at Rhys. For a moment there was something behind his eyes that Rhys didn't expect to see. Regret. It was only there for an instant before it disappeared back behind a sneer. "I'll take it into consideration, Captain."

"Most appreciated, Mr Briggs, thank you," Rhys said with a nod to dismiss his services commander for now.

Briggs grunted and turned fully. "Come on then," he growled to the two starats.

Steph hurried forward, but Twitch lingered by Rhys's side for a few moments. "Will there be any windows I can look out of?" the starat whispered in Rhys's ear. "I want to see a comet or something!"

"We're in subspace at the moment, so there's nothing to actually see out there," Rhys replied with a shake of his head.

"Subspace? Isn't that a... never mind," Twitch giggled. He fled after Briggs and Steph before David could swat him over the ears.

Rhys turned to the larger starat with a blank look in his eyes, his ears curled in curiously. David laughed. "I don't think you want to know, Captain Rhys."

Rhys twitched his tail and shrugged his shoulders. "If you say so," he said quietly. He frowned for a few moments and thought it through, before he shrugged his shoulders. "Come on though. Doctor Sparks will be expecting us."

David's eyes lit up. "You mean I'm really getting to work with Doctor Anthony?"

"Of course. And if things settle down a little more, Twitch will work closer with Chekolin and learn some piloting," Rhys replied. His reward was a tight hug from David, whose powerful arms squeezed around his torso. He gasped, barely able to breathe for a few seconds until David released him. The starat kissed him on the muzzle.

When David let him go, Rhys winced and felt over his ribs to make sure none had cracked in the starat's tight embrace. Everything felt intact. "Ow, do you always hug Twitch like that?"

A mischievous glint immediately appeared in David's eye. It was a look Rhys was more familiar appearing in Twitch's eyes. "Not exactly like that. I can demonstrate if you like."

Rhys's ears pinned right back. "I think I'll pass there. Shall we just got and see Doctor Sparks?" he said. He spoke quickly as he tried to ignore the heat of his blush.

David's smirk was almost unbearable, and Rhys had to keep his eyes away from the larger starat as they started to make their way back through the ship. Thankfully, David tended to stay behind Rhys, as most of the narrow and busy corridors were wide enough only for two. Again Rhys was subjected to awkward, delayed salutes and a few muttered greetings that could barely be heard over the rumble of the engines.

"You're walking a lot better now," David pointed out.

Rhys glanced back towards the starat, then down to his own feet. He certainly didn't think so much about how to place them now. The movement had become a little more natural as he no longer tried to push his heels down towards the floor. He'd stopped thinking too much about his tail as well. His body's instincts controlled it now, which allowed Rhys to keep his balance with a bit more ease.

"How bad was I, really?" Rhys asked. He glanced back to David again, his ears curled down.

"Absolutely hopeless," David said with a laugh. Rhys's shoulders slumped, but David wasn't yet finished. He shook his head for a moment and smiled warmly. "You looked like what you were. Someone coming to terms with a new body and all the problems that came with it. Now though... I wouldn't say you look natural, but you're certainly much better."

"I'm glad," Rhys replied. He fell silent for a few moments as they passed more of his crew. He had to press right up against the wall as they hurried by without saluting their captain. Rhys didn't read much into that. Sometimes when the ship was in flight, crew needed to get to their stations urgently, and decorum like saluting the ship's captain wasn't necessarily demanded. It still hurt though, as their eyes didn't once move down to look at him. He twitched his tail and forced himself to think of something else. Again his eyes slid back to David behind him. "It must be weird for you, isn't it?"

"What do you mean, Captain Rhys?" David asked with a flick of his ears.

Rhys stopped and turned to face the starat. He gestured down at his body. "I look like Twitch. Sound like him too. Isn't that strange? Don't you ever think I'm him?"

"Of course I do," David answered. He smiled wryly and stood by Rhys's side. The two starats both leaned back against the wall as they waited for an elevator to come and take them up to the next level. "Every time I look at you I have to remind myself that you're not Twitch. But there are little things that give it away."

"Like what?"

"Well you're not absolutely, insufferably, insane for starters," David said with a laugh. Rhys couldn't help but chuckle as well. "Your accent too. Your voices aren't quite the same. But more importantly, Twitch is special. There's something about him that no one can replicate, not even someone who shares the same body as him. So yes, I might think you're him out of the corner of my eye, but it doesn't take long to realise who you are."

Rhys's immediate response was cut short as the elevator doors opened. The two people already inside snapped to attention and saluted Rhys as he stepped inside. David fell completely silent and bowed his head to stare down at the floor.

They only needed to go up one level, and the doors soon opened again. Despite his discomfort, David waited until Rhys had left the elevator before he moved. From there it was only a short walk to the medical bay, and before their conversation could be rekindled, Rhys already had his hand on the doors to push them open.

Almost as soon as the door opened, Doctor Sparks poked his head out from the small adjoining office. "It all worked then, Captain Griffiths?"

"All fine, yes. Scott was able to get them all on board. Twitch and Steph are with Briggs at the moment," Rhys replied. He hopped up to sit on the edge of one of the beds. He still didn't like how much his legs dangled over the side.

"Sorry I couldn't help out. I had a few urgent messages to send before we jumped into subspace," Sparks replied apologetically.

Rhys flicked his ears. "I wasn't aware of any transmissions that needed to be sent," he said slowly. His head tilted slightly to one side, and he pulled his hands away from his tail as he realised his fingers had started to stroke it again.

"Oh, just some medical records that needed to be sent out. Nothing I thought to worry you with," Sparks said. The doctor seemed unable to suddenly meet Rhys's eye, but the starat was too focused on trying not to be distracted by his tail to notice. The conversation quickly turned as Sparks switched his focus to David. "So you're to be helping me out around here then?"

David brightened up immediately. "I will be, yes. Captain Rhys said that I could," he said. He bounced on his toes in excitement. "I always helped out with any treatment the starats needed on Ceres." His ears drooped slightly. "I hope they'll all be alright. I'll miss them."

"I'm sure they'll be fine. Admiral Garter will make sure nothing bad happens to them," Rhys replied quickly, though he wasn't totally convinced. He knew the admiral would do his best to protect the starats, but he could only hope that the likes of Cardinal Erik would not take out his anger on them. He supposed it would be a tough time for the new starats on his ship, especially if they had never left Ceres before. Rhys was used to moving on from friends when being restationed, but David, Twitch, and Steph would have little experience of that.

"I hope so. And maybe one day I can see them all again," David said.

Doctor Sparks patted David on the shoulder. "I'm sure Captain Griffiths will do his best so you can go back one day."

Rhys grimaced. He was not ready to make any such promise.

***

Rhys had returned to the bridge some twenty minutes before the ship was due to fall out of subspace. They couldn't jump in too close to Terra, as the gravity wells that surrounded the planet distorted the pull of the Denitchev particles, which could have detrimental effects on the ship. Not only that, but any slight miscalculation could result in the ship jumping out inside a celestial body. That made Aaron's jump so close to Ceres all the more remarkable. Neither Scott nor Chekolin had been able to work out how that had been done.

Chekolin took no risks when he pulled the *Harvester* out of subspace. They were still over an hour away from Terra, but almost immediately McDonald raised his hand to advise Rhys that he was in contact with the Star Hub.

As soon as they had returned from subspace, it was time to start applying the brakes to slow the ship back down so they could cut off the ionic engines well before they reached the Terran atmosphere. Again, Chekolin and Riley were in close conversation as they timed everything to absolute precision. A delay of something as small as a couple of seconds could result in catastrophic consequences.

All went well, and soon Terra and Luna were visible to the ship's sensors. An image of the two celestial bodies flashed up on the front screens. Their speed rapidly decreased, and the artificial gravity systems worked hard to dampen the massive g-forces being applied to the ship. Rhys could feel a slight tightening in his chest, but otherwise the extreme effects of space travel were largely insignificant in the modern ships used by the empire.

Rhys gripped onto the sides of his seat as the image of Terra grew ever larger. A tingle always ran up his spine as he came closer to the brilliant blue and green of his home planet, though it was a new experience to have that tingle go down as low as the tip of his tail.

The rumble of the ionic engines had long ceased, to be replaced by the dull roar of the reverse thrusters that sought to shed the last of the ship's incredible speed. There, in the upper echelons of the Terran atmosphere, they approached one of the greatest feats of human engineering. The Star Hub had been conceived almost a century earlier, and over several decades had slowly been constructed in geosynchronous orbit above the chill white of Antarctica.

The Star Hub acted as a central point where all spacecraft docked on Terra, both military and commercial alike. One half was controlled by the Terran government in association with the military, while the other was a commercial spaceport that dealt with all civilian traffic. Both were protected by the very best defence network the empire had ever conceived. It was utterly impregnable.

Their weapons were likely already trained on the *Harvester*, ready to destroy it should they be identified as an enemy ship.

"Stable orbit achieved. Waiting for permission from the Hub to approach," Chekolin called out. The projected image of the Star Hub gleamed on the ship's screens.

McDonald's communication with the Hub had been fast and detailed. He had quickly verified their identity, and permission was soon given to approach. Small amounts of thrust were applied from the ship's hydrogen engines, lining up the massive bulk of the *Harvester* with the small docking bays. When they were close enough, several tug ships came out to greet them and guide them in with powerful electromagnetic grips.

The ship clanked and rattled as it was pulled in to the Hub, but Rhys wasn't alarmed by any of those noises. He recognised it all as normal behaviour, and it wasn't long before there was comparative silence from beyond the bridge.

"Docking complete. We're free to board the Star Hub at our discretion," McDonald confirmed a few moments later. The communications officer then removed his headset and leaned back in his seat, exhaling heavily.

Rhys clapped his hands together and rose up to his feet. "Excellent work, everyone. Welcome back to Terra," he said. He had to hold onto the side of his chair for support, his feet felt a little wobbly as he tried to get used to the small shift in gravity. "Take advantage of the Hub's facilities while you can. I'm not sure how long we'll be here for. We could get the summons to the shuttles anytime."

"The shuttles, Captain? Not the teleporters?" Dewson called out as Rhys was turning around towards the back of the bridge. His tail lowered, and his ears pressed right down to his head, despite his best efforts to ignore his sensory officer. He didn't know if Dewson was trying intentionally to scare him, but the mere thought of the teleporters utterly terrified him. He never wanted to go through them again.

No one appeared to notice his discomfort, despite how obvious his reactions had been. Either his crew was being polite, or they simply didn't know how to read his body language. He assumed it had to be more the latter. After all, he was still learning how to interpret and control the movements his own body made naturally.

"Not... not this time, Mr Dewson, no. I don't think they'll be necessary," Rhys replied, a small stutter in his voice. He took a deep breath and tried to straighten out his ears and tail. He glanced back at Dewson and flashed a little smile. "Besides, I'd recommend double and triple checking any teleporters before you use them. Unless you're willing to grow a tail too."

Dewson's eyes widened. He shook his head. "No, sir."

Rhys smirked. "I didn't think so. Nasty things. Get in the way of sitting down." A small chuckle ran through the bridge. "But unless you're wanting to hear all the intimate details about this body, I think we should disembark."

A rowdy cry ran around the crew. "Aye, sir!"

On the military side of the Star Hub, each docking bay was kept separate from the adjacent ones. Each was completely independent, able to house the crews of each ship indefinitely. They provided all the facilities required for long-term stays, as well as providing accommodation for short visits before the trip down to Terra.

Rhys waited for his crew to make their way into the Hub, before following out behind them, making sure everything in the bridge was fully powered down. Soon after, a call came up from Briggs confirming all the support systems were likewise deactivated. The *Harvester* was now running fully off of the Hub.

Through the efforts of Rhys, Briggs, and Scott, the ship was soon emptied of all its crew. Once it was confirmed no one was left on board, the *Harvester* was locked up so that no one but those three could gain access again. Rhys tried not to think about the possibility it could be the last time he could ever set foot on his ship. After dismissing his services commander for the next few hours, Rhys stepped out of the airlock that connected the Hub to his ship, and into a gleaming corridor of polished metal and glass.

He was not alone.

"Captain Rhys, this is amazing." Twitch's voice quivered as his face was pressed against the reinforced windows that lined the corridor. The glass was fogging up beneath the starat's breath, and he had to keep wiping it away with his furred arm. "It's even bluer than I thought it would be!"

Rhys slapped Twitch's shoulder as he walked past him. "You haven't seen anything yet," he told the starat. The other two Cerian starats were gazing down with wonder at the planet below too. William, having seen his share of planets already, was less interested in what lay below. He had already limped his way to the far end of the corridor.

"There's more?" Twitch asked. His eyes were wide with wonder as he dragged them away from the blue and green vista below. "What does it smell like down there? I always thought it would be nice. Like strawberries, or something. Is it like that?"

Rhys suppressed a chuckle, and just gestured for Twitch to follow him, with David and Steph. All three starats continued to stare down through the windows as they walked, holding onto each other's hands in excitement. From the corridor, there was a short elevator down to a communal area, of which branched all the requirements and needs the crew would need. Dormitories were on the outer side, with windows that overlooked the impressive view of the planet below, and on the inner were the kitchens and bathrooms, as well as the leisure centres.

Most of the crew were using the time to just rest and relax, taking advantage of all the modern technology they had been denied in the backwater of Ceres. Gaming systems, movies, and e-sports were just a few of the many things on offer within the dormitories and common room. It was a marvel how clean the Hub looked, coming from the dirty and decrepit port at Normandy.

Over by one window, Richard was sat nervously. His tail twitched as he was surrounded by Briggs and a few other members of the services crew. At first Rhys was a little alarmed, but then he noticed that they were just engaged in conversation. He smiled, glad that Briggs appeared to have taken his advice. Even as he watched, William limped across to them as well and placed a hand on Richard's shoulder. He exchanged a few words as well, but Rhys was too far away to hear what was being said.

Rhys turned to the starats behind him, a mixture of wonder and indifference on their faces. "Stay here for a bit. I'll need to meet a few people here to see what needs to be done. I'll catch up with you again when I can down there. Until then, just enjoy yourselves."

Twitch nodded exuberantly. "Sure thing, Captain Rhys!" The starat bounced on his feet as he looked around the place in excitement, but his eyes were always drawn back to the wide windows.

Calling for his first officer to follow him, Rhys left his crew and the starats behind. Beyond the area set aside for his crew was the entry into the communal areas of the military half of the Hub. From the inside, it looked like another network of slightly curved corridors, but Rhys knew that the true splendour of the Hub couldn't be seen from within. On each side of the Hub was half a dozen layers of wide rings that served as the docking bays, all leading towards the two central spheres that housed the civilian areas and central command rooms.

"Thank you for doing that for me," Rhys said, glad of the opportunity to talk quietly and alone with his first officer. Even as they stepped out into the corridors beyond their quarters, there was no one within earshot. "With the starats. And talking to the admiral as well. I didn't expect you to do that."

Scott glanced down to his captain. "It was nothing, sir."

"It was though. It really was. You lied to a commanding officer. They'll have your stripes as well as mine if they find out," Rhys said with a small shake of his head. There was a smile on his muzzle though. "I just want you to know it's appreciated. Makes me glad I've got men like you around."

"I'd do it again if I needed to, sir. Some people are worth lying for."

A maze of corridors and elevators led Rhys and Scott slowly towards this central hub, though thankfully it was signed well enough that there was never any danger of getting lost. He just had to remember where they were docked: D7-70.

Scott stretched his shoulders as they started to pass a few more people, muttering beneath his breath about how the artificial gravity on Ceres had been messing with his back. "Looking forward to a hit on the tennis courts when I can."

Rhys flicked his ears. "Feel like a hit myself. Want to see how this body works. Game?"

"Game? All I'd have to do is lob you every time, sir. Where's the challenge in that?" Scott laughed. Rhys lightly punched him, but he started to laugh as well.

Rhys was glad to have Scott by his side, joking and talking with him. It made things seem normal. None of the unfamiliar faces he passed seemed to notice him. That much at least hadn't changed from Ceres. No matter where he went in the empire, he doubted he would be noticed very often. Not even the stripes on his shoulders made any difference. Humans simply didn't expect a starat to hold any authority, so they could be conveniently ignored without consequence. That was something Rhys would have to fight hard to change. But for the short term, maybe even use.

The small, spider-web like corridors that linked the central hubs to the docking rings always looked small and fragile to Rhys, but at the same time he placed more trust into them than anything at the Normandy port. He knew these weren't about to break apart.

"Do you know what sort of reaction you're going to get in there, Captain?" Scott asked as they began to cross over from the docking circles to the command hub.

Rhys glanced up at his acting first officer and shook his head. "They know about all of... this," he replied, gesturing down to his body in general. "I think. But beyond that, I don't know. Windsor wants my stripes, so lukewarm at best. Anything has to be better than Favre."

"I've got your back, Captain. Whatever they say," Scott said.

"I appreciate that, Mr Scott. But I hope it won't be necessary." Rhys's mouth twitched into a small smile at the show of support. They had almost reached the far end of the corridor, where a large double door cut off any vision of what lay beyond. From memory, Rhys recalled a large, open reception-like area that served to direct and regulate the flow of personnel throughout the facility. Though it was not the official headquarters of the interstellar corps, the Star Hub often functioned as such, given it was the first point of access into the Terran atmosphere.

The doors opened smoothly, well in advance of Rhys and Scott actually reaching them. There was none of the hesitation and grinding evident in the doors back on Ceres. This was clean and efficient, working as it should.

Rhys's memory had been good. One large desk dominated one wall of the large waiting hall, behind which were several men and women in uniform. Two were in conversation with a couple of captains on the other side of the desk, but most were idle and free. Above the desk were situated about two dozen clocks, all displaying a different time with a tag indicating which city they represented. The Hub operated on New Zealand standard time.

As the door closed behind Rhys, the nearest attendant turned towards him. Her smile faltered as she looked at Rhys, though it did return as her eyes moved to the tall human by his side. Her shoulders were unadorned with any indication of rank. "Good afternoon. How can I help you today?"

"Captain Griffiths of the *Harvester*," Rhys said as he approached the desk. He had to clamber up onto one of the chairs by its side in order to even see over the top. "We just docked at D7-70."

"Oh. Let me, uh. Just give me a moment," the attendant replied. She glanced over her shoulder, before darting off towards a few of the other attendants. The quick conversation broke out amongst them, with a few jabbing of fingers in Rhys's direction.

Rhys frowned and shared a glance with Scott. The same reaction again. It was a struggle not to growl. "This is going to be interesting," he muttered beneath his breath.

The attendant returned soon after, this time accompanied by an older man who appeared to be an officer in the terrestrial land army. There was often some cooperation between the armed forces in the running of the Hub, but Rhys was still surprised to see him here. He looked between Rhys and Scott with a deep-furrowed frown that reminded Rhys of Admiral Garter.

"So you're Captain Griffiths?" he asked in a gruff voice. "I'm Major James Wilson. I was sent up from Sydney to expect you. You're to be escorted down to the surface. Sir."

"Escorted?" Rhys flicked his ears. "You make it sound like I'm under arrest, Major Wilson."

"Let's just say you've been causing a bit of a stir here, and that we'd rather keep any fuss to a minimum. We don't want a media circus following you," the major replied.

Rhys hadn't even considered that. He nodded. That made it sound much less like he was being arrested, though he still wasn't too enamoured by an escort down to Terra. It wasn't how he had envisaged returning.

"And the rest of the crew, sir?" Scott asked, directing the major's attention towards him for the first time.

"You're all to follow down tomorrow," Major Wilson replied, a clearly prepared answer. Rhys wondered how long this had all been planned for, whether it had just been in the few hours since their departure at Ceres, or had it been almost since the moment he had become a starat? He wasn't sure he wanted to know the answer to that question.

"I'm to go down now, Major?" Rhys asked. He looked around the room, noticing that there were quite a few stares being cast in his direction. He tried to ignore them, but he couldn't help the fact that his tail lowered down a little. It took a lot of effort not to grasp it in his hands.

Major Wilson nodded. "Unless there's any urgent matters you still need to address with your crew, I was ordered to bring you down as quickly as possible, sir."

Rhys sighed and tapped his hand on the desk for a couple of moments, before sliding down off the chair and looking up to Scott. "Explain the situation to the crew. I'm sure I'll get the chance to see you tomorrow, once you've landed. I'll seek you out for that game of tennis," he said, before grabbing hold of Scott's arm, pulling him down so that he could speak quietly in his ear. "Keep an eye on the Cerian starats. They've never left Ceres before, so they could be a bit overwhelmed by it all."

"Understood, Captain." Scott placed his hand on Rhys's shoulder before standing up again, towering over the diminutive starat once more. "I'll catch up with you tomorrow. Good evening, Major."

With that, Scott turned and started to make his way back to the *Harvester*, leaving Rhys alone with the major and the room of curious, possibly hostile humans. The starat suppressed a shiver as he turned to look up at the major, barely visible over the desk from his lower vantage point. "Shall we then, Major?"

The major cleared his throat. "Give me a few minutes, Captain. I'll be with you soon. Just wait here until I'm back."

Rhys wasn't thrilled about being left by himself, but he nodded and assured the major that he'd wait where he was. He hopped back up onto the chair and gripped the side of it, gazing around the room and meeting the eyes of anyone who stared at him too long. Most looked away almost immediately. It didn't stop them talking about him. He could hear whispered conversations all around. They probably didn't think he could hear them, but his ears were easily sensitive enough to pick up their hushed words, questioning who he was and what he was doing. Why was there a starat who seemed to think it was a captain?

Eventually, Rhys turned his back to the watching humans, trying to ignore them. It was difficult. The whispers were his thoughts made real. Doubts about his abilities, and his chances of keeping his rank. He didn't realise he was playing with his tail again until Major Wilson returned. He dropped it in a hurry and jumped up to his feet, smoothing down some wrinkles in his shirt.

Major Wilson was stern as he frowned down at Rhys. "Ready then, Captain?"

Trying not to think about his cabinet of wine back on his ship, Rhys took a deep breath. "Yeah, let's get this started."

The small gathered crowd quickly parted as Rhys followed the major across the open hall. The mutters didn't stop until they went through the doors on the far side, passing into another narrow, glass-lined corridor. The smooth floor was cold beneath Rhys's bare feet, and his claws clicked with every step. It was a little annoying, but he couldn't raise his toes up off the ground as he walked, or else he'd topple backwards without any support.

A short, silent elevator ride followed, carrying to two up toward the upper echelons of the Hub. The view of Terra was soon lost behind the metal superstructure, instead replaced by the dazzling brilliance of the galaxy. To one side, the stars' illumination was overwhelmed by the fierce light of Sol, but the other was a glorious canvas of light and colour. And they said space was dead and empty. It felt like every hair on Rhys's body stood up on end at the wonderful sight. It never failed to awe him, no matter how many times he saw it; no matter how many times he flew out into that great expanse.

Situated at the top and bottom of Star Hub were the two shuttle bays. There were several ways to and from the Hub, but the shuttle system was by far the most common. Rhys had never quite trusted the shuttles, but given recent events wasn't about to choose the teleporters over them. The other option, the space elevator, was horrifically slow in comparison, and was generally just reserved for those who couldn't handle the powerful g-forces in the shuttles.

The shuttle bay was massive, with two rows of shuttles stretching almost as far as Rhys could see. There must have been nearly a hundred of the small, dozen-capacity crafts, with empty bays for several dozen more. The air was cold, and even with his thick coat of fur Rhys could feel the crisp chill emanating through the barely-heated hangar.

A shuttle was already prepared and ready to accept Rhys and the major. They were directed to one about halfway down the hangar. Green lights around the open doors made it obvious which was theirs. No one else was ready to board, and as soon as they took their seats, the doors closed behind them. They were to be alone. In all that time, no one had spoken to Rhys. The major had fallen into silence. The engineers who had guided them to the shuttle and ensured they were buckled in correctly spoke amongst themselves, but none addressed Rhys directly. He had been met with silence and indifference.

Unlike the shuttles on Ceres, these were manned. Terra simply had too many destinations, with too much air traffic to risk fully automated craft zipping around through the upper atmosphere. Autopilots still controlled the shuttles, but there was always a pilot ready to intervene if necessary. The pilot soon ran through the safety briefing, advising her two passengers to remain seated at all times. It would take them just over half an hour to reach their destination.

With the major still seemingly reluctant to talk to him at all, it promised to be a quiet journey, giving Rhys time to think about what was going to happen next. The closer to Terra they got, the more a cold dread spread through him. He almost wished they had taken the teleporters after all.

chapter eleven

The shuttle came to rest in a large, open field. A couple of hundred metres away was a sprawling complex of buildings that made up the Mount Cotton Space Exploration and Research precinct, on the outskirts of the city of Brisbane. Though it was one of the smallest research facilities in Australia, it was still considered one of the best. Rhys still wasn't sure why he had been summoned there of all places. Sydney would have been the more obvious place, but this was evidently where Admiral Garter and Major Wilson had expected him to go.

The sun was low in the sky when the shuttle doors opened. Rhys flung his arm in front of his face as he stepped out onto the hot bitumen tarmac, yelping as the heat sent stinging pain through his bare footpads. Combined with the heat emanating out from the engines, which had yet to shut down, and the hot evening Australian air, the temperature was almost unbearable to Rhys.

He quickly jumped across to the nearby grass, not wanting to linger on the scorching landing pad for any longer than he had to. It wasn't until he turned around, that he realised the major hadn't come out of the shuttle with him. He just caught sight of Major Wilson as the shuttle door closed. The engines didn't power down, instead starting to rumble and roar louder again. Clapping his hands over his ears, Rhys recoiled as the shuttle started to gather speed, before launching back into the air a short distance away.

There was one person out to meet him from the precinct, though they said nothing in greeting. Instead they just gestured for him to follow, and the human turned around without waiting for him to respond. Already he could feel sweat trickling through his fur. That had been something untested in the cool, air-conditioned corridors on

Ceres. He knew most animals weren't able to sweat, but apparently starats were still capable of it. His shirt was going to be drenched even before he made it to the nearest buildings. With a weary sigh, Rhys started to walk after his silent greeter.

The Mount Cotton precinct consisted of three large, modern buildings grouped together at the top of a low hill. The large grounds were mostly empty, just pale yellow grass that looked like it hadn't gotten enough rain for a long time. It felt slightly crispy beneath Rhys's feet. Away to his right, near the distant border wall, was a large, brick structure that looked rather out of place, especially when compared to the gleaming metal and glass of the main precinct. There was none of Twitch's imagined strawberry scent on the air.

A few other smaller buildings dotted the grounds. Their purposes weren't immediately apparent to Rhys, but he was able to hazard a few guesses for some of them. He knew there had to be an armoury, a research workshop, and likely a detached barracks or dormitory for the ground forces that were based here. Some facilities kept the teleporters separate to the main building too. Rhys wondered how much time he would have to explore the grounds, if any at all. He knew it was possible he wouldn't be allowed to walk around by himself at all.

"Who am I even here to see?" Rhys asked his silent greeter. He was not particularly surprised when he didn't respond at all. He didn't glance back, or even make any acknowledgement he had heard Rhys. He may as well have been mute and deaf.

Rhys sighed and dropped back into silence as they came to the access road that led up to the front of the facility. At least inside he would be able to get out of the oppressive summer heat that beat down on his back. Though the human ahead walked on the road, Rhys stayed on the grass beside it to avoid blistering his feet on the hot tarmac.

The access road terminated at a wide car park that was sparsely filled with only a couple of vehicles. At the far end, a small rise of stairs led onto an open plaza surrounded on three sides by the nearest of the towering buildings. The empire's insignia was suspended above the plaza between the two rows of flags that represented the historical nations that had come together to support the global defence organisation. It all felt rather grand and intimidating.

Rhys dashed across the carpark as quick as he could behind his escort, staying on the cooler white lines as much as possible. He was grateful when the doors opened for them both. Rhys stumbled back at the blast of icy cold air that poured out from the air-conditioned reception. He shivered as his shirt, plastered against his fur, started to cool. "Fucking Australia," he muttered beneath his breath.

Rhys turned his attention to the reception area. His escort had already disappeared behind the desk and into one of the back rooms. Rhys paused, not sure if he was meant to follow. He decided to wait, sure the human would come back out to fetch him if he was needed.

The reception area was open to the authorised public, and so it was designed to be a face of the organisation to civilians. Recruitment posters plastered one wall, with sign up forms just beneath them. A television was suspended from the ceiling in one corner of the room, a news story about something in Sydney playing. His ears flattened when he heard the words 'starat captain'.

Cursing quietly again, Rhys spun around so he could ignore the news report. They had been expecting him in Sydney. Perhaps that explained why he'd been shunted away to somewhere like Mount Cotton, seemingly without much notice.

Someone emerged from the room out behind the desk, not the same person as before. He didn't seem to have noticed Rhys until the starat approached and cleared his throat. The human looked up. "Ah, good timing, starat. I need you to take this up to E14," he said, holding out a thick folder of papers.

Rhys blinked a few times, making absolutely no effort to take the bundle from the human. Instead he tapped the insignia on his shirt. "I'm Captain Griffiths. I just landed in a shuttle from the Hub with Major Wilson. I was following someone, but they uh... I didn't see where they went."

The folder was slowly lowered down to the desk again as the human stared at Rhys. His eyes flicked beyond the starat, towards the television, then back to Rhys again.

"Ah. Um."

Flustered, the receptionist tossed aside the bundle of papers and left the desk, disappearing into the back room once again. The door slammed shut. Muffled conversation reached Rhys's ears, though he couldn't make out the individual words. The door soon opened again, and the receptionist returned. He squinted down at a small scribbled note. "You need to go to B9."

"And how do I get there?"

The receptionist seemed to put all of his will into not rolling his eyes. Instead he pointed to something behind Rhys and to his left. An elevator. "Up to floor B, then to your right. I trust you won't get lost."

"I'm sure I'll be fine," Rhys retorted. He didn't like the thinly veiled insult in the human's words, but nor did he have the desire to correct the receptionist either. It was a bother he could deal with later. Instead he just made his way to the elevator. There was a swipe pad to open the doors for an ID card. He was about to turn back to the receptionist to ask for one, before there was a small buzz from behind the desk. A few moments later, the door opened. All the while he could feel the human's eyes as they bored into his back.

Rhys was grateful for the doors to close behind him, so he could get away from the strange looks the human had been giving him. He pressed the button for the elevator to take him up one level, then waited as it slowly worked its way upwards. When the doors opened again, Rhys stepped out into a long corridor that reminded him of a school. Doors opened out on both sides of the corridor, stretching out an equal distance either way. Each door had a small number on it, evens on one side, odds on the other. It didn't take him long to find B9.

What he found behind the door was a small room with a single table and two chairs. A small water cooler was pushed into one corner, with an air-conditioning unit just above. A clock ticked on the opposite wall, and a lone window provided light. The whole room was barely larger than a supply cupboard.

After checking the number above the door was indeed right, Rhys helped himself to some water in a little plastic cup from the cooler, then flopped down in one of the supplied chairs and rested his feet on the edge of the table. He looked out the window. He wasn't very high up, but the facility was built on top of a hill, and he could see the rolling grassland for quite some distance. Not far away was a vineyard, and close to the horizon he could see the start of the urban sprawl that surrounded the nearest city of Brisbane.

Minutes ticked by, but no one came in. An hour came and went. A few people walked past, but though Rhys kept the door open, not a single one looked in. Even when he called out to a human's retreating back, he was completely ignored. There was no sign of anyone with any sort of authority.

Rhys started to pace around the small room. He wanted to go back down to the reception and demand to know what was going on, but nor did he want to leave and risk missing the person who was meant to be meeting him. All he could do was refill his cup of water from the cooler and wait.

Eventually his bladder started to protest the water he'd been drinking, and he was forced to leave the room in search of some bathrooms. He paced through the unfamiliar corridors slowly, trying to find any signs to guide the way, or any staff to direct him. He found neither. Activity could be heard on the floors above, but whatever this floor was used for, it was quiet and near deserted.

He found what he sought at the far end of the corridor. Taking a few minutes afterwards to give the fur around his face a quick groom and clean, Rhys returned back to his isolation room feeling a little better about himself. His fur was still a little damp, and he wanted a clean shirt, but he felt he was as presentable as he could be, given the circumstances.

Rhys was surprised to find the room was not empty when he got back. Someone was sat in the chair opposite where Rhys had been sitting before. His shirt and epaulettes indicated he was a captain, but Rhys couldn't recall crossing paths with the man in front of him before. It was hard to tell, given he was sat down, but the captain didn't appear to be too tall, though Rhys supposed the human still had reasonable advantage of height on him. On the table was a tablet and a folder, which appeared to be full of paper.

"Door," the captain commanded, before gesturing down to the chair opposite. Rhys quickly obliged, tucking his tail to the side before lowering himself down onto the seat. As Rhys sat down, the human switched on his tablet, angling it up so Rhys couldn't see the screen. A small red light started to shine on the back. "Captain Rhys Griffiths?"

"That's correct. May I ask who I'm-" Rhys started to say, before he was interrupted by a raised hand from the human and a sharp glare. Rhys swallowed and fell silent.

The human picked up the tablet and spoke into it. "This is Captain Adam Rivers of the Terran Inquisition and Investigation

Unit. This is the preliminary interview with Captain Rhys Griffiths, captain of the *Harvester* and most recently posted at the Normandy Spaceport on Ceres. This interview is being conducted at the Mount Cotton Exploration and Research Centre and is being recorded."

"Why am I here?" Rhys asked. He leaned forward in his seat and slipped his tail beneath the table, mainly so Captain Rivers couldn't see how puffed up it was.

The captain slowly turned on his heel to look down at Rhys. With the tablet still in his hand, he said, "You are being investigated over a number of matters, Mr Griffiths. We have a number of concerns about your continued ability to serve in relation to your treatment of starats, and your proximity to the former Captain Aaron Lee."

Rhys had expected something like that. "You think I helped Captain Lee defect?" he growled. His hands gripped onto the table, claws digging into the wood. "I've already explained my case to Chancellor Roberts. I have said everything about it, and there is nothing there to connect me to Captain Lee in his last few months. I don't know why he chose to defect, but I had nothing to do with it."

Captain Rivers waited for Rhys to finish. Slowly, he placed the tablet back down on the table, then leaned down to press his palms flat either side of it. "You are here because Chancellor Roberts found your position to be highly suspect. You are here because we know you helped Captain Lee escape. A confession now will certainly improve your standing, so what's it going to be, Mr Griffiths?"

"I did not do it," Rhys replied. His claws scratched at the table as he gripped it tightly.

"We have logs. Proof of communication between *Harvester* and *Terrestrial Dawn*."

Rhys flicked his ears and blinked. "Well, yes. I sent some messages to Captain Lee to arrange when we would be able to catch up on Mars."

"While you were on Ceres?" Captain Rivers grinned wolfishly.

"What? No. I never sent anything to Captain Lee then. I didn't speak to him at all between my departure from Romulus and his arrival at Ceres," Rhys replied. He knew that for a fact. Not once had he spoken to Aaron during that time. A cold shiver ran down his spine and into his tail.

"Slipped your mind, has it? Maybe I should remind you," Captain Rivers growled. He opened the folder and scattered a number of pages across the table. With trembling hands, Rhys picked up the one that had fallen closest to him. It was a list of communications, and as Rivers had suggested, they were all between his ship and Aaron's. The dates correlated to his time on Ceres, starting the day after he had landed at Normandy.

"I never authorised these. This wasn't me," Rhys whispered.

"Full status reports of the Normandy defences. Rosters of staff and crew. Tell me, does this sound like the messages of someone who knew Captain Lee was going to defect?" Captain Rivers demanded. He slammed his hand down on the table when Rhys didn't answer. Rhys could only shake his head in shock, sifting through page after page of incriminating evidence. This wasn't him. He couldn't explain it.

"Someone on my ship did this," he said quietly. He swallowed and looked up to Captain Rivers. He tried to stop his hands trembling, but he could not manage it. "Give me access to my crew. Accompany me if you must. Let me question them. Someone betrayed the empire, but it was not me."

"So you can spread your lies to the rest of your crew? I don't think so," Captain Rivers growled. He started to gather up the scattered pages and snatched some of them from Rhys's hands. "I know those messages required your authority to send. You knew of them, and your confession will be required."

Rhys shook his head. "It wasn't me. I will prove it to you. Just let me speak to my crew."

"If that's the way it's going to be." Captain Rivers picked up the tablet and started to speak into again, pacing around the room. "Captain Rhys Griffiths has shown reluctance to confess. He shall remain detained within the confines of the detention facilities at the Research Centre, and he will not be permitted to leave. His behaviour shall be monitored, and should any further interviews be required, they shall be recorded and submitted as evidence."

"Please, just give me this chance," Rhys protested, but again he was interrupted by Captain Rivers.

"Would you rather be handcuffed in a cell? Nothing would please me more, but I'm forced to stick to protocol here. But if you push me, then I will not hesitate to use force. And yes. I am willing to say that on record."

Rhys hissed in displeasure, but he didn't say anything to argue. He knew he was innocent, and while he knew that Captain Rivers would be biased against him at every step, he would clear his name. The evidence Rivers had presented was false. It had to be. There could be no evidence against him, because there wasn't any. There was no way he would be found guilty. He just had to ignore all the jabs and insults the human used to get a rise out of him. He took a deep breath.

"I will prove myself. I am innocent," he said. The words felt like barbs in his throat. "I'll do whatever you want, but I will never confess to this."

Captain Rivers nodded once. He pushed a couple of buttons on the tablet screen. "Captain Rhys Griffiths has accepted the terms of his detainment. This concludes the interview."

The red light switched off as Captain Rivers lowered the tablet down to the table. "A room has been prepared for you on Level J. I'll escort you."

Rhys shook his head and suppressed an annoyed growl. "I can find my own way up."

"The elevators can only be controlled using a passcard. One which you will not be issued with," Captain Rivers explained. He gathered together all the reports and transcripts and returned them to the folder, then tucked the tablet beneath his arm and straightened his shirt. "Just remember that we will be watching you very closely, do you understand? You will not be allowed any communications outside of this facility. Now come."

Rhys reluctantly followed Rivers out, taking the plastic cup with him, which he turned over and over in his hands. Not a single word was spoken between them as they shared the elevator up towards one of the top floors. Rhys didn't want to think about how he was being confined to the building, if he wasn't being issued a passcard. No matter how they might call it, he was being held a prisoner here. His tail twitched back and forth, but despite his aggravation, he still felt surprisingly calm. He knew what he needed to do, and it wouldn't help matters by getting stressed about it all.

The doors opened, revealing a small corridor which led to just a single door, which had been left ajar. Captain Rivers didn't even attempt to leave the elevator, just gesturing for Rhys to get out. The door started to close, before the human put his arm out to prevent it. Rhys half-turned to look up at him. "And one more thing," Captain Rivers said, as though there hadn't been any pause in conversation. "I don't want to hear or see anything of you, outside of our little interviews. Understood?"

Rhys smiled bitterly at the captain. "Of course, sir." The captain let the door close at last. Rhys waited until he could hear the elevator whisk the human away to whatever floor he needed to be on. Only then did he push open the traditional, wooden doors. He stepped out into a large, open room that had the look of a communal lounge. The first thing he noticed was the cameras. There were dozens of them wired up around the room. From a quick glance, Rhys could tell that they were able to see everything in the room. Several couches were spread out across the floor, loosely centred around a massive television that dominated the wall closest to the entry. What looked like several gaming systems were tucked beneath it. A little kitchen and a dining area were over by the wide windows that replaced most of the walls. In one corner was an automated service hatch. A small corridor led away to six more rooms, all with an engraved number above the lintel.

Rhys pushed open the door to the nearest room. Inside was a surprisingly comfortable looking bedroom. A wide double bed took up half the room, with a walk-in wardrobe hidden behind a full mirrored door opposite. Another door led through to an adjoined private bathroom. Nowhere was free of cameras. They appeared to be able to see everywhere. If Rhys was to be kept as an effective prisoner here, then his quarters were better than he could have expected. There were no windows inside the little bedroom, but out in the lounge, Rhys had an incredible view. This high up, he was even able to see the distant glittering of the ocean. If this was to be his prison, then at least he was going to be comfortable.

He didn't expect anyone to disturb him and he didn't worry about the cameras. Rhys removed his shirt and tossed into onto the bed, before he spread himself out on one of the couches. At least he had a beautiful vista out the window. Here he was. Getting ready for a fight to keep his career. Maybe even his life. One more night where he could maintain any hope of relaxing.

***

Rhys hadn't meant to fall asleep on the couch, but he woke with the early-morning sun blazing in his eyes. He shielded his eyes with his arm as he slowly sat up. His neck was sore from where he had been lying awkwardly.

Sometime during the night he'd managed to slip free of his trousers. He didn't bother putting them back on again, just letting his underwear preserve his modesty. He didn't expect anyone to see him from ten stories above the ground. Rummaging around the small kitchen for some breakfast, he found supplies for some toast and a cup of coffee, but nothing else. To his annoyance there was no tea. The only cup he was able to find was almost comically oversized for him, but it would do.

As he ate, he wandered around the floor, exploring what else was up here. He poked his head into the other five rooms, but they were all identical to the first, with nothing interesting to see. There was a fire escape too, but a quick test proved the door to be locked. He could only hope it would unlock if the fire alarms ever went off, or else he'd be in a bit of trouble.

He returned back to the lounge room and froze. A human was stood in the doorway. She scoffed at the sight of Rhys's mostly naked body but said nothing. In her hands was a large bag, which she tossed onto the sofa before she turned to leave.

"Will I be expecting Captain Rivers today?" Rhys asked to her retreating back. He got no answer. Not even an indication that he had been heard. She just closed the door without a word. Through the door, Rhys could hear the elevator open and close. He sighed and scratched behind his ear.

He shook his head in frustration and took a sip of his coffee. He let out a fierce curse as he did so too quickly, and the hot liquid slipped out the side of his muzzle and spilled down his chest. Carefully but quickly, he put his cup down on a table and wiped away most of the coffee before it burned him too badly, before taking a much more careful sip from the cup.

Trapped where he was, Rhys knew that he should probably do something a little productive with his time, if he could. After carefully draining the rest of his coffee, he started to rummage through the bag. It was mostly full of uniform with empire insignia on the shoulders, and a few basic supplies. At the bottom was a small laptop. He powered it up and placed it on one of the coffee tables, only to find it had been wiped clean.

He contemplated putting some clothes on, but he decided that he probably wouldn't get any more visitors. He expected some sort of warning before someone like Captain Rivers arrived to interrogate him further. Besides, it wasn't like he had much to wear. The provided uniform would never fit him, as he noticed it was all designed for a human to wear.

Instead, Rhys settled down with a fresh cup of coffee and a nice view. He started to record down everything he could recall about his last meeting with Aaron Lee. He didn't want to miss anything out, providing every possible piece of evidence he could that there had been no collusion between the two old friends. This had been entirely Aaron's decision, and Rhys had had nothing to do with it. He just had to prove that to Captain Rivers and any other doubters.

For most of the day, Rhys sat and worked. He only got up for more coffee, or to take a quick bathroom break. There were no summons from Captain Rivers to distract him, and no word about the arrival of his crew, though he doubted they would be following, given the charges that had been laid against him. He was left alone to work, and by the onset of evening, his hands were starting to cramp up from the amount of typing he'd been doing. Unsure if there was enough to exonerate him, he had nevertheless compiled a reasonable list of everything he could recall, covering a vast majority of the day he'd spent in Romulus. All of it had been spent in areas where security footage could be pulled up. If they doubted his memory, he would be able to demand the evidence that backed him up.

Standing up and stretching his arms above his head, he could feel his back crack a couple of times as his spine straightened for what felt like the first time in hours. He decided to indulge in a long shower to get his fur properly cleaned from the dirt and grime of a few days of travel. The water was nicer than it was on Ceres, cleaner and fresher. It soaked through his fur and made him feel heavy and slow. As always though, the problem was with drying out again. Only a single towel had been provided, and it wasn't long before that was even wetter than he was, and his fur was still drenched.

He tried to put the cameras out of his mind as he wandered around the small apartment with only the soaked towel around his waist to preserve his modesty. He was sure there would be someone watching his every move. A half-naked starat probably wasn't what they had wanted to watch as he rummaged through the kitchen, but he didn't have any other choice. He would have to talk to Twitch and ask him how starats usually dealt with drying off. If he ever saw him again. His ears and tail drooped.

Not only was there no food but for half a loaf of bread, but the realisation that he was probably never going to see his crew again really hit home. It had been a thought that had lingered towards the back of his mind for most of the day. Now it came to the fore. He closed his eyes and sighed softly. There had to be something he could do, but right now he really didn't know what. Captain Rivers had already made up his mind. Or made up the evidence. Neither benefitted Rhys or gave him a way out.

Rhys had almost resigned himself to another meal of unbuttered toast when he noticed a small beep from the corner of the room. He could vaguely recall it a few times previously, but he had never gone to investigate it before. To his surprise, it was from the service hatch. When he opened it up he saw a small tray of food inside. On the plate was a surprisingly generous serve of meat, potatoes, and vegetables. All covered in cold, half-congealed gravy. There was even a small glass of wine – in a plastic cup, Rhys was quick to notice.

He took hold of the tray and paused. There was a piece of paper on the bottom. He shifted his position slightly to try and place his back between the tray and the nearest camera as he slipped the sheet out. He quickly glanced down and read the single handwritten line, then scrunched up the piece of paper and secreted it in his palm as he took hold of the tray and carried it away from the hatch.

Tonight. 9pm. Fire Escape. Wear nothing.

Rhys didn't know who the note was from, but he tried not to think about it too much. He didn't want to look too deep in thought, lest he attract unwanted attention from the invisible onlookers through the cameras. Instead he just focused on his meal. It was cold, and it had likely been in the hatch for over an hour, but it was still enough to ease the hunger in his stomach.

As he ate, he looked out over the view from his windows. The sun was low and cast long shadows over the grounds and the nearby vineyards. He still had a few more hours to wait. For that time he would have plenty of time to think about the note and wonder who had sent it. He knew he was asking for too much to expect it to be from his crew. They didn't know where he was, and surely couldn't have acted so fast. It had to be someone within the facility, and for that his attention wandered to starats. Were there any of them here? Had they sent the note? From what he knew of them, the request to wear nothing wasn't too surprising, though he did have to wonder why.

He wouldn't learn anything until then. Aware that he could be awake late, especially if this was some improbable rescue, Rhys lay back on the couch. He would allow himself to have a quick nap so that he was awake and alert for whatever was about to happen, as he had always been good at waking up when he needed to. He closed his eyes and tried to let his mind relax.

***

It was dark when Rhys woke up. He suffered a moment of panic, afraid he had slept too long, but then he caught sight of the clock on the laptop. Still only 8:30. He breathed a quick sigh of relief and rubbed his eyes as he sat up. His fur finally felt mostly dry, but it stuck up unevenly in some places where he had been lying on it. Much of the half an hour he had left was spent trying to flatten down the rough patches, but without much success.

The last few minutes he paced back and forth around his confines with just the towel to preserve his dignity for the hidden onlookers through the camera. He managed to keep his eyes away from the fire escape, despite the temptation to keep looking in that direction. He couldn't give his watchers any indication that something was about to happen. To keep up the pretence he twirled a pen in his hand and tapped it against his chin a few times, as though he was in deep thought about something. Occasionally he'd even run to the coffee table and scribble something down in rough handwriting on the paper provided there.

When something finally did happen, Rhys almost missed it. A small noise caught his attention. His ear flicked and he quickly glanced towards the fire exit, which had opened just a crack. Wide brown eyes stared from the small crack. He dropped his pen mid-toss, but he regained his senses quickly enough that he was able to kick the pen before it landed to send it skittering across the floor. It came to rest just where he wanted it; right by the open fire exit.

For show, he muttered a curse to himself and hurried after it. He crouched down to retrieve the pen, expecting to have a quiet, muttered conversation with the starat behind the door, but instead two hands tugged on his shoulder and pulled him through. A second starat quickly darted back into the room and stole Rhys's towel in the same movement. The door was closed again almost before Rhys had a chance to protest it, and a finger was placed on his lips before he said anything.

"Up. Quickly," the starat whispered. She stared at Rhys with wide eyes, then flicked her head up. "Go, now."

Rhys didn't need to be told again. Still in a daze about what was happening, he hurried up the flight of stairs that wound up the middle of the building. All around him was grey concrete and red metal handrails. No cameras. No one but a single starat to see his nakedness. His tail tucked up between his legs to cover his crotch as the other starat pulled him to a halt on the next stairwell up. She handed him a bundle of clothes, which looked like they had once belonged to a human child. He quickly dressed into the torn and faded jeans, and a t-shirt that bore the logo of a superhero. One of his favourites when he had been a child, as it happened. The jeans hung low on his hips as there was no hole for his tail.

"Give me a boost, will you?" the starat said when Rhys had fully dressed. She pointed up to a red metal pipe that ran around the wall near the ceiling. The fire sprinklers.

Rhys cupped his hands together for the starat to stand on, then he lifted her up so she could reach the sprinkler system. He grunted a bit with her weight, but it didn't take long for her to fiddle with one of the valves and replace it. When she was done, she gestured for Rhys to lower her down.

The starat appraised Rhys with interested eyes for a few moments, before she grinned widely. "Well, here you are. I'm Emilia. Nice to meet you." She held out her hand for Rhys to take.

"Captain Rhys Griffiths. Can I ask... what's going on?"

Emilia's eyes widened. "Oh, you are him! Leandro thought you might be. He wanted to meet you, so we arranged for Taylor in there to cover for you while you're away. Just for a few hours, but we thought you might like to get out of there as well. Cameras have a little blind spot, just by the fire door. Quick bit of emergency maintenance in the fire escape later, and here we are."

Rhys blinked as he struggled to follow all of that. He didn't quite have it all, but he nodded anyway. "I see," he said. He paused for a moment and pointed back down the stairs. "He looked nothing like me."

"Because humans will notice the difference," Emilia said with a smirk. She then grabbed at Rhys's hand and pulled him along. "Come on, Leandro is dying to meet you."

"And who is that?"

Emilia glanced back up at Rhys as she pulled him down the stairs. "Oh, he is wonderful. You'll love him, don't worry. Everyone always does." She grinned widely. "I think he'll love you too. Especially if you have a good story to tell."

Rhys had to hurry to keep up with Emilia. She bounded down the stairwell with a dexterity and grace that Rhys still wasn't able to achieve. He was so much better with his gait now, but he didn't feel ready to sprint down a set of concrete stairs with so many abrupt turns as it descended. She waited for him on the ground floor. Her finger went to her lips. "Out there try and look like you know what you're doing. There may still be a few humans around, but most would have gone to their quarters by now."

Rhys nodded and pinned his ears back as Emilia pushed open the door. He half expected someone to shout out as he stepped through, but everything was silent in the reception area. The lights were dimmed, with just the out of hours lights still illuminated. It gave everything a slightly eerie feeling.

Emilia led him out the front doors. The air was still sticky and warm, even so long after the sun had set. Already it felt like Rhys's fur was plastered down beneath his clothes. He glanced up. The sky was clear, and the half-moon shone bright in the sky. Even the dark side was lit up with a spider web of lights from all the factories and workshops that were active non-stop. Luna was called the beating heart of the empire's industry for a reason.

Rhys's eyes dropped to a closer focus. Their destination was a small, brick building that backed onto the perimeter wall. It looked old, and it was crumbling in a few places. Small holes were visible near the roof, and most of the windows had no glass in them. To the side was the remnants of a brick gateway that had long ago been closed off by the construction of the more modern perimeter wall.

The wooden front door was swollen from the heat and humidity, and the wood felt soft to Rhys's hand. It was held ajar, and when Rhys pushed it open it resisted the pressure, scraping noisily on the stone floor. The stink of mould made his nose twitch.

Inside, the air was warm and still, with barely a breeze to speak of. It was oppressive. Rhys couldn't imagine living in a place like this. It was dark and dingy, with just a couple of lights swinging from the high ceiling to provide illumination. The constant drip drip drip of a pipe leaking made Rhys's ears twitch.

Directly to the left of the entry was a tiny antechamber. The door had fallen off its hinges, and was now simply propped up against the concrete wall. Inside were some rolls of blankets and bedding, all dirty and torn.

"Come on, through here. They're expecting you," Emilia encouraged, directing Rhys through the dark corridors. A quiet murmuring emanated from further along, the whispering of a few dozen voices.

Further down the corridor were two doorways. One opened to a crumbling set of stairs that led to a lower level beneath the surface. The smell of rot and decay wafted up from down there. Emilia guided Rhys towards the other archway, which opened out into a large hall. The room was a little lighter thanks to the row of windows that ran down one wall at human head height. The starats were all sat together in one corner. A few kits were amongst them, all gathered around an old, grey-furred starat with just one ear.

Everyone turned to look towards Rhys and Emilia as they entered the hall. A hush fell across the room as the old starat rose to his feet.

"I have been to every planet and desolate rock in the Terran Empire, and yet you are like no starat I have ever seen before," the grey-furred starat said as he approached. Rhys got the impression his aged eyes saw more than was in front of him. Behind him the other starats looked at Rhys with curiosity. "Would you care to introduce yourself?"

Rhys stepped forward, looking around the small group of starats. "My name is Rhys Griffiths, captain of the *Harvester*. At least, I think I still am."

A stunned silence met his words.

The grey-furred starat was the first to compose himself, holding his hand out to Rhys. "So you are him? There is a story there, I can feel it; more interesting than any I have to tell."

"Leandro, you do yourself an injustice. Your stories are fascinating," a starat said from amongst the crowd. Another voice approved this, and then another and another. Soon it was a cheer in defence of Leandro and his stories.

Leandro smiled at the praise. Though he bowed his head, his ear had perked up. It was obvious to Rhys that the older starat enjoyed the attention his younger companions gave him.

"You may call my stories fascinating, but already I can tell this starat must have seen and done far more than I could even dream of," Leandro said. He gestured to Rhys to follow him back to the others. "Come Captain Rhys. Take a seat with me. Let us hear your story. It would be good to hear a new one."

Rhys nervously approached the expectant group. "I don't know if I can do such an introduction justice, but I can try," he said. He took a seat a little outside the circle, which quickly reformed so that he was in the centre anyway.

Once again, Rhys started to go through the story of how he had come to be a starat, telling them everything that had happened to him since he had learned of Aaron's defection to the CGP. His audience drank in every word. An awed light shone in Leandro's eyes. When he told them about how Cooper had attacked him there was a collective intake of breath; fear evident in everyone's eyes and ears. He was sure there were more than a few starats present who had felt the wrath of their human owners before.

Another ripple of fear passed through the starats when he mentioned his confrontation with Cardinal Erik. He wasn't surprised. The Vatican's view on starats had always been poor, ever since the very first had been paraded out from the nearby Carindale Research Centre. They had failed in suppressing the genetic research that had gone into creating starats, and they had failed again in preventing their release into public life, but they had succeeded in ensuring they had no freedom or independence. A mentality Rhys himself had bought into.

Upon the conclusion of his tale, recounting his arrival at Mount Cotton and the unpleasant allegations placed before him, Rhys looked around the room at all the starats. They were all rapt with attention, hanging on to every word he said. Never before, not even during his small spell lecturing at the Cardiff Academy, had he experienced such a devoted audience. There hadn't been a single interruption while he had been talking.

"A starat who was once a human?" Leandro breathed. A wide smile cracked across his muzzle. "Captain Rhys, you are most welcome here."

Rhys nodded his head and returned the smile. "I don't know how much freedom I'll be allowed. I doubt Captain Rivers would approve of my presence here at all, but I couldn't turn down the opportunity to introduce myself at least."

"The thought is most welcome," Leandro replied. He took hold of Rhys's hands in his own, cupping them between his palms. "We are quite unused to visitors of your glamour down here. Only prisoners thrown in the cells beneath our paws. The dungeon down there makes our abode look like luxury, and the poor folk who are sent down there are never in any mood to talk. Not since Toledo have I spoken with a captain of the empire."

"I'm really no one special," Rhys said. He pulled his hands free of Leandro's grip and idly scratched behind one ear. He wasn't sure how to describe it, even to himself, but he felt a little unworthy of the attention. Like a fraud. They were welcoming him as a starat, but he wasn't one. Not really. They hadn't known him as a human. They didn't know who he truly was.

"Be that as it may, we would still be happy to do anything you wish to make your stay here more comfortable," Leandro said. His words were met by several other voices speaking out in affirmation.

"There is one thing." Rhys lowered his hand and lightly gripped onto the tip of his tail. "My crew was meant to follow just a day behind me, but I've not seen any presence of them at all. I'm not permitted any outside contact here, and I doubt I could get hold of something easily. Can you find out where they are? I need to know they're safe. If you could pass a message on to them, that would be even better."

Leandro nodded, slapping Rhys on the shoulder as he did so. "Of course. That will be easy for us, Captain Rhys. We are given access to almost everything here, as the humans think we're too dumb to understand what they show us." He grinned a toothy smile and his eyes twinkled with mischief. "We have learned a lot, and we spread that knowledge throughout Terra. We're far from just dumb animals here. This is Essie's land, after all."

"I can see that," Rhys whispered. Once again he looked around at all the bright, eager eyes around him. How could he ever have thought that these were dumb beasts, worthy only of serving humans? They were more than intelligent enough to stand amongst humans as equals. Seeing them in this dark, mouldy hovel was difficult, somehow more difficult than it had been on Ceres. They deserved better, but Rhys didn't feel like he was in any power to help them here. He couldn't even help himself.

As much as Rhys wanted to stay amongst the starats long into the evening, to hear the stories everyone had been praising Leandro for, the old starat soon turned to Rhys and explained about the ruse they had created to bring Rhys out. They had created a false error in the sprinklers around the fire escape. A second error had just flagged in the system, one that required immediate attention. The parts that Emilia had installed had not fixed the problem, as was their intent. Unfortunately for Rhys, that meant he had to return back with another starat so they could swap him back around with Taylor.

Leandro himself volunteered to take Rhys back up to his rooms. Together, they made their way out of the dark and damp building and back across the grounds. The older starat walked at a pace that surprised Rhys, and Leandro chuckled when Rhys pointed that out.

"I may be over ninety, but I still have my health, Captain Rhys. I have been lucky in my owners," Leandro said. He smiled sadly, then looked up to the sky. "I have seen it all, you know. Half of starat history, nearly. So much has changed and yet so much has stayed the same. But you, Captain Rhys. You are different. You are new."

Rhys shook his head. "I'm no one special," he said as they pushed open the doors into the reception.

"There has been no starat as special as you since Essie." Leandro paused at the fire escape. A blissful smile passed across his face. "I met his son once. I was only a kit, but he was... He was everything I could have ever hoped for. I just wish I could have met Essie himself, but he died ten years before I was born."

Rhys didn't have the heart to say he didn't know who Essie was. The name was vaguely familiar to him, but he couldn't recall where he had heard it. He could tell that whoever Essie was, they were a messiah-like figure to the starats.

Then he had it, he remembered. Twitch had told him once. Essie had been the first. The first generation of starats had all been created in a laboratory, so not all starats were descended from him, but still they revered him as their father. Not Rhys though. He had never even heard of Essie before Twitch had mentioned him. There was so much about him that made him stand out from starats. He didn't know if he could ever truly call himself one, but he was so obviously not human either.

He ascended the concrete staircase in silence. Leandro respected that and didn't say anything until they reached the right level. Once they made it, Leandro placed his hand on Rhys's shoulder. "It has been a pleasure to meet you, Captain Rhys, but here is where we part for now. And I do apologise, but you will need to undress."

Rhys grimaced, but he started to strip down as Leandro opened the door by a few centimetres. The older starat dropped his voice to a whisper. "I shall pass on a message to your crew. Is there anything you would like to say?"

Rhys flicked his ears, then nodded. "Address it to Lieutenant Scott. Ask if he'd still like to play that game of tennis. He'll know it's me then."

Leandro flashed another smile. He pulled out a square of folded blue fabric and put it in Rhys's hands. "Hide this in the towel when you swap with Taylor. If you need our help in an emergency, put this up in a window. We'll see it and come as soon as we can," he said, then flicked his tail. "We'll signal with a red cloth in the trees by the perimeter wall when we plan on fetching you. Go now, Captain Rhys. Be safe."

Rhys was aware of a shadow moving on the other side of the door. The door opened a little wider, and Taylor darted out. The towel quickly exchanged hands, and Rhys tucked Leandro's gift down the front. He hurried in and the door closed behind him. He was alone once more.

As Rhys walked away from the fire escape, the joy of his brief freedom started to ebb away. Already it had started to feel like a bizarre dream, and only the presence of the fabric down the front of his towel made it seem real. He rubbed his muzzle and sighed as he looked down across the grounds from his vantage point. Through the gloom he could just about make out the trees Leandro had mentioned. He knew already that he would long for a flash of red amongst them.

He turned away from the windows and sat down on the still unused bed. He lay on his side and peered down into the towel to see what Leandro had given him. He couldn't help but smile as he recognised a flag. It was the historic standard of Australia. It hadn't been used in any official capacity since Australia had joined the combined Terran Empire two centuries ago. He slipped out of the towel and folded it and the flag up, before he tucked them both under his bed. He would only use it when he absolutely had to.

There wasn't much left to occupy Rhys's time. The internet required a password he didn't have, and the television couldn't access any external channels, just the official recruitment videos looping over and over again. The gaming systems were all wiped clean, with no games to run. If Captain Rivers was trying to bore Rhys into a false confession, then he just had to wonder how long he'd be able to last.

Lying back on the bed with the recruitment videos playing as background noise, Rhys closed his eyes and tried to sort out some sort of plan. There had to be something he could do, both for himself and for the starats. Their species had started here. Could he help them take the next step forward as well?

***

It was agonising for Rhys to just wait around, knowing there should be a sense of urgency to everything he did. For two whole days he debated various solutions to himself, but all of them had the same, major flaw. He simply had no way of influencing the world outside of his room. He hadn't even seen Captain Rivers in all that time, and nor had the starats come to see him again. It had been a lonely and frustrating time.

When finally the isolation ended, it didn't bring Rhys any relief from the frustration. He could hear the elevator doors open, and he quickly hurried to get some clothes on. He slipped on his shirt just as Captain Rivers opened the door.

Captain Rivers took a seat on the couch and placed his tablet and cup of instant coffee down on the table. He gestured for Rhys to stand in front of him. "So," River said. He leaned back. The tablet was already recording. "Whatever it is you're trying to do with the cameras, it won't work."

Rhys tilted his head to the side, confused. "What? I'm not doing anything with them. I haven't even touched them."

"Then why do they keep glitching like there's some interference coming from in these rooms?" Captain Rivers pressed.

Rhys spread his arms wide. "I can't answer that, Captain. I haven't been doing anything."

Captain Rivers frowned and narrowed his eyes. "We'll be watching you. Don't think you can do anything and have it escape our attention. And for Veritas' sake, wear more clothes."

Rhys huffed and twitched his muzzle. "Provide more clothes that fit me then. And a hairdryer so I can actually dry my fur," he growled. He plucked at his shirt, which was dirty from a few days of not being able to wash it. "And someone to come and do my laundry at least."

"I'll consider it. But if you provide a confession, you won't need to stay here at all."

Rhys tried to grind his teeth together, but the needle-like things weren't designed for that. Instead he just let out a low growl. "I'm telling you, Captain Rivers, I did not do it. I'm willing to help you find the real traitor, but it is not me."

"Don't try to weasel out of this, because it will never work. We have the evidence," Captain Rivers retorted. He took a sip of his coffee. "Do you want me to bring that all up again?"

Rhys shook his head and rubbed his muzzle. "That won't be necessary," he said. His voice quivered slightly as he picked up the laptop. "I compiled together everything I can remember from my meeting with Lee on Mars. If you wanted to read through it, I'm sure there will be something that conflicts with your evidence."

Captain Rivers sneered as he took hold of the laptop. He didn't even look at it as he tucked it beneath his arm. "You must understand that there's no use in denying it. Either I will extract a confession from you, or the Vatican will. They're already itching to get their hands on you."

Rhys flicked his ears and clutched at his tail. "I have done nothing to them. I have done nothing to you, or to TIE," he whispered. He lowered his eyes. "Please. Just let me speak to my crew."

"They're not your crew anymore. A new captain has been assigned to the *Harvester*. Once the crew has been interrogated for any lingering, misguided loyalty towards you, the ship will be redeployed," Captain Rivers said. The force of his words felt like a punch to Rhys's gut. The captain stood up and loomed tall over Rhys. "If you confess, then maybe I could even get you a position in the services crew."

Rhys remained silent. He had barely even heard the offer. His thoughts were still on the abrupt declaration about his crew. All he had worked for was in danger of being removed with just the stroke of someone's pen. If someone was appointed captain of the *Harvester* without properly dismissing Rhys, then the empire was effectively admitting he no longer existed. Found guilty of associating with Aaron or not, there could be no recovery from that.

"I'll be back tomorrow," Captain Rivers said.

Rhys barely responded. He couldn't talk. His whole body felt numb. Even if he was able to clear his name, he was about to be erased from all official documentation. He slumped back on the recently vacated sofa and closed his eyes.

"Fuck."

chapter twelue

For so long, Rhys had fought hard against the depression that had almost overwhelmed him after his transformation. Now it returned with the force of a sledgehammer to the chest. He collapsed to the floor and started to cry, sobbing to the uncaring silence. It wasn't that he wanted to be human again. He had accepted that he had the body of a starat now, but he didn't know how he would be able to fit in amongst them. He just wanted the humans, his old friends and allies, to treat him with the same respect he had always taken for granted.

Rhys didn't know how long he had been lying on the floor. When he finally sat up again, his facial fur matted with the dried remnants of tears, night had fallen and a few bats were swooping around the window outside. He was utterly lost.

He managed to drag himself to the shower to clean himself up. While he was in there, he could hear the doors open in the main room, but no one called out to him. He knew then that it wasn't a starat who had come. Just a human. He didn't care enough to go out and see them. When he got out of the shower, he realised that the only towel was still beneath the bed, wrapped around the flag. He trudged out into the main room and dripped water over everything.

On the sofa he found a new bag. Like the first, it was mostly filled with clothes. These appeared to be smaller than the first lot, so he could only hope they fit him better. But beneath them, he was happy to see a bundle of towels and, best yet, a hairdryer. The shadow of a smile came to his lips as he pulled them out and started to properly dry himself down. It did little to ease the numbness that had set in. Everything he did was listless and dull. He couldn't even bring himself to scrawl down any more notes on what to say to

Captain Rivers next time. The captain had completely ignored everything he'd prepared last time, so why would the next be any different?

Rhys lay on the sofa with the recruitment videos repeating over and over. He soon drowned them out, and his eyes began to droop. He was just about to close them completely when he heard the snick of a door unlocking. He snapped awake in an instant. The noise came from the fire escape, but he hadn't been expecting anyone. He approached the windows and glanced outside, and gasped. There was a red cloth hanging from the trees.

The door swung open as Rhys turned back around. This time there was no attempt at subterfuge as a starat poked his head out. The starat came into the apartment without any worry.

"Cameras," Rhys hissed, but instead of retreating, the first starat beckoned out another. Leandro emerged from the fire escape. It took Rhys a moment to recognise the first starat as Taylor, his body double from the other day.

The older starat smirked. "Don't worry, Captain Rhys. They're playing a recording from last night. We don't have too long, but it should do for the moment."

Rhys blinked and glanced up to the closest camera. "Captain Rivers said they were glitching earlier."

Leandro nodded. "We did that deliberately. If they kept on flickering like that, then they wouldn't notice when we started the recording," he said with a bright grin. "That was Johnnie's idea. Though we might have to think something new for getting you in and out. They're starting to get suspicious of the fire escape."

"We should hurry though, Leandro," Taylor said. His hand rested on Leandro's elbow.

"Yes, you're right, of course," Leandro said. He beckoned towards Rhys. "Come on Captain Rhys. Taylor will fill in for you again, just in case anyone comes up here. We need to get you downstairs. Your Lieutenant Edgar is expecting a call from you."

Rhys gasped. "You got through to him? What did he say?"

"Nothing, yet. He just gave us a time and a contact number," Leandro said with a shake of his head. "But hurry. Get something to wear and we can go."

Rhys glanced down, and only then noticed that he had been wearing just his underwear. His tail came up to cover himself a little more, before he quietly excused himself and fled to his bedroom. He quickly threw some clothes on and returned to Leandro and Taylor. The younger of the two starats smirked at Rhys, who did his best to ignore the amused expression.

"Thank you again for doing this," Rhys said to Taylor. "I know how much danger you're putting yourself into by helping me. You don't have to do it if you don't want to."

Taylor flashed a quick smile. "Don't worry, Captain Rhys. We help any starat that needs us. That's what Leandro has always taught us."

Rhys squeezed his eyes shut, feeling a couple of tears threatening to trickle down the side of his muzzle. "You think I'm a starat? Knowing I was human? I never even treated starats well…" Rhys trailed off, barely able to force the words from his mouth.

Leandro stepped forward and placed his hand on Rhys's chest. "You are a starat here, where it matters. Your heart is what makes you. Your past is forgivable."

Holding Leandro's hand in place, Rhys bowed his head forward, pressing his forehead against the other starat's chest. Slowly, Leandro's free hand came up to gently stroke over Rhys's neck. "Come on, Captain Rhys. Let's see to your first officer, then we can worry if you're really a starat or not."

Sniffling a little, Rhys pulled back and nodded. "Yeah, that sounds good. What's the plan?"

"We hurry downstairs. Lock ourselves in a computer lab and call your Lieutenant Edgar. We get you back up. No one knows you were even gone," Leandro said. He spoke quickly, and with a little nervousness beneath his excited words.

"Sounds simple," Rhys muttered beneath his breath, all too aware how horribly it could all go wrong. He straightened his shoulders and smiled at Taylor again. "Back as soon as we can."

Rhys hurried down the stairs after Leandro. This time they didn't descend all the way to the ground floor. Instead they stopped just a few floors down. So late at night the corridors were mostly empty, but a few lights still remained on in some of the rooms. Rhys could only hope that they didn't run into someone who recognised him, like Captain Rivers. He shuddered at the thought, but thankfully no one even looked down at the two starats.

Leandro came to a halt outside a small supply closet. It took the grey starat a couple of minutes to find what he needed, emerging with a pair of toolkits. They would provide them with a reason to go into the labs, a disguise to prevent any humans from questioning them. They could only hope that, once in, they would be ignored until they were left alone.

Unfortunately, there were still a few people using the computer lab. Just one looked up when Rhys and Leandro pushed open the door. Choosing a computer at random, Leandro crouched down next to it and slipped beneath the desk. He flicked the power off and started to unscrew it, revealing the complex wiring and components, none of which Rhys knew the purpose of.

"Get down here and look busy for a bit," Leandro hissed. "We may need to unplug everything if they take too long."

Rhys dropped to his knees and poked his head into the confined space beneath the desk. He held his tail up, hoping to block them from view from any prying onlookers.

Five minutes of fiddling followed. Rhys just stayed back and let Leandro unplug a few things, then plug them back in where he found them. A few wires were untangled and tidied up, but little of any particular progress was made.

One by one, the humans started to leave until just the one was left. Footsteps approached, and before Rhys could react he felt a sharp kick to the ribs. He yelped and recoiled, smashing the back of his head against the underside of the desk. Dazed, he whimpered as he felt a booted sole crunch down on his tail.

"Locks this time. Get it into that little head of yours. I don't want the lab unlocked all night again."

Another kick, this time aimed at his hip, had Rhys whimpering in pain again. By the time he was able to retreat from beneath the desk, the human had already started to make his retreat. Slowly getting to his feet, Rhys winced as he rubbed his ribs. He chanced a quick display of his middle finger towards the human's back as the door clicked closed behind him.

"Are you alright, Captain Rhys?" Leandro asked as he emerged from beneath the desk.

Rhys nodded. A deep growl rumbled at the back of his throat, reserved for the human. "Yeah, I'll be fine."

After patting Rhys on the shoulder, Leandro glanced around the room. He then pointed to a computer that wasn't in line of sight to the small window in the door. "Log in to that one. I'll go and lock the door."

Hoping that his credentials hadn't been revoked, Rhys booted up the computer. It didn't take long. Before he had even finished adjusting the seat so he could reach the keyboard easily, it was ready for his information. Muttering a rare prayer beneath his breath, Rhys entered his username and password, then clicked enter. It let him in.

He punched the air in delight and booted up the program he needed to call Scott. Once Leandro gave him the signal that the door was securely locked, Rhys started to type in the provided contact number. The camera and microphone both switched on automatically as the call attempted to connect. A few seconds later, Scott's face and torso appeared on screen. He looked like he was in a hotel room.

"Captain, it's good to see you again," Scott said. He adjusted the camera his end to focus more on his head.

"Good to see you too," Rhys replied. He leaned back in his chair and closed his eyes for a moment, letting out a relieved chuckle. It was so good just to hear a familiar voice. He then started to explain what had happened to him, why he had been separated from his crew. He kept nothing back, wanting his first officer to know absolutely everything there was to know. If Scott could help him, then there was no point in holding anything back.

"Things aren't good our end, either, Captain" Scott replied tersely. He looked off-screen for a moment. "We have a new captain assigned. Captain Uwele. I believe he was Lee's first officer, but he remained loyal when the *Dawn* defected. We're not sure when he's starting, but we're expecting the next week or so. Most of the crew is being questioned by the Inquisition and Investigation for loyalty towards you. I've been doing the same, but I think our goals are different."

"What about the starats? Twitch and everyone. Are they alright?" Rhys asked.

Scott nodded. "Yes, they're all fine, Captain. Doctor Sparks is looking after them at the moment. Someone from Ceres did meet up with me yesterday to retrieve them, but I said they ran away in the confusion of losing you."

Rhys breathed a sigh of relief and leaned back. "Thank you for looking after them. It is most appreciated. And the rest of the crew, of course."

"That's what I'm here for," Scott replied. "I look after the crew when you're not able. But what can we do to fix this?"

"I don't know how I can get out of this," Rhys sighed. He glanced between the computer and over to Leandro, who had remained by the door to keep watch for any possible danger. "The only ones who will listen to me are the starats. Beyond them I've been ignored at best. Beaten at worst."

"I wish I had a solution as well, Captain, but the best thing I can think of is bringing you back here and at least letting you remain on the *Harvester* under a new captain," Scott replied. He spread his hands. "There's really little we can do. Short of drastic methods."

Rhys flicked his ears. "How drastic are we talking?"

Scott leaned closer to the screen and dropped his voice low. "Just how much did you know about Captain Lee's decision?"

It felt like a massive current of electricity sparked through the desk. Rhys leapt back out of his chair, crashing back into the desk behind him. "You had better not be thinking what I think you're talking about."

"I fail to see any other solution that works for you, Captain."

"I fear he is right, Captain Rhys," Leandro interjected, cutting across Rhys before he could answer. The starat left the door and made his way across the room, coming to stand between Rhys and the screen. "You know the empire will never tolerate starats. There is only one place where you will keep your ship."

Scott had tensed up when he first heard Leandro's voice, and didn't relax until the starat had come across the screen, though his eyebrows did rise a little in surprise. "He's right," the first officer added. "I don't know what you hope to achieve there, but you have been put there for a reason. They're hiding you away, stripping you of your voice. Already the media interest in you is fading. Rumour is swirling that it was all a hoax anyway. In a week, you'll be forgotten entirely. Unless you act now."

"Your Edgar speaks well, Captain Rhys. If you want a happy ending to your story, then you must do something that truly makes a difference," Leandro said.

Scott smiled and nodded. "I've rarely heard a starat speak, but I think I like him already. I'm Edgar Scott, first officer of the *Harvester*."

"Leandro. A pleasure to meet you, Mr Edgar. If you are the chosen first officer of Captain Rhys, then you must be a human worth knowing," Leandro replied, giving a little bow towards the computer screen. The starat then turned back to Rhys. "And you should listen to your first officer, Captain."

Rhys sighed and closed his eyes, resting his hands either side of his muzzle. The worst thing was, he could understand what they were saying. The empire didn't care for him anymore, so why should he care for it? That's what loyalty was. Never wavering from the cause, no matter what may try to turn your head. He had told Aaron that, chastising him for betraying the empire and fleeing to Alpha Centauri. Could he really do the same?

"I can't make this choice now," Rhys whispered.

"That's understandable," Scott said. Rhys squinted open his eyes to look at the computer. "But you don't have long to make that decision. I think I may have delayed it for a few days at least. I just 'discovered' that Twitch was born in Brisbane, so I'm coming up with him for a day or two so he can meet his family. I'll try to get in to Mount Cotton while I'm in the area, so hopefully we can arrange something more face to face."

Despite his worries, Rhys couldn't help but smile at that news. "They believed that?"

"They thought I was an idiot for caring about him." Scott shrugged and leaned back. "I don't know what we can do, so I want you to think about my suggestion. I've already spoken to some of the crew about it, and they're still behind you. Whatever you decide, we will follow."

"I appreciate that," Rhys sighed. He tapped his claws against the desk and glanced up towards the clock. He knew they couldn't stay too long, or else they risked discovery and put Taylor in greater danger. "I can't stay any longer. I'll try to contact you when I can, or else I'll see you here. I'm up in Floor J, by the way. If you can't make it up to me, then send Twitch to the starats in the old guardhouse. They'll find a way."

"Until then, Captain Griffiths. Stay safe."

Scott reached forward, and the screen flicked black for a moment, before returning to the desktop. Rhys pressed his knuckles into his forehead and groaned. The situation was no less complicated than it had been before. He could barely sort his thoughts out as he struggled to work out what he truly believed. Did he think that betraying the empire was his only option, or was he prepared to fight for his cause here until he was finally defeated? If he was not truly defeated already.

Leandro placed his hand on Rhys's shoulder. "Come on Captain Rhys, we should start heading back upstairs."

Rhys nodded and switched off the computer. Despite his promise to start moving, he remained sat in his chair for a few moments longer. "Why are you helping me, Leandro?"

"I already told you, Captain Rhys. I like what's in here," the older starat replied as he placed one hand over Rhys's heart. "And I sense that you have many great chapters to write in the story of our kind. You will not be writing them in here. For that you need to be out there."

"Don't you ever get scared?"

"Scared? Life isn't worth living if you don't get scared. If you're scared, it means you're doing something worth doing," Leandro replied. He held onto Rhys's hand. "I would never let fear get in the way of something I knew must be done. I'm too old to start new habits like that."

"It must get boring sometimes. The stars are up there in our reach, and you're stuck following orders," Rhys said sadly. He bowed his head.

"When there's so much to learn, Captain Rhys? No. There's always something new to know, and that keeps me going. More than once has death wrapped his spindly little fingers around my heart, but every time knowledge has saved me." The grey starat clicked his tongue against his teeth a couple of times. "Remind me to tell you some of those stories sometime."

"I'd love to hear them," Rhys replied. He finally rose up to his feet and stretched his hands above his head. "You make my life sound quite dull in comparison."

"I can't imagine how your life could be dull, Captain Rhys," Leandro said with a laugh.

Together, the two left the computer lab, and Rhys pulled the door closed behind him. For just a fraction of a moment Rhys forgot about his tail, and before he could yank it out of the way the door smashed hard on it. The door bounced open again, and Rhys held his tail gingerly in one hand. The tip fell limply down as he struggled to twitch it. "Jesus fuck that hurts!"

Leandro looked over with sympathy in his eyes. "Every kit does that at some point, Captain Rhys. How badly does it hurt?"

"Like stubbing my toe. Only much, much worse," Rhys whimpered. The sharpness of the pain was already beginning to recede into a deep, dull ache, but he couldn't move the tip of his tail at all. He slowly ran his fingers along it and winced.

Leandro's fingers joined Rhys's. The older starat gently probed Rhys's tail. "I don't think it's broken, but I can look at it closer once we get back upstairs."

Rhys shivered and nodded. As he walked he tried to ignore the pain in his tail as he held it out stiffly behind him. The corridors were quiet, with no humans around to disturb them. They started to climb the fire escape, and once again Rhys started to worry about being left alone, but he knew he had no choice. Leandro couldn't stay with him, and nor could he slip out of his confinement for too long. Should Captain Rivers discover him, he and all the starats would be punished.

Taylor was waiting for them in the apartment. He had only remained behind in case someone like Captain Rivers had come up the elevator and a starat was needed to maintain the ruse. He also showed concern over Rhys's stiff and kinked tail, but nervously hopped from foot to foot as Leandro lay Rhys belly-down on the couch. "We can't guarantee they're not watching us now," Taylor muttered quietly.

Leandro waved Taylor away. "Go listen out for the elevator if you're that worried," he said. His hands slowly rubbed up from the base of Rhys's tail. "I need to make sure nothing is broken."

Taylor retreated away and mumbled something beneath his breath.

"Don't worry about him, Captain Rhys. He's just anxious," Leandro said.

"So am I," Rhys replied. He then yelped as Leandro pressed around a sore part of his tail, around halfway along its length. "What if they fix the cameras and see you here?"

Leandro shook his head. "They won't even know there's a problem with them. There's only one person down in security today and, quite frankly, he's not very smart." His fingers gently probed further up Rhys's tail. "Nothing feels like it's broken. Just sprained."

"I suppose you'll need to go now, won't you?" Rhys asked sorrowfully. He was glad his tail wasn't badly injured, but he was worried about being alone. Especially after the conversation he had just had with Scott. He was scared where his thoughts would lead him. He felt like he teetered on the edge of a decision he would never be able to pull back from.

"Not just yet, Captain Rhys," Leandro said. The grey-furred starat sat down on the sofa beside Rhys. "I feel like I should tell you one of my stories. I think you need to hear it. Just the abridged version though. I don't feel like there is time for the whole thing."

The logical part of Rhys's mind wanted to turn Leandro down, to warn him not to linger and to get back to safety. But he found himself nodding instead. He enjoyed the company too much to let it go so soon. "I'd like to hear it," he said quietly.

Leandro beamed widely. "I am glad, Captain Rhys." He paused for a moment and cleared his throat, before continuing in a voice that was clearly rehearsed and familiar, but still passionate like he was telling the story for the first time. "I was owned by Masterson Minerals, and was sent to a small asteroid in the middle of the Belt with two other starats. Christie and Ellen, their names were. We were probably the only souls for thousands of miles in all directions, forced to work on this little rock to dig for minerals. We were tethered to the asteroid, or else we would literally float off into space with the smallest stumble."

"Sounds terrifying," Rhys said quietly. A shiver ran down his back at the thought.

Leandro nodded, but otherwise didn't acknowledge the interruption. "Every movement was with hook and tether. We drilled for minerals and transported it back to the small silo that had been landed with us." He stopped again and laughed. "The minerals had better shelter than we did. Our space suits barely fit us, and we were uncomfortable for every second of the three months we were there. We had enough food and air for three months and one day.

"Everything was going well though. About as well as you could expect for being on such a desolate rock with nothing to eat but plain nutrition bars and nothing to do but work. Constantly. Work, sleep, eat, work, sleep, eat. But still glorious and majestic. Few can imagine the view of sunrise over the nearby horizon of a rapidly spinning asteroid, and we experienced it thousands of times over those three months. Always made us stop and stare.

"Then things went wrong. Badly. There was a small leak in the oxygen tank. It wasn't a big one, but it was enough. It took me too long to repair it, and in that time we had lost nearly five days of oxygen. We didn't have enough to survive the remaining four weeks. We sent out a distress beacon right away, but we're just starats. We didn't expect anyone to answer."

Leandro bowed his head, but Rhys could still see the small smile on his muzzle. It was all for show. The older starat enjoyed this. "Ellen volunteered to remove her helmet. She would be dead in seconds, but the rest of us would have enough oxygen to survive until Masterson Minerals returned to collect us and their precious cargo. I refused. I wouldn't have anyone die out there.

"I won't lie, Captain Rhys. That was when I was most terrified. I was scared I had killed not only myself, but also Ellen and Christie. We kept working. We kept breathing. We kept looking towards the stars, waiting for our rescuer that never came. The stack of minerals kept growing, but our supply of oxygen kept depleting.

"Then, when we had mere hours left, the impossible happened. Lights in the sky. A ship had come. We were being rescued. Captain Rhys, do you know what ship that was?"

Rhys shook his head. He hadn't realised he had gripped his knees hard. He slowly released them and relaxed as he let Leandro finish the rest of his tale.

"It was the *Emperor's Revenge*. I was the first thing the Silver Fox ever stole. To that day, I have owed him a debt I have never been able to repay. He was an enemy of the empire, but he was a friend of starats." Leandro paused and clasped his hands over his lap. "I hear he's on a desolate rock now, like I once was. I sometimes wonder if his story will have the lights of my ship rescue him."

"It was my first officer who turned him in," Rhys mumbled. His ears folded in and he hunched over a little, pulling his legs up onto the couch and curling his tail over them.

"Your Edgar?"

Rhys shook his head. "The one before him. Cooper, the one who attacked me."

"Oh, good. I like Edgar. I didn't want to think he locked away the Silver Fox." Leandro turned to Rhys and placed a hand on his leg. "The empire left me to die then, Captain Rhys. I was so replaceable, they would have let me die and send a new starat to complete the work. It was a pirate, an enemy, a good for nothing scoundrel, who rescued me. Sometimes, Captain Rhys, the good guys are not who you want them to be."

Rhys bowed his head and remained quiet. He had been given even more to think about.

Leandro rose to his feet. "I should not remain any longer. I think poor Taylor will be shedding his fur soon. Please do think about my story, Captain Rhys. I think it is important to you."

"I will, yes," Rhys said. He had no choice but to think about it. Rather than distract him from his painful decision, he felt like the story had pushed him closer to the edge. His mind was unbalanced, and he wouldn't be able to put those thoughts away until he made a decision.

"Thank you, Captain Rhys. I'm not sure when we will be able to come up next. We may need to find a new excuse to sneak in here, but I assure you we will keep looking out for you, and get messages from your crew," Leandro said. He smiled at Rhys and gave him a quick salute. "You're a good starat. Remember that."

Rhys felt tears spring to his eyes. He quickly wiped them away and saluted Leandro back. "Get back to safety. I'll be fine here," Rhys said. He smiled at Taylor as the other starat returned. "And Taylor. Thank you for all your help as well."

"Goodbye Captain Rhys, for now."

From almost the moment the two starats were gone, Rhys felt a wave of intense loneliness wash over him. He wanted nothing more than someone to hold. It was a feeling he hadn't felt for years. He hugged his arms around his chest as he slowly trudged off to bed to think. He knew the thoughts would consume him and keep him awake all night. He had one important decision to make.

For the Emperor or against him.

chapter thirteen

Captain Rivers was waiting for Rhys when he woke up the following morning. He had heard the human in the other room, but Rhys had taken his time to get himself dressed and ready. He already knew what the first question would be, and he didn't want to face it so quickly. Instead he just rubbed his face and tried to sort through his worried thoughts. The human didn't give him long though, and within just a minute Captain Rivers barked out a demand to hurry up.

"I know you're in there. Get out here and face me."

Rhys grumbled beneath his breath. He adjusted his clothes and smoothed down the fur on his tail, before he left the comfort of the small bedroom. He froze at the sight before him. Captain Rivers was not alone. One man stood next to Captain Rivers, with two more just behind them. The man standing by the captain's side was the last human Rhys wanted to see. The ugly face of Cardinal Erik leered at him.

Captain Rivers cleared his throat. "Given your lack of cooperation, I have called in assistance from the Vatican. Cardinal Erik was only too eager to come to our aid. He will be tasked with extracting a confession from you," he said, before a smirk broke across his face. "Unless you are willing to confess now."

Rhys swallowed nervously. His eyes flicked between the two humans. He felt trapped, but he knew it was suicide to make a false confession. He shook his head.

"Then you are under the jurisdiction of the Vatican now," Captain Rivers said. He made to turn around, but Cardinal Erik placed his hand on the captain's elbow.

"There are starats at this facility?" the cardinal asked. A smirk spread across his face as Captain Rivers nodded. "Kindly inform them that our prisoner has already been transferred to Mars. I don't want them to know he's still here."

"I assure you there's no way they've been communicating," Captain Rivers protested, but the cardinal wasn't having any of it.

"This one has a particular way with starats it seems. Corrupts them with remarkable ease about ideas of equality and unity," the cardinal spat. Rhys stayed tight-lipped as Cardinal Erik's attention turned back to him. "Besides, it would remind this one that there was no hope for him. No way his ratty friends can come rescue him. Oh. And disable the cameras. I don't want anything recording us."

A shiver ran down Rhys's spine and tail. He didn't know if Leandro and the starats would believe such a declaration from Captain Rivers. If they didn't see through the deception then there would be very little chance for him to escape. He closed his eyes as Captain Rivers nodded.

"If you think it's necessary," the captain spat. He muttered beneath his breath as he turned to leave again. "Waste of my time if you ask me."

This time, Cardinal Erik didn't stop Captain Rivers as he pushed past the two burly guards in front of the door. Instead, the cardinal's hungry eyes bore right into Rhys's. It took all of Rhys's strength of will to keep standing with his back straight. He didn't step away, despite wanting to flee into the next room.

"So here we are. Me and you," Cardinal Erik said, gesturing to each of them as he spoke. "Human and beast. Blessed and tainted."

"I am not a beast," Rhys replied. His voice shook with fear, despite his best efforts to keep his voice even.

Cardinal Erik folded his arms across his chest. He sighed softly. "You still believe yourself to be human. Pure and untainted. I almost feel sorry for you, but I cannot allow sentiment to get in the way of my purpose. For my purpose is to cleanse you of the sin that is your body. But to do that, your mind must repent first, and for that, you must accept what you are. Beastly and lesser to the purity that is mankind."

"With no respect intended, go fuck yourself," Rhys snarled in response. His anger flared anew. For a brief moment it was able to overwhelm his fear of the cardinal.

"Tut tut," the cardinal replied. He waggled one finger in Rhys's direction, before gesturing to the guards behind him. "We will teach you to control that mouth of yours as well."

Rhys recoiled at the sight of the two massive humans as they approached. He bumped into the sofa behind and almost fell back onto it. He didn't want to know what the guards had planned for him, but he knew he was about to find out anyway.

Rhys doubted he would have been able to fight off one of the guards. Two was definitely too many. He dodged the slow lunge from one, only to feel the fist of the other smash into his chest. He wheezed and collapsed to his knees, unsure if any of his ribs had been broken.

Rhys was barely given a moment of respite before he felt a heavy weight press down on his back. Rough hands gripped his muzzle, pinning it shut. With one human holding down his shoulders, and the other keeping his mouth closed, there was nothing Rhys could do but struggle helplessly. He could barely move, and he certainly couldn't make any sound but a few wordless grunts.

Cardinal Erik kneeled down in front of Rhys. "I don't trust that mouth of yours. It's been getting you into a lot of trouble recently, with all those words of treason and heresy spouting from it." The cardinal's voice was dangerously calm and quiet. "I think it would be much nicer if you just listened to what I had to say, instead of thinking you could speak in my presence. As though you were worthy of such a thing."

At the click of the cardinal's fingers, Rhys's head was slammed down to the floor. He howled in pain as he tried to writhe and twist free from the powerful grip holding him down, without any success. He could feel blood welling in his mouth, but he was unable to spit it out with his muzzle pinned closed. Chest heaving, Rhys felt like he was choking on blood.

The humiliation was not complete. The hands shifted their grip around his muzzle. For a moment Rhys was able to open his mouth again, but immediately a gag was forced between his teeth. A leather band was wound around his muzzle before he could spit the gag out. It pinched tight and prevented him from working his jaw at all.

A red-robed knee then came up into Rhys's chest, making the starat groan and collapse to his knees. "I will break you, starat. Before I'm done you'll be praying for it to end, to sink into mindless oblivion. Maybe I'll let you have it. It depends how much I like your whimpers." Cardinal Erik's voice took on a predatory snarl as he whispered right into Rhys's ear. "I own you now. You're mine."

As Cardinal Erik started to pull back, he lashed out and struck Rhys hard over his muzzle. The thick leather strap absorbed some of the blow, but the starat was still knocked back from the force, his vision spinning. The cardinal winced and shook his hand as he stepped away. He clicked his fingers to the guards, who roughly hauled Rhys back up to unsteady feet. They pinned his arms behind his back.

"If you think a confession to Captain Rivers will save you from my reach, then you are mistaken," Cardinal Erik continued. He held one hand on Rhys's forehead. "You are mine until you break. And then you die. Slowly. Painfully. And you will know, during every moment, that you deserve it."

Cardinal Erik removed his hand and wiped it on his robe. He snapped his fingers again. "Collar and cuff him."

Rhys struggled and tried to kick out, but it took just one of the guards to keep him still. One thick hand was wrapped around his wrists, and the other arm squeezed around his chest. He grunted and growled, but the stream of curses he wanted to unleash on the gloating cardinal remained sealed behind his bound muzzle.

The second guard held Rhys's head back as he affixed a thick leather collar around his neck. A couple of metal hoops were embedded into the leather. Despite his kicks and attempts to thrash out of the powerful grip holding him in place, the collar was soon secured in place. It pinched around his fur, but it wasn't so tight it hindered his breathing.

Rhys was then dragged off his feet and pushed to the floor. One guard placed a heavy boot on his back to stop him from rolling away, while the other wrestled his arms into position above the base of his tail. His wrists were bound by a pair of heavy metal manacles, and a leather strap looped between them and around his tail, before being attached to one of the rings in the collar.

He was finally released by the two guards, but there wasn't much he could do to move. His arms were both locked in position, and his tail was forced into an uncomfortably raised position. He felt humiliated and vulnerable. Just as Cardinal Erik wanted of him.

The cardinal crouched down in front of Rhys. He placed a hand on Rhys's bound muzzle and closed his eyes. "The mouth that blasphemes: silenced." He forced Rhys's head down and slowly brushed his hand down the starat's back until it came to rest on the manacles. "The hands that sin: bound."

Rhys growled and twitched the tip of his tail, but he was otherwise helpless to resist as his jaw was wrenched up again. He was forced to stare into the blazing eyes of the cardinal. "May Jesus and Veritas have mercy upon your soul," Cardinal Erik said softly. He placed his hand gently on the side of Rhys's muzzle, then gripped tight around the leather bindings. "For as their weapon, I certainly will not."

In one quick motion, Cardinal Erik slammed Rhys's head down against the floor. His jaw struck hard against the ceramic tiled floor. His breath caught in his throat as his limbs became heavy and numb. The floor's reflective shine grew brighter as his mind slipped into unconsciousness.

***

Rhys didn't want to wake up. He felt the handcuffs before anything else, a constant reminder of his imprisonment. Already, the metal chafed his wrists, cutting in to his flesh and leaving a raw ring of skin where the fur had been torn away. The second thing was the headache. A dull throb that spread from beneath his eyes to the underside of his jaw. He closed his eyes to try and ease the pain, but that only made the sharp throbs more intense. What he needed was water and painkillers, but both were out of his reach.

After ten minutes on the floor, Rhys decided the pain in his shoulders was getting too great to bear. He slowly struggled up to his knees and shuffled across to the sofa. He wasn't feeling confident enough to bring himself up to his feet, already suffering from nausea and dizziness merely from kneeling up. Again he closed his eyes as he rested against the sofa, before manoeuvring himself up onto it.

He couldn't lie on his back. His tail was forced up into a position that crushed it when he tried, and nor could he move his hands out of the way. Unable to move his arms, he wasn't comfortable on his side either. Lying down on his belly was the only way he wasn't in immediate pain, but the burn in his shoulders and tail slowly increased, meaning he couldn't stay there for long.

He eventually just ended sat upright, perched on the edge of the sofa as he struggled to loosen the manacles around his wrists. He didn't know how they were locked as he couldn't turn his head around far enough, but they were too tight to do anything. All he did was rip off a bit more skin and fur.

It wasn't until the scent of blood increased his nausea before he stopped. Blood already stained the straps around his muzzle, but he could now feel it trickle down his wrists and hands. He closed his eyes and took several shallow breaths, but the nausea only increased. He did not want to know what it was like to throw up in his bound mouth, but thankfully the feeling slowly started to recede again.

As he waited for something to happen, Rhys tried to take stock of his situation. Outside was still daylight, but he didn't know if it was still the same day or not. He had no way of knowing if he'd been out cold for a full day, or just a couple of hours. By now, he was sure no one was aware he was here, other than his captors. All of his friends and allies would think he was on Mars, but the real question he had was why wasn't he actually there already? There had to be a reason why Cardinal Erik was keeping him here. He was making him wait. But for what?

Rhys expected Cardinal Erik to return to inflict more punishment and pain, but the door remained closed. He didn't know how much time ticked by. Each second melted into the next. Minute by minute, hour by hour. Time was meaningless when there was nothing to do, and no way to track the passing of it, but for the movement of the sun outside. He didn't know why, but the clocks had been taken from the walls.

By the time the sun had sunk below the horizon, Rhys had been drifting in and out of uncomfortable rest. His shoulders and wrists ached, but he hadn't found a comfortable place to hold them at all. He hadn't even attempted to stand yet, unable to trust himself to balance with his tail in such an uncomfortable position, or his stomach to remain uneasily settled.

Nothing else changed for Rhys. Instead of sitting on the sofa in the sunlight, now he was sat in the darkness. No lights had turned on in the room, so the only illumination was a small red light blinking from the TV. There wasn't even any moonlight to brighten the dark sky.

There were few times Rhys had ever felt so lonely before. He closed his eyes and wept silently.

***

Two further days passed without any contact. No visit from Cardinal Erik or Captain Rivers. Two days of agonising torture for Rhys. The constant pain in his wrist and head had become a thudding pulse that felt like it grew worse with each beat of his heart. He couldn't ignore it, but nor could he ease it.

He had managed to remove his trousers before his first attempt to use the bathroom, and he hadn't bothered trying to dress again. He had attempted a shower once, but the effort of switching the water on had only caused his wrist to flare in unbearable agony. He had screamed into his gag until his throat hurt, if only to distract from the other pains.

Beyond all the pain, his mouth was parched and his stomach was constantly rumbling with hunger. He felt faint, but all he'd had to consume was the occasional drops of blood that dripped from the roof of his mouth and his tongue.

By the time the doors finally opened, Rhys barely had the energy to lift his head. A flash of red passed by his vision, and even the stab of a needle into his forearm barely drew a reaction from him. Even so, he felt a hand at his throat in warning.

"Stay still or I make this worse for you," Cardinal Erik snarled.

Rhys blinked his eyes to focus as he looked up at the cardinal. Even lying down, his vision swam uncomfortably. He could just about make out a small, plastic tube connecting the needle to a transparent bag suspended over his head. It was filled with a clear fluid that was slowly trickling down into his arm.

"I don't trust these teeth, or that tongue," Cardinal Erik said, flicking Rhys on the muzzle. "From now on, this is how I keep you alive. No food. No water. So you had better behave, or I might suddenly forget to put a new bag in for you. I wonder how long it would take for you to starve to death."

Unable to answer, Rhys could only glare back at his captor, but he was too scared of the needle in his arm to move. His stomach growled loudly, prompting a barked laugh from Cardinal Erik.

"Get used to that, beast," he said, before pressing a single finger against Rhys's forehead. "Captain Rivers wants to shoot you. Right here. A mercy kill. I almost considered letting him, but then I thought about all the glory I would miss out on. I get to flay the sins from your soul. You should be on your knees praising me. Worshipping me. I am your saviour, but what do I get? Hate and scorn."

The cardinal shook his head sadly. "One day you will thank me. And on that day, when I know you truly believe it, I will set your soul free to join Veritas, should he deem you worthy." He paused to adjust the IV drip, before he wandered over to the window. He stood with his arms behind his back. "In one week the ship will come to take us to Mars. Enjoy the sunlight while you can, beast. It will be the last time you get to see it."

At that, Cardinal Erik whipped around and stalked out of the room. He slammed the door behind him, leaving Rhys by himself once more. The starat didn't dare move for fear of dislodging the needle and pricking open a vein or artery, though maybe that would be preferable. At least then he wouldn't be in pain, with the prospect of endless torture to look forward to. But he couldn't bring himself to do it. At least the nutrients in the bag had started to ease his dizziness, though his stomach still ached for something substantial.

As he whimpered softly into his muzzle, Rhys closed his eyes and tried to think about anything but his hopeless situation. He didn't know how long his mind would be able to hold out. Even through the worst of his troubles after his transformation, there had always been that little seed of hope to nurture. Sometimes that had been all that had kept him going, but it had been enough. Now that had been taken away. He had nothing left.

***

"Do you feel it yet, animal? Do you know your place yet?" Cardinal Erik whispered into Rhys's ear.

The words delved deep into Rhys's mind, but he tried his best to show he was ignoring them. He was rewarded by a powerful punch to the stomach. He wheezed and doubled over, only for the cardinal to strike him across the cheek.

At least two nights had passed since Rhys had first been fed through the IV, though to Rhys's confused mind, it could have been three. Just once more had he been given any fluids, and he was struggling to keep conscious. The pain in his wrist had mercifully ceased. Instead he felt nothing beneath his right elbow. He didn't know what was better. The pain in his head had only spread, fuelled by the cardinal's hand striking him. His tongue felt swollen in his mouth, and his throat ached for something to quench his thirst.

The cardinal dug his fingers in between Rhys's neck and the collar and pulled him off the bed. Unable to fight back, Rhys just resigned himself to being dragged along the floor, not putting up any resistance at all. If anything, that seemed to annoy the cardinal more. He was roughly thrown to the floor once more.

"I can still see that fire in your eyes, but it is starting to flicker and fade. Soon it will be extinguished entirely," the cardinal said. He knelt down by Rhys's side and toyed with a small dagger in his hand. In his other hand was a small vial filled with a clear liquid.

Rhys's vision blurred in and out of focus as the cardinal carefully emptied a few drops of the vial onto the blade of his dagger. The starat squirmed and tried to push himself away, but the cardinal quickly reached out and grabbed hold of his collar. The wet blade was held over Rhys's chest.

"May the blood of the beast be cleansed," the cardinal muttered beneath his breath. He then quickly slashed the knife vertically down from each of Rhys's armpits, opening up a small cut several centimetres long each time. Blood welled from the wounds, and Rhys howled into his gag as the cuts burned. His chest heaved as he struggled to draw in breath, and he tasted blood on his parched tongue once again.

"Feel the hellfire of sin coursing through your veins," the cardinal continued, his voice growing a little louder. "You are a sinner. A beast, unworthy in the eyes of Veritas our saviour. Only with my blessing will you meet him and our creator."

In the depths of Rhys's mind, through all the distractions of pain and suffering, one thought coalesced in the chaotic maelstrom. Veritas was not his creator. His creator was Essie. Essie was the first starat, and Rhys was a starat in his image. He was not human, bound to the same creator Veritas had preached of.

The thought crystallised in his mind, and he was able to use it as a shield against the poisonous words that Cardinal Erik whispered in his ear. He was a starat, and he would never break. He would never give the cardinal that satisfaction.

Slowly he opened his eyes and glared at Cardinal Erik was as much force as he could muster. For just a moment the cardinal's steady stream of whispered words faltered. The fire in Rhys's eyes burned fiercely. It would never go out.

His display of insolence was rewarded with a fierce slap across the muzzle. His head cracked against the floor and for a few moments his vision was marred with black spots. Before he could recover, the cardinal jabbed a needle into his neck. He howled in pain, struggling against his gag as it felt like ice was being injected into his bloodstream.

As the chill cold spread through his body he realised he was losing his already diminished ability to move. His fingers had gone cold and stiff, and the sensation was rapidly spreading. The cardinal gloated down at him as his weak struggles slowly ceased. Rhys's mind raced, but less than a minute after the injection he felt completely paralysed. His heart still beat in his chest, and his lungs still drew breath, but nothing else in his body moved.

"How do you like the mindlock? It's a powerful drug I helped develop. Great for torture. Don't worry, it only lasts a few hours, but that's plenty of time to do what I want," the cardinal snarled. He moved away and quickly vanished from Rhys's limited field of vision, but the frozen starat could still hear him moving around. "This wouldn't have happened if you'd submitted willingly. You only have yourself to blame."

The cardinal stood over Rhys. An insufferable smirk spread across his face. "That's much better. I can see fear locked into your eyes. That will make you much better to work with."

Rhys was roughly rolled over onto his belly. He couldn't resist it at all, and again his head struck the floor. He would have whimpered in pain, but not a single sound emerged from his mouth. He could still feel everything as Cardinal Erik tugged on his arms, but no matter how hard he tried, he couldn't even twitch a finger. He tried to think of Essie again, but he didn't know what the first starat looked like, and without the ability to close his eyes, he couldn't summon a powerful enough mental image.

To Rhys's surprise, his cuffs were removed. His arms immediately fell to the floor, and a jolt of pain stabbed out from his wrists. He was dragged out into the middle of the floor and kicked over onto his back again.

The cardinal held Rhys's right hand up, making sure the starat was able to see it. The cardinal held what appeared to be a pair of pliers in his free hand, which filled Rhys with impotent terror. He wanted to struggle. He wanted to push the cardinal away, especially with his arms now freed of their bindings, but he couldn't.

The pliers squeezed down on the claw on Rhys's index finger, and with a sharp realisation he knew what the cardinal was going to do. He could do nothing. Even his breathing was smooth and regulated, doing nothing to betray his surmounting panic and fear.

The cardinal wrenched the pliers, and Rhys's mental scream of pain almost overwhelmed him. His body didn't react, but his mind screamed over and over as waves of pain radiated out from his finger. The claw had been pulled out in a bloody spray, and the cardinal simply flicked it to the floor and prepared the pliers again, this time on his middle finger.

He couldn't brace. He couldn't prepare. The cardinal didn't even give him time to recover from the first, before he ripped the second claw from his finger.

Cardinal Erik squeezed the two fingers together as he gloated down at Rhys. "Shame I can't hear your screams, but I can see the pain in your eyes," he said, before pulling Rhys's hand up. The human sniffed at Rhys's palm and grinned. "Oh yes, I can sense your pain. Your fear. Your anger."

The cardinal threw Rhys's hand to the ground. Blood leaked from the tips of Rhys's fingers, but the starat was helpless as it dripped onto the tiles and slowly pooled. He could smell a metallic tang mixed in with a cinnamon spice, and it sickened his stomach.

"You must wonder why I'm doing this," the cardinal said. He stood over Rhys, one foot either side of the starat's chest. He crouched down and pulled up Rhys's hand again, pressing hard where the two claws had once been. Pain throbbed through Rhys's hand and up his arm. "How does this cleanse your soul? Truth is, it doesn't. I just enjoy feeling your pain too much."

Rhys longed to just close his eyes, but he couldn't even do such a simple task. He was forced to watch as Cardinal Erik dug his fingers into the wounds he had created. "That's it," the cardinal crooned. The human closed his eyes and tilted his head back as though he were drinking in Rhys's pain. "Scream for me. Share those thoughts."

Rhys could do nothing else. His internal thoughts were nothing but screams of pain, intermingled with an occasional mental tirade at the cardinal, but he could do nothing else. He was locked inside his body with the cardinal free to do whatever he wished.

The cardinal's hands released Rhys, and the starat's arms dropped limply to the floor again. Rhys knew more pain was coming, and it soon pulsated through his arm as the pliers squeezed around another claw. This time, the cardinal trod down hard on Rhys's right hand as well. He could feel a few crunches and cracks as the human's weight came down hard on him, but even that pain was nothing compared to another claw being ripped from his finger.

The two remaining claws soon followed. Rhys's right hand was nothing but absolute agony, and for the first time he was glad he couldn't move. He knew every twitch or spasm in his right hand would send waves of pain rippling up his arm, but instead it was left flat against the cool floor in a pool of blood.

For a few brief moments, the cardinal left Rhys alone. The pressure on his hand was released, and the human disappeared from view. Despite the pain he was in, Rhys's heart still beat normally, and his breaths came in slow and regular. Whatever drug was in his system, it was maintaining his vitals to a standard level. Rhys hated it. He wanted to use the pain to fuel his anger, and to overwhelm the drug and force himself into movement, but it was too strong. He couldn't even blink.

"Hands are such a curious thing, aren't they?" the cardinal said. Rhys couldn't tell exactly where he was. His ears usually moved to work out where a sound was coming from, but they were stuck perked upright. All he knew was that the cardinal was somewhere behind him, but couldn't tell how close. "They're used for so much sin. Our saviours both had their hands crippled because of that. How proud must you be to share their pain."

Rhys whimpered mentally as his right arm was suddenly pulled up. It was dragged into position so it was held at a right angle to his torso. His left hand was then crushed beneath the boot of the cardinal as the pliers found their grip around his index finger again. He knew what was coming, and his screams of mental anguish began anew. Somehow, they seemed to fuel the cardinal, as he growled in bestial pleasure with each tortured silent scream.

One, two, three, four, and all five claws were ripped from his fingers, even as his hand was crushed beneath the weight of the human's boot. The cardinal snarled in sadistic delight as each claw was tossed to the floor. One landed on his chest. He could feel it pricking into his skin slightly.

Once the cardinal was done mutilating Rhys's hand, he forced the arm up into the same position as the right. Rhys lay on his back with both arms outstretched. The martyr's pose.

Cardinal Erik kicked Rhys in the ribs to shift his torso slightly. He laughed down at the paralysed starat. "You may suffer the same pain as our saviours, but you will never be worthy to be a martyr like them. You will be forgotten, just another starat killed in humanity's quest for perfection."

Rhys's hands were wrenched together, palm to palm. His ruined fingers were pressed together, and the cardinal wrapped his wrists up in a small length of rope to keep them held in position.

The cardinal gently tapped the blade of a knife against the back of Rhys's hand. Even the soft touch sliced through Rhys's skin, producing another line of red as blood trickled down onto his wrist.

"May the stigmata drain the sin from your body," Cardinal Erik muttered in quiet prayer, before he plunged the blade into the back of Rhys's right hand. The keen blade slipped between muscle and sinew, puncturing right through one hand and into the other. The blade was withdrawn for a moment, before it was plunged back in with greater force.

Rhys screamed in mental anguish as this time the knife sliced through both hands. When the knife was withdrawn fully, it left behind two bleeding, ragged holes. The cardinal then threaded a thick length of semi-flexible metal through the two holes, securing it in place with an electromagnetic lock.

Rhys mentally pleaded for the relief of unconsciousness, but nothing came to ease his pain. He barely felt it as the cardinal undid the rope tied around his wrists, but he did feel the surge of pain that blossomed as the cardinal let his hands drop to the floor.

Still the cardinal was not finished. He prepared his blade with a new vial, letting a thick, black liquid drip over the keen blade. He grinned down at Rhys as he did so, making sure the starat could see his every movement.

Once he was ready, the blade was pressed against Rhys's forearm, first his right, then his left. It sliced through his flesh three times on each arm, depositing the thick liquid right into the wounds. It burned like fire flickered over his flesh.

"Devil's Blood," the cardinal whispered in Rhys's ear. "It will eat through your flesh quite nicely. Those hands will sin no more, beast."

The knife tapped lightly against Rhys's ears, but it didn't cut through his flesh. "I wonder what I'll take next time. Perhaps I should target the source of your lust. Or silence your sinning tongue permanently. I'll let both possibilities weigh on your mind, I think."

The cardinal reached down, and for a moment Rhys was terrified the human was going to press down on his eyes, but instead the cardinal simply pulled his eyelids closed. His vision was robbed, and he was surprised by a few firm kicks to his ribs.

"May Jesus and Veritas cleanse your wounds should they find you worthy," the cardinal said. It was his parting shot, as Rhys heard the human packing up his instruments of torture, before footsteps retreated and a door was closed. Rhys was left all alone, with nothing but pain for company.

Unable to move, Rhys could only lie in agony as blood dripped from his hands and onto his belly. He could barely thread together two thoughts as he was constantly distracted by the pain radiating from his hands and arms. He tried to think of Essie. Without knowing what the first starat looked like, he filled in the blanks by imagining the grey fur of Leandro. In his heart though, Rhys knew the truth.

Not even Essie could save him now.

chapter fourteen

Rhys hated every moment of being awake. His hands were utterly ruined, and he could feel the Devil's Blood eating through his arms. Sharp, stabbing pains erupted every few minutes, barely giving any time to settle down before flaring anew. There was no relief from it all.

His tail was freed from its uncomfortable position as the cardinal hadn't secured him to his handcuffs again, but they weren't necessary. Rhys had tried several times to remove the loop of metal threaded through the holes in his hands, but it was a futile effort. It was locked in place, and it hurt to even move the bar a few centimetres as it rubbed and scraped against his exposed flesh and bone inside his hands. He tried to loosen his gag, but his declawed fingers couldn't grip onto anything without unbearable pain. Once they had healed, then perhaps he would be able to free himself, but until then he couldn't manage it.

The only glimmer of positivity was that the cardinal didn't return. For three whole days Rhys was left by himself, to suffer in silence. His hunger and weakness only increased as the hours and days ticked by, exasperated by the constant loss of blood that seeped from his wounds.

He usually ignored the windows, but as the sun was starting to set on yet another evening, he staggered towards them. He closed his eyes and rested his forehead against the cool glass. It helped ease his consistent headache slightly, but more than anything, he wanted to feel the sunlight on his fur. He doubted he'd get many more opportunities of that.

Tears flowed as he opened his eyes again and looked down on the grounds. There were a couple of starats wandering around. He almost looked away, before he realised something unusual. They were accompanied by a human. Then he saw who it was. Even from this distance, Edgar Scott's height made him stand out. Rhys wanted to shriek and howl, to bash his fists against the glass until his first officer heard him, but the only sound he could make was a pitiful squeak that hurt his throat. He was so close, but he had no way of telling his first officer he was here. No way of communicating with the outside world.

But he could.

A sudden clarity overwhelmed Rhys's mind. Thoughts came easily to his head for the first time in days, and his limbs were filled with a desperate urgency that belied his weakness. He stumbled and staggered through to his bedroom and dropped down to his knees. He reached beneath the bed, whimpering as his ruined, broken fingers clasped hold of the hidden flag.

At the sight of the deep blue fabric, Rhys's vision blurred beneath a fresh wave of tears. It felt like so long since he had been given the flag, it seemed like a different lifetime. One where he hadn't been enduring through constant pain and humiliation.

With the flag held gingerly in one hand, Rhys rolled back up to his feet and dragged it back into the main room. He was thankful Cardinal Erik didn't choose that moment to burst through the doors.

There was no way he would be able to pin the flag up as normal, but with a bit of work he was able to wedge it against the frame of one of the panes. It hung limply, but he hoped that one starat would look up and see it. He could do no more than that.

Something other than pain was starting to spread through Rhys's limbs. Hope had returned.

For the first time in several days, Rhys tried to pull his hands apart and free himself from the piercing bar, but immediately he had to stop. Both hands were utterly ruined, he knew that already. He could barely move his fingers, and blood still slowly oozed from the gaping holes where his claws had been.

Grunting into his muzzle, Rhys turned his attention to the collar. He had noticed it was a little looser than it had been, but he doubted it was enough to slip free. If his hands weren't in agony, then maybe he would have been able to tease it loose.

There had to be something more he could do. Some way to break free from his confines. Even if the starats on the grounds saw the flag, they wouldn't have any way to come up to rescue him, not without taking control of the elevator and risking the wrath of Cardinal Erik and Captain Rivers. That was surely much too great a risk, even for the bravest of starats.

His eyes turned to the other door in the room. The fire escape. He had tried that door a few days earlier, but it had been firmly locked. But perhaps there was a way he could force it to open.

Rhys's eyes flicked up to the ceiling. A number of sensors and sprinklers were situated above him, ready to deal with any fire that broke out. If he could set them off, he would create a window of opportunity for someone to reach him. It wasn't much of a hope, but it was worth the risk. All he needed now was something to set the alarms off, and for that he searched around the small suite of rooms, looking for something that could create a little fire.

His eyes eventually fell on the hair dryer, left beside the sink in the bathroom. He knocked it down to the floor, then carefully dug his toe claws into the insulating coating of the electric cord. They stripped away at the plastic until there was a large section of exposed wire. Once he was satisfied, he worked the dryer back up again so he could place it in the sink. The pressure on his fingers was agony. The dryer didn't weigh much, but it may as well have been made from solid metal for the effort it took to lift it back up to the sink. On two occasions he dropped it, but finally on the third attempt he was able to lift it high enough to fall into the sink.

The surge of energy that had coursed through his limbs was starting to fade. Feeling faint, Rhys had to lean against the wall and take a few deep breaths before attempting to carry on. The intravenous nutrients had been keeping him alive, but it had been so long since he'd even had that luxury. Every action cost so much, his limbs aching and head spinning.

Bracing himself for the act of stupidity he was about to do, Rhys turned the hair dryer on before reaching for the taps. Rushing water met the whirring drone of the dryer, and Rhys hurried out as quickly as his tired legs could manage, before the dangerous mixture started to spark. He cowered in the kitchen for a few seconds, before there was a frightful explosion from the bathroom. Porcelain shattered, and an instant later a deafening wail started to tear through the building. A cacophony of noise echoed from floor to floor as the fire alarms were triggered. It was the most beautiful noise Rhys had ever heard.

Shouts and scraping chairs accompanied the alarms, soon followed by thudding footsteps on concrete stairs in the fire escape just beyond his closed door. No one came in to collect Rhys. It only took a minute or so before the sounds of movement upstairs had ceased. Those floors had been quick to evacuate.

A second explosion ripped through the bathroom. Rhys lifted his head up, eyes wide with fear as he noticed a few flames starting to break out around the rooms. At the same time, the sprinklers started. It took just a few seconds to drench Rhys's fur. Rather than put the fire out it only seemed to fuel it. The hair dryer had long stopped, but he could hear the wires were sparking and spitting with the increased flow of water.

Then the lights went out and the hideous sparking ceased. Power had been cut to the building, and this time the water started to subdue the flames.

Rhys let the sprinklers drench him. He closed his eyes and arched his muzzle up, hoping that a little moisture trickled through to his lips. Nothing made it through the gag, leaving him as desperate for water as ever.

Using the last of his rapidly fading energy, Rhys staggered over to the door and pushed down on the handle. It didn't move. The door was still locked.

He would have yelled in frustration if he could, but instead he just sunk down to his knees and bowed his head. He prayed, but it wasn't to Jesus or to Veritas. He prayed to Essie.

Footsteps approached, pattering against the concrete stairs. It didn't sound like the heavy boots of a human. He lifted his head up and squinted open his eyes as someone slammed into the door. A few seconds of frantic hammering followed, before the door swung open.

Two starats burst into the room with such speed that they almost tripped over Rhys. One shrieked in anguish as they both knelt by his side. Rhys's face was already so wet, he wasn't sure if he was crying or not, but he was in Twitch's arms, with Leandro holding onto them both.

"Are you alright, Captain Rhys?" Twitch asked. His hands stroked over Rhys's chest.

Rhys shook his head as Leandro's fingers felt over the collar around his neck.

"Come on, let's get you out of – ah shit."

The alarms had abruptly cut out, and in the relative quiet a new sound could be heard, one that none of them wanted. Heavy footsteps coming up the stairs.

"We'll be right here, Captain," Leandro said. The older starat placed his hand on Rhys's cheek for a moment, before the two dived away and disappeared into one of the bedrooms. They weren't a moment too soon, as barely had they hidden away was the fire door slammed open again.

"What have you done?" Cardinal Erik snarled. He towered over Rhys, aiming a kick at the starat's ribs. He could feel a couple of them crack under the blow, but he was powerless to defend himself.

The human then grabbed hold of Rhys's collar and flung him across the room. "I have been too soft on you, clearly. Too lenient. I had thought to start gently, that you would be more malleable to the stricter punishments on Mars, but I see now that I was mistaken. You are so far taken that nothing will get through to you. You are a beast and nothing more."

Dazed from the impact against the floor, Rhys struggled to raise his head as the human prowled towards him, pistol in hand. Rhys squeaked in terror, flicking his tail and trying to kick out at the cardinal, but to absolutely no effect at all. As the sprinklers finally turned off, the barrel of the pistol was placed against Rhys's crotch. "I have decided what I will do next. I will do everything. But we shall start with the sin of lust, shall we?"

A loud shriek came from the nearest bedroom. "No!"

Cardinal Erik whirled around, but too slowly to prevent the starat from diving on top of him. The impact wasn't enough to knock him off his feet, but Twitch was relentless in his attack, trying to scratch and bite at the human's face and neck. The human still had the advantage of strength though, and he was able to tear Twitch away and throw him across the room.

The cardinal had three deep scratches on his face, blood trickling down onto his neck and dripping onto his crimson robes. Again, he aimed the pistol for Rhys's crotch. This time, he pulled the trigger, but a second starat crashed into him at the same moment.

Rhys howled in pain as the bullet punctured into his hip. He arched his back and writhed on the floor as his whole body burned from the pain. It was agony, somehow worse than all he had already endured.

He didn't even notice what was happening between the starats and Cardinal Erik, barely even cared. He ignored the pain in his hands as he tried to wrench them apart. He could feel a couple of fragile bones snap from the force as he tried to clamp his hands down on the bullet wound, but still the metal bar held sturdy.

A hand touched Rhys's shoulder. He squeaked and recoiled, before realising it was just Twitch. The starat's muzzle was bloody, and he was panting with exertion.

"I... we should hurry..." he gasped. He looked down at his hands, which were also stained with blood.

Cardinal Erik was lying still on the floor, completely unmoving as Leandro's hands patted over him. Rhys couldn't tell if the human was still breathing. Blood trickled from a wound on his forehead. The grey starat crowed in victory as he pulled a set of keys from the human's pocket.

Twitch's bloody hands fumbled around Rhys's collar. After a few attempts, he found the right key and unclipped it. The collar fell away and the weight around his neck was shed in an instant. The gag and strapping around his muzzle was next, and he was able to open his mouth for the first time in what felt like forever. He tried to speak. No sound made it out from his throat.

"Sit up please, Captain Rhys," Twitch whispered. The starats fumbled around the metal between his hands, trying a few more keys before the loop loosened and allowed the bar to painfully thread out of his hands. It clattered to the floor with a fresh leak of blood. The two starats then lifted Rhys up to his feet, their hands supporting him beneath his arms. Rhys whimpered in pain as the movement aggravated the fresh wound in his hip, as well as his damaged ribs.

He was losing blood from the wounds in his hands and the various cuts over his body. He didn't know how much he had left to lose.

"Can you walk?" Twitch asked, taking most of Rhys's weight as he leaned into him.

Rhys tried to take a step forward, but even with the two starats supporting him, his right leg almost gave way as he placed his weight on it. Pain ripped through his hip. "No," he croaked. He spat a thick, sticky ball of bloody saliva onto the carpet.

Twitch glanced to Leandro. "Do you have that stuff from Edgar?"

Leandro rummaged through his pockets and pulled out a couple of syringes. Rhys tried to pull away, momentarily fearful of the needles, but Twitch kept a firm grip on his shoulders. In quick succession, Leandro stabbed the two syringes into Rhys's arm. The first numbed Rhys of his pain, and the second clarified his mind and gave him a powerful surge on energy. He gasped and took a deep breath.

"What was that?" he whispered.

"Painkillers and adrenaline. The most powerful stuff that Doctor Antony had in his supplies," Twitch said. The starat put his arms beneath Rhys's shoulders. "Do you think you can walk now?"

Rhys nodded, and with Twitch's help he was able to take his first few steps. Though his legs shook, he was able to make the few unsteady steps towards the door. The stairs were a challenge, and several times Rhys almost slipped and fell down the concrete staircase, but each time Twitch grabbed hold of his hand in time. Even through the painkillers, Rhys howled in pain as Twitch's hand squeezed around his. He didn't dare look down to see how bad his hands were. Twitch's whimpers were enough.

With the adrenaline and painkillers running though his system, Rhys felt stronger than he had done in a couple of weeks, but he knew he had to reign in his newfound energy. The pain was muted for now, but he knew he could still cause more damage to his many wounds.

It wasn't until they reached the ground floor before they heard the first sounds of humans. At first, Rhys cringed away from the sounds before he realised that it was Captain Rivers barking orders at the station staff. The fire alarm had caused chaos, and the captain was still trying to wrestle everything back into order.

Twitch guided Rhys away from the front entrance and led him instead to a small entrance out the back. Scott was waiting for them just outside, and the first officer was unable to hide his shock at Rhys's condition.

"Are you alright, Captain?" Scott asked.

Rhys opened his mouth in an attempt to answer, but no sound came out. He closed it again and simply shook his head.

"Do you have something to wrap his hands?" Twitch whimpered quietly. His voice shook.

Scott had some bandages in his pack, and he gently wrapped Rhys's hands up. It took just a few seconds to stain them crimson, but at least the open wounds were protected slightly. Rhys hissed and grimaced as the bandages were tied off, but he didn't pull back.

"We should hurry," Leandro said once Scott had finished. "I don't know if the cardinal is still alive, but I don't want to wait around and find out."

Scott pursed his lips and nodded. "Right. Better get him to the car then. Hopefully they're busy enough sorting themselves out to pay any attention to us."

Rhys followed after Scott as the first officer led them around the side of the grounds. His heart was thudding in his chest, and Rhys wasn't sure that was solely down to the adrenaline shot he had been given. He feared what would happen if Rivers did see him. It wouldn't just be him in trouble, but Scott too. The sooner they were away from Mount Cotton the better.

Leandro ran along with them, and it took Rhys a few moments to realise that. He wasn't able to vocalise his confusion, but the older starat picked up on his gaze. "You think I would miss this story, Captain Rhys?" the grey-furred starat said quietly. He then held a finger to his lips as they neared the large car park where most of the human staff were gathering. "Nearly there."

Rhys felt a surge of anger as he caught sight of Captain Rivers. The human was facing the other direction as he tried to do a body count of his staff. Rhys tried to ball his hand into a fist, but a combination of the dull pain, broken bones, and bandages prevented him from moving his fingers.

With one eye on the gathered humans, Rhys followed Scott to the lower end of the carpark, furthest away from the gleaming buildings of the station. There was only one car at that end, plugged into the charging ports that designated each bay. Scott quickly unplugged and unlocked the car, before gesturing for the three starats to hurry.

Despite the adrenaline rushing through his system, Rhys was starting to struggle again. He stumbled over the smooth tarmac a few times, only saved from falling by Leandro's steady hand. His body felt weak and his head started to spin. His throat burned. But he made it to the car and fell in through the door Twitch held open for him.

With a barely perceptible whine that did nothing to mask the sudden shout of alarm from further up the carpark, the car started to move. Rhys hauled himself up to look out the back. They had been seen, and from out the front doors came a flash of red robes. Rhys fell back into his seat and cowered. He hugged held his hands close to his chest as he started to shiver. He had gone so far beyond the limits of his endurance, but he still had to push himself that little bit further. He could feel Twitch's hand gently brush over his shoulders. The contact felt nice.

"Can you shoot?" Scott asked. Rhys glanced forward to the front seats for a moment before realising his first officer had been addressing Leandro by his side. Ahead of the car, Rhys could see they were approaching the security checkpoint by the main gates to the complex. His vision was blurred and darkened around the edges.

"Better than most humans, I'd say," Leandro replied. Even from behind, Rhys could see the smirk on the older starat's muzzle. He could hear it.

"By your feet will be a pistol. Keep it hidden, but close to hand. We may need to use it," Scott said. His voice was terse and tight, and Rhys could see he gripped the wheel so hard his knuckles had gone white.

Leandro nodded as he reached down beneath his seat. Rhys caught sight of the pistol for a moment before it was hidden in the side of the door. Everyone was quiet as Scott brought the car to a halt, and two armed guards stepped up to meet them. Their hands rested close to their firearms.

"Reason for departure?" one of them asked. Both guards had eyes only for Scott. They had briefly glanced at the starat occupants, but their attention was all on the lone human.

"A few injuries in the explosion. Getting them up to the facility up at Carindale to get them replaced," Scott replied. He handed the closest guard his military identification card.

"I didn't hear anything about starat transportation."

"I don't think everything is quite under control yet. Message must have got lost in the chaos," Scott replied. He flashed a quick smile as the guard handed his ID back.

One guard tapped his fingers on the side of the car, before stepping back and waving Scott through. Ahead of them, the gates started to open. "Go on through."

"Thank you," Scott said. "Have a good day." The car started to roll forward again, inching its way towards the gates and the freedom that lay beyond.

Before they could make it, a frantic yell reached them. "Stop them!"

Rhys glanced back to see Captain Rivers leading a battalion down the hill. Aware of the danger, Scott accelerated before the guards could react and close the gates in time. A few shots were fired, but none hit their target. Before anyone could stop them, they were through the gates and onto the road. Scott wrenched at the wheel to get them in the right lane and filter into the thin stream of light traffic with a squeal of tyres.

Somehow, Rhys was free. He glanced once more out the back window. He knew they would be pursued, but just for this moment there was no one following them. A shadow of a smile spread across his muzzle as he lay down on the back seat and rested his head in Twitch's lap.

chapter fifteen

As the adrenaline faded from his system, Rhys found he was barely able to stay awake. Though the occasional jolt and bump in the road sent shockwaves of pain through his broken body, Rhys soon found himself drifting in and out of consciousness. Through it all he was aware of Twitch's gentle hand stroking over his head and neck, but everything else descended into an unknown blur of light and noise.

The next time he woke, he felt a burning in his throat that he couldn't ignore. He struggled to move, and he felt Twitch's grip on his shoulder tighten a little. "Water," he gasped, the word feeling like knives on his throat.

A quick conversation followed, the words too fast for Rhys to hear, before a bottle of water was placed at his lips. He tried to reach up and grab it, but his arms were too weak.

"Slowly," Twitch warned as he gently tipped the bottle back, enough to let a few drops of liquid pass between his parched lips. The warning was needed, as just that small amount rekindled the taste of dried blood on his tongue, making Rhys cough and gag. Twitch waited for him to recover before trying again, and after a few attempts Rhys was finally able to swallow. It did little to ease his thirst, but he felt marginally better for it. His belly rumbled for food, but he didn't think he'd be able to manage anything solid just yet.

"Thank you," he whispered quietly. He slowly sat up and looked out through the windows. They were in suburbia somewhere, though Rhys couldn't work out exactly where. The roads were wide and smooth, and the houses that lined the roads were generally clean and spacious. A few humans walked the streets. They passed a garbage truck with a team of starats crewing it.

Rhys realised that he had been clothed while he had been asleep. It was something as simple as jeans and a t-shirt, but he was glad for it. He had been so caught up in the panic and adrenaline before that he hadn't even noticed his nudity, but through the fog of pain he could feel his cheeks reddening slightly at the thought of it. The jeans were already stained red as blood dripped from the wound in his hip.

"Where are we going?" he asked quietly. Despite the drink of water, his throat still felt hoarse and dry.

"Brisbane starport, Captain, and then up to the Star Hub," Scott replied. "Should be about ten minutes away."

Rhys bowed his head. "How were you there? It doesn't make sense." The words cut into his throat, feeling like it was ripping open new wounds each time he opened his mouth.

"They delayed my trip with Twitch," Scott explained. "I think that was when they claimed to move you to Mars. They probably worried that we knew you were there, so they wanted us to think you were actually gone before allowing us anywhere near Mount Cotton."

"I just don't know why they didn't actually move you," Twitch added. He pulled Rhys across the back seat and held him gently. "I'm glad they didn't, of course. But it doesn't make sense."

"They wanted me to see you," Rhys said slowly. He frowned, then winced as the movement sent pain stabbing down his back. "If I saw you and couldn't escape... that might have broken me. That's what they were counting on."

Speaking so much sent Rhys into a coughing fit that spat up more blood and bile. He felt Twitch's had squeeze around his shoulder, but there was nothing anyone could do until the fit subsided. He grimaced and wiped his hand over his muzzle, only to hiss in pain as he moved his right arm. For the first time he glanced down at his arms. The white bandages that had been wrapped around his hands were already crimson. Below his elbows, his arms were almost furless, and the three scratches on each were black. His flesh was emaciated as the poison had eaten through his muscle, just as the cardinal had promised.

"Fuck," Rhys whispered. He closed his eyes and tried not to think about the ghastly sight.

"We'll get you to Doctor Anthony," Twitch said, squeezing Rhys's shoulder again. "He'll get you fixed up in no time."

Rhys tried to swallow, but only coughed again. His whole body trembled, and he found it hard to think properly through the pain that was starting to increase again. "Do you have any more of those painkillers?"

"Can you wait until we get to the starport, Captain Rhys?" Leandro asked. The older starat looked back at him, eyes full of worry. "We have no tablets, and I do not trust these roads to stay smooth if we're injecting you."

Rhys gritted his teeth and nodded. He shuffled back into Twitch's arms and tried to ignore the burning pain that radiated out from his hip and ribs. He didn't know how he would make the journey up to the Star Hub in his condition. Everything hurt, and he was barely able to keep his eyes open anymore.

His eyelids drooped for what felt like just a moment, but he woke up to feel the punch of a syringe in his shoulder. He cried out and gritted his teeth as his mind was wrenched from blissful unconsciousness. He opened his eyes only for a moment before they were burned by the bright sun blazing down from the clear blue sky.

After throwing his arm up to shield his eyes, he slowly sat up and blearily blinked clear the dazzling afterimages. They were in another carpark with towering, gleaming buildings overlooking the massive area of black tarmac, but this felt different. This was no military base. It was the Brisbane civilian starport, and Rhys allowed himself to sit and watch the humans going by. Most appeared to be tourists, though there were some in smart black suits going to or from their jobs. He immediately spotted two starats, but both appeared to work for the starport. One pushed the luggage belonging to a human family, and the other was emptying a bin.

"We should hurry. They'll be following us, I'm sure," Scott said, breaking Rhys out of his reverie.

With Twitch's help, Rhys got back up to his feet. He felt a little steadier, but his head still felt light and his vision spun slightly. He didn't know how long the new burst of adrenaline and painkillers would last, so he squared his shoulders and took a couple of steps towards the terminal.

Scott led the way. Despite the three starats following behind him, no one paid him any particular notice as they crossed the carpark. Rhys tried to avoid standing directly on the blistering tarmac, and he followed Twitch's lead in moving along the white lines or walking down the central grassy embankments as much as possible.

By the time they reached the terminal, Rhys could feel sweat dripping down his whole body. It stung as it trickled over his wounds, especially the one on his thigh. He grimaced and flicked his tail in annoyance, but then the automatic doors of the terminal slid open and he was blasted by the powerful air-conditioning within. He hurried inside and delighted in the feel of cool tiles beneath his feet.

The queues inside were massive. Lines upon lines of humans waited outside the kiosks of various airlines to be guided through to the right gates for their flights. The starport combined both atmospheric travel and interplanetary, with both departing from the same terminal. Flights to destinations like London and New York were as common as those to Luna and Mars, with all interplanetary services departing via the Star Hub.

Only one kiosk didn't have a queue at all, and it was to this one that Scott led the three starats. Rhys glanced up to see the military insignias above the doorway behind the kiosk. One attendant was stood behind the kiosk, though two armed guards stood either side of the doorway. Rhys trembled as they approached.

Scott had his ID in his hand even before he was asked for it. The woman behind the counter took it from his and scrutinized it with a careful eye. "Reason for travel, Lieutenant Scott?"

"Star Hub medical centre for urgent starat treatment."

The woman sighed slightly as she handed Scott's ID back. "Don't know why you even bother. Just get new ones," she said as she waved them through. "First right to processing. They'll sort everything else out for you, Lieutenant."

Twitch gave a little growl, but the woman either didn't hear him, or she ignored him entirely. She didn't even look at the starats as they passed by and were let through the door by the guards. Scott was the only one they cared about.

A couple of sterile white corridors followed. They were stopped in another short queue in a small room. Wide windows opened up on one side, showing a much larger room where civilian passengers were queued. A few more questions were asked about their destination, before they were given a gate to go to.

More corridors followed, but it wasn't until Rhys caught sight of some signs at the ceiling that he realised where they were going. He stopped dead in his tracks and trembled. "No, Scott. No."

Leandro was the first to speak as the others all turned to face him. "What's the matter, Captain Rhys?"

"We must. It's the quickest and safest way," Scott said. He held out his hand for Rhys, but the starat didn't take it.

"I'm not taking them, no," Rhys squeaked. He shook his head and took a couple of paces back. He closed his eyes and dropped his voice to a whisper. "I... I just accepted it. I can't go through it all again."

"I don't understand," Leandro said. Rhys could feel a hand on his shoulder.

"Teleporters. We're taking the teleporters," Rhys said.

"You could be human again," Twitch said. His voice was bright and cheerful, but Rhys could hear the worry in it.

Rhys slowly opened his eyes and lifted his head. He looked right into Twitch's eyes. "That's what I'm scared of," he said quietly.

Twitch's hand slowly stroked down Rhys's cheek. "I'll go through ahead of you. That way if anything goes wrong you'll just be me again. Don't worry, Captain Rhys. We'll keep you safe. We'll keep you as my beautiful self. But please, we can't stay here."

Rhys took a deep breath and nodded. Every instinct he had was screaming at him to turn around, but he ignored them. His legs shook as he followed after Twitch, but he kept walking. He kept his head low and didn't look around as they walked down a couple more corridors. They were walking past the shuttle bays, instead heading deeper into the spaceport were the teleporter pods were located. Rhys could almost imagine he could smell them. They smelled of cinnamon.

"Here we are," Scott said. He opened a door with his ID card and held it open. Rhys could make out the side of a teleporter inside. His tail went rigid in fear, and once again he fought the urge to turn and run. "Leandro, you first."

The grey-furred starat slipped into the small room first. He immediately hopped up into the pod and closed it behind him. A burst of bright light followed, and the door unlatched itself and swung back open again. It was empty, with no sign of the starat at all. Rhys whimpered slightly in involuntary fear. He knew that Leandro was fine, and was already on the Star Hub, but a small part of him refused to believe this simple fact.

Scott crouched down in front of Rhys. "Captain, you can…"

The first officer was interrupted by a loud tannoy message. "Lieutenant Scott, report immediately to security. I repeat, Lieutenant Scott, report immediately to security."

"Damn," Scott muttered. "We'd better hurry. Rhys, come on. You first."

Rhys shook his head, and he took a step away from the door. "Twitch first, please." He turned to glance down the corridor as he heard a distant door slam open. Someone shouted in the distance, and footsteps started to pound down the corridor, still around a few corners. "They're here. Go through, Twitch. Please."

"Not before you," Twitch replied, but Rhys gave the other starat the firmest push he could manage.

"You first, please," he pleaded. Tears sprung to his eyes. "Please, you have to go first. I need to be… I need to be you, because that's me. Please."

Twitch flicked his ears and nodded. He squeezed Rhys's shoulder. "Just make sure you follow, alright?"

"I'll be right behind you, I promise," Rhys said. He looked up to Scott and took a deep breath as Twitch stepped up into the teleporter. The sounds of pursuit were closing in as Twitch disappeared in a flash of bright light. Faced between the choice of teleporter or capture, there was only one option. As the teleporter door slowly swung open again, Rhys staggered towards the pod.

"Hurry, Captain," Scott said. The first officer closed the door to the room and wedged it closed with a stray chair.

The tangy scent of electricity still filled the air, and Rhys eyed the smooth metallic inner walls of the pod with distrust. The pod door remained open, and everything would remain inert until he closed it and pressed the small red button beside the lock. He took a deep breath and tried to slow his racing heart. He reached out with one trembling hand for the door and muttered beneath his breath. "Essie keep me safe, please."

His hand tugged on the handle just as someone slammed against the door. It almost fell off its hinges, and the chair propped up against it fell back to the floor with a clatter.

"Go, Rhys, go!" Scott yelled. He drew his pistol and aimed it at the closed door.

The door slammed again, and this time it shattered open. Rhys closed the pod as the first shots were fired. Scott recoiled as he was hit in the shoulder. The first officer staggered back and locked eyes with Rhys in the pod.

Rhys's ruined fingers found the small red button beside him. He pressed it just as Scott's arm came up, finger on the trigger of his pistol. Aimed right at the pod. Rhys realised what Scott's plan was just as he pressed the button. Scott's finger squeezed the trigger just as Rhys was lost to a bright light.

Rhys screamed. The pod door opened, and he tumbled out onto the cold floor. Hands touched him, but he thrashed and pushed them away as he looked up at the teleporter. An angry red light flashed above the open door, with two words displayed. 'Signal Lost'.

"Where's your Edgar?" Leandro asked.

Rhys was numb. He was gone. Scott was gone.

Rhys screamed in anguish, hurling abuse at the teleporter as though the machine was responsible, but his throat didn't hold out long. He descended into tortured sobs as he knelt in front of the teleporter, his head bowed.

Hands touched his shoulder. "We can't stay here, Captain Rhys," Twitch said. His voice trembled, sounding on the verge of tears. "They'll find another way up. Another pod won't be far away."

Rhys allowed Twitch and Leandro to lift him up to his feet. He didn't want to move, but slowly his legs started to work again. His foot was slippery with blood that trickled down his leg. Despite the cool air in the Star Hub, Rhys felt hot and drenched with sweat. His hands felt like they were the source of the heat, and they burned with pain every time he moved his arms. The pain was becoming unbearable again, and he stumbled several times as he tried to keep up with the two starats. He was sure he was imagining things too; the cracking of glass all around him, the voice of Aaron in his ear. His old friend whispered to him, telling him he would never look down upon Terra as a friend.

The planet was visible through the windows, looking as it had always done. Beautiful Terra, the home of humanity. Rhys no longer belonged there. His head dropped down. Terra vanished from view.

Everything had turned into a blur again, but somehow through the confusion, Rhys was able to recognise when Twitch led them through into the quarters set aside for the *Harvester's* crew. There was only one person present. They were just a blurred silhouette, completely indistinct to Rhys's failing vision.

"Shit. Is that him?" Chekolin asked. The silhouette stepped closer. "Where's the lieutenant?"

Twitch didn't answer. No one did. Everyone was silent, and that was all that was needed.

"Come on through then. Hurry," Chekolin said, breaking the pained silence. Rhys felt a human hand rest on his shoulder, before the ship's pilot simply picked him up. Rhys hissed in pain as his weight settled in Chekolin's arms, but at least he didn't have to walk anymore.

 Rhys was vaguely aware of being carried through the rooms and then down the corridor that connected to his ship. His eyes closed as they passed through an airlock. Doors hissed open, and the scent on the air changed slightly.

Another pair of arms took hold of Rhys and carried him away from Chekolin. Rhys recognised the voice of Doctor Sparks. "Welcome back to the *Harvester*, Captain Griffiths. You've certainly looked a lot better."

"Take him to the medical bay," Chekolin said. "I'll deal with getting away. I'll... I'll step up for Scott."

"Scott is...?" Doctor Sparks said, but he was interrupted by Rhys.

"No," the starat mumbled. He forced his eyes open. He tried to push against the doctor's shoulder. "I need to be there. Give me another one of those shots."

"You need urgent medical attention," Doctor Sparks said, but he didn't start carrying Rhys away.

"I need to be on the bridge. I'm captain. I'm responsible for this. It needs to be me."

Rhys could hear Doctor Sparks suck his breath in, but it was Chekolin who spoke. "Come to the bridge with him. Keep an eye on him."

"Fine, but this is your last one, Captain. I don't know how many of these a starat body can take. Even a human shouldn't have this many is so short a time," the doctor replied. He gently lowered Rhys to the ground and let him find his balance. A few moments later Rhys felt the sharp jab of a needle again, shortly followed by the familiar rush of clarity and energy to his thoughts and movement.

"Thank you," he said, his voice trembling slightly. It took him a moment to find his bearings, before he led the way up to the bridge. Even the two starats followed after him, but once he actually stepped onto the bridge, Twitch and Leandro hung back.

"Captain on bridge," Chekolin barked, trying to disguise the grief in his voice.

A shocked ripple spread through the bridge as his crew came to attention. There was surprise and relief amongst them, but confusion started to spread when they noticed the absence of the first officer. He stumbled forward until he was able to take a seat in his chair.

"You don't have to do this," he said in the strongest voice he could manage, but Chekolin cut across him.

"Everyone present wants to do this. We haven't been idle while you've been away. I questioned the crew with... with Lieutenant Scott, testing their loyalty to you. Everyone you see here passed that test," the pilot explained. He gestured his arm around the bridge. "The services and operations crews are both loyal to you, and we are all aware of where our next step will take us."

"And where is that?" Rhys asked, already knowing the answer.

"Alpha Centauri," Chekolin answered.

Rhys nodded. "Then let's do it." He leaned back in his chair and draped his hands over the armrests. He let Chekolin take control of preparing the ship for departure, and everything seemed to progress smoothly. Being back on his ship didn't erase the torture he had endured, but it did make it feel like he was slowly waking from a bad dream. The mere thought about what he was about to do both thrilled and terrified him. He was leaving the empire behind. He was chasing after Aaron.

"Engines primed and ready to fire." Rhys squinted to see that Chekolin's understudy, Mathers, was in control of the ship. The regular pilot was still going through the final checks with the navigator.

"All clear here," Chekolin called out a few moments later.

"Launch when ready," Rhys said. He leaned forward slightly in his seat, but for a few seconds nothing happened at all. "Is everything good, Mr Mathers?"

"Uh, slight problem, Captain," Mathers replied. Chekolin quickly hurried to the side of the junior pilot. His words sent ice through Rhys's heart. Not now. Not after all of this. "I thought the engines were strong enough to overcome the electromagnetic grips, but there's a failsafe I didn't expect."

"Shit," Rhys muttered beneath his breath, before he addressed his communications officer. "Are they aware of us yet, Mr McDonald?"

"Not yet, Captain. Can't be long though," came the immediate reply.

Rhys tried to tap his fingers against the chair, but the pain where his claws had been forced him to stop. A voice called out from the far side of the bridge. "Captain Rhys? I have an idea." Rhys turned to Twitch in surprise, before gesturing for the starat to join him. Twitch's eyes went wide as he stepped onto the bridge, before he quickly scampered across to Rhys.

"What's the idea?" Rhys prompted.

Twitch beamed as the words spilled from his mouth. "The Denitchev Particles stay close to the ship because of the electromagnetic shields, don't they? We could use that."

Rhys shook his head. "No, we can't use the jump drive this close to Terra. The gravity well is too strong."

"No, no. Not that. The shields. Electromagnetic, aren't they?" Twitch babbled. "Same thing as the grips. They'd cancel each other out. Shields go up, grips go down. It'll work, trust me."

"Did you catch that, Mr Chekolin?" Rhys asked.

The pilot shrugged his shoulders. "It could work, I suppose. Don't know if the shields are strong enough to totally cancel out the grips, but it might be enough to squeeze free."

"Then that's enough for me," Rhys said, before he raised his voice. "Van den Burgh, shields up to maximum please."

"I'm afraid Van den Burgh isn't here, Captain. You'll have to make do with me."

Rhys blinked and glanced over to Van den Burgh's usual station. His weapons officer wasn't present. Instead her cadet officer was manning the station, Simms. She had turned her back on Rhys, and she was already preparing to activate the shields. So that was one person who hadn't come. Rhys couldn't help but feel saddened at that. It felt like a betrayal of his trust that he hadn't been able to rely on the support of all his crew.

"Thank you, Miss Simms," Rhys said. It felt like he had been punched in the stomach, and he sunk back into his seat.

"Shields active," Simms called out.

Her words were greeted by an immediate response from Mathers. "Full power on the engines. We're getting some movement, but they still have a hold on us."

"We're being hailed, Captain," McDonald said, adding his voice to the mix. "And they sound pissed. They're demanding immediate shutdown of our engines."

"Ignore them," Rhys barked. He coughed and winced as his throat protested the sharp command. "Simms, increase power on the shields. Give them everything."

"Any more and we could fry the systems," Simms warned.

"Just do it. We have to break that hold."

Creaks and groans echoed through the ship as the sound of the engine roar increased. The *Harvester* lurched forwards a couple of times, but it was always caught again by the Star Hub's powerful grip. The hum and crackle of electricity as Simms fed ever more power into the shields grew louder until, with a deafening whine and screech, the ship abruptly launched forwards.

A whoop of delight spread through the bridge, but it was quickly overwhelmed by a frantic rush of commands from Rhys as he leapt up from his seat.

"Riley, get co-ordinates for Alpha Centauri. The quickest jump possible. Cheko… sorry, Mathers, get us there as soon as possible. Simms, prepare the gunners for defensive shooting only. If the Star Hub sends any ships after us, do not return fire on their ships. And focus all shields around the engines," the starat barked out. No one hesitated to obey his command, even as his voice cracked and failed.

Rhys's knees felt weak, but he remained standing. "McDonald, put me through to Star Hub. Transmit audio to all."

"You're through," McDonald confirmed after just a few moments.

An urgent voice boomed through the bridge. "Stand down immediately. I repeat, stand down immediately. You do not have authorisation. The fleet is on standby and will be deployed if you do not comply."

"Do you know who I am?" Rhys asked the unseen voice. He spoke quietly, but it was enough to throw the speaker off their scripted commands.

"What? No. You are unauthorised for launch, that's all I know. Return to the Star Hub and surrender now. This is your final warning."

Rhys took a step forward and straightened his shoulders, though he knew the speaker could not see him. "I am Captain Rhys Griffiths," he said, his voice growing louder with each word. He could taste blood again. "Captain! Rhys! Griffiths! You will not take me or my ship."

"Then we have no choice," the speaker said, before a burst of static announced the end of the communication.

"Riley, how far?" Rhys called out.

"Ten minutes until jump point. Luna is still too close."

Rhys growled softly beneath his breath. "Then we shall hold them off for ten minutes." He raised his voice again to address the full crew. "This is the finest ship in the empire, and you are the finest crew. Let's do this."

Both sensory officers were on deck, and it was Pool who called out first. "Ships are being deployed. Two, no, four… no, five, six. Looks like six ships have been scrambled."

"They're trying to lock on to us. The Hub's ionic cannons are powering up," Dewson added. He swiped across on his screens to transfer the co-ordinates of the ships to Simms so she could arrange the defensive measures.

"We're being hailed again, Captain. This time from the *Unity*," McDonald said, adding his voice into the mix.

"Ignore it," Rhys barked immediately. He didn't need to be speaking to anyone else. He knew they weren't about to negotiate. The torture he suffered at the hands of Cardinal Erik would be nothing compared to what he would face if he were recaptured. They had already killed one of his own. He would never allow another to be taken. He would never surrender.

Rhys knew he didn't need to give any more orders. His crew were amongst the best, and he was confident that they would be able to work best without him over-managing them. He used the opportunity to sink back into his seat before his legs gave way entirely. He hissed in pain as his right hand brushed against the armrest. Already he could feel himself start to fade, but he had to see this through.

"Incoming energy weapon fire," Simms warned. "Shields holding up for now."

Rhys hissed gently. They needed the shields to use the Denitchev Drive, so there was no use in burning them out entirely. The pursuing fleet would know that. "Direct fire to take out their turrets and engines. Do not shoot to destroy," he ordered. Simms raised her hand to show she had heard his orders. He turned to his first officer. "Can we get visuals? I need to see this."

By his side, Doctor Sparks and Twitch worked at the first officer's terminal. A few seconds later, the screens at the front of the bridge flickered to life. Rhys held his hand to his mouth as he looked out over the view behind them. Six ships lined up with the Star Hub receding in the background. Flashes of red burst out from the ships as they fired their energy weapons, which were met by white flashes as the shields dissipated the energy into harmless light and heat. But for the flashes of light, everything looked like a frozen image. The ionic cannons from the Star Hub fired. The screens briefly lit up with bright light as the energy was dissipated across the shields. Rhys knew they would not be able to take many more hits from such a powerful weapon.

Twitch gasped and stared at the slowly moving image with wide eyes.

The six ships were slowly spreading out as they gradually gained on the *Harvester*. Rhys could see that they were trying to get the better angle of attack in an attempt to circumvent the shields, but Simms was able to divert enough power to maintain their integrity.

"Missile fire incoming," Dewson called out.

Rhys saw it a moment later on the screens. Streaks of white quickly cut the gap between the six pursuing ships and the *Harvester*, but they were met with return fire from the picket guns down the spine and belly of the ship. One by one, the missiles burst into a brief flare of bright light. Not a single one reached its target intact. Some of the inert shrapnel thudded against the hull, but no damage was reported.

Rhys grimaced. The pursuing ships didn't seem to be holding back. They were not looking for a surrender anymore. They were going for the kill. He gripped his armrest a little tighter. "Can we go any faster, Mathers?"

"Not if we want to make it to Alpha Centauri with any fuel, Captain," came the quick reply from the junior pilot. "I'm giving it everything, but most of our power is going to the shields."

"Do not cut power to the shields," Simms cried out. Her face was red and glistening with sweat as she frantically worked at her terminal. "They're already being overloaded with heat energy. I don't know how much more we can take. Two more hits from their ion cannons, maybe?"

"Riley, can we jump yet?" Rhys asked. His closed his eyes for a moment. The constant talking was ripping shreds from his throat, and he could taste blood again. He took a deep breath, then tensed as he felt Doctor Sparks's hand on his shoulder. He felt like he should brush it off, but he didn't feel like he could summon the strength to move his arm.

"A few more minutes, Captain. Luna's gravity is still too strong to safely jump."

"We have another request come through," McDonald called out.

"Ignore it," Rhys hissed. He didn't want to hear their final demands, but McDonald hadn't finished.

"It's a tightbeam from the *Europa*."

Rhys blinked. "Admiral Garter? Show me. Full visuals. Chekolin, oversee the defences."

The screens flickered. Gone was the sight of the pursuing ships, and in their places was a slightly blurred image of Admiral Garter alone on the bridge of his ship. His hair was dishevelled and his eyes were red.

"Rhys…" the admiral said. He looked lost for words.

Rhys tried to salute his former commanding officer, but the movement hurt too much. "It's been a pleasure serving under you, Admiral Garter, but this is the end now. They killed Scott. I can't go back. I can't stay."

Admiral Garter recoiled at the news of Scott's death, before he composed himself and nodded. He saluted Rhys. His voice trembled as he spoke. "I just wanted to say sorry. I didn't do enough for you, and now…" He took a deep breath and composed himself. "Good luck, Rhys. Take care of yourself. I wish you all the best in your new life. May you find happiness there you could never find here."

"Goodbye, Admiral."

The screen went black and returned to the terrifying image of the following ships. They had gotten even closer, and their missiles were beginning to overwhelm the desperate defence of the *Harvester's* gunners. They didn't have long left.

"Under one minute, Captain." Riley's voice sounded so quiet, and it was a moment before Rhys realised that he could barely hear anything around him. He opened his eyes again, and it felt like he was moving in slow motion as everything blurred all around him. The ship rocked beneath him, but it wasn't until a red light started to flash that he realised it wasn't in his own mind. They had been hit.

Rhys tried to focus, but every movement brought pain and distraction. He could barely see, barely hear. He could feel Twitch at his side, trying to hold him up. He couldn't even remember getting out of his chair.

"Scott..." Rhys whispered. He heard an echo, louder than his quiet whisper. Then he realised it hadn't been his voice, but Twitch's. The starat had said something different, but Rhys couldn't work out what.

A blurred figure that looked like it could have been Scott crouched down in front of Rhys. If the figure said something, Rhys couldn't hear him. Rhys tried to clear his throat as darkness started to creep in around his vision. "Order the jump. Now."

Chekolin's voice bellowed out to Riley.

Rhys craned his neck to look up towards the screens. The dark blur burst into blinding white before everything faded to a calming black. Rhys slumped forward into Twitch's arms and knew no more.

chapter sixteen

Rhys woke up slowly. He resisted it at first. Sleep was somewhere he didn't hurt, and he longed to stay there for as long as he could, but his body resisted his mind's wants. He could feel himself drift towards wakefulness, and in his drowsy state he wasn't yet convinced that everything since the teleporters on Ceres had been nothing more than a vivid dream.

His eyes snapped open. He was in the medical bay of the *Harvester*, lying on one of the beds. He groaned and tried to move his arms, but they felt stiff and weak. With his mind still fogged by exhaustion, he wasn't able to remember why that was. A hand rested on his shoulder as he noticed a starat lying on the end of his bed. He glanced up to see David by his side, just as Twitch lifted his head.

"Good morning, Captain Rhys," David said. The starat tried to smile as he carefully removed an IV drip from Rhys's wrist. "How do you feel?"

"Like I've been run over by my own ship," Rhys replied. He felt groggy, and his words were as slurred as they had been when he had first woken up in his new body. He tried to sit up, but David placed a hand on his shoulder again to stop him moving. Twitch leaned into his partner's side. The joyous light in Twitch's eyes was gone. The fur on his cheeks was wet from recent tears.

"It will take some time for the pain to go away. You've been out for six days already, but we thought you needed to be awake now," David said. He sat on the side of the bed and placed his hand on Rhys's chest. "We're only a few hours out from Alpha Centaura."

"Shit," Rhys mumbled. His head sunk back into the firm pillow. He closed his eyes and took a deep breath. "Who's been running things?"

"Chekolin and Dewson, mostly," Doctor Sparks said. The human stepped out of his office to stand behind David. His hand rested on Twitch's shoulder. "This one helped us immensely. You lost a lot of blood, Captain. Thankfully we had someone around with a perfect match to help you get through it all. There were times I thought we were going to lose you."

Rhys's ears pinned to his head. "What was the damage?"

His mind was starting to clear as he woke up further. He knew there was something terribly wrong with his hands, and already his breathing had started to quicken. He forced his thoughts elsewhere.

"Four broken ribs, two fractured bones in your tail, severe abrasions around your neck and mouth, gunshot wound to your hip, dehydration, and starvation," the doctor counted off. He paused for a moment and sat down on the next bed next to David. "But the worst were your arms. I was lucky I recognised what that bastard gave you, but it had eaten away almost all the flesh in your forearms, and it was starting to spread to your upper arms. I was able to get an antidote to stop further damage, but I haven't been able to repair much. I'm not certain it can be repaired."

Rhys's ears flattened down as he nodded. He slowly pulled his arms from beneath the bedsheets. They were swathed in bandages, but even through them he could see how thin and frail they looked. His hands trembled from the exertion of lifting them, and he had to lower them back down to rest on the bed.

"I'm sorry," Doctor Sparks said. "I wish I could have done more."

"It's not your fault," Rhys replied in a strained whisper. He couldn't blame the doctor. He was sure that Doctor Sparks would have done all he could to protect his arms from the wasting poison Cardinal Erik had inflicted upon him.

Rhys felt a furred hand seek out his shoulder. His eyes opened enough to see Twitch on the bed with him. "At least there's a way to tell us apart now," Twitch said. His hand slowly stroked over Rhys's bandaged upper arm. "Besides, you'll have all the guys fawning over you now as they try to help you. Or the women. I don't even know who you're into. Is it both? Neither?"

Rhys couldn't help but smile despite the tears that came to his eyes. Twitch was always able to do that. He sat up fully, letting the sheets fall from his bare chest. His arms hung limply by his sides. "I'll keep that a mystery, shall I?"

Twitch stuck his tongue out, before wrinkling his nose. "Though at the moment you won't be attracting anyone. I know you've had a tough time, but phew do you need a shower. Perhaps you need my magic hands again." David swatted Twitch across the ears, but the starat just grinned wider.

Rhys flicked his ears and glanced down. He swung his legs out over the side of the bed. He was glad the sheets still covered his naked crotch. His fur was matted and dirty, though at least the bloodstains had been cleared up. Doctor Sparks had been able to heal his wounds, but his personal grooming had been entirely neglected for too long. He definitely agreed with Twitch. He glanced up to the starat. "Can you go get some clothes from my quarters? I'll get cleaned up. Then I should get to the bridge."

Twitch beamed widely as some light came to his eyes again. He nodded. "Be right back," he said. He kissed David, and then scampered out of the ward. The door closed slowly behind him, but not before it let in some heat from the ship. With Twitch gone, Rhys looked down again. His eyes lingered on his wasted hands.

"Once we get to Alpha Centauri, maybe we'll be able to find a better regenerative cure," Doctor Sparks said, breaking the momentary silence. "I looked for some support prosthetics to give you some better strength or grip, but Briggs didn't have anything at all."

Rhys glanced up to the doctor for a moment, then across to David, before looking back down to his arms. He could move them, but there was little he would be able to do with them. He could barely even move his fingers without any pain. "This is all just another new thing to overcome. I got used to this body once. I can do it again." He sighed and lay back down in his bed. "Though first, I think I need something to eat. Do you have anything?"

"I thought you might be hungry. Just lie back and rest for now, and we'll get you something your stomach can handle."

***

Food turned out to be a simple gruel, but Rhys ate it as quickly as David allowed him. It tasted plain, but to Rhys's deprived tongue it was the sweetest, most beautiful thing he had ever had. He couldn't even finish it, much to his dismay. The bowl was only a small one, but barely halfway through he found himself unable to eat anymore. His stomach protested, and he was forced to turn aside the bowl in favour of some icy water. Being fed was a humiliating experience, but Rhys couldn't even hold a fork. He was able to overcome his shame by his sheer need for food and water.

By the time he finished draining the cup, Twitch returned with a set of his uniform in hand. He wasn't alone either. Another starat followed just behind him.

Upon hearing the distinctive clack of William's ill-fitting foot against the floor, Rhys raised up his right arm to the starat. "I know what it feels like now," he said, a bitter smile on his muzzle as he showed the starat his clawless fingers. His bandages had been removed, and his palms were a mess of scar tissue where the metal bar had punctured through his hands. His fur had only barely begun to grow back.

"I didn't wish this on you," William said quickly. He didn't quite meet Rhys's eye as he approached the bed. "For all my anger at you, I didn't want you to feel the same pain I do."

Rhys pinned his ears back and raised his arm. "I know, I understand. I was just trying to make a joke. Guess I should leave that to Twitch."

"I do keep all my jokes in my claws," Twitch said solemnly, before breaking into a little giggle. "Dunno why you were so serious and grumpy before though."

Rhys chuckled softly and shook his head. "I guess you still have a lot to teach me, don't you? But I suppose I must ask you for your magic hands again. I don't think I can groom myself yet."

"With pleasure, Captain Rhys," Twitch said brightly. He held out his hand, and Rhys placed his into the starat's grip, wincing in pain at the light pressure. Slowly he got out of the bed, letting the sheets fall down around him.

"I'll give you a moment," Doctor Sparks said. The human retreated towards his small office. "Let me know when you're ready, and I'll make sure you're ready to go back to the bridge."

With the human gone for now, Twitch helped Rhys across the ward. His leg still hurt, and his hip was stiff with pain. He winced slightly with each step, but with Twitch's support he was able to make it into the small bathrooms. There was a single small shower in the white-tiled room. David followed them in and placed Rhys's uniform down in the corner where it wouldn't get wet.

Rhys was eager to get into the shower and feel the dirt and grime from his time with Cardinal Erik get washed away. Instinctively, he tried to reach out for the taps, but pain flared through his hand as it touched against them. He felt like crying again. His hands were utterly useless. He was completely helpless until he was able to build strength up again. Assuming he ever could.

"Don't worry, Captain Rhys. I'm here for you. I'll make it feel better."

Rhys rolled his eyes. "Ugh. Why do you always need to make everything sound so... dirty."

"Don't know what you mean, Captain Rhys," Twitch giggled. The starat reached around Rhys to turn the water on. Rhys closed his eyes as he let the hot water steam the dirt away.

Twitch's hands did the rest.

***

Rhys could barely remember what being clean felt like. By the time Twitch was done with him, his fur felt soft and silky. He didn't have any knots or tangles left, and the few lingering bloodstains had finally been washed away. It took almost twenty minutes to properly dry his fur, but it wasn't long after that before Rhys was finally dressed again. Twitch made sure he was careful around Rhys's arms, ensuring the ruined hands touched the fabric of his shirt as little as possible.

Once he was done, Twitch stepped back and beamed widely. "There. A proper captain again." The starat's smile faded a little. "We're all here to help you, Captain Rhys. Anything we can do to make it easier... if we'd have made it there a couple of days earlier..."

Rhys leaned into Twitch and clumsily hugged him. "You got me out, that's all that matters."

"I know. But still, seeing you like that with that cardinal about to…" Twitch shuddered and took a deep breath to compose himself. He shook his head and grimaced. "It's going to be a long time before I get the taste of his blood out of my mouth. Nasty. Can tell why you didn't like biting that human before."

Rhys rested his head against Twitch's. "Thank you. You saved my life, and that's all there is to it. But as much as I'd like to rest a bit more, I really do need to go up to the bridge before we reach Alpha Centauri."

Twitch nodded, but he held his ground for a moment longer. His ears flicked and he tilted his head to one side. "Hey, Captain Rhys. If we're going to Alpha Centauri, is it true they have actual centaurs there?"

Rhys couldn't help but burst out into laughter. He leaned into Twitch's shoulder and shook his head. "No, of course not."

"Oh, that's a shame," Twitch replied. He sighed forlornly as he rubbed his hand down Rhys's back. "Maybe we can find a planet that does, sometime."

Rhys chuckled as they walked back into the ward. David and William were sat on one of the beds together, and their conversation came to an abrupt halt. David banged his fist on Doctor Sparks's door.

The doctor emerged a moment later as Twitch scampered over to sit by David's side. Rhys briefly swayed as he tried to put his full weight down on his right leg. He limped forward a couple of steps, glad he was able to make it without falling over.

"Hold out your arms, please," Doctor Sparks said. He held up a roll of bandages, which he gently wrapped back around Rhys's hands and arms, covering up his wounds and the furless areas. Rhys grimaced as the doctor worked, but he didn't pull back at all. He was then given a new shot of painkillers, but this time he didn't need any of the adrenaline to keep him going. His stomach still felt unsettled, but slightly warmed after he had been fed.

"Do you think they'll heal?" Rhys asked the doctor.

"I don't know," Doctor Sparks replied. He shook his head as he finished wrapping up the bandages. "It all depends what they have on Centaura. If they have more than I have here, then perhaps. I can't make any promises though."

"I hear they have better prosthetics there," William said, sounding a little hopeful.

Rhys glanced across to the other starat and smiled. "If that's so, then we can make sure you get something better. You deserve it at least." His smile faltered as he glanced down at his weak arms and sighed. "But I should go back to the bridge, if we're getting close to Alpha Centauri."

"I'll walk you up, Captain Rhys," William offered.

William wrapped his arm around Rhys to provide some support. Rhys's legs shook slightly as he took a few steps. He paused for a moment at the door and turned back.

"Can't bear to leave us?" Twitch giggled.

David pulled Twitch back. "Go do your captain stuff," the larger starat said. He kept one arm around Twitch, who simply looked up at his partner and stuck his tongue out. David squeezed him a little tighter.

"I'll try to see you before we arrive. Thank you all for your help," Rhys said, before stepping outside the ward. Twitch waved, before the doors closed behind them.

Outside the sound-proofed medical ward, the engines were an almost ubiquitous roar that felt like it nearly deafened Rhys. He could feel the ship vibrate through his feet. Everything felt warm, like being in the baking Australian sun. Just walking through the narrow corridors caused him to break out in a sweat, and he couldn't imagine having to work in the lower levels constantly when the ship was in flight. In subspace there was nowhere for ships to vent excess heat, and it used too much energy to constantly jump in and out of realspace. At least they didn't have much longer to go, and that thought gave more urgency to Rhys's feet. He wanted to be on the bridge before they emerged into CGP territory.

Though the ship's engines were as loud as they always were, the ship felt much quieter to Rhys as he made his way up to the bridge. He passed fewer crew, and it appeared to be running on barely a skeleton crew. If Chekolin had told him how many they had been forced to leave behind, then he couldn't recall. It must have been quite a significant number who had refused to follow their captain, but he had always had less influence over the services crew. They were beholden to Briggs, and Rhys doubted the services commander had chosen to join them.

Rhys finally made it up to the bridge. Though William hesitated, Rhys still leaned on the other starat for support. The two stepped onto the bridge together.

For the first time, Rhys was able to see for the first time how many of his operations crew had remained. But for Van den Burgh and Scott, no one was missing. Everyone, senior and junior, was present. He wasn't surprised. This was a monumental event, and no one wanted to miss it.

"Captain on deck," Chekolin called out.

Immediately, everyone but Dewson on the sensors came to attention. He waved them down weakly, his arm hurting from the simple motion. He said nothing as he walked towards his chair in the middle of the bridge as he worked out what he was going to say. He still didn't know exactly what, even as he opened his mouth to speak.

"I didn't get the chance to say this before, but thank you," he said. He looked around at everyone, his eyes lingering on each member of his crew for a moment before moving on to the next. "You have all chosen me, and I will never be able to thank you enough for that support and loyalty. We have already paid for that loyalty. There is one man who should be standing here with us, but he is not. I will do my best to prove to you that I deserve your loyalty, and that Edgar Scott's death was not in vain."

Chekolin spoke up. His voice was unsteady. "We've seen what the empire can do, what the Vatican can do. To you, Captain, and to other starats. To other humans, too. To Scott. It's not right."

"Some of us do have family and friends on Terra," McDonald added. The communications officer stood up and looked around the bridge. "I don't want to leave them behind, but I owe it to you to remain, Captain. I don't want this to be a permanent exile. I hope you will return the favour someday by finding a way to reunite us with those we have given up."

Rhys nodded. "If it is in my power, then I will do all I can. But before all of that, where are we and how long until we jump into realspace again?"

Riley sucked in his breath. "Depends how close to Centaura you want to get, Captain. We can drop out in five minutes and be in the outer reaches of the system, or we can go for another couple of hours and get close to the planet," he explained. He muttered beneath his breath, which Rhys's sharp ears could pick up. "If I could work out where exactly Centaura is."

Rhys slowly sat down in his chair and tapped his clawed hand on the armrest. "Drop us out in the outer reaches. Any closer, and they might interpret it as an attack. If they have good subspace sensors, they may already be aware of us."

"Understood, Captain." Riley and Chekolin leaned in close to each other to co-ordinate their efforts to bring the ship out of subspace. Knowing it was so close set Rhys's fur on edge. His tail had already fluffed out as it draped across his lap. The temptation was there to stroke it, but he tried to keep his hands away from his tail, not wanting to suffer the pain of stroking his clawless fingers through them.

"I can't detect anything in the target jump point," Dewson called out. His voice didn't sound completely confident, but it was enough for Rhys.

The starat slowly breathed out, before he rose to his feet. "Prepare for emergence into realspace. Simms, deactivate all weapons and defences. Mr McDonald, as soon as we do so, I want you to open communications for broadcast on all channels. Signal me when you've done so."

Both Simms and McDonald responded in sync. "Understood, Captain."

Rhys wanted to pace, but he forced himself to stay standing still. He wanted to project to his crew that he was confident, but his curled up tail and folded ears displayed the opposite. He couldn't do anything about those but hope his crew couldn't read his body language.

Chekolin began to count down from ten.

They were almost there, with no chance to turn back now.

"Seven."

The screens at the front of the bridge flickered on. They displayed the unending white of subspace.

"Six."

Rhys could only hope he had made the right choice. Both for him and the rest of his crew. It was a better place for starats, but would the CGP welcome them?

"Three."

Rhys straightened his back and cleared his throat.

"Two. One."

The white of subspace gave way to the darkness of realspace. In the distance was not one, but two suns. Rhys felt his breath catch in his throat as he gazed on the binary star system. He wasn't sure which was Rigil Kentaurus and which was Toliman, but he was looking on the pair of stars that made up Alpha Centauri for the first time. He was so awestruck that he almost missed McDonald's signal.

Rhys cleared his throat again, before he spoke loud and clear for the entire system to hear.

"This is Captain Rhys Griffiths of the Terran warship, *Harvester*. Our weapons are deactivated. We surrender."